An Unexpected Enemy

Diane Kozak

From expectations Comes power.

Diane Kozak

Cover art by Jason Gregory & Diane Kozak

Contact Diane
www.dianekozak.com
(508) 636-8230

To my friend and inspiration
Phyllis Bourassa
and her students at the
Bristol Community College
in Fall River, Massachusetts

An Unexpected Enemy

Diane Kozak

*Introduction to
An Unexpected Enemy*

My name is Abia Haddad and I am known world-wide as the sister to the Islamic Extremist terrorist, Mohamed Haddad. This may seem like an odd way to introduce myself, but ever since my brother helped to mastermind a series of horrific terrorist attacks on American soil two and a half years ago, being related to him has dominated my life. I was in high school when this nightmare began. Back then my biggest problems revolved around being bullied because I am a Muslim in a post 9/11 world. That changed when I noticed hidden messages within terrorist attacks in Europe; a message that forewarned of terrorist attacks on American soil. As if being a Muslim who happens to discover the imminent attacks wasn't bad enough, I also discovered my elder brother, Mohamed, was a mastermind of the terrorist acts. By the time the nightmare was over I was no longer "Abby" Haddad the high school student. No, I was Abia Haddad - the terrorist Mohamed Haddad's sister.

Even though everyone promised me that time would heal the wounds I carry because of my brother's evil and traitorous actions, two years passed and I was still notoriously the sister of the country's most wanted enemy; Mohamed Haddad. But, I could do nothing about my reputation so I went about my life. While attending college in Boston, I was shopping at a bookstore near Harvard University when there was a terrorist attack on the campus. The attack was made to look like the work of Islamic Extremists and so these were the enemies blamed for the horrendous loss of life. How did the extremists take responsibility for the attack you may wonder? It was simple. They used my brother as a scapegoat! I never believed Mohamed was behind the attack. In fact, he helped to expose the enemy and bring the group to justice, well most of the group. You see, two members, a mafia crime boss and the unknown ninth Eurabian, got away. Some people believe Mohamed is the unknown ninth Eurabian, but I know he's really a hero that helped fight these creeps, well at least that's how I see it.

Now, six months later, law enforcement is rounding up the last members of the vast country-wide Eurabian network. Meanwhile, I am still going to college in Boston. Besides a new apartment, my life also now includes being monitored by federal officials for security sake. (I think they watch me to make sure I'm not in contact with Mohamed, but they won't admit that). Of course, I am still notoriously Mohamed Haddad's sister, which has consequences such as making me unemployable and inhibiting my social life.

Things are going along fine until Boston is hit by a bizarre storm that seems like something from a science fiction movie. The winds are crazy, hail stones are bigger than normal and there is a hurricane spinning out tornadoes with fires inside of them. It occurs to me this is no normal storm, meaning something or someone who is not Mother Nature, is behind it. Could this storm be related to the escaped Eurabians? If so, can finding them prove that Mohamed is not the unknown ninth Eurabian?

And so, with the help of my friends and Mohamed, I am determined to find out who the enemy behind the storm is. And in doing so, I will prove that Mohamed is a reformed man turned American hero who deserves a second chance at life.

Chapter 1
The Storm

There was a time in my life when I accepted everything around me at face value. This time was over two years ago before I had to expose my older brother Mohamed as a terrorist with plans to attack Boston with the small pox virus among other intended atrocities. As if that weren't enough, just six months ago, he was held captive by an American branch of an international enemy group consisting of nine powerful men who used his terrorist history as an alibi for their own evil actions against this country. To save my brother I had to expose this enemy, called Eurabia, before it succeeded in murdering some of the most powerful politicians in the United States including the President. Of course, I didn't do these fantastic things alone; I had a lot of help including my three closest friends, my brother Abdul, and his fiancée Chelsea. But no matter how many people I shared these experiences with I still felt alone inside because I am the only one who has zero doubts that Mohamed was a true patriot during the Eurabian crisis and that he sincerely is trying to make amends for his prior mistakes. I believe in him so much that I've been harboring a secret from everyone these past six months; a secret that could destroy my life and possibly lead to Mohamed's death. It is this secret that brings me to where I am at this very moment in time; walking a familiar route while I look around me and wonder why the brewing Boston wind storm feels wrong to me. As the wind blows my long curly hair from all different directions something inside of me is screaming that this storm is different and I should not take it at its face value.

I've walked through this ancient and isolated cemetery so often it almost feels welcoming to me; that is until now. When I started my walk earlier this afternoon the skies were cloudy but calm; the sort of blue heavens that promise neither bright sunshine nor stormy weather. In the last few minutes, however, a harsh and unbelievably uncanny wind has developed. It feels like the gusts of moving air are alive in some way; as if the wind can think and strategize where it goes. I know this is impossible, yet I can't shake a growing belief that I am the wind's target. My paranoid fear intensified when, moments ago, I passed by the side of the stone Episcopal Church to which this cemetery belongs. As I walked through the creaky wrought iron gate a sweeping burst of wind lifted me completely off my feet. Yes, I am short and petite making my weight less burdensome than perhaps most adults, but still for this force to lift both my feet off the stone pathway, well, to me, that seems incredibly intense. After all, to think that today began as an ordinary spring day in the city of Boston with flowers poking up through the dirt, birds flying home from the warmer regions in the south and no chilly air expected until the sun went down. How I now find myself in the midst of such a bizarre storm I simply can't understand.

From the corner of my eye I notice what I can only describe as a mini tornado whipping up from behind the first row of cracked and crooked slate headstones. I estimate it to be about two to three feet tall and spinning at a high enough speed that whatever debris entangled within it is indistinguishable. When my curiosity with this freak of nature fades I quickly walk to my right, which, I predict, will easily take me out of the twister's path. The wind tunnel changes its course once again, putting me directly in its line of fire. I attempt several more dodging strategies before I accept the fact that I will be struck by this mini tornado no matter where I go and no matter what I do.

After having spent a great deal of time caught up in my terrorist brother's dangerous life, I have learned how to react quickly in a crisis. Preparing myself for what I expect to be a heavy physical blow I clutch on to the nearest sturdy headstone and wait to be struck by the moving wind tunnel. Ironically the names of the deceased that are chiseled on to my temporary security post are Albert Windermere and his wife Priscilla. Although my body is fairly well braced for impact the pressure from the twister smacks my head repeatedly against the stone marker while it squeezes the air out of my lungs. When I am finally able to breathe without pain I evaluate my situation. The bad news is that the wind is still raging and sleet drops are beginning to drop out of the sky. The good news is that I don't see another tornado forming – yet. After checking myself for injuries I continue to make my way to the last row of graves. If my reasons for being in this place were less important I would run back to my apartment because I am, quite understandably, frightened by what I now know is an unusually dangerous storm. But I have a purpose for being here and I will fulfill it despite becoming a victim of what very well may be some type of supernatural event.

I am Abia Haddad, the sister to the world's most wanted terrorist Mohamed

Haddad, and I have found myself in quite a few life threatening situations in the past couple of years. I don't claim this experience lightly, it is the regrettable truth. It began when I was in high school and my friends and I discovered and helped to divert terrorist attacks on this country that my brother masterminded. All of these planned terrorist hits were bizarrely linked to the 9/11 attacks which we discovered by deciphering hidden clues and messages sent out by the Islamic extremists. In the end the attacks were stopped and the government covered up our involvement in everything that happened; well, as well as they could cover things up. After all, Mohamed did escape and I am his sister.

Just when I though the nightmare was over I was almost killed in a bombing at Harvard University. The reality of being who I was while also being so near to a potential terrorist attack frightened me so I fled. Unbelievably this event caused me to re-connect with my fugitive brother. The next thing I knew my friends and I were exposing a criminal group called Eurabia who had infiltrated the very underpinnings of America. For decades this group of nine men and its informal army of followers were secretly destroying this country from within. Luckily all but two of them were brought to justice. Carlo Bertoni, the Eurabian representing the mafia, managed to escape. And another one, the ninth Eurabian, has not been identified. Many believe this mysterious evil doer is my brother Mohamed but I don't believe that. If I did I wouldn't have been semi-communicating with him in this old graveyard since the whole Eurabian thing busted open months ago. Yes, that is my purpose for being here while this storm rages. I come here to communicate with who I believe to be my brother Mohamed. Right or wrong, I love him. Without a second thought I am willing to risk prosecution to have peace of mind that he is, at the very least, alive.

The sleet drops are coming down more intensely now so I use my leather wristlet as an umbrella while I pass through the familiar ancient grave markers. I am a mere couple of steps away from the last row of graves when the wind yanks a low lying branch from a nearby decaying oak tree. I am momentarily hypnotized by the sight of the airborne limb flying toward me. When I finally react to this bark and moss covered missile my attempt to jump off to the side fails. My body, entangled in leaves and tree limbs, hits the ground with a thud. Once again my head takes a blow, this time leaving me dizzy and dazed. My patience is tested while I untangle myself from the branches which, for some reason, seem to be fighting with me. When I am finally free of the leafy octopus like obstruction I am wet, dirty, and throbbing in pain.

Thankfully I make it to Mohamed's and my unofficial message spot without further incident. From the distance comes the sound of emergency vehicle sirens; they seem to be coming from many directions at the same time. I also see smoke in the sky; its origins unknown since the wind could be carrying it from just about anywhere. Another wind gust blows at me, this time seemingly coming directly down from above. I am almost too frightened to look for its source but when I do I see another mini tornado hovering above me. My reflexes and instincts kick into action pushing me to run into the nearby trees. The mini twister follows me; however, it dies out while it whips through the dense cluster of branches. As much fear as I have I also am in disbelief at what I am experiencing. There are no words to describe how I feel at this moment except for the military term 'shock and awe.'

For the first time since I got to the cemetery I think of my roommates; my boyfriend Frank Stiller, my best friend Sarah Brady and her boyfriend Randy Arruda. With an unexpected need to communicate with those I am closest to, I instantly regret having left my cell phone on the kitchen table before I left the apartment. Even though Randy and Sarah are out of town I feel a need to tell them about what is happening here. As for Frank, he's still at the apartment or at least he was when I left for my walk. I have no doubt he's out looking for me right now. The thought of him being hurt in this storm because of me fills me with regret. Of course, I've had this same sentiment many times before because, like me, he has put his life on the line fighting terrorists and enemies these past two years because of Mohamed and I. But somehow this is different because Frank doesn't even know the real reason I'm out here. No, I've lied to him about my contact with Mohamed because I wanted to protect him from the consequences should our contact be discovered. I know he may never truly forgive me for this lie but I honestly believe that keeping him unaware of the risks I'm taking is the same as giving him a gift; the gift of innocence.

My deep thoughts are broken by the annoying blare of honking car horns. The traffic jams bother me because I don't know where all these drivers are trying to go and why they all want to get there at the same time. The scene screams emergency evacuation; an understandable but horrifying possibility under the circumstances. Knowing time is now a major factor I ignore the bruising pain that is shooting up my thighs and find the charcoal colored slate headstone marked with the name of Jeremiah and Mary White. Out of habit I take a good look around to make sure no one is watching me before I crouch down and look behind this grave marker for a plastic baggy hidden under a sizeable gray rock. As it always is, there is an empty Ziploc bag in this secret spot. This is as it should be because the routine is for me to leave money and notes inside the bag and someone, who I refuse to believe is anyone other than Mohamed, takes it away. He never writes anything back to me, not even when

I leave him a pen. I know he doesn't do so because it isn't safe for either of us to have real contact. After all, it isn't a crime to leave things inside a plastic bag but it would be a crime to communicate with a terrorist fugitive. I get that, but, I wish he'd give me more than an occasional hint that the person I am communicating with is him. After all, how much faith can I put in the fact that I once found inside the plastic baggy a letter M, as in Mohamed, ripped out of a newspaper? How am I to be sure it was put there by my brother's hand? Even the time I found a dirty empty Sky Bar wrapper, which was our childhood favorite candy bar, in the bag seems to imply less and less of a definite bond as time passes by.

From my wristlet I slide out an envelope with a $50 bill tucked inside. This is a large sum of money for me; after all I'm a poor college student who is basically unemployable because I'm Mohamed Haddad's sister. As I do every week, I include clippings of the latest news articles about the Eurabian bust. This week there is another article about him being the assumed ninth Eurabian. There is also an article about a sighting of Carlo Bertoni and Mohamed together; something I can only hope is incorrect since I'd hate for my brother to be in contact with this criminal. Lastly, there are more jailhouse stories from the Eurabians who are tucked away in prison and, as has always been the case, they are sticking to the rehearsed story they have all told since day one. Unfortunately for Mohamed part of their story is that he is the ninth Eurabian. The last thing I place inside the baggy is the engagement announcement of our brother Abdul and his fiancée Chelsea Rosenfield. Even though Abdul now despises Mohamed and he somewhat believes that our brother is an enemy of the United States, I try to convince myself that someday my brothers will reconcile. I secure the bag behind the gravestone with the heavy rock, checking twice to make sure the powerful wind will not carry it away. To be extra careful I walk to the edge of the cemetery and retrieve a second rock to place upon the bag.

On my way out of the cemetery the slight incline up from the graves and toward the church is extremely difficult for me to maneuver because a steady stream of gusting wind is blowing down upon me. Unlike any other storm I've ever witnessed the winds are almost continuous and coming from ever-changing directions. The sleet drops are getting heavier; perhaps they are considered hailstones now. Worst of all the sky is a collage of eerie gray shades. My instincts are screaming that something is very wrong with this storm; something diabolical in nature. Because the screeching wind is encircling me, I have so far taken at least fifty steps forward and yet I haven't moved more than a few yards. It takes more energy and determination than I ever imagined I'd need to reach the rear of the church.

Taking a look back upon the cemetery before making my way to the street, I surmise that this storm is an unforeseen hurricane. Of course in this day and age this is not anything that I ever imagined I'd encounter; no, on the contrary. Storms coming up the East Coast in the Gulf Stream are watched closely and reported on the news incessantly from the time they form. They are tracked minute by minute from even before they are officially declared a hurricane…tropical storms they call them. How in the world could a force of nature such as this have slipped up to Boston without anyone knowing? It's impossible I tell myself. Yet, from where I stand I can plainly see that a storm with more power than I personally have ever witnessed is consuming the ancient cemetery and the woods around its border.

A quick look at my watch tells me it is almost three o'clock in the afternoon. This means I've been out for my so-called half hour daily walk for almost an hour and a half. I am positive that Frank is out looking for me. Since he knows I like to walk through the ancient cemetery I predict this is one of the first places he will come. With the big stone church as a shield against the storm I decide I should just wait for him in the corner formed by the grand church steps and the front of the building. I feel temporarily relieved until a bolt of lightning cracks overhead. I have seen many lightning bolts in my lifetime but never one as long and with as many arms as this one. If a normal lightning bolt generates the light of a 25 watt light bulb in the sky then I'm guessing this bolt had the power of a 500 watt bulb. The rolling thunder that follows the brief light show is so intense it shakes the ground beneath me. Another lightning episode occurs and this time I think I actually see fire in the sky; fire that spins into mini tornadoes. I am overwhelmed by so much horror that I have a desperate desire to get inside the church and be closer to the Christian God. From all that I've heard he's a good guy that'll welcome a petrified Muslim young lady into his home, which, at this moment I most definitely am.

It takes as much courage as determination to get to the steps that lead to the red front door of the Christian God's house. The wind is spinning so rapidly I fear my body will be sucked into a tornado. During this relatively short walk I actually witness a cat flying by; a live cat which will undoubtedly perish when it is slammed against some immovable object. Even though I can't explain what protection the front stairs of the church offer me I do feel safer when I get to them. The railing and the worn stone steps are covered with leaves, branches and bits of garbage that the wind has deposited upon them as it whirled by. Although I can't imagine the church door is unlocked I am determined to try it. I make it almost halfway up the stairs before the combination of the wind and the slippery steps causes me to tumble backwards. My head takes a third beating as I roll down one stair after another. Sprawled out between the bottom step and the sidewalk, my now bleeding body appears defeated. I remind myself I am not a quitter and get up into a sitting position. I know I need to rest and scrounge up some much needed perseverance but I have to push this need aside when I witness the formation of a mini tornado just sixty or so feet from me.

The tornado is growing in size as it travels. It is seemingly grasping its energy from its surroundings. It also inhales things in its path. It takes hold of a garbage can as if it is weightless. First the cover of the container flies off and then pieces of garbage are thrown out of the cyclone randomly. I am so enthralled with this weather based monster that I don't notice a fully formed twister coming at me from the opposite direction.

This one, which is an odd reddish gray color, is bouncing up and down off the ground like it is doing some type of ritualistic dance. It is traveling in an erratic pattern yet it appears to be focused on making contact with me. I witness it flatten a bed of tulips, knock over a stone bird bath, and obliterate a clothesline and the sheets hanging from it. I notice various objects getting sucked up into its tunnel while others are spewed out of it. If I'm not mistaken screaming live animals are traveling inside this atmospheric phenomenon. I'm not sure how long I am watching the reddish gray swirling devil before I notice Frank fighting his way down the street.

As I expected, my brave boyfriend has come to rescue me. His tall well built frame is swaying as he walks amid the wind. He tries uselessly to prevent his unruly brown hair from whipping about his face. Aware that my screams will be muffled by the loud noises of the storm I pull myself up the stair railing and begin to wave my arm furiously about me. Frank waves back. I don't take note that his waving becomes more panicked until I see that he is trying to scream something to me. Suddenly I remember the reddish gray twister which is now less than twenty feet away. I take cover between the cement walls and railings that frame the church entrance stairway. I lie as flat as I can on one of the lowest stairs and wait for the twister to pass over me. I see and feel the wind tunnel pounding the steps as it sweeps some of the church's bushes and plants up within its cyclone. I feel my body being pulled by the wind force as if a giant vacuum nozzle were hovering just over my head. I hear the church railings rattle while I pray that the old iron stays connected to the stone in which it is embedded. Pieces of my hair are being yanked out of my head; the pain is becoming unbearable. Worse of all is an ever present slapping sensation on my body that is so intense I have to close my eyes to endure it. Finally the suction begins to abate and the stinging slaps come to a stop. I am exhausted and emotionally drained but the swirling wind beast seems to be gone.

I hear Frank talking before I open my eyes. The tone of his hysterical voice frightens me. My fingers feel a sticky sensation all over my body and I smell an unpleasant metallic odor. When I finally am able to focus on my surroundings I make out that I am covered in some sort of reddish brown substance; a sticky substance with a peculiar yet familiar smell. Frank kneels over me protectively; he is saying something to me that I can't hear well enough to understand. He is wiping the substance from my face. Then he is inspecting my arms, then my legs and my back and...

"It's blood, Abby, you're covered in blood and I don't know where it's coming from!" he yells over the wind.

"But I'm not hurt," I tell him. "I'm not bleeding that badly."

"Then where is..."

"Wait...the twister had red in it. I saw it, didn't you? The smell, it smells like blood. Could the red be blood? Did it shower blood on me? It was huge is it possible..."

Frank pulls himself up using the iron rails to keep him steady. He is looking at the path of the twister with a confused intensity that assures me he's made a discovery. Without announcing where he is going he leaves me to investigate something I assume was discarded by the reddish gray wind monster. When he returns his voice shakes when he tells me the blood I am covered in likely belongs to the corpse down the street; that is the corpse of a young man we both were familiar with as he worked part time at the gas station down the street.

Chapter 2
Evacuation

The dead body of the young man from our neighborhood gas station has been torn at in a manner which I can only describe at as mangled. It has been cut, hacked, slashed crushed, maimed and mutilated by the wind tunnel in so many places that not even an animal attack could produce this many injuries over such a large area. I've seen pictures of a man who survived a grizzly bear attack who looked in much better shape than this young man. Despite Frank's insistence that we get back to the apartment I refuse to leave the corpse exposed like a discarded piece of rubbish. With so much miscellaneous debris flying about it is fairly easy for me to spot a covering for the body; a piece of a canopy torn off of somewhere that is now plastered against a house across the street. While Frank reluctantly retrieves what will provide a dignified covering for our young acquaintance I silently pray that one of the fire tornadoes I saw coming from the lightning bolts doesn't make a surprise appearance. We wrap the canopy around the body while saying a hasty prayer. I leave the dead body behind with a feeling of helplessness draining me of my strength to fight the raging storm.

Frank, on the other hand, leaves the scene with his usual determination to succeed. He is also insistent on figuring out what exactly is happening around us which, he believes, will best enable us to make proper decisions as to what to do when we get back to our apartment. However, his logic based thinking is tortured by all that we encounter on our short but treacherous journey. The storm itself is terrifyingly odd in that we have never experienced or heard of anything like it in the past. The changing winds, growing hail balls, and dark skies are too eerie for a logical mind to accept as real. Even if Frank could believe the atmosphere of the storm was somehow true to life as we know it, he cannot explain how or why the small twister demons are attacking human beings, including us. The little monsters are sweeping up just about anything in their paths that they are strong enough to grab on to, and, without a doubt, their paths lead to the closest and largest groups of people. We soon learn to avoid the crowded streets and traffic jams even though the roads are the quickest and most direct route back home. Even though we stay to ourselves the wind tunnels find us making it necessary for us to take temporary shelter from them many times along our way. We hide in doorways, under parked cars, behind sheds, and even inside the bed of a landscaper's truck to stay clear of the dangerous demons.

"I heard the mayor tell people in our part of the city to evacuate before I went to find you. I should've packed and taken my car to get you. Now there are traffic jams everywhere. I hate it when I don't take the time to make good decisions," Frank complains. "Of course when I left to find you the storm wasn't the insane thing it is now. Had I known…"

"You couldn't have known and I couldn't have either," I say. "There's no way to evacuate part of a big city like Boston without huge traffic jams. It's not possible. We'd have been caught in traffic no matter what."

Frank shields us from a sheet of tar paper whirls in the wild winds. Inspecting his arm for damage he says, "I'm thinking getting in a traffic jam is not our best interests. Perhaps it's best if we stay on foot."

"Maybe we can get to the subway. I know the T system may be dangerous during a storm but if the trains are running underground then maybe we can get out of the city. Or maybe we could find a secure building somewhere; a place where the officials want people to go while they wait out the storm, like a shelter."

"What you say makes sense except going out on foot is more dangerous than being in a car. It also heightens the possibility of you being recognized."

Shielding my eyes against a surge of wind-powered dirt I say, "I know, but I can hide my face. I think the most dangerous things are the little tornadoes. I've even seen some come from lightning bolts…with fire inside of them. If we figure out what attracts them to people then maybe we can figure out a way to outsmart them."

"Interesting thought, yes, interesting indeed."

With Frank's reasoning mind now somewhat focused on what causes the wind demons to target human beings, I am on higher alert for flying debris. I call out whenever I spot a potential danger. Thankfully, we don't come across any other human corpses.

When we reach our three story apartment house, I'm amazed to see that the damage done to our old brick and stone building is minimal in comparison to the other houses on the street. The bushes near the front and side entrances are uprooted, an overturned empty garbage barrel is lodged against the side of the house, and what appears to have once been a wooden wind chime is dangling from the gutter, but other than these oddities everything seems to be okay. Knowing that Sarah and Randy are in New Hampshire checking out campgrounds for the escape the four of us are planning this summer, I expect to be greeted by silence when I burst into our apartment. Instead I'm greeted by the voice of Boston Homeland Security Chief, Agent Brown, being recorded on our answering machine.

"…me and I will give you details. I caution the four of you to be extremely vigilant during this emergency as there are many people who blame Abby for what her brother has done and will turn their fear of this storm on to her. Since agents of this office will not know where you are it will be impossible for us to ensure that people who wish Abby harm cannot get to her as we have been doing these past few months. Although you do not see my agents you have been living under my watch, do not forget that. Cell phone service is not likely to work reliably during the storm so I can only hope you do hear this message. Call me when and if you can. I wish you luck and safety. Do not take risks. Remember, Abby, you are not an ordinary American caught up in an unexpected storm. You are Mohamed Haddad's sister, and, whether you are in contact with him or not, many believe you are. In times of panic they will assume he, and you, are somehow to blame for their misfortune."

Frank bolts past me and grabs the phone just as the voice message ends. When he begins speaking I realize he's caught Agent Brown just in time. I don't listen to him because I think of the warning I just heard. I then sadly envision the angry words painted on my car and on the sidewalk in front of the house. The horrible insults I've had to endure while finishing my classes this semester had lessened once the other students realized federal agents might be around to protect me and learned harassing me was a punishable offense. I suppose I allowed myself to believe that fewer insults meant there were less people hating me, which, of course, was an illusion I chose to entertain. Frank, Sarah, and Randy shopped, ran errands and did anything else that required being in public so I've been shielded from the horrible looks of people all this time. My parents are in hiding in Connecticut, having abandoned our homestead, without any hope of ever living there again. My brother Abdul has somehow managed to melt into his fiancée Chelsea Rosenfield's elite family in such a way that he doesn't carry the stigma of having a terrorist brother the same way that I do. The fact that he openly and outwardly exhibits his disdain and hatred of Mohamed certainly boosts his popularity with the public masses. I, however, cannot bring myself to behave this way which is why I know Agent Brown's call to me today is so important; like it or not, many people in this city, and probably all over the country, despise me.

"He's given me every phone number he has but if only land lines work we still might not get him. It's weird how he's hoping you're somehow in contact with Mohamed. Hmmm, I don't know why he's so suspicious of you sometimes. Anyways, while you clean up, I'll pack. I'm taking essentials only because Agent Brown is suggesting we go out on foot. The highways are deadlocked." Frank nervously cracks his knuckles; a habit he's had since childhood. "I have some emergency cash. If you have any tucked away somewhere you better grab it."

"I already did," I answer." You haven't told me yet what Agent Brown wants us to do."

"He wants us to get out of here for starters. He also doesn't want you in a crowd of people because he feels that'll be dangerous for you. That eliminates taking the train or going to a shelter."

"Great, so he's got the '*don't do's*' covered which leaves us with what?"

"Basically hiding out in a safe structure - a building made of stone or something sturdy like that - a below ground location being ideal. I even suggested here because our building is weathering the storm fairly well, but he insists we leave because some fanatics know you live here and they're bound to come here looking for you sooner or later."

"Did he say anything about the storm itself, like what is up with this thing and how could a storm like this pop up without any warning?"

"He absolutely wouldn't say a thing about the storm. All I know is what I'm getting from the news, which is broadcasting that this storm is coming from the east, from off of Cape Cod. Unlike all the hurricanes in New England that travel north up the Gulf Stream this one just blew in off the ocean from the east. It's totally bizarre, in the true sense of the word. There isn't any explanation for it and the experts really don't know how to explain it."

"I'm scared," I say, before entering the bathroom with my clean clothes. "We've been through so much in the past couple of years because of Mohamed and the attacks and all that and…I know I should be immune to fear by now. But this storm is different. It feels supernatural, you know? Like this is the end of the world or something."

As he usually does, Frank wins my confidence over with a calmly stated logical summation.

"This storm is most certainly an oddity of nature but it is unlikely to be the end of mankind. No, it will take more than hail stones and twisters to kill off human life. With that in mind I suggest we venture out and make our way toward Boston University. I've thought this through and I believe the stone buildings on the campus offer us the best protection we will find in the area. It is a reasonable distance from here with a web of side streets we can use as we attempt to limit our visibility. Also, the university houses a NSF Science and

Technology center. I'm almost positive that this one studies weather, which, I'm thinking, will be full of scientists right now trying to figure out what's going on around here. Maybe, with some luck, we can sneak inside the place."

*****

Darkness comes before nightfall. The rain and hail filled skies turn slate black in color. Frank and I have been walking for hours. We are soaking wet, exhausted and battle worn. The mini twisters are not quite as small as they once were and now average about five to six feet in height. Thankfully, the wind devils move slowly enough for us to dodge them without getting hurt. When forced to stay out in the open we grasp on to whatever looks solid and sturdy while the wind tosses us around as if we were made of cloth. I find that the newest tornadoes have wind suction that is much stronger than the twister I battled on the stairs of the Episcopal church several hours ago. In fact, I have seen these larger wind demons take hold of grown people, lift them off the ground, and toss them aside. I've also seen them uproot grown trees, topple cars, and rip off the roof of a shed with ease. My fear is growing exponentially with every twister attack we witness.

When we reach Commonwealth Avenue and look upon the great old buildings of Boston University I am taken aback by the number of people gathered in the area. We take temporary refuge beneath a now branchless tree on St. Mary's Street to assess our situation. I soon realize that the subway stop beneath the street is overflowing with anxious evacuees who still hope to get a place on one of the trains leaving this part of the city. These people are mixed in with a group of folks who apparently are trying to gather inside the university's Marsh Chapel. There are also several groups of people from city buses who can no longer continue on their route as the traffic jams have them helplessly locked in place. The bus riders seem to be undecided as to whether or not they should give up their seats on the bus and seek alternate shelter. It's not possible to identify why the countless other people within our sight are out here but I know that, like Frank and me, they don't have anywhere better to be.

"If people start breaking down the doors to the Boston University buildings what will the police do?" I yell over the noisy winds to Frank.

"The cops won't let that happen. No looting and no breaking down doors."

"It's good that school is out for the summer and most of the students are gone."

Frank nods and shrugs; as if to question why I'd bother to make such an observation given the circumstances we're in.

"I have tools," I tell him. "I brought some of the house tools."

Without speaking Frank reaches for my backpack. I proudly pull out a wrench, screwdriver and hammer.

"There's a couple more at the bottom," I say.

"The university buildings have ground level windows. They have protective wire mesh on them, but…" Frank taps the wrench against the palm of his hand and smiles. "If we go to the back of the buildings we can find some trees or bushes to hide behind. Maybe, just maybe, we can get inside."

"We should try. If we stay here I'll be recognized." I adjust the hood of my sweatshirt to hide my face and point to the street. "Let's just do it before we have time to worry about it."

With a renewed sense of determination we haven't felt in hours we march across Commonwealth Avenue. While we inspect the various buildings that line the sidewalk I'm careful to hide my face without appearing to be guilty of a wrongdoing. The presence of the police unnerve me a bit, as they always do because of who I am; however, the officers are clearly overwhelmed with their duties making it somewhat easy for us to scope things out unnoticed. Several police officers are on the steps of the university chapel; one appears to be speaking on a two way radio to someone about the possibility of opening the place.

"This one," Frank screams over the loud winds while pointing to the building to the east of the chapel. "The back door."

Frank leads me to a large building, which, to me, looks like many of the others on the campus. He manages to try to open the back door unobserved for quite some time; unfortunately, the door is locked and there isn't a tool in my backpack that will get us past it. We check the ground level windows along the rear of the structure only to find them covered with secure iron grates. Trying not to let my discouragement and disappointment overwhelm me I enter an alleyway created by the building and the one next to it. This area is empty except for old trees, bushes, and a considerable amount of garbage that the raging wind storm is depositing. Because the windows on the neighboring building are also covered I expect to find the same to be true of the ones on this east side of the building we're currently inspecting. While I inspect the first window I notice Frank passing me to get to the next one. With every ounce of force in my body I try to move the grate only to find it is cemented in place. I don't need to ask Frank how he is making out as I can see his frustration as I pass him to get to the next window. I feel a twinge of hope when I notice the weedy bushes near the ground level window are noticeably flatter than the plants at any of the other windows. As I bend down I see what appears to be a partial sneaker print in the damp dirt.

"Look!" I yell feeling rather than seeing Frank behind me.

"Damn, it moved. I saw it. It's loose! Move over and let me get at it!" Frank bends down grabbing on to the heavy iron bars. Although they are firmly embedded in the cement they do move enough for us to realize that someone has broken through them before now.

I hand Frank the tools he needs while he works on the bars. I feel a bit like a surgical nurse handing the surgeon tools during an operation. Despite his grunts, groans, and occasional swears, Frank masterfully wedges the loosened grate away from the window. He discovers the window itself to be unlocked. Without a flashlight to see what awaits him inside, he bravely lowers himself down into the darkness. I hear furniture move and something fall over before I see Frank's up-stretched hands.

"Let me help you down," he calls up. "Hurry before someone notices you. Throw down the backpacks first. Hurry!"

His strong arms effortlessly lower my petite body. I'm greeted by an odd smell of bleach mixed with salt, an uncomfortable coolness, and just enough grayish light to see shadows of unknown objects scattered inside a wide open area. While I nervously hold Frank's legs as he balances on a high laboratory stool, he replaces the grate and closes the window leaving them exactly as we find them.

"What are the odds that we'd find a way into this place?" I ask, thinking our luck is changing for the good.

"The odds were higher than you think. This is the building that houses the NSF Science and Technology Center. Like I said before, I think this center deals with integrated space weather modeling. If any building on this campus has someone sneaking inside of it during a storm like we're having today it would be this one. I can see I'm right." Frank points to the floor. "I can see dirty foot smudges that aren't ours. Whoever broke in through that window before came prepared with better tools than we had and they're here for a purpose. And that's why I wanted to come here. If anything weird is happening with this storm I'd like to know what it is."

"Like what are you thinking?"

"I don't know what to think but I do know weird when I see it. I also think it strange that Agent Brown was so concerned about you. Sure, he makes an excellent point about your safety but I sense there was something else about his reason for calling. I don't know what but it was like he wanted to make sure we disappeared until he could reinstate the surveillance he has on you. And, mentioning Mohamed like he did. It's not logical for me to rely on feelings like this but...he seemed...off."

I store Frank's instinct driven observation in my memory and say, "Hmmm, I guess the humming noises I hear and the moving water sounds make this room a science lab of sorts. I can't quite make out what all the equipment is from here but I can see dim light shining off of many metal objects."

"We'll only know for sure if we take a look around. We need to be careful and quiet though. We don't want whoever else is inside this place to know we're inside."

We discover an intricate water system made up of various vats running along one entire wall of the room. The presence of sea water explains the salt smell that permeates the air. There are scattered desks piled with paperwork, glass beakers, and computer equipment. There are tables with chemistry set ups arranged in neat rows and white boards covered with letters and numbers of which I can't make sense. The largest object in the laboratory is unidentifiable. It resembles the sort of light a dentist uses while working on your teeth except it has more metal on it and it is almost one third the size of the room. A large and powerful light is the source of the constant humming noise that has haunted me since we arrived.

"Whatever they're doing in here they certainly do like things clean," Frank comments, while we pass by the biggest and best stocked cleaning cart I've ever seen in my life.

"That explains the fine aroma of bleach I've been smelling."

"Given a different set of circumstances I'd be real interested to learn what they're doing in here."

"I'd just like to know why they have all this sea water and no animals. I'd think if they were going to go through all the trouble of maintaining sea water they'd at least have some fish or a lobster or something."

"They have a variety of marine plant life which, I assume, is the object of their research."

"Well let's see if they have a variety of furniture for us to rest on and maybe, if we're extra lucky, some vending machines."

"Good idea."

Frank slowly leads me out of the lab into a hallway that is lit only by emergency exit signs. I'm a bit surprised when he dares to go up the stairs since venturing to a new level is a bit risky. Of course I follow after him like a sheep following a shepherd, hoping to spot the welcoming bright colored lights of a soda machine. I find the ground level floor, which I assume to be the first floor as opposed to the basement from which we just walked, to be much warmer and more hospitable. In fact, I am quite taken with the oil portraits that grace the Ivy League hallways when my thoughts are interrupted.

"Who are you and why are you here? Tell me now or pay the price!"

Face to face with a wild haired big boned mad man with a gun aimed at our faces, I try to scream only to find my voice is hopelessly out of my reach.

Chapter 3
Arnie

Since I have come face to face with several guns during these past couple of years I have experience in how to react to people with their finger on the trigger: tell them whatever they want to know. Unfortunately, in this case, I sense that the wild eyed giant looking down on my less than five foot body will not be satisfied with my answer to his question, but I deliver it with most accommodating pleading voice all the same.

"We're here trying to get out of the storm and we were curious about finding scientists in the NSF office who might be able to explain…"

"You look familiar. Are you a reporter?" the now drooling maniac asks.

"No, no…I'm a student."

The madman re-aims the gun at Frank while asking, "You then, are you a reporter?"

"Whoa…hey now, put the gun down, okay? I'm not a reporter, either. We're just here to get out of the storm, that's all. I knew this building was where the NSF was so I figured with this weird storm hitting Boston that some scientists would have this place open," Frank explains. "My name is Frank Stiller and this is…"

"I know who she is. Yeah, I see it now. She is Abia Haddad, sister of Mohamed Haddad. Am I correct?" The armed man inspects me like a horse breeder looks over a newly born foal.

I make a brave, but weak, attempt to shake hands. The strange man's free hand feels damp and cold; it doesn't respond to my touch. "You're right, I am Abby Haddad. I assure you that although my brother is believed to be a threat to this country, I am not. And your name?" My attempt to make casual conversation in these circumstances sounds ludicrous even to me.

"My name is not your business. May I suggest that you get out of here before I make your trespassing in this building my business?"

"Listen, please lower the gun so we can…" Frank begins to suggest when a distant hallway door sweeps open. "Hello, hey, can you help us here? Can you get this guy to put the gun away? Please? We're just college students coming in from the storm and mean you no harm."

The wild haired stranger continues to stare at us with his gun drawn. Without turning to see the second stranger he says, "Arnie, this is the infamous Abia Haddad, and, I believe, her boyfriend Frank Stiller. As you just heard they claim they came to this building to get out of the storm. Frank states he selected our building because he knew the NSF was here and suspected there would be people, like us, working during this unprecedented weather disturbance. I, however, do not know if we can believe him. After all, how many people know what the National Science Foundation is and that its Center for Integrated Space Weather Modeling is located here at Boston University?"

Arnie looks like he could be cast in the part of the college nerd in a Hollywood movie. He is tall, thin, awkward, plain looking and wears thick glasses. He is also clad in the typical nerd attire of khaki pants and a plaid short sleeved cotton shirt. His mannerisms are odd in that he will not make eye contact with us, or, for that matter, look much at us at all. Without bothering to turn to his friend he announces, "Rocky, you may put the unloaded weapon away. I believe these people mean us no harm. It is not logical to treat them as a threat as there is no evidence they have knowledge of who we are or why we are here."

Rocky sneers as he obeys Arnie's commands. Without as much as a nod he turns on his heels and strides down the hallway. Alone with the odd man named Arnie I feel less threatened by violence but no less comfortable with what is happening in this odd place.

Frank, who is biting at his fingernails, looks at Arnie and says, "Okay, I'm totally confused by what is happening here and I'm not even sure I want to know more. Obviously you and Rocky and whoever else is here are doing something without permission because it seems from the window that we used to sneak in that you all snuck in here. And I know that you're here because of the crazy storm that is blowing west off the Cape instead of up the Gulf Coast. Well, blowing mainly west, as in that is where the storm is coming from. The actual wind gusts appear to be rather erratic; they're coming from various directions simultaneously. Anyway, I'm willing to bet you're in here trying to figure out more about this unpredicted storm and why the little tornado twister things seem to target people. And the tornadoes with the fire in them; they must fascinate you too. But even knowing all of this and putting the pieces I have together I don't get why you're so afraid to get caught doing research. But, hey, it's no problem. Abby and I will go back downstairs and hang out with all the water and equipment located there and pretend we never saw you or your bulldog pal named Rocky, deal?"

"Arnie, don't worry about us saying anything about you and your friends being here because we're really good at keeping secrets. Hey, you know all about me and what I've been through because of my brother, right? If nothing else our messed up terrorist plotted political haunted conspiracy theory past proves we can keep a secret, right?" I add. "I just need to be away from people because…well… Mohamed is…"

"Because they fear you as they fear your brother?" Arnie asks. "This is understandable although it is neither logical nor sensible."

"Excuse me?" I ask.

"Your brother's past behavior is not evidence that you are personally involved in terrorism. Although the enemy called Eurabia was a nine headed team of which eight members are known and one is unknown, this does not make Mohamed guilty of being the unknown enemy." Arnie explains.

"So you don't believe my brother is the ninth Eurabian?"

"No. That is my personal opinion."

Moving to where Frank thinks he is in Arnie's line of vision, he says, "May I ask why you believe Mohamed is innocent? Is your opinion based on any facts?"

After a fleeting glance into my face he states, "Three of the eight Eurabians represented: the House of Representatives, the Senate and the Supreme Court. These members were needed to control the government. There was a mafia boss, a well-connected business man, and a Hollywood powerhouse. These members were needed to handle the logistics. The enemy had two specialists: a terrorist mastermind and an inside Homeland Security agent. The specialists provided knowledge, resources and needed protection. The question is what did Mohamed Haddad have to offer this group called Eurabia? I can think of nothing beneficial. In fact, having Mohamed Haddad, who is a wanted criminal, on the panel was a detriment to the Eurabians, not a contribution. Also, the members of Eurabia were connected to the group directly or indirectly through their families for decades, this could not have been true of Mohamed? No, Abia's brother had nothing to offer the Eurabians but to be a scapegoat. That is, he took the blame for their wrongdoings. Was he a member of Eurabia? I think not. He was a pawn of the evil enemy and nothing more."

The open dialogue about Mohamed has changed the tense atmosphere to one best described as careful camaraderie. The possibility of friendship is yet a distant thought.

"I totally agree with you and we've been stressing this to the big guys in Washington for months but they don't seem to be buying into it," Frank explains.

"Like you, I think the evidence overwhelmingly indicates the unknown Eurabian cannot be Mohamed."

"They don't want to believe he's changed, or, they don't want us to know that they think he has. Either way, Mohamed remains a hunted man and I am his hated sister," I complain. "So, tell me, who do you think the ninth Eurabian is?"

Arnie looks up and past us. "I will share my suspicions only after you share yours."

"Okay. We believe it is someone else with some kind of connection to the New England area. This person may live here full time or part of the year, or own a company here, or something of that nature. Since all the other members have solid reasons for being in the Boston and Cape Cod area we believe this person has to have ties to the area as well. We also think the person is a government type, but more in a branch or agency of the government than in elected office. They had a guy in Homeland Security for physical attacks but we're thinking about someone who could work with Eurabia on more unconventional kinds of terrorist attacks," Frank explains.

"We're thinking the ninth Eurabian could be someone at the FDA, or in the Transportation Department, or a computer systems person, or…well, someone like that." I feel my excitement growing as it always does when we talk about this topic. "Think about what could happen if a powerful person in the Energy Department could somehow bring down the power grids across the country. What if our food supply was tainted or we had an epidemic of a disease that we couldn't control."

Arnie cocks his head to the side appearing as if he is processing our thoughts. "We think much alike. I, however, have knowledge that you do not. I know from my own research that this unconventional attack you speak of has already begun."

"What?" I ask, dumbfounded that this curious young man would make such a profound announcement.

"The storm we are experiencing today is, according to my scientific analysis and calculations, an attack. In this case the weapon is the weather and we are the targets. Just as Frank stated earlier, the small cumulonimbus tuba, I mean tornadoes, have been weaponized to hunt for and attack human life. This is being done by sensitization of body heat, carbon dioxide, movement, um and, well …other scientific methods which I believe you may not understand or be interested in." Arnie looks directly at us for the first time. His apologetic smile softens his rather sharp features. "Applying weather modification methods for the purposes of military operations is a science that has been studied for quite some time."

"Are you suggesting that the ninth Eurabian is someone from the military who is involved in a program that is modifying weather activity to use it as a weapon? Are you saying that the United States is developing a weather weapon that can attack a country by starting a hurricane or a blizzard on the enemy's land instead of shooting missiles and bombs at them?" I ask, stunned at the enormity of Arnie's accusation.

"Yes, such a program exists. You see, weather-modification is part of our national security policy with both domestic and international applications. It is defined as the alteration of weather phenomena over a limited area for a limited amount of time. So, to answer your question, yes, such things as creating hurricanes and blizzards would fall into this definition." Arnie cocks his head adding, "My reasons for believing Mohamed Haddad is not the ninth Eurabian is partly based on the fact that I believe whoever is this enemy is indeed responsible for this weapons-based weather storm. I do not believe Mohamed has the knowledge or the capability of creating this storm."

"Wait a minute here. We've all heard the conspiracy theorists talk about weather weapon technology in the United States and Russia but most intelligent people believe it's a bunch of hype," Frank points out. "I mean, there isn't any evidence that weather weapons exist, is there?"

"What more evidence do you need than the storm you are hiding from at this very moment?" Arnie asks sincerely. "Are not the attacking twisters, irrational wind patterns and irregular hail precipitation enough proof that something has greatly impacted the weather patterns of this area? Is it not believable that the storm phenomena we are experiencing today are the result of an alteration or modification of the weather?"

Frank and I share a few confused thoughts before I ask what I believe to be the next obvious question. "Let's say that you're right and this storm is really a weather weapon. Who made the storm and why?"

"I believe the ninth Eurabian is at the root of this attack; however, I do not know if he or she is solely responsible. I cannot begin to assume who would initiate a storm such as this or why he or she would do so. I can theorize that the only person or persons with the capability to do so are or were connected to the military, have control and knowledge of at least some parts of the weather modification program, and are enemies of this country." Arnie scratches his head and adds, "Considering what has transpired just months ago with the exposure of the enemy called Eurabia we know that two of these dangerous enemies are not captured. One is Carlos Bertoni, the New Jersey mob boss. The other, as we have discussed, is unknown. With enemies such as this unaccounted for it is logical to deduce that they are somehow connected to the weather attack of today."

"That's crazy," Frank mutters. "Okay, so let's assume you're right, what could they gain by attacking Boston with a storm?"

"I know little of the Eurabian enemy other than what I hear on the news. This information, of course, has been filtered through the government which makes it incomplete at best and possibly even misleading. For this reason I cannot begin to consider the motivation for today's attack." Arnie checks the time on his oversized black band wrist watch. "I do not have an objection with you remaining in the building. I will speak to the others."

Arnie's short direct dismissal takes me off guard. "Are you their leader?" I ask.

"Oddly put but yes, I am in charge."

"How many are with you?" Frank asks.

"There are five of us. We are all scientists." With a hint of a smile Arnie adds, "Rocky is a scientist as well as a second amendment enthusiast. I allow him to carry his handgun as long as he allows me to hold the bullets."

Frank initiates a hand shake in which Arnie hesitantly engages. His discomfort with being touched is obvious. "Tell me something straight. There's no way you and Rocky and the rest of your scientist team would be bothering with a gun unless you're all afraid of someone or something. So, of whom or what are you so frightened? Who is threatened by your research of weather modification weapons?"

"Carlos or whoever the ninth Eurabian is, of course," Arnie replies.

"Have you seen Carlos or the ninth Eurabian? Have you been contacted by them?" Frank presses.

"No, not them."

"Have you been contacted by anyone that you think may represent them?" Frank insists.

"I believe so. You see, my team of scientists is working on a grant funded project through the NSF and Boston University. We have had free access to this building and our laboratories for months now. Inexplicably, this morning, the locks had been changed on the front, back, and side doors. So we broke inside earlier today to study the storm, which incidentally, is related to our research. Whoever changed the locks is most surely related to the ninth Eurabian. Of this I am convinced."

Arnie looks past us for a long silent moment. When his dark eyes finally meet mine he squints, as if the contact is physically painful.

"I have Asperger's syndrome; a high functioning form of autism. I am extremely intelligent and articulate although I am also somewhat socially awkward. This condition makes me hypersensitive to the things in my immediate surroundings, such as in my apartment and in the work area I am assigned to use in this building. I am very sure, no I am positive, that a person or persons have looked through my work papers in both of these locations. I cannot prove it to be true, nor can I convince the authorities that my privacy has been violated, but I assure you that it is so."

"Who do you think is monitoring what you're doing?" I hear Frank ask.

"The person spying on me is not important as he or she is unlikely to be more than a hired thug taking pictures of my work. It is whoever hired him or her that is important and that person is a mystery." Arnie breaks the limited eye contact he has with us and adds, "Oddly, it is you who is more likely to identify the person in question than I. After all, if I am correct in assuming this storm is a weather attack spurred by an enemy related to Eurabia or a member thereof, then your intimate knowledge of the group may hold the key to his or her identity."

*****

When Frank and Arnie fall into a deep discussion about weather patterns and the military's effort to weaponize them, I attempt to organize the information that is overwhelming my now overloaded brain. First there is the storm; an oddity of nature in and of itself. Even I, a person not known to be a weather watcher, could tell that the storm I met up with in the cemetery was unlike anything I had witnessed before. The existence of the intimidating mini tornadoes is frightening enough, nevermind the fact that these impossible wind tunnels are somehow able to detect and target human life. The fire filled wind demons are most frightening of all. The flame throwers, I can only hope, are rarities.

Next I am informed by Homeland Security that the people who have been unofficially watching me will be taken off my tail because of the magnitude of the storm. Okay, this makes sense, except that Homeland Security agents don't normally get involved with weather events; I don't think. Why is Homeland Security concerned with a hurricane unless this storm is not just any storm but really a weaponized storm just like Arnie suggests?

And now I'm in a science building of Boston University, where we run into a mildly autistic scientist and his team of four workers; one of which is a hulk of a man named Rocky who carries an unloaded gun. As odd as this place is, the fact that Arnie has built a bridge between today's storm and the Eurabian battle I was fighting just months ago has me convinced that I was meant to come here for a reason. But surely I can't get myself involved in hunting down Carlo Bertoni and the last Eurabian or whoever else is involved in this so-called weather attack on the country. Why would I even want to get myself involved in such a thing? The very thought of it is ludicrous. No, I need to figure out a way to earn money this summer selling my handcrafted jewelry at craft shows with Sarah because that is the only way I'll ever earn a buck. Yeah, making money when no one will hire you because your brother is a terrorist isn't easy and this jewelry thing seems my only way out. So, getting involved in this storm thing and hunting down the ninth Eurabian shouldn't even cross my mind. Yet, Arnie is right about one thing…my friends and I probably are the best people available to figure out who the unknown Eurabian is. That makes us the best people to solve the mystery as to who is waging this weaponized weather attack on us. Well, actually, we're not the best. There is one person who has even more knowledge about this mysterious enemy in his head than we do, even if he's unaware that he knows as much as he does about the matter, and that is Mohamed himself. Yes, Mohamed lived among these men for two years and in all that time surely he got to know who all nine of the Eurabians were, wouldn't that make sense? Yet he states he never knew the ninth one…the unknown one. If Mohamed is telling the truth, then why was the identity of the ninth Eurabian kept such a mystery? Is it possible that Mohamed does know the identity of the unknown enemy and refuses to tell us? If that's the case then….is Mohamed really as reformed as I believe he is? Of course he's reformed; why do I even think such stupid thoughts. You know, the only way to prove that Mohamed isn't the ninth Eurabian is to prove who really is. Maybe that is reason enough for me to get involved in this mystery Arnie is trying to unravel.

My thoughts are interrupted by the echoing sound of a distant explosion. Arnie and his team run downstairs.

Frank hands me my backpack. "Come on, we might as well follow them and see what is happening out there."

We are careful not to be seen as we slither up from the window and out from behind the bushes. There is no sign of Arnie and his scientist team anywhere. There are, however, chaotic people all around us; screaming aimlessly as they run in no particular direction. A louder explosion blasts my ear drums. I look to the east expecting to see a building on fire, a bridge collapsing, or some other major calamity. Instead, off in the distance, is a gray twirling mass of wind with a firestorm at its core. The eye-piercing light emitting from this dark monster is shooting lightning bolts out of its center in every direction; including down on the people below. The bolts of lightning shed spark showers as they move, leaving a trail of small fires in their wake. The explosive noises, I soon learn, are a form of thunder traveling inside the tornado, which, for some reason, neither precedes nor follows the lightning strikes but rather just explodes arbitrarily. This horrendous monster seems to be traveling along the Charles River which means it is heading our way. Like the frenzied people around me I cannot begin to process what I am witnessing.

"That thing…the fire tornado… it's moving slowly. Do we have time to get away from it?" I ask.

"I'm estimating it to be at least a mile and a half in circumference. No, escape is not possible." Frank replies.

"Maybe we should head for the water because at least in there we'd be safe from the fire?"

"Safe from the fire but in the direct line of the storm. Also, water is a conduit for electricity which would attract the lightning to us. No, not the river."

"Okay, so what do we do?"

Frank looks at me with fear and frustration in his eyes. "There is no place safe for us to go because there is no way for us to get out of this section of the city. So, I guess, the only thing to do is to go home."

Like an unthinking robot I follow my boyfriend to our new destination; dodging people, flying objects, and storm precipitation as I do my best not to be recognized. In fact we make solid progress until a streak of fire zips over our head and lands amid a group of parked cars. The shrieks of human terror momentarily drown out the ugly noises of the horrifying tornado. I feel my legs weaken when a human form engulfed in fire rolls out into the street.

Chapter 4
Sempre Forte

My stomach churns when the smell of burning human flesh blows past me. Not even the smoke from the human fireball's clothing can cover up the horrible odor. When the crowd thins I see that the two men who ran to this victim's aid have successfully put the fire out before he perished; however, his injuries look painfully severe. Frank's arm pulls me away from this tragedy only to enmesh me in the chaos of a panicked crowd. With people screaming as they run about randomly, I can't help but get caught up in their frenzy. It is Frank's unwavering calmness that guides us out from the center of this growing mob. Once we're safely at the edge of the Boston University campus we stop to examine our situation. Toward the east I see that the fire in the core of the huge tornado that looms above the Charles River radiates against the uncanny darkness of the black cloud crowded sky. Hypnotized by a sight I cannot convince myself is real, I do not notice when Arnie and Rocky join us.

"It is both fascinating as well as astonishing, is it not?" Arnie asks in the most animated tone I've heard from him yet. "It is on course to hit the University NSF laboratory as we expected."

"Which is why we were there taking all of our research data," Rocky explains. "Now we can keep working from a new location."

"You and the team can, yes. I will be going to the Otis Military Base, remember?" Arnie says to Rocky. "That is imperative in regard to gathering all of the critical information we need to continue on with our work."

"You speak so freely about what you're doing in front of us. I know you can trust us but how do you know that?" I ask the scientists.

"We just decided we could, that's all." Rocky scans the area from his extremely tall vantage point. "I'm going to check on the others. Meet us over there, okay boss?"

"Affirmative." Arnie dismisses his team member during this crisis with less emotion than I feel for an ant when I step on one. With his now familiar head tilt he steps uncomfortably close to us and says, "It is not just a matter of trust it is a matter of logic. I trust you because I need you. I believe the answer to the mysterious weather storms is related to the United States' weatherized weapons program. I believe this weapon is being used against our country by an enemy. I believe that enemy either is or is related to the ninth Eurabian. I believe the only people who have any hope of discovering the identity of the ninth Eurabian are you, your friends and, most importantly, Mohamed Haddad. Therefore, it behooves me to trust you so you will work with me to solve the mysterious things that are unfolding around us. Does this not make sense?"

Frank waits for me to nod before saying, "Yes it does. So tell me more about the Otis Military Base. Be quick because that tornado is on the move and its only a matter of time before someone recognizes Abby."

*****

The short time we speak with Arnie is long enough for the huge fire based tornado to spin out more small fire demons. Each one of the life threatening horrors creates stampeding crowds of terrified people. As frightening as being swept up into one of the human tidal waves feels to me, I am even more afraid of being cornered by a fire breathing wind tunnel. What has me most on edge is that once these horrors are launched from the core of the mother tornado they can linger about until they find a human being to attack. This means that deadly danger is lurking all around us all of the time. It also means that my nerves are sharply on edge making me react to every sound regardless of how threatening it may be. I am mentally exhausted before we are one third of the way back home. By the halfway mark I am physically exhausted from fighting the powerful wind. I am also questioning our decision to go back home.

"Are you sure this is the smart thing to do?" I shout at Frank. "We're supposed to be evacuating our apartment not going there. Besides, Agent Brown absolutely doesn't think I'm safe there because people will come looking for me."

"I know all that but you're safer there than on the streets. There is no where else to go. Agent Brown didn't know a fire tornado was going to come ripping through the city when he told us to try to leave."

"True, but…"

Frank jerks me into the doorway of a brick building seconds before cars on the street explode. Although I don't actually witness the gaseous vapors turning to flames and the twisting metal ripping apart, I do see the aftermath of the numerous blasts that I hear. I also glimpse enough human debris to know that the fire tornado's destruction took innocent casualties. I am sickened at the sight and smell of what we witness when we finally gather our nerve to leave the safety of our shattered glass filled entryway. While I consider the odds that such a horrific thing would happen so close to where we are walking, I hear a blast that dwarfs the one we just witnessed. Turning, I see flames rising into the dark grey sky. While Frank guesses which structure has fallen victim to yet another fire tornado, I allow a numbness to creep over me. Rather than engage my brain in thoughts of Boston geography and possible tragedies, I silently pick shards of broken glass from the back of my boyfriend's jacket. Thinking of how the windows in the building entryway blew inward when the gas tanks in the pack of cars began to ignite I remind myself that, like glass, human life is fragile.

It takes us four long and torturous hours to get home. Along the way we witness enough horror and heartache to break the spirit of even the most hopeful of mankind. The crazed storm with the tornado of fire has taken many lives; probably far more than I can even make sense of in the state I'm in. The damage to the buildings, cars, landscape, and other physical things is so vast I can't begin to process it other than to think of my surroundings as a war zone after a bomb has hit. Each time I point something out to Frank I hear myself saying the word devastating which is likely the best description of our surroundings. Although our apartment house is quite some distance from the direct path of the biggest flaming tornado, the wind and hail damage is considerable. There are also rumors going about that looters are beginning to hit the streets; an added threat to an already dangerous situation.

"I figured the power would be out but I didn't expect this street to be so empty. I'm starting to wonder if we're the only people even on this block," I murmur while following Frank inside the dark entryway of our building. "What ever happened to the emergency lighting requirements?"

"This hallway had emergency lighting but something made them die," Frank tells me in a tired voice.

"Or looters took the battery out so they could go through all the apartments without being seen."

While fumbling through his backpack for a flashlight, Frank says, "Stay a distance behind me just in case things aren't as they should be, okay? Not that I'd expect anything weird to be happening in the apartment but you never know, right?"

Frank's fear spreads over me like fog does after a rainy night. The fear turns to terror when we find the door to our apartment is open. Not sure whether or not the person who broke into our home is still there, I grab on to Frank's arm. He quietly unclenches my clinging fingers and points for me to go downstairs.

When I obey his order, he inhales deeply and slowly pushes the slightly ajar door open. Although my first intention is to wait for him below, where I am safe from one or more intruders, my conscious tells me I can't allow my boyfriend to take all the risks alone. I remind myself that if there is some evil doer waiting for us in the apartment this person is most likely after me as I am Mohamed Haddad's sister; therefore, it should be me that comes face to face with danger. Frightened but determined, I creep back up the stairs and am about to call out Frank's name when I hear furniture banging around and a muffled male voice yelling. With no advantage except the element of surprise I crawl though the door and hide behind the coat tree. I feel along the carpeted floor for Sarah's umbrella, which I quickly realize is not where I last remember it. Thinking of what else I can use for a weapon I visualize the gaudy bowling trophy Frank won years ago that he stubbornly insists be put out on display. Unfortunately it isn't actually being displayed but rather it is being used as a doorstopper in the bathroom. Since I don't know the exact location where Frank and the intruder are fighting I need to figure a safe way to cross the apartment to retrieve it.

Despite the darkness surrounding me I feel sure there is no one in the living room area nearby or the kitchen to my left. Forcing myself to crawl across the cool tile floor I am careful not to allow my shoes to make a scraping sound. My rescue effort is cut short when Frank and a man about his size come brawling into the kitchen. When Frank's bloodied body crashes against the sink I can hear his breath being pushed out of him. Allowing my survival impulses to guide me I jump up, grab a chair, and crash it down as hard as I can on the mysterious man's head. I expect him to fall to his feet, at which time I assume Frank and I will easily subdue him, but that doesn't happen. Instead he manages to regain his composure remarkably fast and grab hold of my shoulders. I kick him, scream, bite his arm, spit in his face, and pull his hair to no avail. It is the knee to his groin that slows the intruder down just enough for Frank to whack him with a frying pan.

"Good grief this guy is some sort of animal! I can't believe he's this tough. And mean…" I'm saying, as I nervously look through the kitchen drawer for something to tie the stranger up with.

"Go under the sink in the tool box. There's electrical tape in there," Frank says. "And hurry, he's already coming around."

"You do his mouth and hands and I'll do his ankles."

Frank rips the tape with his teeth and hands me every other piece. Having little experience with hostage taking I am about to wind the tape around the man's socks when Frank tells me to tape his skin. Doing this I notice his legs are tattooed; not a little tattooed but seemingly covered in tattoos. A quick inspection of his arms confirms that the mysterious intruder is indeed covered in ink.

"Okay, now that he's secured what do we do with him?" I ask, trying my best to keep my senses about me. "I'd like to call Agent Brown and make this his problem, but, of course, given this storm and his earlier call, that isn't possible. For that matter, I doubt any police at all will be available to come on by and deal with this."

Frank points the beam of the flashlight into the man's face. "He's not some looter or anything like that. He knows we live here and figured we wouldn't be home so he came here. Why?"

"To get something that we have that he thinks is valuable. We don't have money so that's out. We don't have…"

"Maybe he thinks we have clues to Mohamed's location?"

"What makes you think that? Who could he be that he'd want to find my brother? And why wait for this incredible storm to come around to look for clues and…"

Frank's eyes widen as he says, "I think he's waking up. This guy is made of iron. Damn it, we're going to have to whack his head again."

I retrieve the frying pan with a deep sense of trepidation. I fear we will accidentally go too far with keeping this stranger under our control. With no logical alternative course of action to suggest, I hand my boyfriend the pan and inwardly pray that a light tap will knock the consciousness from the intruder's head. As it turns out the deed requires far more than a tap. The egg shaped bump on the stranger's head is a bulging mass of ugly red and blue tissue which, as I watch it, is melding into the color purple. I have no doubt the bruise will be sizeable. What I do have doubts about is whether or not the damaged head can recover without blood clots, concussions, or brain damage of some sort.

Frank and I soon learn that it is much harder to move a heavy lifeless body around a dark apartment than it would seem. By the time we have the stranger bound, gagged, tied securely to a radiator, and checked for any hint of identity, we are both physically spent. Our mental states are equally diminished.

"Okay, so we know by the words on this dude's tattoos that he's Italian," I surmise. "And we know by the fact that he doesn't carry an ID that he's probably a professional thug who doesn't want to be identified. What we don't know is why he's here and what he wants."

"We know more than that. One thing I took the time to learn after Carlo Bertoni escaped the big Eurabia bust was what kind of weapons the mafia uses. Well, of course they use just about anything they can get their hands on but they execute people with small caliber weapons because it reduces blood and brain spatter when they shoot victims in the head. And, if I'm not mistaken, the weapon this guy has is small…like a 22 caliber."

"You know that? Really?"

"I also know that the tattoo on the man's right arm that reads *Sempre Forte* with a fist in it is a typical mafia tattoo. In Italian it means 'Forever Strong.' The fist, of course, speaks for itself."

Re-examining the thug's rather handsome slim face I now recognize the ethnic features of a man of Italian heritage. The olive toned skin, somewhat large nose, and his dark arched shaped eyebrows indicate that the man leaning up against the wall in my kitchen has Italian blood running through his veins.

"So is it safe to assume that Carlo Bertoni sent him here?" I ask, hoping that my logic based boyfriend will find a reason to answer in the negative.

"I believe it is reasonable to believe that is the case. This leads me to conclude a couple more things."

Frank helps me to my feet and leads me away from our hostage. I recognize his tender touch as a precursor of his need to tell me something that I do not want to hear. Although I've never been able to totally prepare myself for bad news concerning the incredible mess my brother Mohamed is in, I do manage to brace myself for the inevitable bad theories I know my boyfriend is about to tell me.

"If this man was sent here by Carlo Bertoni during the storm, that means Carlo Bertoni is either in control of the United States' weather weapons program or is connected to someone who is. I doubt that the New Jersey crime boss has infiltrated the weather weapons department of the US Military which means Carlo is in partnership with whomever has such power; the mysterious ninth Eurabian." Frank cracks his knuckles while leaning closer to me. "So the question becomes why is Carlo interested in us? Or is it the ninth Eurabian who wants us? After thinking about it, though, I'm not sure it is us they're after. It can't be us because we don't know anything so… that leads me to believe they're after Mohamed. So, Abby, I have to ask you something straight up. As far as I know you haven't been in touch with Mohamed since the Eurabia bust six months ago; is this true or is there something you need to tell me?"

I think Frank could tell by my nervous shake and misty eyes that I was guilty of being in communication with my brother before I admitted it to him. As I explained my walks to the ancient cemetery and the exchanges behind the gravestone in the last row my beloved boyfriend's face was absent of emotion. As I finished my confession I braced myself for a look of anger and scolding harsh words. This is not the reaction I witnessed, however. Instead, Frank said nothing. In complete silence he looked at me and allowed his dark eyes to speak on his behalf. Without words his eyes told me my boyfriend felt betrayed.

*****

With a heart heavy with regret I listen as Frank thinks aloud about our options. Yes, we need to get rid of this mafia hoodlum. Yes, we'd like to know more about why he's here first. Yes, it is very risky for us to question the mafia man who could then repeat whatever we say to Carlo Bertoni. Yes, calling Agent Brown is a wise idea. No, getting in touch with Agent Brown will not be easy. No, talking to Agent Brown about the entire weather weapons program at this point is not a good idea. No, Agent Brown will not believe Mohamed is not the ninth Eurabian even though Arnie's theory makes perfect sense. Yes, this strange mafia man may know all about Abby and Mohamed's secret cemetery communication.

"When I weigh it all out I see no alternative but to call Agent Brown and let him deal with this guy. If we let the intruder go we have too much to lose. We've learned what we need to know from him. Carlo and possibly the ninth Eurabian want Mohamed for some reason and that's a fact," Frank announces.

"I think that reason is extremely important. I could…"

"In the future I'd prefer it if we discussed contact with your brother. Perhaps we need to contact him. We will consider this when we are under less pressure. For now let's try our best to get Agent Brown to help us with the goon we have tied up in here. I'm also thinking he may be able to get us jobs on the Otis Military base."

"What? Why would we want to do that? We already have our summer jobs, remember? Going to craft shows throughout New England selling crafts? Sarah and Randy are booking shows up north right now."

"This thing with your brother will never end unless we make it end. You'll never let it go until Mohamed is proved not to be the ninth Eurabian. You'll continue to do anything and everything to be in contact with him as long as you believe there is a chance he can redeem himself and live a normal life. Besides all of that, the Eurabian fiasco isn't really over until all nine of the enemy are down and that just isn't the case. Carlo Bertoni is on the loose and so is the mysterious ninth Eurabian." With his eyes softening just a bit Frank adds, "We have to go to Cape Cod and get jobs on the Otis base if we're going to work with Arnie on figuring out what the weather weapons storms are all about. Arnie told me if we had the right connections we could get jobs on the base, which has this program where they track animals in the wild. They research endangered species and how they adapt to mankind and the changing environment and…"

I stop Frank's rambling words by putting my hand up.

"What are you talking about? We are getting jobs on an Air Force base? Are you out of your mind? I'm Mohamed Haddad's sister and you think this government will put me on a military base?"

"Abby, listen to me. Agent Brown knows how much danger you're in as long as people believe Mohamed is loose and trying to harm this country. I know when he finds out about our Italian mafia visitor he will freak out about what could have happened to you…to us. So, we tell him we know about the program and we want to be taken there for safety reasons. We say that Randy and Sarah will stay close by on the Cape and presto…we're on the base."

If I didn't still feel the deep hurt of having betrayed Frank I might have laughed off his suggestion but instead I ask, "Okay, so if this works out at the base what exactly will I be doing this summer?"

"Turtles, we'll be finding turtles in the woods on the base and logging their weight, size, and locations. You see, I believe how this program works is that each tutle is numbered and…"

Although he keeps babbling out words of explanation he loses my attention when visions of turtle hunting sweep into my mind. Never having had a pet turtle my experience with the creatures is restricted to children's books and cartoons. This means that my knowledge of them is equally limited. I know turtles are slow movers, have shells, and hide inside their shells whenever they get scared. I know they're reptiles, at least I think they are, and some people make soup out of them. I also know that they have teeth but I'm not sure if their bite hurts. Deep in thoughts of turtles, I am aroused back to reality at the mention of Agent Brown.

"If we call the Boston office and tell them who we are and that we have an intruder in here that we believe is related to Carlo Bertoni, then I'm sure they'll locate Agent Brown no matter where he is."

"There's only one hitch."

"What's that?"

"If we call Agent Brown and tell him Carlo Bertoni sent a thug to our place looking for a clue to find Mohamed then, in a way, we're dragging Mohamed into all of this."

"Then we don't tell him that. We're just guessing that, anyway."

In a matter of minutes Frank puts our plan into action. As he expected, his call to the Homeland Security office is blown off until he states he is calling on my behalf and there is an intruder in my apartment who we believe to be connected to Carlo Bertoni. Agent Brown has a staffer return our call. He and his team are in my apartment within 40 minutes. There are, however, a few pieces of our plans that don't work out quite so well. First, Agent Brown is in no mood to discuss getting us jobs on the Air Force base. Secondly, his staff is pounding us with questions that we are ill prepared to answer. And lastly, the intruder is apparently far more banged up than we thought he was. In fact, according to one of the Homeland Security agents, the guy may have an internal bleed which could lead to death.

Chapter 5
Father's Day

The words tattooed on the dead man's arm lift off his skin as if they were nothing more than stickers being plucked off a poster board. A string of them twist and turn into the shape of an arrow. The point of the letter-made weapon is level with my forehead when it starts to spin; slowly at first but gaining speed rapidly. I see the black blurring shape is about to come for me when...

"Wake up." Frank shakes me violently enough for me to know this is not his first attempt to rouse me. "You're having another nightmare. Is this another one about the intruder?"

"Of course it is. Have you heard anything more from Agent Brown?"

"No, which means the man will survive the crack to his head. He told us the initial report from the emergency room was promising. It's not like I meant to kill the guy with that stupid frying pan."

"But the EMTs said..."

Frank hands me my worn terry cloth robe as he interrupts my thought. "I know they said the man could have had an internal bleed but he doesn't and that's that. So forget about him for now, because we have way more important things to discuss. Randy and Sarah came back last night after you fell asleep. I caught them up on everything, and, like I am, they're aching to get a plan set up and into motion."

"I'm sure Randy is but Sarah, nope, I don't think she's aching to do anything of the sort. Sarah needs time for all of this to sink in before she convinces herself that getting involved with Arnie and his nutty storm theory is a good idea," I state unemotionally. "Furthermore, I'm sure Randy put up quite a fight that he won't be with us on the Otis Military Base hunting turtles with us. He has to be steaming that he has to stay on the sidelines doing the craft show circuit with Sarah while you, me, and Arnie have all the excitement on the base. So you can stop pretending the catching up talk went smoothly because I know our best friends too well to believe that."

"Point taken, Abby."

"So, tell me, what's the plan for Agent Brown and Mohamed?"

"Mohamed?" Frank raises his eyebrows at the mention of my brother.

"Oh come on. If Carlo Bertoni is out to get my brother I refuse to leave Mohamed out there like a sitting duck. Obviously, I have to leave him some kind of communication today about what happened yesterday. He's obviously in danger; I refuse to not help him. We should even wait around for a reply. He's never communicated back to me before but, this time being such an emergency, he might."

"What if Carlo is watching our every move? He must suspect we're in contact with Mohamed if he sent his goon here to question us, right?"

"What if he's not anymore because of what happened to his goon last night? By now he must know we're on to him."

"I need to think about this Mohamed thing. I wasn't focusing on him being part of our plans because it's so dangerous having him anywhere near us. I assumed he'd benefit if we proved he wasn't the ninth Eurabian but I didn't exactly consider him being part of our team."

"Really? I'd say he's key to our plans. Even your new friend Arnie believes that. Mohamed may not be aware of it but he may know who the ninth Eurabian is. As we investigate the storm and other matters at Otis, information will be gathered that may help Mohamed figure out who this enemy may be."

"That's true but…it's not like we can take him with us to Cape Cod. I mean with us gone from here how could we even stay in touch with him?"

"Prepaid cell phones?" I suggest.

"As in you have one and you leave one for Mohamed?"

"Yeah, as in just that."

"Well, that could work, especially since Agent Brown and his posse of agent followers is officially off our case. But even still…"

"I say we pick some up today while we're out doing the official Father's Day visits. I saw on the news last night that there's minimal damage in our home town so we'll have no problem getting the phones down there."

Frank slides a bowl, a box of cereal, and a carton of milk before me and says, "We also need for you to retrieve the bullet. With all this going on I want that thing in our possession. In fact, I'll be shocked if Agent Hanscom doesn't insist on you handing it over to him as a condition of his cooperation with the Otis Air Force Base assignment. He didn't exactly say that last night because there were too many other agents and EMTs around but he certainly dropped enough hints."

"I know, I heard it too. So, should I give it to him? That bullet is our protection from Uncle Sam and any dirty dealings anyone within this government could possibly have with us or Mohamed. That bullet is proof that we, a group of kids, prevented a mind blowing terrorist hit which would have resulted in a biological attack of the small pox virus that would have killed off thousands, if not millions, of Americans. That bullet proves that we, not Uncle Sam, killed Dr. Azar, who masterminded the entire small pox terrorist plan. That bullet came from a gun that we had, not from a federal Homeland Security weapon as was claimed in the official story. And that bullet proves that the American government covered up our involvement and took all the credit for what we did. Sure, the cover-up was in our best interest and in the best interest of American national security. But it was also in the best interest of Homeland Security who would have looked ridiculous if it was known how they missed the unfolding of such a terrorist plot that even a group of teenagers saw coming."

"I know all that and I totally get how important it is for us to keep it in our possession. That damn bullet protects us from the people within the government who would like to see us so-called heroes erased from the blackboard of recent factual history. And, I admit, giving it to Agent Brown is one heck of a sacrifice."

"It is also protection for Mohamed, who, if we didn't have the bullet to wag in front of the faces of the media-crazed reporters, would never be given a fair trial should he ever be apprehended."

I see the excitement that had grown inside Frank at the prospect of working with Arnie on the Otis base deflate as my passion-inflamed arguments connect with the logistical centers of his brain. As he sits in the chair across from mine he says, "You're right, Abby. I'm sorry if I allowed my excitement to distort my reasoning. The bullet is vital to our future and we cannot give it up unless circumstances require us to do so. At this point, I must agree that we have yet to meet that juncture."

Relieved the subject is, at least, temporarily postponed, I turn our discussion to Sarah and Randy. Frank's rendition of their actual response to the news of the weather weapons storm, my contact with Mohamed, Arnie, the Otis Military Base plan, and Carlo Bertoni's intruder into our shared apartment was very close to what I predicted it was. Randy is excited at the prospect of another country-saving, patriotic, intriguing, and high-adventure mission. Sarah would rather crawl under a rock than be involved in yet another dangerous situation; however, she is willing to go along on the mission if she is convinced it needs to be done.

When I see her this morning she is already convinced of exactly that.

Although we have no electricity, the apartment's gas powered appliances and our several flashlights allow us to cook and shower in the scantily lit rooms. As is always the case, Sarah looks marvelous despite the inconveniences. Her blond hair flows flawlessly down her back, her make-up is applied with the skill of an artist, and her clothes are wrinkle free. The men are donned in wrinkled clothes but their rather short hair looks normal. I, on the other hand, look a mess. My clothes are in need of ironing which the lack of electricity prevents. Without a hair dryer, my naturally curly hair is untamable making it appear like a lion's mane of curls. My make-up is messy and my good sandals are still damp from yesterday so I have to wear my older pair, which are embarrassingly worn out.

Without Father's Day gifts in hand, the four of us pile into Frank's silver Ford Explorer; Sarah and I in the back, Randy rides shotgun, and Frank drives. The thought of going home to see all the folks was a welcome one before the storm hit. Now all discussion focuses on the dangers of being in temporary shelters all summer as we travel around New England selling jewelry at craft fairs. Our parents will, understandably, prefer us all to stay at our homesteads where we will be relatively safe. This option, of course, is not possible for me as my old homestead is now empty. My parents are temporarily living in an undisclosed location until it is safe for them to return to the childhood home of Mohamed Haddad. Unfortunately, this may never happen especially if Mohamed stays on the run.

After considerable bickering it's decided that we will visit Sarah's father and young wife first. Her father's surprise marriage to a buxom thirty something year old beauty does not sit well with Sarah who remains totally devoted to her mother. Sarah may never forgive her Dad for cheating on her Mom throughout their marriage; however, I give Sarah credit for staying in touch with him despite his serious morality flaws. Although she wanted to postpone seeing him as long as possible by visiting him last, she accepts the earliest visiting slot with dignity. We are welcomed inside the huge colonial mansion-like house by Sarah's step-mother, who is wearing a sassy outfit better suited for a teenage girl. Her father awaits us in the formal living room. I give him the customary hug and kiss before I sit on the couch and take in the modern art that adorns the room. While Sarah and Randy chat with the mismatched couple, I try to figure out what the oil paintings in the room are supposed to represent. As I am entirely unsure how the orange, yellow and black blobs of paint relate to each other I focus on the shape of what appears to be patterns the colors may or may not be forming. My lack of enthusiasm for the art leads to an easily straying mind. It is in this unlikely moment that it occurs to me that if Carlo Bertoni sent someone to question me as to the whereabouts of Mohamed then he does not know where my brother is. If that is the case, then Mohamed and Carlo have no business together currently nor is it likely they will join forces with each other for a future project. So, this must mean that Carlo wants to find Mohamed for some other reason. That other reason can only be to kill him. But why does Carlo Bertoni want to kill my brother Mohamed? I'm completely obsessed with this unanswerable question until our visit with the newlywed Bradys is over.

"Well wasn't that awkward?" Sarah asks, as we pile into Frank's car. "Did you notice how the home wrecker checked out our boyfriends? What is up with her? Please don't tell me she's already on the prowl for a younger man. Isn't my dad's money enough to keep her faithful at least until the ink on their marriage license is dry?"

"Not to be picky, but the new Mrs. Brady did not technically break up your parent's marriage," Frank points out unnecessarily. "Your father was, as they say …"

"He was a lying butt cheat the whole time he was married, that's what he was. And now he has her and I hope he cheats on her size three little butt too," Sarah says, while reaching for a half eaten bag of corn chips. "I swear that woman makes me insane with all the fake niceness and that thousands of dollars veneer smile. Who is she kidding? No one is born with perfect pearly white teeth like that."

Randy, who is known for losing his temper easily, is being remarkably quiet during Sarah tirade. I am considering prompting him for his opinion about the new Mrs. Brady when he finally weighs in.

"Your father is a jerk, Sarah. Always has been and always will be. At least he's keeping up with his financial obligations to his kids and your mom. As for his wife, she's so into herself it's a wonder she could make any conversation at all."

"Is that why you kept leaving the room? You went to the bathroom, got a drink of water, and went out to check the car? What was all that about?" I ask Randy.

"No, I did all of those things because the current Mrs. Brady is a reporter for the city newspaper which means she has a press pass. A pass that reads Nicole Brady can easily be altered for us to use if ever we need to get in somewhere that the public isn't allowed to go. So, I went searching for her press credentials which I eventually found clipped to her camera case."

Randy holds up a 5 inch by 4 inch plastic coated badge with a picture of Nicole on the left and a bar code on the right. At the top the word 'PRESS' is boldly written in white letters against a black background. At the bottom is the name of her newspaper; The Standard Times. Complete with a black neck lanyard, the pass appears very official.

"Now that's good work, pal," Frank says, smiling. "If we're really careful we can make that pass good for any of us."

"I'm thinking it's for me. If you and Abby are gonna be counting turtles on Otis Air Force Base and Sarah has to be minding the jewelry booth at craft shows to make our cover believable, then I'm the best candidate to play reporter."

"That is if you can rein in that temper of yours," Sarah says.

Randy kisses the press pass and presses it against his heart.

"I can do whatever I have to do if it means stopping Carlo Bertoni and whoever else he's working with from conjuring up any more killer storms."

*****

The visit to Randy's parent's house is, as always, a pleasant trip back to the days when families were uncomplicated. Randy's parents are still happily married, his siblings are great and everyone loves one another. No one is doing drugs, has an eating disorder, or is self absorbed in any way. In fact, not one family member is in therapy for anything. The Arruda family is so idealistic I've often wondered what skeletons are hiding in their perfectly organized closets. But, after years of looking for at least one blemish on the pristine clan, I've come to accept that with the exception of a few bumps in the road, which they gracefully work out together, the Arruda family is the real deal.

Next we visit Frank's father house. Mr. Stiller is an extremely wealthy man who aspires to accumulate even more wealth. The fact that his son is in love with me, despite the incredible family complications and problems I bring as part of my package, is not something Mr. Stiller easily accepts. If he had his way Frank would dump me and begin focusing on a business education which he could use to help his father make even more millions of dollars. Although he has never been outright cruel to me, or even cool for that matter, he has never made me feel one iota welcome in his presence. With Randy and Sarah beside me the visit isn't nearly as bad as past visits have been. Mr. Stiller politely ignores us as he makes conversation with his son. The three of us gladly accept the snub while gorging ourselves on the platters of hors d'oeuvres host has so generously laid out for us. Frank ends the visit not a moment too soon as far as I'm concerned.

This leaves the visit to my parents for last. Since my parents moved out of their home months ago, because of the Eurabian scandal and Mohamed's involvement in the international mess, we visit them at their temporary home which is a rented cottage on West Island. West Island is connected to the mainland by an old causeway which is often overcome by ocean waves when a storm hits during high tide. The island does not have affluent summer homes, luxurious yachts, or vacationing millionaires. Instead it is an island of ordinary folks who do ordinary things the ordinary way. Although many homes on the island are not winterized, some of them are and the owners of these places live on the island year round. My parents are renting one of these homes; a gray two bedroom cottage that sits on the right side of the main road onto the island not very far from the causeway. When we walk inside my dad is waiting for us in the quaintly furnished living room. My mom is in the kitchen which is the next room in. Their greeting is genuinely enthusiastic.

In between the talk of the storm, my mother's home baked pies, and the latest gossip about our home town, I get the sense that my father needs to speak to me in private. My father was always a stern old school man with a bit too much old Islamic tradition in his bones up until the trouble started with Mohamed. Somehow, witnessing his beloved oldest son become a radicalized Muslim extremist changed my dad; it made him more understanding of things that I never thought he'd accept. For example, although we never speak of our living arrangements in our apartment in Boston, my father accepts that I share an apartment with Frank, Sarah, and Randy for monetary reasons as well as safety reasons. This is not a situation my dad would have even considered just a few years ago. He also attended a wedding at a Catholic church with my mom, which he considered to be sinful at one time. Other evidence of his loosening attitude includes his choice of reading materials, music, and TV shows. Gone is the strict unbending man of my childhood. Instead my dad is a wiser man with a desire to learn and accept that which he knows little about.

"Come, Abia, I wish to show you the bracelet your Sitto wore. You know, the one we spoke of," my dad announces, as he strokes his beard.

Since I've never spoken to my dad about a bracelet that either of my grandmothers wore, I recognize his statement as a ploy to get me alone and play along. "Great. If it is from the Middle East then it is pure 24 carat gold and it must be worth a fortune. You shouldn't be keeping it out here in this place."

My mother smiles as we excuse ourselves; her way of letting me know she is aware of what is about to transpire. My dad leads me into one of the two small bedrooms; this one they are using as a combined office and sewing room. The small beads of sweat on his bald head make me nervous.

"This storm in Boston. You must tell me the truth, Abia. Is there something about this storm that connects to your brother? I realize that your mother and I are quite paranoid that everything is somehow his doing but this storm…it is unusual. All over the news they are saying that the storm is not normal. The consensus is that the storm could be a result of global warming, but others are saying it may be a scientific experiment gone wrong? Or a weapon of some sort? An act of terrorism? The rumors and conjectures are…"

I take both of my father's hands in mine. "Dad, this has nothing to do with Mohamed. I'm positive of that. I think it may have something to do with Carlo Bertoni but I don't even know that for sure. Listen. I'm not mixed up in this and neither is Mohamed, okay?"

Every muscle in my father's face relaxes. His eyes close before the water in them can form into grateful tears.

"Listen, if I can get that job on the Cape that Frank was telling you about, the turtle counting gig at the military base, I'll be far away from Boston and any of the trouble that may be happening in the city." I lie, being careful not to mention how I'm hoping that giving Agent Brown the mafia thug found in our apartment will propel the official to get us the coveted positions on the military base. "And you know as well as I do that Abdul won't be getting involved with anything even remotely related to Mohamed, terrorism, political intrigue, or scandal of any kind. After the Eurabian mess he's totally done with it all. I swear he'd change his identity if he could."

"Ah, but indeed he has."

"What are you talking about?"

"Abdul Haddad is now Abdul Smith. Haddad means blacksmith in Arabic; hence many Haddads assume the name of Smith when they come to America. He has chosen to do the same."

My stomach twists into an unforgiving tight knot. The various cheeses, crackers, hand sandwiches, and dips I ate while visiting Mr. Stiller are threatening to erupt from my gut. Abdul's betrayal is so heartbreaking I cannot stop myself from sobbing aloud. My tears drip onto my shaking hands. I am speechless.

"I am also hurt, Abia, but I cannot blame Abdul for taking this action. For that matter, I would not blame you for doing the same."

"Never." I spit out the word rather than say it.

"There is also one more thing I must inform you of, my dear Abia. Abdul has been looking for Mohamed these past six months and believes he may know the vicinity in which Mohamed is hiding. He intended to inform Homeland Security of his suspicions. I believe the storm has bought Mohamed some time, but not long. Although I can not bring myself to turn Mohamed in, since I believe in my heart and mind that he changed from an enemy of state to a national hero, I cannot criticize your brother for doing so. Abdul is convinced that Mohamed is the unknown ninth Eurabian."

"That's not true."

"Abdul called me today and insists that Mohamed is responsible for the killing storm that spread fire through Boston."

"Dad, absolutely not. I know that for a fact!"

"Abia, Abdul tells me that Mohamed is hiding somewhere not too far from your apartment. I do not know if you are in contact with him nor do I wish to know; my ignorance and your mother's is an asset to you if you are. However, if you know of Mohamed's whereabouts or can contact him then you must decide how best to handle the information I just gave you about Abdul's plans."

"You want me to warn Mohamed?"

"I cannot and will not ask you to do that, Abia. No, I shall never do such a thing. You have been through a great deal in these past couple of years and have proven yourself to be far wiser and stronger than I could have ever hoped. I am honored to have you for a daughter and I trust you with my life. You make me most proud, my dearest, Abia. I trust you to do whatever the right thing is, my precious daughter, as even I do not know what the right thing is."

Chapter 6
Mohamed

Wise people say that everything looks better in the morning, but from what I can tell this philosophical tidbit doesn't apply to my situation. I am incredibly disappointed that we are no further along with plans for our mission to identify the enemy behind the weather weapon storm this morning than we were when we returned to the apartment last night. To add to our burden we also must now cope with the problem of warning Mohamed about Abdul's betrayal, involving him in bringing down the unknown ninth Eurabian, and telling him of Carlo's attempt to locate his whereabouts through us. All this must be done without it being discovered that we are in contact with Mohamed. To add to my misery we are still without electrical power which has caused the food in our refrigerator to take on a peculiarly unpleasant odor.

"Still no call back from Agent Brown," Frank announces, as I enter the kitchen. "Randy took off to see if he could find him downtown or somewhere else. I told him it was fruitless but you know how Randy is; he always needs something to keep him busy."

"Is Sarah with him?"

"No, she's not up yet. After you fell asleep last night I heard her puttering around in the living room. She's either still stewing over her stepmother situation or getting all wigged out about the weather weapons and our plans to investigate what's going on."

"Sarah won't admit it but she hates being involved in all the dangerous stuff we've dragged her through. You know, she really is an unlikely hero. She was always been afraid of her own shadow as a kid; the first one to freak out at horror movies and all that. Remember the time we convinced her we were vampires?"

Frank's sincere laughter instantly lightens the eerie atmosphere.

"How old were we, like six or something? She was such a spaz."

"But through everything she's hung in there with us and bravely done whatever needed to be done. And now, just when she probably thought it was over, we're jumping back into the danger game."

"And this time we have no real reason to. The first time we were the only ones that could put the pieces together about the upcoming smallpox attack because we knew what Mohamed and Dr. Azar were planning. The second time we had to stop the enemy called Eurabia from taking control of the country because we were the only ones who could work with Mohamed. But this time we could just sit back and let things unfold by themselves."

"Not exactly," I say. "We have to let Mohamed know he's not safe. Not only is Carlo Bertoni looking for him but Abdul is about to report his whereabouts any day now. I was stressing about why Carlo is looking for Mohamed while we were visiting Sarah's father and I came up with an idea. Before you tell me you don't like it please listen to my reasoning from start to finish."

"I assume this has something to do with Mohamed?"

"Of course."

"Let me guess, you want to hide him?"

"Maybe. Just listen," Before laying out my plan, I settle down with a steamy cup of coffee. The caffeine rush propels my brain into action. "If anyone knows who the ninth Eurabian is it's Mohamed; even Arnie the genius scientist nerd believes that. Now, Mohamed may only hold clues to the mysterious man but, with our help and investigation, we might be able to uncover his identity."

"Okay, of course, this assumes that Mohamed is not the ninth Eurabian."

"Do you really think he is?" I ask, truly shocked at the insinuation.

"No, but I'm not sure Sarah and Randy are ready to stake their lives on it. I've never talked to them about how they feel now, since the storm thing happened."

"Fine, let's assume they agree that Mohamed is innocent. That means Carlo Bertoni and the ninth Eurabian are responsible for the storm. The question is why? Why make a storm like this? Why do they need to find Mohamed? Why are they still together even though the group called Eurabia theoretically fell apart? Why hasn't Carlo been caught? Why would a military person with knowledge of the Weather Weapons program be connected to Eurabia?"

"Enough with the questions, I get that we have much to discover while having few answers. So what do you suggest we do?"

"Work with Mohamed again. He was instrumental in exposing Eurabia and he can be just as instrumental in uncovering whoever these enemies turn out to be. He has answers he doesn't know he has. And, with the storm becoming the new threat for Homeland Security to focus on, we aren't being watched and the hunt for Mohamed is probably not as huge of a priority as it was…

so…it's sort of now or never."

"And where, exactly, do you plan on hiding him? Surely the military base is out of the question which leaves the camper Randy and Sarah will be in while they do the craft show circuit. You think they should risk harboring a terrorist in that camper?"

"No, I couldn't ask them to do that, at least not for long."

The computer printouts I made at Randy's parents house slide out of the orange folder onto the kitchen table. Frank examines the maps of the Otis Air Force Base carefully, glancing up at me with a quizzical look when he notices my pencil markings. Without the need for me to explain the details of my idea he says, "Okay, the base is hundreds of square miles of wooded forest; much of which is never used. You want Mohamed to camp out on the base?"

"Maybe."

Frank shakes his head while biting at his already gnawed fingernails. I don't want to interrupt his intense thinking so I stay quiet as he murmurs to himself, re-examines the map, and hopelessly attempts to access the internet. After about fifteen minutes of torturous silence he speaks.

"Mohamed can't stay on the base. I agree that the military doesn't use every inch of the place but they do use it for military training exercises and things like that. There is absolutely no way of knowing where and when a soldier will pop up on that property; be it in a vehicle, on foot, or in the air. No, it's totally out of the question. This is a post 9/11 world and places like Otis are secured to the utmost so hiding Mohamed in the forest there, no matter how possible it may seem, is simply not a good risk. And, if Arnie is right and there is information about the Weather Weapons program on the base, well now that the storm has hit, I'd expect security to be ramped up even higher."

"Okay, fine. So, what's your idea? You haven't been mulling around all this time thinking about nothing?"

"True enough. There's a place called the Otis Trailer Village close by the base. It's a place with mobile homes. Some are for rent; you know, like for summer rentals. It's here on a map you printed out last night and you even have an advertisement for the place on this other paper…"

"Trailers? Like the trailer parks people live in?"

"Or sometimes it's older people who want to live in smaller homes. Anyways, this place also has a campground attached to it so I doubt that it's as elite, as in an ultra expensive, place to live. I can't tell all that much about the place from looking at this map and the ad but maybe, just maybe, we can rent a place for Mohamed to stay."

"That could work. That could really work. It would be even better if we could live in the trailer instead of in the barracks on the base that Arnie told you about. Tell me again about how students live dormitory style."

"According to Arnie, the buildings that used to serve as barracks have been renovated into tiny efficiency apartments which students stay in while working on the base. Each apartment fits two students, well Arnie says they don't actually fit two humans but two are assigned to live in each one, nonetheless. Because all of the apartments are in two adjacent buildings Arnie says there will be a serious lack of privacy. So, I would love to find a way for us to live in that trailer park instead of on the base but at this point we have to wiggle our way into the job first."

"You're right."

"As for this morning, we go hunting for Mohamed, under the circumstances that has to be our number one priority."

*****

Sarah decides to hang out with me at the cemetery rather than stay alone in the electricity- void apartment. I can tell by her non-stop junk food snacking that her anxiety is growing rapidly. Unlike me, Sarah doesn't feel a screaming angry fight of patriotism burning inside her which is why, I believe, she has such a serious lack of enthusiasm today. But, having her with me in the ancient cemetery is not only a wise maneuver, as two people are always safer than one in a dangerous situation, but she is also a great comfort to my slightly weary thoughts. Once we've left the envelope and message in place for Mohamed to find at Jeremiah and Mary White's grave marker Sarah and I hide in the wood line and wait to see who comes to pick up my communication. Of course we expect it to be Mohamed but we can't assume anything, hence we stay hidden until we are sure.

"It's been over an hour and a half. Frank said he'd be checking in with us in two hours, should I go up to the church and wait for him near there?" Sarah asks in between bites of a now stale banana muffin. "I'll have him take me somewhere to get more food, I'm starved. And I want to check up on Randy. I wish our cell phones were working. This old fashioned electronically challenged communication world is horrible."

"Randy isn't due back until after noon time. I bet he won't even come back if he doesn't get Agent Brown to agree to come see us or get us jobs on the base." I break off a small piece of the muffin with hopes that is will quiet my rumbling stomach. "You know, Randy was way too eager to be the one to go after Agent Brown this morning. Does he have something else up his sleeve?"

"Like what?"

"Like seeing if he can get a job on the base too?"

"Maybe, but I think he does understand how important it is that some of us be on the outside and out of sight so we are free to do whatever has to be done. Whoever is working on the base is, in a way, under a microscope. He gets that. But, I have to admit, you never know what Randy is up to sometimes."

"He's also been unusually quiet about everything that's happening. You know, as in less opinionated than his normal outspoken bull in a china shop self."

"I agree. He's been acting almost…normal."

"So what gives? What's he up to?"

"Abby, I honestly can't figure it out and believe me when I tell you I've been trying. I've snooped in his stuff, checked his cell phone messages when we were at his parents' house and even went through his precious 'not so secret' journal. Nothing…I found nothing."

I know Sarah as well as I know my own reflection and it is obvious she is telling the truth. This means that our dearly beloved and trusted Randy is up to something secretive. This fact is hardly surprising, because after all, Randy is quite an unpredictable character at times. He is also a very patriotic young man who is easily fired up at the thought of defending his country. It is this patriotic personality quirk that is making me wonder what unexpected thoughts are rolling around inside his head.

While Sarah goes up to the street to tell Frank that we have yet to see Mohamed, or anything else interesting for that matter, I, once again, test my cell phone connection. As it has been since the storm hit, my phone doesn't work for reasons I don't truly understand. What I do know is that once the batteries die I don't have electricity to charge the phone anyway so reception will become a moot point. Temporarily distracted by the unusable device, at first I don't notice the flash of dark color moving between the trees. In fact, it isn't until it is within twenty-five or so feet of where I am crouched down against a damp tree that I become aware of the approaching danger. My first reaction is to scream but miraculously I stay silent long enough to assess my situation.

"Abia, it is me. Please, make no noise. I do not want Sarah to hear me," Mohamed states in his deep even toned voice. "I am not prepared to speak to anyone but you at this time. I beg of you to keep silent until you have heard me out."

With the exception of his black penetrating eyes and a few undisguised features my brother is unrecognizable. His hair is long and matted as is his beard and mustache. He is so thin he appears to be suffering from cancer or some other terminal illness. His skin has the olive tone of our shared heritage yet it has a sickly hue I've never seen on anyone but my dying grandfather so many years ago. His clothes, or should I call them rags, are filthy and tattered to the point I can not tell what they were once meant to look like. On his feet are two old sneakers; one was once white but now is dirty gray and the other is a faded black with broken shoelaces.

"As you can see, my dear little sister, I have been able to keep myself hidden for these past six months by becoming exactly the type of person that no person is willing to look at; a homeless person. I have been hiding in full view, yet I have been invisible. My disguise is poverty and hopelessness; two things in life that no one whishes to face let alone look beyond."

"You've never left Boston?"

"I've never had to. I live among the unfortunate. They ask no questions of anyone. Those with nothing expect nothing; not even answers. With the money you gave me I've lived rather well. You would be surprised at how far money goes in the world of the destitute." My six-foot tall brother smiles. "I appreciate your kindness."

"How did you know I'd be here today?"

"I did not. I saw you when I came to see if you left me anything at the grave. I saw Sarah as well. Such a nice girl she is; such a loyal friend to you. However, I am not yet sure who I can trust so I hoped I would somehow arrange to see you alone. I am quite fortunate to have this chance."

"This storm...how did you make out? What do you think of it? Do you think Carlo Bertoni..."

Mohamed interrupts me before my questions turn into a stream of ramblings. Glancing up the slight hill to the church and the street he says, "I know nothing of this storm other than it is unusual and the topic of much speculation. I know nothing of Carlo Bertoni after the night he escaped other than he was smuggled to safety through a tunnel beneath the Catholic cathedral in this city. I assume, however, that you believe this storm is related to the escaped Eurabian. Am I correct?"

"Yes, and I can prove it but..."

"There is no time for this now. Are you staying in the city for the summer?"

"No."

"I feared that would be the case. I am aware that your presence in this neighborhood is slowly becoming known and, because of your relationship to me, this is problematic. I realize it is better for you to leave here, at least temporarily. I am grateful I've had the opportunity to say goodbye to you and to, once again, thank you in person. It is better if now we part ways. It is safer for you if we do. Please do not worry; I can take care of myself from now on."

His unexpected farewell speech ignites my deepest emotions and I begin to gush out all of the reasons he has to stay with me. I explain about the storm and Arnie and how we all believe he holds the secret to the mysterious ninth Eurabian even though he may not yet be aware he has this knowledge.

I tell him about the weather weapons research on Cape Cod and how we are trying to get jobs on the Otis Air Force base so we can better snoop around for possible links between this research and the people who unleashed this murderous storm. I tell him about Abdul's betrayal and how Carlo Bertoni is looking for him. I am in the middle of telling him how we intend to hide him in a trailer park near the base when he says,

"Sarah is coming around the church. You must go to her. I will wait here, for now."

Linking my little finger with his, as we did as a sign of an unbreakable promise as children, I trot out of the woods before Sarah notices I am not alone. Her long blond hair is whipping around her face as she jogs toward me. When I am able to see her eyes and mouth I instantly know that she has important news to tell me.

"Randy is back…at the house…with Agent Brown. He wants to see all four of us…now!"

*****

If there is one thing I've learned how to do very well while dealing with insane terrorist- laced espionage it's how to come up with a believable lie under pressure. Without a moment's hesitation I say,

"You go to the apartment now and I'll follow. We have to make it look like we weren't together."

"Frank is waiting in the truck in front of the church," she says. "He wants us to go together."

"Agent Brown will know something is up if all three of us show up together."

"When Frank went to the apartment earlier to get something he told Agent Brown we were together; something about waiting in line to use a payphone at the Stop and Shop."

Sarah looks past me and into the distant tree line. With arched eyebrows she asks, "Are you hiding something? Is Mohamed back there?"

I wordlessly nod.

"I'll cover for you," she says with a grunt. "I'll tell them you'll be at the apartment in less than a half an hour."

"Tell Agent Brown that I was next in line and I wouldn't give up my spot. Frank will go along with it once he knows why I'm staying here, I know he will. And," I add, putting my hand on my best friends arm. "Thanks."

"Never a problem, Abby, you know that."

As promised, Mohamed is waiting for me in the exact spot where I left him. The difference with him is that he's had time to process the limited information that I gave him about the circumstances surrounding me and the storm. When I add the new twist that Agent Brown is waiting for me at the apartment I detect a bit of fear flashing in my his sharp eyes.

"I cannot commit to this proposal of yours for several reasons. First, I do not wish to endanger you with my presence. Having me in your custody is harboring a federal fugitive which is a federal crime. To do so to protect me from capture by Carlo Bertoni or federal agents due to the betrayal of my brother Abdul…I do not wish you to take risks for these reasons. If either the federal government or Carlo discovers you helped me I fear your punishment will be death. I cannot risk that."

"Those are risks that the four of us are willing to take. Furthermore, in return for our help, we are asking you to help us battle the enemy behind the weather weapon attacks."

"This attack, as you call it, is neither your business nor your duty to investigate. I believe it would be best if the enemy behind the storm is left to the officials." Mohamed's piercing eyes deliberately bore into mine. "You cannot fool me, Abia. I believe you have only one reason for getting involved in this affair and it is transparent to me what that reason is.

Knowing that further deception is fruitless I say, "Okay, I want to prove to Agent Brown, once and for all, that you're no longer a threat to this country. I'm hoping that if I do this he'll help you make some sort of life for yourself somewhere. Is that so bad?"

My elder brother nods, indicating he believes what I've said are my true intentions.

"No, it is understandable although it is unwise at the same time," he says, followed by a sigh. "The question now becomes what is motivating your friends?"

"Frank is a die hard patriot for one. He also knows how I feel about you and wants to exonerate you so I can go on with my life with him without always worrying where you are and whether you're alive or not. Just because you don't see me doesn't mean that you don't impact my life. I've been leaving messages and money near a grave for months hoping and praying that it was you receiving them. Don't you realize how crazy my behavior is? But it is motivated by my love for you. Frank knows I cannot let go of you until I am at peace with your living situation."

Faced with the impact his life has on my own, Mohamed shivers. For a drawn out moment he turns his face away from mine. I watch his expression wishing I was able to read his thoughts.

"And Sarah is motivated by your feelings as well?" he asks, turning back toward me. "Or does she have her own reasons for getting involved in what is sure to be an extremely dangerous investigation?"

"Sarah hates all of the danger and drama, believe me. Given a choice, she'd make her costume jewelry and sell it at craft fairs all summer while eating hotdogs and drinking milk shakes. But Sarah will stick with the rest of us no matter what. Her loyalty is far stronger than her desire for comfort."

"Which leaves Randy? His motivation, I would guess, is that he loves all the intrigue and danger. He is also a man with a fire burning inside of him; a fire just waiting to be released on an enemy who he can outsmart. Yes, Randy Arruda is a brave man. He is also impulsive and impatient; less than redeeming qualities when working on a mission such as you describe."

"Randy is what he is," I'm saying when Mohamed quickly backs away.

"I will go to your apartment after Agent Brown leaves, "Mohamed whispers, while pointing toward the church.

When I turn around I see a crowd of people congregating near the cemetery entrance. It isn't until I am near them that I realize they are mourners of the young man who was killed in the storm yesterday; the young man who worked at the local gas station. I am about to offer my condolences when a middle aged woman spits on me and shouts,

"You! You are Mohamed Haddad's sister and he is the one who made this storm. The storm that killed my innocent son! I don't know how he did it but he did. Your brother is a murderer and you are Muslim filth!"

Chapter 7
The Deal

Agent Brown is a handsome, well-built middle aged man who, despite the enormous stresses of his job, manages to appear completely comfortable with every solitary thing happening around him. I assume, of course, that he is far from comfortable with the weaponized weather storm and having to drag a half-crazed mafia thug out of my apartment. However, his persona today is so relaxed that not one bit of his tension is seeping through his official 'in control' mask. I greet him with affection because, after all, we've become quite close fighting terrorists together over the past two years and I genuinely like the man. His guarded, yet sincere, hug gives me the sense that he is actually glad to see me. I wish I could return the sentiment but I am not glad to have this official visit us right now because I greatly fear he will discover that Mohamed is nearby and that I have broken many federal laws by being in contact with him. Luckily, I am able to overcome my initial reaction to seeing him while I change into dry clothes. When I join the others I take my seat on the couch near Frank, which happens to be situated very close to our tan corduroy recliner where our visiting agent is seated. I look about for a moment while my eyes adjust to the lack of electricity and sunlight in our small living room. The shadows cast off by Sarah's grandmother's old kerosene lamp are almost ghost like. The smell of burning oil is mildly unpleasant.

"Agent Brown was just telling us how he suspects our interest in working at the Otis Air Force Base is related to the storm that hit Boston yesterday. He is curious to know what we think of the storm." Frank keeps his face expressionless because he is aware the agent is sizing up his every move. Not knowing what he, Randy and Sarah have already told the agent, I don't respond. The awkward silence slowly fills the room.

Unexpectedly, Agent Brown slams a fist on the chair's arm and says, "Let's cut to the chase, shall we? I know you four realize that there is something highly unusual about the storm and also that the deadly nature of the storm may tie back to the military. I also can conclude, by the fact that a mafia hit man was here yesterday, that you realize organized crime, possibly at the leadership of Carlo Bertoni and the unknown ninth Eurabian, are connected to the storm, am I right?"

Agent Brown is focused on me. I sense this is the case because he has already heard from the others and now needs to know where I stand on leveling with him. Although I recognize the stickiness of the situation I am in, I don't know how to get out of it. I decide on using diversionary tactics to play for time.

"You could be. What I find interesting, though, is that you say the unknown ninth Eurabian. Does this mean you don't agree with Homeland Security's public statement that Mohamed is this unknown enemy?"

"I'm not here to discuss that, unless, of course, you know where your brother is. If that be the case, I will remind you that it is a federal crime not to turn him over to me immediately. A crime punishable by imprisonment or worse."

I actually feel blood leaving my face. To hide my guilt from the agent, I turn from him and pretend to be offended.

"Oh come on," Randy interjects, saving me from what is already a very bad confrontation. "You and your people have been watching us constantly since the Eurabia bust and you haven't seen anything that even suggests we're in touch with Mohamed. Let's not rehash stuff that we both know isn't even true. The issue at hand is the jobs on Otis Air Force Base. Now, my proposal to you is that two of us get jobs on the base and two of us work from outside the base. And, in return for getting us the jobs, we agree to give you any information we find out. Since you insist the weather weapon storm isn't connected to Otis then you stand to lose nothing by letting us snoop around on good old Cape Cod, right?"

Agent Brown hasn't stopped staring at me when he says, "Yes, Abby, your friends already explained to me about your suspicions about the storm. I was simply testing whether or not you would be honest with me. You were not. This tells me I cannot completely trust you. I needed to know that."

"I didn't lie to you," I insist.

"You didn't have to for me to know that I can't trust you to be completely honest with me." Agent Brown turns his attention to Randy and Frank. "Otis is a military base and Abby is Mohamed Haddad's sister. Do you really think it's easy for me to get her a job there?

"It may not be easy but it's possible. You can say she needs to be there because of the threats on her life," Frank suggests.

At this point I explain exactly what just happened to me at the entrance of the cemetery. Although I can not say my life has been threatened I am able to honestly say that given a different make-up of the gathered crowd, it may have been. Frank reacts to my story with concern, as does Sarah. Randy, as usual, is angry at my assaulter. Agent Brown is, curiously, more concerned than I thought he'd be.

"It's become too obvious that you live in this neighborhood, which I've always stated, was dangerous for all of you; particularly Abby. I have never shared with you the intelligence Homeland Security has gathered on people who we believe would like to harm you, but, I must say, it is likely more serious than you are aware. I am particularly concerned about... You see, Otis is a place where...."

Agent Brown grits his teeth while, again, making a fist and slamming it down on the arm of the recliner. His always unreadable agent face is expressionless but I sense that he is on the verge of bringing us into his confidence about something important. I also sense that this mysterious thing somehow concerns us.

"So, you too have secrets?" I ask.

"Maybe, but if I do I keep them for good reason." The agent says in his stern authoritative voice. He turns his entire body toward Sarah, whom, I think, he assumes is the most reasonable of the four of us and asks her what she has to say about the situation. For a second Sarah reminds me of neutral Switzerland caught between the fighting world power countries.

Sarah tosses a bag of pretzel sticks on the table and says, "My concern is what happened yesterday. Even though we don't know where Mohamed is doesn't mean that Carlo doesn't think we do. If he sent a goon after us yesterday in an effort to hunt down Mohamed he'll keep doing it. Our plans for the summer were to hop from campsite to campsite and sell jewelry at craft fairs. It was a fun idea where we knew we could make money. And, because Abby can't get hired anywhere else because of her...connections to Mohamed...well, it was a way for us to help her make money with us. It was a great plan until we found out that Carlo Bertoni is after us...or Abby. You owe it to her to put her somewhere she can be protected."

"And that place is Otis. Face it, with everything happening in Boston right now, never mind if more storms hit, you can't spare enough people to guard Abby and you know it. So, putting her on a military base makes sense," Randy argues. "You can't just leave her to fight off people like Carlo, can you?"

"And I go wherever she goes. So that's two jobs on the base. Is that so much to ask?" Frank rubs his knuckles before giving them a quick snap. "In return, if we do find out anything important that is connected to the storms and whoever is responsible for them, then we let you know."

"The thing is this. I don't want any of you anywhere near whatever is happening with the storm. I admit that the storm that just hit Boston was abnormal, and, very possibly, weaponized by an enemy. I admit that it is my job to investigate this matter from every and all angles. And I admit that Carlo Bertoni and the unknown ninth Eurabian, be that Mohamed Haddad or someone else, is a suspect in this crime if a crime does, in fact, exist," Agent Brown pauses to look around at each of us. "But what I don't admit is that I'm willing to let you four become any part of this. Regardless of your motivation for wanting to get involved, which, by the way, I am unsure of what these reasons truly are, I am having a very hard time paving the way for you to get on the inside track of this suspected terrorism attack. I am also concerned about putting you at Otis Air Force Base because there are people there that I...let's just say, that I don't want near you. I will not explain who or why but I will say that I suspect someone of being an enemy that is associated with the base. "

The three men break into a deep and detailed argument about what should happen, who should trust whom and who knows what. Even though there are two men, Randy and Frank, pushing the reasons why we should be given the jobs on the military base and Agent Brown is alone on his side of the debate, the fact remains that the agent has all the power. The agent announces this fact several times leading to much frustration on my part as I know that we have some power, too. He is not sure of the power we hold over him because we have lied to him about it for so long and so convincingly that he cannot know what we have or don't have with any certainty. I slide my hand inside my pocketbook until I feel the cool metal of my keys. I silently slide my key ring into my hoodie pocket and then I think about the events of two and a half years ago.

Back when Mohamed was involved in masterminding terrorist attacks in Boston he worked with an evil man named Dr. Azar. Because my friends and I uncovered the terrorist's plans through watching my brother, we knew what was going to happen when the police and federal law enforcement officials did not. In the end it was one of us, a friend named Sam, who shot and killed Dr. Azar in a school in Dorchester, Massachusetts. Because the US government could never admit to not discovering the plot, never mind that a group of students actually saved the day, Agent Brown said he shot the evil Azar. For reasons unknown to me at the time, he gave me the real bullet that killed Dr. Azar, the one with the exact markings that matched up to the precise measurements of the wounds as measured on the corpse of the doctor during his federal autopsy. This bullet proves that we, not the mighty U.S.A., brought down the biggest and most horrific terrorist threat to which this country has ever been exposed. We, four teenagers sitting in this room right now, saved this entire country from a biological attack using the smallpox virus that would have annihilated the population of this country and then spread throughout the world. Yes, I have that bullet in my possession and if I want I can offer it to Agent Brown in exchange for the jobs on Otis. This is exactly what Frank predicted Agent Brown would demand from us in exchange for his cooperation, yet the agent isn't asking us for it. So, now what? If Agent Brown isn't going to ask for the bullet, do I just offer it out to him? If I do, what's to stop him from taking it and then not following through on his part of the deal? For that matter, he could demand I give the bullet to him and I really can't say no after I've admitted I have it, can I?

As if he can read my mind I feel Frank's hand touch my arm.

"It appears we are at a bit of an impasse," he says. "What if we give you something that we know you want to prove to you our good faith?"

*****

If given one word to describe Agent Brown's reaction to our offer of the bullet that killed Dr. Azar in exchange for two jobs on the Otis Air Force Base I would have to choose the word furious. Apparently, he truly believed that the bullet was misplaced during the Eurabia crisis; a lie the four of us have told him so many times it almost began to feel true. The truth of the matter was I gave the bullet to Mohamed before we parted ways during the crisis because I thought he would need it to protect himself from unfair prosecution. This may seem like a rather crazy thing to believe, given the fact that my brother is a known and confessed past terrorist; however, the lies and accusations about him since he has changed have mounted so high I thought he needed some way to sort out truth from falsehood. Having the power of the truth of this bullet at his disposal guaranteed him the ear of the most powerful people in the country; that is the best form of protection a person in his position can possibly have. Since I could never admit to Agent Brown that I gave the bullet to Mohamed, a federal fugitive, we decided then and there to say the bullet was misplaced. However, the bullet was mailed back to me in an envelope with no return address. This was Mohamed's way of telling me he was alive. Since then the bullet has been safely tucked away in a hiding place that only the four of us know about. However, since the lie to Agent Brown about the bullet being lost had already been told…well…we kept saying it thinking… hey…we just may need that bullet as proof of the government's unyielding power to cover-up and lie to the American people after all.

"That bullet is more powerful than the pristine bullet theory that surrounds the John F. Kennedy assassination," the agent roars. "That bullet proves that a Homeland Security agent… me…did not truly shoot and kill Dr. Azar who was the mastermind behind the biggest and deadliest attack by which this country has ever been threatened. That bullet has the exact markings that prove it was the one that passed through Dr. Azar's body; every nick from hitting bone and every…"

"We understand how important the bullet is and how it can be used to prove that the bullet the government has is really one you planted using some spent bullet from your gun. We totally get that, believe me," Randy says, his natural excitement starting to bubble. "We also know that we betrayed you when we lied about not having it, when, in fact, we did. We totally get that too. But, this is where we are now, okay? I mean, let's face it you haven't always been exactly honest with us either. For example, you've admitted you've had us under 24-hour surveillance since the Eurabia crisis and you never told us you were going to do that. That's a betrayal too. Not to mention the little stuttering pause you had just a little while ago about getting us two jobs on the base."

"You dare to question what I do, me, the leader of the Homeland Security Office on the east coast?" Agent Brown roars. "I do not report my doings to you or any other civilians regardless of who you are or what you've done! I admit that there is a special relationship between you and me. How can I not admit that the secrets we share have created a bond between us? But do you really believe that should the four of you decide to rebel against me and the might of this government that you couldn't be stopped? Do you really believe that I couldn't erase you right now, at this very moment, before you had a chance to retrieve your magic bullet and present it to the media?"

For the first time since I met this man I truly feel his immense power. I feel frightened, foolish and insignificant. While the agent continues on with his tirade both Frank and Randy try to calm him using logic, a plea for understanding, but eventually they beg for mercy. I gather Sarah is too afraid to even move since she does not speak or eat the entire time the tirade is being delivered. I, on the other hand, take this opportunity to observe the agent's behavior. I've taken enough psychology courses with body language chapters to know that the body sometimes says things that the mouth does not. For starters, Agent Brown's body is not tense nor is he blocking what the men are saying by crossing his arms across his chest or turning away from then. In fact, his body indicates that he is very much interested in what they are saying; as if he is using his angry outburst to draw information from them. I also notice that when he tells them he never suspected we had the bullet he takes a step back while saying it. This is called distancing yourself from the lie. In other words, he always suspected we did have the bullet and his make believe anger is the real lie. When I am as convinced as I can be that my body language theory is correct I take center stage.

"If you want honesty then I'll give you total honesty," I say, as I stand on somewhat shaky legs. Various levels of shock register on Sarah's, Frank's and Randy's faces. Agent Brown's pretend rage seems to dissipate into thin air. He looks at me now with questioning eyes. "If you've been watching us all these months then you know I go for regular walks, right?"

The agent raises his eyebrows and nods.

"So tell me, where do your spies tell you I go and what do they tell you I do?"

"You go around the neighborhood, always careful to take different routes whenever you notice them following you. Yes, Abby, they are aware that you suspect you are being watched. You have been extremely cautious with your walking habits."

"You haven't answered me which means you're not being honest. If you want me to show a little more of my hand to you before you reveal your secrets to me I will."

Not knowing exactly what I am about to announce, my three friends are outwardly shaken. Since Sarah and Randy have just learned this morning of my secret meetings with Mohamed, they are even more nervous than Frank is since they've had less time to process the consequences of my illegal actions. In an effort to hide her fear Sarah is gulping down handfuls of pretzel sticks. Randy is up and pacing around the room; his trademark nervous habit. Frank, who has cracked all of his knuckles, is now chewing on his fingernails. I suspect he will begin ripping off his hangnails soon.

"I go on those walks to check on the bullet," I state, as if my words were fact instead of fiction.

"Then that explains your routine and your secrecy," Agent Brown replies, peering at me with skeptical eyes. "So where is the bullet hidden?"

"It was hidden in the cemetery behind the Episcopal Church near a particular old grave. It doesn't matter which one. That's where I really was before I got here. I wasn't making a phone call at the Stop and Shop. I was at the cemetery getting the bullet in case we needed it while meeting with you."

I see clearly that admitting I was lying about where I was before coming home has paid off. The agent's eyes soften and a small, but certain, smile appears on his otherwise expressionless face.

"I am aware that you visited the cemetery on many of your walks. The agents never risked following you inside in fear that you would notice them because the cemetery slopes downhill and has no large trees to hide behind.

Your visits there were short, too short for you to be meeting anyone such as your brother Mohamed, so it was assumed you were simply walking. I admit it never occurred to me that you would hide the bullet in such a place."

"I did. I didn't want to leave it here where you or any of your people might find it," I say, allowing the second lie to spill out gracefully. "Since you know the truth I will get it now."

I walk out of the living room with a determined stride, which I hope will discourage the agent from following me. The truth is the bullet has been close by me the entire time it's been in my possession which will become obvious should Agent Brown call my bluff and accompany me to its hiding place. I catch a whiff of the vanilla sachet on my dresser as I slide my key ring from my hoodie pocket. Careful to minimize the sound of jingling metal, I remove the bullet, which has been carefully wrapped in paper and electrical tape, from the inside of my key ring flashlight. It is nuzzled in the place where the batteries are intended to go; a tight fit I have learned to maneuver with ease. Of course the flashlight is inoperable which is something I blame on burnt out batteries should ever I have to explain why it is useless. I am proud of the ingenuity of my hiding place which has allowed me to keep the valuable bullet close at hand with little fuss. It was simple to keep it with me as I could attach the key chain to my keys, use it as a medallion on my pocketbook or clip it to my backpack. It is small enough to be put inside a coat pocket, a wallet or even some change purses. I've even hooked it on to a belt loop on occasion. Like Mohamed, who has been hiding in plain view as a homeless man, I hid the bullet in plain view camouflaged as just another American doodad.

I return to the living room where I am greeted with four pairs of expectant eyes. With a steady hand I place the bullet on the coffee table. Agent Brown quickly picks it up to inspect it.

"I see I may have misjudged you, Abby. Perhaps I need to understand that you hid the fact that you had the bullet out of fear. Was that why you lied to me?"

"Of course. Fear for me, us, and the future. If you were me wouldn't you be afraid?"

"I don't have to be you to be fearful. Like all of you I've come to realize that people I know and trust are not who they appear to be. I've been tricked and used. I've been misguided. I've seen the unimaginable while uncovering truths I never would have considered possible. I know and understand fear of the unknown and the unthinkable. I've lived with betrayal just as you all have."

With one smooth sweep of his hand the agent removes an overstuffed envelope from inside his suit coat.

"These are for you and Frank," he tells me, as he places the envelope in my waiting hand. "Congratulations on your new jobs. I hear counting endangered species of turtles is quite an exciting job."

And so I was tricked by Agent Brown into giving him the bullet to obtain jobs he already had for us on the Otis Military Base. Well, I'm not the only one being tricked though, am I? I still have one up on him; I have Mohamed waiting outside to come in and I'd bet a whole lot of money our big cheese agent friend would love to know that.

Chapter 8
The General

"Agent Born came here playing the role of being betrayed and really mad with every intention of scaring us into handing over the bullet! I don't believe for one second he bought our lame excuses that we lost the damn thing. No way. He knows us too well to believe we'd lose something as valuable and as powerful as a bullet that could expose the biggest cover-up in this country's history!" Randy roars. "He was playing us all along. Agent Brown came here with the two jobs on the base already sewn up nice and neat. Those jobs were his bargaining chips to get the bullet back from the get go."

"I don't blame him, really," Sarah comments. "He knows we're interested in the Weather Weapons Program and he knows that Carlo Bertoni is involved with this threatening storm problem. He also suspects that there is an unknown ninth Eurabian mixed up in all this; a person of whom we, more than ordinary citizens, are in a position to have clues. So, to prevent us from losing the bullet to the enemy he had to get it from us."

Frank nods. "He also doesn't want us to have any power over him to while we're tied up in this mess."

"I don't think he totally believed we did still have the bullet. His reaction to Frank's offer of the bullet was rather intense which makes me think there was a bit of surprise in it. So, this makes me wonder of what else he's unsure. He acts like he knows so much about our motives yet...well...I don't think he's totally on his game. For example, he seems to be very willing to allow us to get involved in this Weather Weapons Program stuff despite his claims to the contrary. Is this because he assumes that he can't stop us from interfering in this thing? Does he secretly want us to get involved so we can report things to him?" I ask.

"Who knows? The guy is impossible to figure out," Randy complains. "He got you and Frank the jobs but not housing on the base. What's up with that?"

Frank unfolds the white pages of information from the envelope Agent Brown gave me. Straining to move the pages close enough to the kerosene lamp light to make out the words, he reads, "Due to the late date of your employment into the program I must report that all student housing on the base is occupied. There are, however, a number of economical accommodations in the immediate area that will be perfect for the students' needs. They've arranged for us to have a unit at the Otis Trailer Village."

"What about the jobs? How did they manage to come up with two more turtle counting positions on such short notice?" Randy asks.

Frank flips through the paperwork before reading from a different typed page.

"Additionally, as all of the positions within the Eastern Box Turtle Conservation Program have been filled, the positions assigned to Frank Stiller and Abia Haddad are new this season. These individuals will be assigned to hunting for turtle specimens in areas which have yet to be identified as turtle nesting grounds. The enclosed map highlights…" Frank reads.

"We're going to be turtle hunters?" I ask.

"From what it says here the turtle program has only been able to cover a select area on the base due to a shortage of funding for student summer interns. We're going to be sent out into the unexplored turtle wilderness to look for turtle colonies that can be added to the study." Frank narrows his eyes.. "Do you think Agent Brown came up with this job to give us flexibility for getting on and off the base? If we're assigned to unknown areas without direct supervision we can pretty much do as we please."

Sarah nods. "Is it possible Agent Brown is looking for help from us? Is he actually hoping to work with us without actually coming out and asking for help?"

"He can't directly ask us for help. The man would lose his career and maybe be put in jail. We're civilians after all," Randy adds.

"Forget about Agent Brown for now. I have something more important to talk about. Mohamed will be coming here soon. He's waiting outside. He wants to be absolutely sure that Agent Brown is long gone before coming up but he's coming here to meet with us." My announcement is greeted with the dead silence associated with horror stricken moments. "I know everyone is upset that I didn't tell you I was secretly in touch with him these past months. I am sorry about that but I didn't tell you because I didn't want to implicate you in my crime. I was trying to protect you from being accused of helping an enemy of the state. Instead I betrayed you and I'm sorry. I won't ever lie to you through omission again. From now on I bring my dealings with Mohamed to the table and that starts here and now."

Although I'm not surprised that everyone is willing to have Mohamed meet with us, I am a bit surprised that Randy is hesitant to agree. I understand that Sarah, Frank, and I have known Mohamed all our lives and therefore have a much stronger bond with him than Randy, who has only known him in recent years, but I expected a more enthusiastic welcome considering everything the group of us has gone through together. I listen close to Randy's words, hunting for a clue to his subtle uneasiness, and surmise that Randy believes Mohamed will be a hindrance to our investigation.

I am about to explain how Mohamed will be an asset to us while we attempt to identify the enemies when Mohamed knocks on the back door. I hurry to let him in. Despite having warned the others that my brother appears to be in very bad shape I can see how astonished they are when they see him up close. It is not just his dirty clothing that is so upsetting but his skin has red blotches, he is incredibly thin and his hair is almost brittle. So concerned by his obvious discomfort, Frank insists that Mohamed shower and change into some clean clothes immediately.

"I just never thought," Sarah fights back tears. "I would never have believed it was him."

"That was the point, wasn't it?" Randy says. "It's one damn good disguise I'll give it that."

"It is a convincing disguise because it is real. Mohamed is, in fact, a homeless person living on the mean streets of Boston. That is, he was. The discussion tonight has to do with us bringing him with us to Cape Cod. It may seem like a risky thing to consider; however, if we expect his help, then it is a necessity. We also have to consider that my brother Abdul is ready to rat him out and Carlo Bertoni is looking for him. These threats make leaving him here in Boston pretty much the same thing as abandoning him to danger. He needs to get out of here." I watch as Randy averts his eyes from mine. "Mohamed also knows things that I'm sure will help us uncover the mystery of the storm. If the ninth Eurabian is behind the Weather Weapons Program that is obviously going astray, then we can prove this person is not Mohamed by uncovering who it really is! Mohamed is the only person who may have clues about who the ninth Eurabian is; even if he's not aware of it."

"We only have one unit at the Otis Trailer Village. The unit was meant for two people and with Sarah and me we're at four. If we add Mohamed we're at five." Randy says. "You know, I don't mean to be a jerk, but that's a lot of aiding and abetting a fugitive of the law. It's not like we could deny we knew he was with us or anything like that."

I hear the water from the shower start to run from behind the bathroom door. Knowing my brother can not overhear our conversation I decide to poke at Randy's passive resistant attitude regarding Mohamed.

"It's a bit surprising that you would feel this way about taking Mohamed in. After all, you've always been the biggest chance taker of all of us. Besides that, we never agreed he'd stay with us. We've never even discussed that. I have to ask why, since this storm thing happened, you've become the model of cooperation with Agent Brown and Homeland Security while seemingly being skeptical of helping my brother."

Randy gulps down, what I assume is, bubbling up anger and says, "I'm not. I'm just being cautious about upsetting them any more than we need to. Why should we deliberately endanger our relationship with them? What does that gain us?"

"Whoa there. When we were dealing with the Eurabian enemies you were ready, willing, and able to hide things from Agent Brown with no trouble at all. And now, all of a sudden, you want to play on the same team as him? Not that we shouldn't cooperate with him whenever we can but, hey, if Mohamed is involved with us we'll be lying to Agent Brown constantly," I say, my voice getting louder as my frustration grows.

"I'm aware of that…" Randy starts to say.

Before he can continue Sarah interrupts, "Okay, that's it. There's no use in fighting amongst ourselves anymore than there's any point in any of us keeping secrets. I'm not sure where any of us stand on what we're getting ourselves involved with but maybe we need to start talking to each other."

Taking center stage in the middle of the living room, Sarah takes a deep breath. "I am scared to death to get involved in another one of these dangerous situations. Just having Mohamed here so close after Agent Brown left makes me so anxious I feel sick to my stomach. I don't have any personal reasons to get involved in any of this except that I want to help Mohamed. I know what he was before but I also know what he is now. I want him to be okay. No, I know he can't ever be really in my life but I want him to be okay somewhere. For him and for Abby I will get involved in trying to discover who the ninth Eurabian is, and if that means we start with investigating the so-called weather weapons storm, then so be it."

Sarah sits down with the dignity beholden a first lady. Randy paces from the window to the couch and back but says nothing. I look over at Frank while he puts down the reclining portion of the chair.

"I'm doing this for Mohamed and Abby. There will be no peace for either of them, or their parents, until Mohamed is proven to have changed from the terrorist he was. I don't believe he will ever be able to prove he is a good guy until the mysterious ninth Eurabian is identified as being someone besides him. At the core of all of this are my feelings for Abby. She will never be free to live her own future until this part of her past is at peace. If she has no peace in her future then I will have no peace in mine."

Tears of gratitude and love form as Frank's words stir up my pent up emotion. His soft eyes look down upon me while he returns to his seat. I feel the warmth of his hand in mine and, for a moment, I allow myself to be happy.

"I believe we all know what Abby's motivation is so that leaves you, Randy," Sarah says. "Try not to be too outraged when you explain your feelings to us. Just a bit of emotion goes a long way."

Randy runs his fingers through his wild red brown hair. Although he is not a tall man, his strong build and charismatic presence fills the room. "I am motivated by all of the same things that you are, but you're right, there is more to it for me this time than there was before. After hearing what that guy Arnie said about the ninth Eurabian likely being connected with a military weather weapons guy…well…I'm more motivated than ever."

"Why is that?" I ask.

"Because I think I know who the ninth Eurabian is. I've thought about it these past few months and I've even done a little secret investigating. That's why I'm not thinking we need to involve Mohamed in this. I think I know who the man is. He's military, he's tied to Cape Cod, and he's super powerful."

"So who is it?" Frank asks.

"Well. This is where the complicated part comes in. He's related to Agent Brown. We need our buddy Brown to be really happy with us and out of our way. Antagonizing him with Mohamed isn't part of my plan, you see?"

"Related to Agent Brown? Are you nuts?" Sarah shouts.

"I wish I were. The thing is it all works out perfectly. He's the father of Agent Brown's wife; his father-in-law. I think even Brown suspects maybe something is up with this man but doesn't want to admit it. I believe Alena Brown married Agent Brown because of what he did for a job and then Brown was elevated up the ranks because of his wife. Get it? She marries Brown, who gets promoted so her father can keep tabs on what's happening at Homeland Security! Agent Brown may be an honest agent; I totally believe that. But whether he knows it or not he was planted in the Boston office by the bad guys who keep a watch over him through his damned wife!"

*****

Cleaned up, Mohamed could easily pass as my father's brother. The resemblance between them has never been more noticeable. When I examine him I am astounded there are such pronounced age lines around his eyes. His hair, now that it is no longer matted down with oily dirt and debris, is speckled with gray streaks. Frank's clothes dwarf his thin body, his teeth are no longer the sparkling white I envied so much as we grew up and he looks to be slightly hunched over. If I didn't know he was not yet thirty, I'd guess him to be a much older man. While he listens to Frank and Randy tell him everything they know about the storm, Arnie, Otis Air Force Base, the turtle program, and Agent Brown's family, Mohamed scribbles on a pad of paper. I lean over to glimpse at what I assume to be notes and instead I see that my brother has doodled pictures of turtles, tornadoes and military insignia.

"Please, allow me to absorb all that you are saying. You must remember that you are mixing together facts with theories which makes it difficult for me to know what I can believe as truth and what I can consider as possible," Mohamed says, as he lay the pad down. "These theories about the storm really being a United States weather weapon attack; this is indeed possible. I am more convinced than not because of this scientific team you speak of at the NSF."

"Yes, the National Science Foundation Science and Technology Center. That's where Arnie and his crew work. He's the one who will be working on the Air Force base this summer," Frank explains.

"But he is not in the turtle program?" Mohamed asks.

"No, a guy with his brains and weather knowledge doesn't count turtles. He just told Frank about the turtle program as a way to get him and Abby on the base." Randy stops pacing long enough to look out the window.

Sarah, who has been noticeably quiet throughout the discussion, turns to face Mohamed. "I think this entire thing is crazy, especially the part about Agent Brown's father-in-law being the ninth Eurabian. I just can't get myself to believe that a guy as smart as Agent Brown was tricked into marrying his wife and then put in a position of such power just to be used like a pawn, can you?"

"As I said earlier, I never knew much about the ninth Eurabian. I knew he was not the leader; Senator LaFlamme was. I knew the ninth Eurabian was more powerful than many of the other members, and, for some reason, did not have to attend many of the group's meetings. I knew some of the others did not totally trust him; an impression I got more than actual knowledge. I never saw him," Mohamed states.

"Let's say I'm right," Randy says.

"Let's say you review your theories one by one identifying what is fact and what is not." Frank moves the kerosene lamp closer and prepares to take notes. "And go slowly this time…in order…say everything in order."

"I started thinking about the fact that the ninth Eurabian wasn't identified even though all the Eurabian information was confiscated. I know things were written in code and all of that but surely there had to be some clues to this person's identity somewhere. So that led me to believe that information was known but not reported; as in another cover-up. So, who would have the power, the ability, and the motive to cover-up the identity of the ninth Eurabian?"

Frank nods for Randy to continue.

"Agent Brown has, that's who. So from there I started to think about the course of events leading up to the Eurabian bust. First, he sent his wife and family out of town after the very first sign of trouble; the attack on Harvard University. Why would he take such a drastic step unless he knew than that attack wasn't to be the last one to hit Boston?"

"That's true," I say. "He did say he sent them out right after the Harvard attack."

"Then, after we are forced to confide in him because we need help, Agent Brown keeps a close watch on us, yet we manage to continue on with our dangerous exploits. If this man had the power to lock us up and keep us out of the whole thing, why didn't he?"

"It wasn't like he didn't threaten us plenty of times. He was livid with us on more than one occasion," I remind everyone. "Maybe he didn't want the hassle of explaining why he had to take us into custody."

Randy scoffs, "He's the head of the whole damn region. He didn't need to explain anything to anyone. No, he let us go because he needed to know if we did or did not know who the ninth Eurabian was. By that point he may have suspected his own father-in-law. If he wanted to make any kind of choice involving the future of his in-law dad he had to be sure we didn't already have the goods on the guy!"

"That makes sense," Mohamed says. "Then, when he determined that the identity of the ninth Eurabian remained a mystery, he was free to handle his father-in-law criminal as he saw fit."

Sarah shakes her head. "No way, Brown is as straight and honest as the day is long. Father-in-law or not, he'd turn the guy in."

"I'd have to agree with her analogy of the integrity of the man," Frank says. "He is above reproach."

"What if he couldn't turn the guy in for some reason?" I ask, finally able to see the assumptions that Randy has knitted together. "What if his father-in-law has something on him or threatens his family? What if Agent Brown is being black-mailed or held hostage or something like that?"

"Agent Brown has a son, right?" Frank asks.

"Yeah, a young son; like four or five maybe. He's got a daughter too. She must be like ten years old or something like that," Sarah says. "His wife, though, now I don't know much about her. I don't even recall seeing a picture of her come to think of it."

"His wife is someone I've investigated quite well. Now she's an interesting and quite bizarre person. Her maiden name is Alena Kulik; no middle name. Her mother is a woman named Raisa Golovkin. Her father is…"

Mohamed cocks his head to the side and asks, "Kulik? As in General A. D. Kulik?"

"None other. General Alexi Dimitri Kulik is Alena's father. You know of him?" Randy asks Mohamed.

"Wasn't he a young up and coming military hero while Reagan and Gorbachev were battling the nuclear arms race?" Mohamed asks.

"You're right again. He's the very same man, a real go-getter who used his Russian heritage to prove that being an American trumps blood lines and family connections to heritage homelands. General A.D. Kulik is Agent Brown's father-in-law, weird, isn't it?" Randy takes a moment to gather his thoughts. "Now I'll tell you exactly why I think he might be the ninth Eurabian. First, there is the current relationship between Agent Brown and his wife Alena. From what I can gather from watching them and visiting the health club where she works out at, she is a cold woman who is totally unattached to her husband. Whether or not she loved him once, I don't know. But I'm getting the sense she doesn't love him now."

"How can you know that?" Sarah asks, skeptically.

"Because she's having an affair with a guy at the club."

"Surely, the man in charge of Homeland Security is aware his wife is not faithful?" Mohamed says, surprised.

"I would suspect so. If he is aware, thought, he doesn't seem to care." Randy shrugs. "Now, for the General himself. He is much harder to get near because he lives in Washington D.C. and only comes here to his so-called summer home on occasion. The home is a year round cottage on Cape Cod; it's in Orleans. It's a nice place down a long lane; totally private."

"The perfect place to break into without being seen?' Frank asks Randy.

"I'd say so. It's at least a great place to peek into windows, which of course I did."

"And what did you see that convinced you this general is the ninth Eurabian?" Mohamed asks.

"Bottles of cranberry wine from the Cape Cod Cranberry Farm. The very same bottles of wine the Eurabians poisoned in an attempt to kill the President, Vice-President and key legislatures of Congress just six months ago. Is it possible this man just happened to buy a few bottles of this very same wine and store it in his wine rack? Yes, anything is possible. Is it likely? No, I don't believe it is."

"The exact same bottle of wine that the Eurabians tried to use to poison the

President?" I ask.

"They have the tan labels with gold letters and the cranberry logo." Randy states.

"It's compelling testimony to be sure, however, it is circumstantial evidence all the same" Frank mutters. "I wish there was something even more incriminating."

"I think there is but we have to watch the property to be absolutely sure." Randy crouches down near the coffee table so he can make eye contact with all of us when he says, "The day I went there, when I was leaving, I swear I saw a man that looked just like Carlo Bertoni driving a car heading toward the cottage. I swear it was him; I'm almost positive!"

Chapter 9
Otis Trailer Village

My first impression of the Otis Trailer Village is that it is in dire need of updating. Perhaps the morning sun is too harsh on this unkempt place. The old wooden entrance sign sways in the breeze; its faded green lettering and peeling paint is too dull to reflect even a glint of light. Dust blows up behind the truck as we drive down the severely worn tar driveway. We dodge overhanging branches along our way to yet another sickly looking sign. This one announces that we have arrived at "The Village Circle." Here we find that the village's office building is really an old mobile home trailer with a neon office sign in the front window. Not surprisingly, the letter "c" in the word "office" is burnt out. I look around the circle to see a fenced off dumpster area which would require access keys if there were still a lock on the gate.

Next, I take in the entrance sign to the campground. This tacky handcrafted relic hangs down from a large pine tree on uneven rusty chains. The sign, which features a black bear and her cub, looks to date back to the 1950's. Next to the campground entrance is, of all things, a rather nice dog park; an amenity that doesn't seem to fit in this otherwise Daniel Boone-inspired place. Next to the dog park is the entrance to the trailer park; the place we will call home over the summer.

As Frank pulls up to the office trailer I inspect a man whom, I assume, is Mr. Jinkins; the owner of this extremely odd place. He is tall, thin, and hairy. As I check him out, the term werewolf comes to mind. He watches us get out of the truck with an interest so intent I feel violated by his staring eyes. Although he is expecting our arrival he appears to be sizing us up as if our presence on his sacred property is a serious violation of some unspoken but powerful rule. To avoid contact with this creepy man I convince Sarah to visit The Village Store with me while Frank and Randy take care of the formal matters in the office.

"This is a store? It looks like a big shack," Sarah whispers while stepping inside. "And Mr. Jinkins, what's up with him? Is it me or is he demonic looking?"

Glancing around at the inventory displayed on dusty shelves, I reply, "He's not exactly friendly looking, that's for sure. As for this so-called store, well, at least they sell junk food."

"This whole place is like you see in old camp movies; you know where a psycho killer goes around chopping up teenagers and…"

"Please, don't draw me that picture, okay? This is our temporary new home and we have to find a way to make peace with it. Jinkins is creepy and this place is, um, weird, that's all."

"Yeah, okay, sure." Sarah points at the store's cracked window and shakes her head. "Any ideas about finding a place for Mo…I mean your brother? I was checking things out on the drive in here and I noticed quite a few old motels that are sort of off the beaten path. It'll be really expensive to put him up in a place like that but it could work."

"I noticed the same places. The money problem is huge, though. We'd have to charge it all and that'll leave a paper trail we could never explain to Agent Brown should he monitor things like that. That's not even mentioning the fact that we'll never earn enough money to pay bills of that size back. We'll have to sell a whole lot of jewelry to pull that off."

"I know. I've talked to quite a few people who sell handmade jewelry at craft fairs and I'm pretty confident I can earn enough to keep us afloat this summer, especially with the money you and Frank will be earning as turtle hunters, but we won't have extra money to finance a hotel."

Suddenly a young girl, who I estimate to be no older than fifteen or sixteen years old, comes out from a back room that is tucked behind the checkout counter. She hesitantly ends her cell phone call before acknowledging us. Her greeting message is short, curt, and without eye contact. Within seconds she begins texting. Like Mr. Jinkins, she is tall, lean, and has a full head of hair. Unlike him she is not hairy elsewhere. Her half crazed grayish blue eyes are identical to his.

"She's got to be Jinkin's daughter," I whisper. "Can't imagine any other reason she'd be here. She's not even old enough to work."

"Spitting image of her old man." Sarah casually picks up a $6.49 jar of no brand peanut butter and giggles. "Apparently the price of convenience is very expensive out here in the woods. Besides being outrageously expensive I bet this stuff is older than I am."

In order to get a better look at the girl at the cash register, I pick up a box of crackers and a local newspaper. At the checkout counter, I grab a handout of scheduled events for the park which include cowboy and Indian reenactments, square dancing, country line dancing, bingo night, and a weekly Saturday night karaoke event at a place called The Campers Cottage. Attached to it is a folded map of the Village Campground and surrounding area.

Back in the truck, while we wait for Frank and Randy to return, I study the map. "I believe that a sizeable portion of the area around Otis Trailer Village is just woods, mostly undeveloped. This means that Mohamed could camp out in the wilderness somewhere if he has to. It's not much but just knowing that gives me a little bit of relief."

Sarah takes a closer look at the map saying, "It looks like there are a whole lot of woods out there. Finding just the right place for him may take time. He needs to be close enough for us to get to him yet in a hidden place; possibly near water…"

"I know," I interrupt. "And I also know that Randy will drive us nuts explaining why a camping idea won't work. As for Frank, mister practicality, he'll spend hours just drawing up a logic based action plan as to how to go about searching for an acceptable spot."

Convinced it is best for the two of us to take matters regarding Mohamed into our own hands, Sarah and I are deep in discussion plotting strategies when the Frank and Randy return.

*****

Our new home, the rented trailer, is taupe colored with pine green shutters and what was once white trim. I walk through the small entryway cautiously, as, in my opinion, it doesn't seem to be properly attached to the trailer itself. The smell of stale cooking grease sticks to the old style veneer cabinets in the eat-in kitchen. A quick glance around the living room assures me it will barely fit our couch, love seat, and TV. The nicest parts of the room are two built-in bookcases which I would actually like if only I could think of a purpose for them. I brace myself before going into the bathroom. Although I expect to see ugly old chipped tiles and stained fixtures I am pleasantly surprised to find it has been updated recently. The room is tastefully done in white and gray with a soft apricot border running just below the ceiling. A set of working, clean, and freshly painted bi-fold doors separate a washer and dryer from the rest of the room.

"The owner of this place is quite a piece of work but he was honest about this, anyways," Randy says, as he looks inside the washing machine. "He said the bathroom was just re-done and it seems he was telling the truth. I can't believe the bath is so nice."

Sarah runs her fingers over the bathroom counter saying, "Jinkins looks like a slimy character, do you think he is?"

"He's a shady dude," Randy says. "And his eyes are like a bloody wolf's eyes. He sees right through you. I don't like him, but hey, we don't need to like him so it doesn't really matter."

Frank unlocks the back door across from the two bedrooms and says, "Mr. Jinkins has a habit of answering a question with another question. For example, he originally told us this unit was being rented as a summer unit so I assumed it would be furnished. When I talked to him over the phone this morning he told me it's not furnished. When I asked him if it isn't typical for summer units to come with furniture, he didn't answer me. Instead he asked if I've ever rented on Cape Cod before. He's a crafty guy using the art of diversionary conversation to connive us. Next thing you know, when we got here, he said he could provide furniture to us for an extra monthly fee!"

"Would we be better off renting his furniture rather than lugging our stuff up here?" Sarah says.

"Ugh, I don't want to sleep on any mattress he provides. Can you imagine? It would probably have bed bugs or maggots." I shiver at the gross thought while I look around the bigger of the two bedrooms. "This one must be the master. The carpet needs shampooing, but overall it's not so bad."

"The other bedroom is actually in better shape, although the color of the paint is a bit loud. It must have been a kid's room," Sarah explains.

Randy leads us back to the living room, puts his hands on his hips and starts to laugh.

"I vote we get our own stuff up here because I don't trust Mr. Jinkins to give us anything clean enough to use either. I've got to say that the thought of sitting on a sofa our manager has in stuffy storage somewhere is rather revolting."

Sarah nods. "I'm with you. The only other bad thing about this place is only being allowed two vehicles. Abby and I will miss our compacts."

We chatter a bit more before Frank announces it's time to return to Boston.

"Um listen." With what I hope is a hidden hand signal to Sarah, I say, "Sarah and I were talking before and since we've already packed everything up at home we figured we'd stay here while you the two of you went back to Boston. If you two unload the boxes we brought with us we can get to work."

"Yeah, we'll start unpacking and getting things in order." Sarah winks at me. "Besides that, this dumpy place needs a lot of cleaning before you start dragging furniture in here."

Although Randy looks at Sarah a bit suspiciously he leaves with Frank without arguing. We head out for the woods within minutes of their departure.

*****

With nothing but a backpack of basic supplies and some pre-thought out items, I lead the way into the tree line hoping to find a path. I don't know what makes me think there will be a hiking trail cut inside the woods but I soon find there is not. As I told Sarah earlier, getting lost in the woods is easy to do so planning to avoid this horror is essential. In this regard I start leaving strips of red ribbon tied to low bushes as a way to mark our way back to the trailer. With the fairy tale image of Hansel and Gretel in mind, I imagine how they must have felt when they discovered that birds ate the breadcrumbs they left behind to mark their trail.

"I don't see how this land can be developed." Sarah complains, as she follows me through the woods. "Doesn't it seem a bit spongy damp to you?"

"In spots, but it has been raining recently. I think with the trees thinned out and the land leveled off it'll be like the rest of the campground area," I tell her, not truly convinced. "The map clearly says future expansion of the campground and the trailer park is planned for this area. But, Mr. Jinkins may have put this on his map because that's what he wants it to be even though it hasn't been approved."

"That's true."

"Well, it doesn't matter. We're only looking for some place Mohamed can hide. A clearing for a tent near water would be nice; or an abandoned building."

"A building? Way out here in pine tree land? Jeeze Abby, you really are an optimist."

"You never know. This land could have been used for something else before the park was here."

"Yeah, like a cemetery."

Careful not to trip over exposed tree roots, I turn to look at Sarah.

"Do you always have to think up the creepiest things to put in my mind? I wasn't thinking about dead people and now I'm going to be looking around for ancient tombstones and unmarked graves. Just help me here without freaking me out, will you?"

"Fine, let's take Frank's approach and be logical about this. What do we know about this place? We know it's near Otis Air Force Base, and, for some unknown reason, it was never made into a neighborhood for typical military families. That means whoever owned it never sold it for development money. That doesn't sound like our greedy Edward Jinkins. This means he has only owned the place in recent years; since the base was downsized from a full service base."

"Exactly right. Now you're thinking."

"So, who originally owned this land? Who would keep it as woods despite its development value?" Sarah picks at a pine cone. "Maybe the original owners were so rich that money wasn't a motivator to them."

"Maybe they didn't want it developed because they loved nature."

"Which means exactly nothing as far as what could be on this tract of land," Sarah points out. "Except, is it possible the owners once lived on this land? I didn't notice an old homestead anywhere on these grounds, did you?"

"No, but I did notice a dirt road on our drive in to the park,"

"Yes, I saw that too. The dirt road near the horse stables! Now that you bring it up that road went back into nowhere sort of. I thought maybe it led to horse riding paths …"

Too excited to hold back, I interrupt, "But the paths were on the other side of the barn! I saw the path signs!"

"So the road leads to…?"

I stop to assess where we are in relation to the campground, the trailer park, and the horse stables. Squinting into the late morning sun, which I know is in the east, I point to our right. Just as I am about to explain to Sarah that I believe the road will be out in this direction I distinctively hear a branch snap behind us. Sarah's quickly turning head tells me she heard it too. Like two frightened rabbits we stare silently at each other without the slightest movement.

"It must be an animal, that's all," I whisper. "Deer, raccoons, opossums… all sorts of critters out here."

"It's daytime and those critters, as you call them, are all nocturnal, aren't they?"

"Well, I don't know. Then it's a fox or something."

Sarah pulls a bag of chocolate covered peanuts from her pocket. While popping open the bag she looks in the direction the sound came from and shrugs.

"Okay, I'll go with the opossum story. So, you were pointing out to the right? Lead the way."

As it turns out we do find the dirt road, but only after a couple of miscalculations. Oddly, we have a tendency to veer northeast rather than just east; a phenomenon I know to be true but can not explain. When we find the road we quickly locate exactly, well not exactly, but sort of, what we hoped to find; an old homestead. There before us, tucked inside the woods is a cozy old farm house that I can imagine once housed a loving family. I have to stress the word once because the house is no longer habitable. It is now decrepit. The windows no longer have usable glass, the front door is hanging off its hinges, and the house is missing a sizeable chunk of its backside. From the backyard you can clearly see a fieldstone fireplace which appears to have once been part of a spacious living room. The stairs leading to the second floor are missing treads. The banister is in pieces on the floor. What wallpaper remains intact is faded, moldy, dirty, or all of these. The roof, or what is left of it, has peep holes into the sky. To make matters worse the abandoned run-down structure was victim to a fire. What is left of a kitchen is so badly fire damaged I can't make out what it once looked like. Although we don't explore the building thoroughly, Sarah and I quickly conclude that the only thing this building is now capable of providing shelter for are four legged furry creatures.

"It won't do for Mohamed," Sarah crouches down to peek inside a ground level cellar window. "It's possible it could be better down there."

"I don't see how. With rain seeping into the stone cellar for who knows how many years it has to be a mold terrarium by now. And rats, I bet rats are down there."

"Good point. So, now what?"

"We head back to the trailer and hope we stumble across something worthwhile."

Sarah is about to agree when I notice her attention is captured by something off into the tree line. Like a hound dog following a scent, she quickly makes a beeline to what she believes is something worth finding. Confused, yet optimistic, I chase after my quick moving long legged friend. The sound of snapping twigs and brushing tree leaves is surprisingly robust; too much so for just us to be making. When she comes to an abrupt stop I literally crash into her. For a couple of seconds after our movement ends I swear I hear lingering movement behind me. I turn around nonchalantly to avoid spooking Sarah, but can't see anyone or anything around us.

"Look past the pine trees and under that big droopy elm. See it? It's a rusted up reddish tractor. I actually caught a glimpse of the red from the old house. If there's a tractor out here that means there was a barn out here at one time, too."

"Aren't barns usually near the farm houses?" I ask.

"You never know."

And so, with nothing more than optimism, determination, and unspent energy, we hunt around for other structures. We do successfully locate the barn foundation, but it was taken over by wild greenery long ago. There is no evidence as to what happened to the barn that once stood upon it. Of course, the entire time we are scouting around I can't stop feeling as if we are being watched. I also imagine sounds of another person moving not far from where we are. With the exception of flattened bushes and ruffled pine needle patches I find nothing that supports my eerie feelings.

Disappointed and tired, we trace back our steps by following the low lying red ribbons I left behind earlier. We are only half way back when we find that some of the ribbons are missing. At first I convince myself that I just thought I tied a ribbon on a certain tree or near a particular stump but really didn't. But, when Sarah is as convinced as I am that red ribbons have been removed, we both begin to panic. Since our hiking skills are lacking, we are soon in an unfamiliar place. I try desperately to get my bearings using the sun, but to no avail. For a better vantage point I climb up a few branches of a tree. Fear takes control of me but not before I spot something off in the distance. "There's something up there; north. It sounds crazy but it looks like a small building," I tell my frightened friend. "It could be the place for Mohamed. We have to check it out."

"Really? I can't even believe this. We're already lost out here and you want to go even further off the path?"

"Sarah, we don't know where the path is now so going a little ways in any direction won't make a difference. Just follow me. It doesn't look far. I think there's a path that leads to it. At least there seemed to be a slight parting in the trees. That's helpful too."

As hard as I try to confidently lead the way to what I am fairly sure is a cabin, I lead us in a circle. My second attempt, however, is successful.

"Wow, this cabin looks to be in pretty good shape. Maybe someone is keeping it up?" I kneel down to inspect an elaborately constructed stone fireplace not far from the old but sturdy structure. "This thing looks like a real mason made it."

Sarah walks with a spring in her step; an indication that she is excited by what she sees. She yells out that the cabin door is latched shut but it isn't locked. She joins me on tiptoes to peek through the cracks in the boarded up windows. Being short is always a disadvantage for me, yet I can make out what looks to be bunk beds. Sarah identifies a door that leads to a second smaller room. I can feel the optimism forming like a cloud around us.

"Stay out here and hold the door open so I can see what's inside, okay?" I take a hesitant step inside. I am instantly overcome by the dense odor of stale air mixed with urine. Convinced this place is the home of some sort of living creatures I carefully feel my way around. The bunk beds feel solid but do not have mattresses on them. In the corner is an old primer pump, the type you have to pump by hand, attached to a cracked porcelain sink. Above this are cabinets that I don't dare open. Slowly, I make my way to the door at the other end of the room. It is ajar so I push it open with my foot. "Sarah, get this. That door you saw leads to a bathroom! How in the world can a toilet work way out here? And a sink? With running water? It has one of those hand pump things…the old fashioned kind!"

"Are you kidding? Do you think someone lived in here? This place has four bunk beds that's room for eight people, right? What in the world is going on out here in the woods?"

"I don't have any idea. Come inside and see for yourself."

"Hey, the flashlight on my phone is working. Try yours."

With the two cell phone lights in hand Sarah and I discover a plaque displayed proudly in the central part of the cabin.

"On my honor I will do my best to do my duty to God and my country and to obey the Scout Law; To help other people at all times; To keep myself physically strong, mentally awake, and morally straight."

"That's the Boy Scout oath. My brother had to learn it," Sarah says. "I bet this place is an old Boy Scout camp."

"So, that's why the original owners of this place never sold out; they must have been honorable scouts who loved the land. Now this place is just sits here abandoned."

"I still think someone has cared for it over the years; maybe an old scouting guy. But anyway, this place could definitely be cleaned up to make a good place for Mohamed to hide." Sarah takes in a deep breath as she steps outside. "I say we forget trying to find our way back the way we came. Let's follow the lane that leads to the cabin and see where it leads us. If we go back in the woods we'll stay lost…"

Sarah's soft yelp pierces through me. I grab hold of her while quickly assessing if she has been physically harmed in some way. Instead, I find the all too familiar petrified expression on her face. Her hand trembles while she points over my shoulder. I see the bright red color before I recognize it as a ribbon tied to a branch of a nearby tree. There is no longer any doubt that someone followed us through the woods today. The question remains; how much did they hear us say about Mohamed?

Chapter 10
Otis

The only nice thing I can say about Randy's beat up old clunker of a truck is that it has a second seat that Sarah and I can squeeze into if need be. That is, of course, when the seat is clear of the many miscellaneous items that accumulate. Randy's high tolerance for messiness makes it possible for such things as drive-in restaurant trash, college text books, countless travel coffee mugs, and plastic bags of stuff to collect in this seat for months at a time. But as much of a monstrosity as I find this vehicle to be I do note its dependability while I watch Randy back it into the narrow driveway. The second he hops down from the cab Sarah comes out of the trailer.

"What's wrong with Randy?" she asks over my shoulder. "He looks shook up."

"Maybe the moving went badly," I reply, assuming Randy's impatience is the cause for the manner in which he stomps over to Frank's SUV.

When I get a closer look at Frank I immediately notice that his face is abnormally flush. Randy looks at each of our neighbor's trailers while pretending to make small talk with Frank. It takes them several minutes before they come over to us. During this short time Sarah speculates that something has gone terribly wrong. I, on the other hand, insist on remaining positive.

"What's wrong?" I whisper to Frank. "Obviously something isn't going as planned."

"For one think Mr. Jinkins is a lot nosier than I'd like him to be. And it's also not a good time for him to be nosing around the truck. You see…" Frank is interrupted by a pale faced and shaking Sarah.

"Abby, come here, quick. Look!" Sarah's panicky but controlled whisper is accompanied by a wave of her hand. When I reach her she holds up a red ribbon hanging down from pieces of bed frame that stick out over the back of Randy's truck. "This is the ribbon we had. Look close. It has the same ridges as the one you had."

The guys instantly begin questioning us about the ribbon as they too have a strange story attached to it. It seems that Mr. Jinkins stopped the guys at the entrance of the trailer park and refused to let them drive inside until all the items that stuck out of the truck beds were marked with red ribbon. Frank is explaining how this marking technique is, in fact, likely a safety motor vehicle law while I fight the urge to shake him so I can explain what happened in the woods earlier today. Finally, unable to control her stress, Sarah blurts out a detailed story about our morning adventure. Randy and Frank are as interested in the Boy Scout cabin as they are in the mysterious red ribbon activity.

"So Jinkins is more than just nosy. He senses that we're up to something and he's determined to find out what it is. But why should he care as long as we pay our rent on time?' Randy growls.

"And, under the circumstances we're in now, his interference is particularly alarming," Frank notes.

"What circumstances? Do you mean having to move Mohamed here?" I ask.

Frank does his two handed knuckle crack and lowers his voice, "We didn't have a choice but to bring him with us today. It appears your brother Abdul has been quite focused on finding him these past few months. He narrowed down Mohamed's whereabouts to our section of Boston assuming, of course, that you would maintain contact with your fugitive brother. He even discovered how Mohamed rotated where he spent nights. Anyways, Mohamed actually saw Abdul. Luckily Abdul didn't recognize him being all hairy and stuff but it's getting way too dangerous."

"And that's not even counting Carlo and his gang of thugs," Randy reminds us. "They're all looking for Mohamed, too."

I feel an emotionally-charged burning sensation growing in my stomach. Although I understand Abdul's feelings about what Mohamed has done and the horrid impact his actions have had on our family, I just can't accept his determination to turn him in to the authorities as anything other than a betrayal. I allow the silent pause to grow rather than attempt to explain my feelings.

"Is he in your truck or Frank's SUV?" Sarah finally asks.

"He's packed in the back of the truck, like a damn piece of furniture," Randy stammers. "This is insane. We've got a fugitive with us and we'd be the first people expected to hide the guy. Then we get here and crazy Jinkins is tying red ribbons to furniture that's literally just feet away from him!"

"Crazy? He's more than just crazy. That creep is up to something." Sarah leans into the truck bed and whispers. "Can you move a bit so I know you're in there?"

Mohamed moves just enough for the kitchen table to wobble slightly. Just seeing this response makes me momentarily overcome by gratitude for his safety.

"I never expected things to get so bad for Mohamed so quickly. At this point all we have is the Boy Scout cabin in the woods as a place for him and even that may be spoiled because of Jinkins. I don't know what he heard us saying but that creep wants us to know he's watching us. He deliberately tied the same red ribbons he stole from us and tied them to the furniture to send us a message," I insist.

"If Jinkins is on the prowl he'll find Mohamed no matter where we put him. Logically speaking, the cabin sounds ideal for what we need and if Jinkins insists on snooping around then we can't do much about it. But I'll tell you, we didn't need this complication." Frank hands out boxes and bags while saying, "But first things first. Let's free up some space so your brother can sneak inside."

*****

Unpacking is a pleasant distraction from the non-stop heated discussions flaring up inside the tight quartered trailer. In fact, the four of us are so hyped up by the numerous disagreements we are having that our work is getting done much quicker than I anticipated. At the core of every argument is differing opinions as to what we should do next. We all agree that finding out who is behind the weather weapons storm is important, as is proving that Mohamed is not the ninth Eurabian. However, none of us seem to agree on how we should go about achieving these objections.

"I believe my joining your group at this unexpected time has caused quite a bit of confusion," Mohamed says from the center of the living room. "I am most grateful that you were willing to take me away from Boston. It is unfortunate that my need to flee the city became imminent at this particular time. Perhaps now that we are in the circumstances that we are, we need to take a break and establish a plan for how we are to deal with all that needs to be addressed. I realize that such a plan will need to be a compromise of sorts as we all have such strong views on the matters at hand. I also realize that as long as we remember we are all working towards the same things then such give and take is not a sacrifice but rather a gift we can offer to each other."

Sarah steps over a bag of towels and leans against the kitchen sink. Having known her all her life I recognize the slight squinting of her eyes that indicate she is fighting an urge to cry.

"Thank you, Mohamed, for trying to restore some semblance of team spirit in our group. I think I may be able to redirect our conversation in a more civil way. I'll begin by telling you all how I feel. While I speak you all listen. No interruptions." Sarah gives Randy a warning look. "I feel as if there are too many things going on at the same time. We all agree that Mohamed has to get to the Boy Scout cabin but then we get sidetracked into an argument as to who and how we should determine if this place is safe for him. Hey, I agree he shouldn't be staying there if some pack of scouts is going to be hiking down there for a camping trip and I agree we need to come up with a way to get more information about who uses the cabin, but every time we start discussing options Randy changes the subject to scoping out General Kulik's cottage. Or Abby reminds us that she and Frank have to go to Otis to pick up their uniforms and fill out employee forms. Then there's Frank trying to tell us a story about the Catholic Cathedral in Boston!"

"We have to go to the base soon," I mention calmly. "According to the paperwork Agent Brown gave us we need to be there 'early this week' which I assume is yesterday or today."

"I believe going to the General's cottage here on the Cape should be delayed until after the cathedral is investigated..." Frank begins to explain.

"Whoa there...going to the cathedral may not even be practical." Randy snaps.

"What is the whole cathedral thing about exactly?" Sarah turns her attention to Mohamed. "You were the one who was there so I want you to explain it."

"When the big Eurabia bust occurred at the cranberry farm, Carlo Bertoni and I went into hiding together until it was safe for us to make our escape out of Boston. I was grateful to him for taking me with him since it was his mafia connection with the cardinal of the Boston diocese of the Catholic Church that provided us safety for several days. Below the cathedral is a secret series of rooms. There is also a tunnel that goes to someplace or places that Carlo would not disclose to me and I was never able to determine. While there all my physical needs were met; however, there was an unmistakable shroud of secrecy looming around me. Unfortunately, with Carlo always so close by I was never able to investigate where I was or any of the things that were down below the ground with us. The three separate rooms had locked doors and I was never allowed inside any of them. My casual questions regarding these rooms went unanswered." Mohamed looks off into the distance, as if he is remembering the sights and sounds of the cathedral's underground rooms. "After about a week, Carlo got agitated and told me that I had to leave immediately. It was a rather abrupt notice for someone in the precarious position that I was in. Nonetheless, that evening I was provided with a disguise and brought to the destination of my choice. I was, however, never provided with an explanation for my eviction. I did overhear enough of a conversation between Carlo and the cardinal to piece together a theory of why I had to go. It seems that someone of great importance was extremely unhappy when he learned that I was allowed to stay there in the first place. I have always assumed this someone was the ninth Eurabian.

"And so, if some of us can get down below the cathedral and inside those rooms we may find evidence of who the ninth Eurabian is," Frank explains. "It may very well be General Kulik, but it may not. I think we need to go there first before we start assuming the general is the ninth Eurabian."

Unable to control his temper, Randy throws both his hands up and says in a loud voice, "If we find evidence of Carlo being in the General's cottage, that is all the proof we need that the man is the ninth Eurabian!"

"Here we go again!" Sarah says, forcefully. Using a wooden spoon as a gavel, she bangs on the kitchen counter until the room goes quiet. "We also need to deal with other matter such as the craft fair I'm supposedly doing this weekend. We should check in with our homes, straighten out the mess in here, get Mohamed settled somewhere and shop for food. Of critical importance is that we need to get some damn extension cords because this trailer doesn't have a whole lot of electrical outlets. So, if you please, stop with the arguing because we do not have time for it. Do you understand?"

Sarah's outburst brings a more focused energy in the trailer. I can almost feel all of our individual energy bonding us together instead of having us fight each other. Frank leans over to retrieve a pen and paper indicating he is prepared to make notes about group assignments. Randy is hooking the laptop to a printer. Mohamed is packing up gear he intends to bring to the cabin once we are sure it is safe for him to hide there. And I, being the diplomat I always try to be, break the stubborn silence.

"I'll go to the Otis Base and get the uniforms and paperwork. I'll make some kind of excuse for Frank not being able to go. That way he can do something else. While I'm there I'll also go look for Arnie. I don't need Frank with me to do that."

"I'll run to the store to get food and extension cords while Randy doctors up the press pass we stole from my stepmother. If he can make it look like it belongs to me I can use it to get into the Boy Scout Council. Even though they sold the land, I bet they'll still know what's going on with the place."

"I will make a map of the cathedral area and its underground rooms. Then I will work with Randy on a detailed map of General Kulik's cottage. When these are completed we can make plans to investigate them. As he and I work, perhaps it will become apparent as to what circumstances are desirable to make it safe for us to go to these places. We must remember that the time to investigate must take into consideration many factors; most of which do not concern us or our desire to do things. No, we must be aware of how other people interact with these targeted destinations before determining when it is best to go to them."

"True enough. I'm glad you reminded us of that. I guess sometimes logic can get lost in too much emotion," Frank says. "Anyway, I'm going to go find the log cabin and map out a route to it before the sun starts to set. I want to leave discreet markers to it in the woods but I don't dare because of Jinkins. "

"That dude is trouble," Randy says. "I don't know what his game is but he's going to cause us a whole lot of trouble."

*****

I'm greeted at Otis National Guard Base by two armed soldiers at an entrance security gate. I hand them my ID while instantly explaining why I am there. My explanations fail to buffer their military reaction to finding the country's number one most wanted terrorist's sister in a car right before them. The driver's door opens and I am yanked out on to my feet. My hands are placed on the hood of the SUV while I am frisked from top to bottom. This is not like an airport search. This is a full pat down by male military personnel. I think I would be humiliated if I wasn't so frightened.

"I'm here to speak with Dr. Theodore Ritter…um…Environmental and Readiness Center…Ah…I have some papers from him in the car…on the front seat….I swear…"

"Dr. Ritter? What do you have to do with him?" The bigger of the two soldiers snaps.

"I'm working for him this summer and I have to see him about my uniform and some paperwork and…"

The two soldiers exchange a knowing glance. The big one stays outside with me while the other goes inside the guard booth to make a phone call. Not daring to make small talk, I look around instead. The base is surrounded by forest and has many buildings, all of similar design and drab color. Camouflage painted vehicles buzz along the roadways as do some civilian vehicles. Because the base is used for training there are soldiers all over the place making the people out of uniform, like myself, stand out from the crowd. I don't quite understand how this busy place can seem so quiet; it's as if the forest's trees absorb the noises generated by the activities they surround. The atmosphere here is best described as busy dullness; robotic without an ounce of emotion. There are few adornments anywhere and even the few I can see, like a flower garden of red and white perennials, appear misplaced.

After a few uncomfortable moments, the second soldier struts out of the booth and reports to his superior that I should be allowed to pass. And so I am. There are no apologies for the rough handling, the suspicion, or the delay. There is only an abrupt order to go directly to the building in which Dr. Ritter waits. I nervously drive away wondering if I will have to go through a similar humiliation every time I come to work.

Dr. Ritter is, not surprisingly, a decorated soldier. He is not, however, a physical specimen of a fighting man. He is chubby, pasty pale, and snivels constantly. He wears black framed, thick-lensed glasses you only see people wearing on old movies and rerun TV shows. His uniform is rumpled, his shoes are muddy, and the hat lying on his desk is stained with I don't even want to know what. His office looks like a dump with a section for paper, a section for dead plants, a section for reading materials, and a special section for unknown scientific specimens. The sights within these walls are intense but not alarming. The smells swirling and mixing in the air are more curious than unpleasant.

"Oh yes, Abia Haddad, yes, yes yes. Agent Brown sent you, yes? And Frank Stiller? He is not here? No?" the doctor says in a surprisingly high pitched voice.

"No, he is moving our things into the…"

"Yes, yes, indeed, yes. You cannot stay on the base since there is no room available in the old bachelors' quarters, correct? Yes, I remember now."

Dr. Ritter stares at me with his head cocked to one side. After an awkwardly long pause I say, "I'm here to get our uniforms and the paperwork?"

"Ah yes, indeed, yes. I do have that ready for you, yes I do."

He scampers out of his office without excusing himself. After waiting ten minutes, I begin to panic that this odd man has forgotten about me. Hoping to find another employee who may be able to help me, I poke my head into the hallway. Seeing no one I venture out to the general reception area, which, as it was when I arrived, is empty. Since I can tell by the size of the building that there has to be much more going on inside this place than just Dr. Ritter and his Environmental Readiness Center Studies, I casually poke around the curved reception desk. From an emergency evaluation map I find taped to the wall I learn that this building has three main sections. When facing the building, the environmental related offices are up front and to the right taking up about one quarter of the total building square footage. Taking up the entire left side of the building are the Weather Center offices. I'm most intrigued to learn that tucked behind the environmental offices and next to the weather offices is a space marked as 'Top Secret Access.'

"Abia? Can I help you?" Dr. Ritter asks while he darts inside the reception area.

"I'm so sorry for walking around but when you didn't come back I was hoping to find someone who could help me find you and…"

"I see, yes, I see you are a curious girl, yes? Well, I think perhaps this will serve you well in your employment for me this summer. Ah, yes, yes, indeed, curiosity and the ability to see things a bit out of place; these are key assets when one is hunting for turtle nests. Think of the poor creatures basking in the sun when all of a sudden their environment is overrun by mankind and the damaging agents… Ah, but how I go on, yes? Let me just say that a keen eye on this base is a very helpful thing for the box turtles; a very helpful tool indeed."

I spend the next forty-five minutes learning about the plight of Eastern Box turtles and the role Frank and I will play in saving these poor creatures from the evil and greedy ways of mankind. During this lecture I learn that there is a black market for these creatures. As with any animal of value, these turtles are stolen from the safety of their nests by poachers. Dr. Ritter gets outwardly angry when speaking of this illegal activity, showing an aggressive side of him I wouldn't have believed existed. Finally, with paperwork and ugly khaki uniforms in hand, I bid my new boss goodbye. Rather than walk me out of the building, he waves to me like a child does from a school bus. As odd as Dr. Ritter is I can't help but like him. Of course, on my way out I look for Arnie. I soon learn that every door I encounter is locked and requires a badge swipe or code to gain access. I also learn that there are cameras everywhere, making it unwise to search for Arnie without any viable excuse to be walking around the building. Feeling like a failure I hesitantly decide to go back to the trailer.

"Abia, here. Over here." A familiar but unrecognizable voice says as soon as I step out of the building. Turning to look at its source I see only an immaculately gardened area and flag pole.

"No, I'm in the parking lot, behind the black Toyota," the voice states factually. "Take approximately eight and one half steps forward and then…"

The exact nature of his words tell me the speaker is the person I came to see; Arnie. He is half squatting behind a car wearing a uniform similar to the ones I have just been issued. When he looks my way he is actually looking to the right of me, his autistic traits evident.

"Hi, how did you know I was here?" I ask. "Did you see me come in? I've been looking for you."

"I have been waiting for you. I have been waiting for you every day."

"Oh, so you saw me coming in?"

"The receptionist came to tell me you were here."

"Oh, so that's why she or he wasn't at…"

"She, the receptionist is female. We are friends and I told her to inform me if you, Frank, or both of you should come in. I heard from Dr. Ritter that you were to be hired. I am most pleased that you took my advice. I am grateful and relieved as well."

Because Arnie has almost no reflection in his voice I carefully weigh his choice of words as I consider what he is telling me. Unable to examine his facial expressions because he still will not look at me, I feel compelled to push him for answers.

"What do you mean relieved? Is there something wrong?"

"Yes, there is something very wrong."

"Okay, is it something Frank and I can help you with?"

"If you cannot then no one else can."

"All right. Then what is the problem?"

"Someone is trying to kill me. I am sure this is the case, Abia. The enemy, whoever it may be, wants me dead."

Chapter 11
The Cathedral

Normally a weeknight represents little more to me than the passing of another day. Tonight, however, is to be a night of high intrigue and possible danger. Safe in the apartment, at first it is simple to speak of our trip to the cathedral while we help Sarah gather, sort, and pack up everything she needs for the craft show this weekend. Of course, as the departure time approaches, all of us display tension in different ways. I am chewing the inside of my cheeks, which, as my friends know, indicates that my nerves are becoming increasingly frazzled. Frank, who has cracked his knuckles and bitten off all his fingernails, is now babbling incessantly about what we can expect to find when we get to the cathedral. Sarah is eating her perfect model stick figure flat stomach way through a huge bag of cheese curls. Her fingertips are so stained by orange food coloring crumbs she is no longer allowed to touch any of the inventory. And Randy, whose patience wore thin many hours ago, is still brooding that he is not getting his way about this evening's plans.

"If we split up we could go to the General's cottage and the cathedral tonight. There's no need for us…" Randy suggests for the third time.

"Come on now. We've been through this already. We've been through way too many dangerous situations together not to know how important it is to be careful. And, as we've learned time and time again, there is safety in numbers." Frank says in an even tone. "We can't be hurrying things just because we feel like it. According to Arnie someone is already on to him and if that's the case then the enemy may be on to us real soon, too. Whatever is happening with the Weather Weapons Program it involves powerful people who apparently have access to all sorts of places. And, they're not the least bit afraid of attacking civilians. That means if we run into them tonight we're in big trouble, so, caution is needed. Our enemy is very dangerous. I mean come on, for them to run Arnie off the road; that's crazy!"

Randy fiddles with the larger jewelry display case in an effort to make it more stable. "That's what Arnie said but how do we know it's true? According to what he told Abby it happened fast and he isn't exactly sure of every detail. Besides that, Arnie is a bit odd. Maybe he has a paranoid personality and just thinks someone is trying to kill him."

"He is odd, but he's highly intelligent. If he says a black sedan followed him, waited for him to be on a deserted side road, and then rammed his car over a ledge, then I'd say he's smart enough to evaluate that this is what happened," I say, a bit defensively. "After all, the bruises and scratches he showed me on his arm from when he jumped out of the car on its way down the sandy slope do sort of scream out real life pain as opposed to self-inflicted pity wounds."

"Could he have just been in an accident? Like he lost control of the car?" Randy challenges me. "Maybe he doesn't want to admit…"

"Randy, if the guy was embarrassed about a car wreck he wouldn't have hunted Abby down to tell her all about it much less expose his body wounds to her in a parking lot. Arnie was pushed off the road and he believes it's because of his suspicions about the storm; plain and simple. Whether or not he is right remains to be seen but it is a logical and reasonable assumption." Frank holds the jewelry case while Randy tightens the corner screws. The silence between them speaks volumes; the discussion ends.

Sarah snaps shut a case and slides it across the floor. Aware that the atmosphere is tense she attempts to lighten it by changing the conversation to the upcoming craft fair. She speaks of necklaces made of semi-precious stones, drop earrings of bright shiny crystal, and her latest creation: scrimshaw inspired charms. I offer out comments and opinions about her pieces with hopes that Frank or Randy will join in. Instead, they remain disinterested and quiet.

"Okay, fine, so we'll talk about the enemy if that's what you want," a frustrated Sarah says to Randy. "I'm picturing the enemy is like an octopus with multiple arms that cover-up its evil doings as it slithers along. We know Carlo Bertoni and the mafia are part of the enemy and we're guessing General Kulik and his military connections are, too. But is that all it would take to get control over the country's weather weapons program? Not just to get control but to make a storm with it? No, I don't believe it is. I think there's a whole lot more to it than that. I don't know who else is behind this nightmare but I have a feeling it's someone no one would ever expect."

"I believe she's right," Frank comments. "Having the ability to make a weather weapons based storm is huge. Someone besides Carlo and the General are behind this. But who could it be?"

"Or whom; as in multiple people," Randy suggests.

"Whoever it is, I believe it's someone we would never expect," Sarah insists.

"An unexpected enemy, how in the world do you do battle with an unexpected enemy?" I whisper to myself.

*****

The Cathedral of the Holy Cross in Boston is a huge, breathtaking stone building with two side by side welcoming front doors. On the drive into the South End of Boston, where this majestic place is located, Frank tells us it is 364 feet long, 90 feet wide and 120 feet high. I'm not exactly sure how impressive these measurements are until I am standing before the building with my head tilted as far back as it will go and I am still unable to see the very top of the spires. Frank also informs us that this place was opened in 1875 and can seat over 1700 people. I cannot even imagine an audience of this size.

"It's just about 7:30 now which means that the mass will be letting out soon," Frank says. "I don't expect it to be packed with people because most of these night time masses are held in memory of the deceased."

"So Catholics don't go to mass much during the week?" I ask.

"No, Catholics only have to go to church once a week and that's usually on weekends," Sarah explains. "I think the churches have the memory masses on weeknights to guilt the deceased's family members into going to church on a weeknight."

"Interesting," I say.

"I want to warn you that there's probably a giant size crucifix hanging up in there somewhere," Randy says to me. "Seeing Jesus all bloody and dead hanging from a cross can be disturbing. As a Muslim whose not used to seeing this image you may be a bit freaked out."

I am about to explain that I am most definitely disturbed when I see a crucifix as the red front doors open. A healthy, but not steady, stream of worshippers meanders down the stone steps. I notice they neither smile not speak as they pass by. Just as we rehearsed, Frank casually walks up the stairs with the three of us close behind him. We wait off to the side until most of the people are gone. We get inside the cathedral with no problem. Looking up the long center aisle which is lined with white archways, pews and dark stained glass windows, it is all I can do not to gasp at the sheer exquisiteness of the beauty before me. The gold, the stone work, and the detailed painted icons are indescribable. As I follow the others to the altar I stare at a burgundy cross to which an icon of Jesus is nailed. As I always do when I see this image, I shudder. Behind Jesus and at the tips of the cross are glittering yellow gold beams of majestic and holy light exuding from the son of God. Even a non-Christian like me understands the message given by this piece of art; the son of God is like no other for he is both human and divine.

As Frank explained earlier, the inside of the cathedral will be in the shape of a cross, and, as expected, there are two side altars representing the arms of the cross right before the altar which represents the top of the cross. Mohamed told us there were stairs to the basement level near both of these altars but advised us to use the ones on the left. With only a few people straggling inside we are much more noticed than I'd like us to be. I'm also uneasy that I've yet to see the priest who performed the mass this evening. Wondering where the church leader could be, I glance up into the dark choir loft.

"Its okay, Abby, can't you hear the low whispery voices? That's the priest and someone in confession. It's that little room on the other side," Sarah whispers in my ear. "The older lady wearing black is waiting for her turn to confess. When the person inside comes out, she'll be next. That's when we'll be able to slip through the doors."

"Got it," I say.

Frank leans over, adding, "The stairway should be just on the other side of that door. We'll just kneel here at this altar until the time is right. Maybe we can light some candles and pretend we're praying for somebody."

Totally unfamiliar with the concept of buying healing for the sick with candles I hesitantly take the wooden stick from the sand box. Following Sarah's lead, I put the stick in the flame of a burning candle and transfer the flame to an unlit one. As I extinguish my fire stick I decide to dedicate my candle to Mohamed, who is, although not ill, the person in my life with the most problems. Before kneeling at the iron bench with the red cushioned kneelers, Sarah touches her forehead, her chest, and the front of both of her shoulders; what she calls making the sign of the cross. Hoping this is not a sin for Muslims, I do the same.

"Okay, it's time. Let's do it," Randy whispers.

In a calm orderly fashion, we walk through the side door and into the silent hall that runs parallel to the altar. I am immediately startled to see a whole line of statues along the wall on my right, each with a small kneeler of its own. A sign tells me that these are the Stations of the Cross; another mysterious Catholic tradition of some sort. On my left is a door to the stairs that lead to the level below. Without a thought we all start to step forward as Randy turns the doorknob. We unexpectedly bump into each other when the doorknob doesn't turn.

"The stupid thing is locked," Randy grumbles.

I would think that the older the lock is, the easier it would be for us to break into it with Randy's locksmith kit, but that is not the case. Despite breaking into locks dozens of times during the many crises we've encountered since we first got involved with Mohamed's troubles, Randy can't get this ancient door lock to budge at all. Fearful that the priest will find us here before locking up the cathedral for the night, I volunteer to check on the stairway door on the other side of the building. Although a good reason why that one should be unlocked while this one is locked escapes me, I convince myself and the others it is worth the risk of venturing over there.

As I walk past fourteen Stations of the Cross, each with a statue depicting scenes from the time when Jesus Christ was crucified, I wonder why the Catholic faith seems to focus so much on the horrible fate of their beloved son of God rather than on the joys their faith preaches his coming to Earth brought them. At the end of the hall there is a large stained glass window with lighting strategically placed to illuminate every piece of the colored cut glass. The intricate mosaic picture is of the dead Jesus' body as it lay draped in the lap of a woman whom I assume is his mother, although she seems incredibly young to be the mother of a thirty-something year old man. I am temporarily mesmerized by the details within the picture and the stunning contrasting colors that seem to melt into each other. My attention is so drawn to the curious piece of art that I almost miss the sudden change in lighting off to my right. There, in a hallway of what I now realize must be offices, an occupant has shut off an office light. I, being mostly hidden behind the fourteenth Station of the Cross, watch a middle aged woman carrying a briefcase walk toward the hallway on the opposite side of the cathedral. She has a purposeful stride, giving the impression she is someone of importance. When the hallway is clear I do a quick scan of the remaining offices which I find to be all empty.

The hallway on the right hand side of the cathedral is much narrower than the one which runs parallel to it. This is because it has three doors that lead to rooms within it. I assume the doors lead to closets or storage space, because unlike the offices, they don't have glass windows for their occupants to look through. The doors in this section are old; two of the three are locked. The door closest to the stairway is unlocked. I make a quick detour inside. I find myself inside a walk-in closet which is crammed full of priest vestments of many different colors. The smell of starch and moth balls overwhelms me. Along the top of the closet are various pieces of headwear; one, in particular, is so large I assume it is reserved for a Catholic boss of some sort. This closet is also uncomfortably warm, lending truth to my middle school science teacher's theory that cloth can be used to insulate a house if need be. As I step out into the cool hallway my sleeve catches on something on the wall. Something jingles as it falls to the floor. The noise startles me a bit, but not as much as the sound of the door leading to the cathedral squeaking open. Instinctively I duck back inside the closet, closing the door behind me.

Gauging how much time has passed while in a dark room is not something I do well. In fact, I am so inaccurate at my estimations of elapsed time in such circumstances that I've made it a habit to count off seconds and minutes in my head. When I believe three minutes have passed I crack open the closet door. Thankfully I don't see or hear anything. I tiptoe the remaining ten or so feet to the stairway door and pray to the woman in the stained glass window holding the dead body of Jesus, whoever she is, that this doorknob is unlocked. My prayers are not answered. The ancient lock stubbornly stays immobile as I twist the door knob. Once again I hear someone coming my way. I revisit the priest vestment closet with less anxiety than I had the first time I hid in this spot.

I am not in the closet very long when I hear the door knob turning. Because I am completely unprepared to hide, I simply push myself into the clothes rack between the vestments. If whoever is in the closet looks down my jeans and my shoes will be visible; a thought I can't get out of my head the entire time I am not alone. Thankfully the person is not inside the closet long. It sounds like the mysterious person is hanging up jingling metal such as…keys? A male voice whistles as he closes the closet door. The sound of the closet door being locked seems amplified to my nervous mind. After a moment I worm my way out from the clutches of the priestly garb. I turn the door knob which opens from the inside despite being locked. I actually hear my sigh of relief. Next I feel along the wall until my fingers touch a wooden rack with metal hooks. The feel of the cool keys on my skin brings a smile to my face.

*****

The keys to this expansive building all hang on a massive wooden rack. Above the hooks that hold the keys are tags that describe what each key opens. Finding this organized system convinces me that the powers to be, whoever they are, are looking out for us. With the help of my phone flashlight I locate what I need in a matter of minutes. I hurry back to the others with a feeling of optimism. I find the others to be less lighthearted.

"Really?" Randy asks, as he looks at the skeleton key in my hand. "The tag on it says it belongs to this door?"

"It says it belongs to this door knob. This key here," I say, holding up a modern key, "belongs to the lock in the door itself."

"It's way too good to be true." Sarah aims a light on the door lock. "So far being in this place hasn't gone very well. I keep thinking that any good fortune that befalls us is secretly laced with bad luck."

Frank, trying to help me lift the mood, says, "We got back here easily and we weren't seen by the priest. Those are hardly strokes of bad luck. The stubborn lock, broken tool, and cut on Randy's hand are unfortunate, but not tragic."

Having not known that a tool was broken or that Randy was hurt, I am busy trying to assess the damage when I hear Randy say that the lock is open.

"Hold on to these keys and we can relock this door on the way out," Randy says to Sarah. "Okay, it's time to find out what's below us."

Not wanting to put a damper on the sudden burst of enthusiasm, I don't ask how we intend to get out of this locked up fortress when we are done investigating the tunnel below the cathedral. Rather, I push all possible problems out of my mind so I can focus on what is happening now. With our flashlights, we carefully go down a flight of stairs. As Mohamed described to us, we find ourselves in a small chapel with several pews, kneelers, icons, and what I think is a crypt. The wall opposite to the stairs has frescoes on it. These paintings, done on wet plaster, depict joyful themes with angels and cherubs; a much more enjoyable environment than the statues of the Stations of the Cross.

"Okay, Mohamed says to pass the fresco nearest the crypt and feel around for a crease in the stone wall. He says the door to the stairway to the tunnel is plastered over and blends in perfectly with the pattern on the old plastered wall. He also said if you don't hit it just right it'll never open. So here goes." Frank's hands slide over the smooth walls for quite some time without any indication that he has found an indentation of a secret doorway. Not one to get flustered easily, he continues his search without as much as a disappointed sigh.

Randy, on the other hand, loses patience after only five or so minutes. He squeezes in beside Frank demanding that he be allowed to try. His hands swirl rapidly about the wall; trying to cover as large an area as possible with the least amount of movement.

"Can you feel anything at all? Even a crack?" Sarah asks.

"The problem is there are too many cracks and creases. How the heck do we know which ones are the door?" Randy complains.

"Do they run from the ceiling to the floor? Do all the cracks run all the way from the top to the bottom?" I ask. "Mohamed said the door was short, remember?"

"She's right! We should be looking waist high; no higher than that," Frank says.

With the new focus we soon find the secret door and we make our way down into the concealed chamber of rooms. The main chamber is quite roomy. I'm surprised to see it is furnished with old cots, chairs, and tables. The dry dust down here makes breathing a challenge, but not difficult. I now understand what Mohamed meant when he said his stay in this room was adequately comfortable. Off at the far end of the main room looms the darkened tunnel entrance. It is a large archway which is lined with bricks. I don't know why I expected to see a small hand-dug dirt hole in the wall but this is certainly not what awaits us. No, this tunnel was built by rich people with a purpose. Off to the side, are three doors to rooms made of wood and brick. This construction appears old but sturdy. Not surprisingly, the doors are locked.

"Now these padlocks I can do!" Randy announces. He flips open his locksmith kit and, with the precision of a surgeon, lays out the various tools. "Just give me a couple of minutes and I'll have us inside door number one."

"Okay. Come on Sarah, let's check things out. I saw some boxes on the floor near the tables." I look about the dark space wondering who constructed this odd place and for what purpose. Then I picture Mohamed hiding out here just six months ago. Oddly, I feel as if I've become part of a secret society now that I'm here.

"I wonder if anyone comes down here on a regular basis. What did Mohamed say about why this place was built?" Sarah asks.

"He said it had something to do with the Italian Mafia and the Roman Catholic Church connection from long ago. He doesn't know any details because Carlo was secretive about it."

Sarah bends down and opens a wooden box. There is a nothing inside but old newspaper. The next box she opens is empty.

"I'll go over there." I walk past a handful of folding chairs that lean against the wall. While I examine two broken wooden crates I hear a muffled scream. I bump into Sarah as I race toward the guys. Randy and Frank are standing inside the first room, blocking us from seeing inside. They are highly agitated.

"What's inside there?" I ask. "I want to see."

"Absolutely not." Frank pulls Randy forward while closing the door behind them. "There are bodies in there…many bodies…in various stages of decay. Plastic vacuum containers or not, the smell of rotting flesh is leaking out. I don't know who they are…or were…or who brought them here or why but I'm not real comfortable being down here nosing around right about now."

Randy grabs on to Sarah. "That room was built for bodies. It's something like a tomb, you know, to keep the smell in but when you're in there…"

A wave of the most rancid stench I've ever encountered hits me full force. I instantly begin to gag. I hear Sarah reacting to the revolting odor in a similar manner.

"Its okay, the door is sealed shut again. It'll pass," Frank's soothing voice is saying.

"This is bad news I tell you; really bad. Whoever uses this place thinks nothing of killing people. I could be mistaken but I actually think I saw parts of a military uniform in there. Who can kill soldiers, dump them down here, and get away with it?" Randy helps Sarah away from the room.

"An unexpected enemy, just like Sarah said, no one we ever expected to be our enemy." My simple words seem to hang in the mysterious dark room below the cathedral. I wait for someone else to speak so my unnerving comment will dissipate but, for some reason, no one does.

Chapter 12
Chambers

It takes a while before the horror of discovering dead bodies inside the sealed room fades enough for us to even consider opening up the second room. Sarah, prone to being more vocal with her fears, has declared that she will return to the crypt area if anything even remotely as disgusting as the corpses is found behind door number two. I, pretending to be braver than my dear friend, falsely claim that I am prepared for the worst. Frank and Randy seem neither hesitant nor anxious to open the second room. My guess is that they are more concerned about us girls than they are about whatever is lurking down below the cathedral. The locksmith tools click together when Randy picks them up and casts them aside. He says nothing about the difficulty of breaking into this particular lock. For that matter he doesn't even make grunting noises nor does he whisper curse words. This is why I am surprised when I see Frank and him stand up straight. They pause for a moment before opening the door. With relief evident in the tone of his voice Randy says, "Nothing dead or rancid in here; just some old file cabinets. Hey, they don't look even look locked."

Frank enters the room saying, "It makes sense not to have locking files in a locked up room, I suppose. Now who would keep office files down here? What in the world could be so secret it would have to be hidden in the bowels of the cathedral?"

"Records on the dead people in the room next door?" Sarah suggests sarcastically.

"I doubt that the deceased down here have any records at all. But I am curious as to why paper files are being used in this day and age?" I slowly walk into the stuffy room. "Check out that desk in the corner. That thing is so old it belongs in a museum somewhere. And what about that thing over there, what is that?"

Randy and Frank follow the ray of light from my flashlight to the heap of metal, wood, and odd piping piled in a corner of the room.

"I can't imagine," Frank says after several thought filled moments. "I'd say that's a barrel of some sort but its use down here completely baffles me."

"Yeah, well maybe they use it to drain blood from the dead bodies or something horrendous like that!" Sarah calls out from the doorway. "Or, even more disgusting, maybe that's how they embalm the corpses. Yeah, this damn place is an underground mortuary for all the victims the serial killers murder, that's what it is. And, incidentally, if we don't get out of here, we'll be the next ones in a plastic body bag! My guess is the third room has an autopsy table and a freaking chain saw!"

"Are you quite finished with your theatrical rendition of Frankenstein below the cathedral?" Frank chuckles, nervously. "Perhaps you girls should stay in this room while Randy and I work on the next door. All kidding aside, there's no reason we should all be exposed to the horrors that may be in there."

"I'll take that offer," Sarah is quick to reply.

Feeling a bit emotionally drained and somewhat curious about the mystery of this room, I also agree. Ignoring the musty smell only very old papers can have, I begin the job of reading through a black ledger book I find in a rickety wooden file cabinet. Considering the book's age, I am impressed at how well preserved it is. The thickness of the dust that covers its surface is evidence that no one else has held this book in a very long time. Although the inked writing is faded, it is legible, making it easy for me to identify the names of saints and locations listed on the left hand column. A glance across the page includes dates, volumes of something measured by a symbol 'g', dollar amounts, 'ship info' with unidentifiable noted descriptions and checkmarks indicating the transactions were completed.

"Okay, this church or whoever was using this place, was shipping something to churches all over the state and even in other parts of New England," I announce to Sarah. "Do cathedrals ship stuff to other churches?"

"Just because I'm a Catholic doesn't mean I know how the church dioceses work. Besides, what dates are in that book? How long ago was it?" she replies.

"Let me see…um…1924…and into 1925."

"It doesn't say what they're shipping?"

"No, just that it's measured by a symbol of the letter g."

"G as in grams?"

"They weren't using metric back then," I remind her.

"Then gallons?"

"Yeah, gallons of what?"

"Holy water? Maybe the cathedral blessed all the holy water for the whole state? Does that even make sense?"

"What is holy water for? How is it made?"

"You know Abby, you being Muslim is certainly trying at times. Holy water is blessed water that Catholics dip their fingers in to bless themselves. The water can be used to bless houses and, well, places and stuff like that," Sarah explains. "And you don't make the water, you bless it."

"I know that. But who can bless it? Anyone? Can you bless water? You're a Catholic, can you make water into holy water?"

"Of course I can't. Priests can, well, I guess priests and people higher up than them can."

"Then that kills the idea of a cathedral with a bishop or cardinal shipping out gallons of the stuff, doesn't it? I mean, why ship blessed water if any old priest can bless the stuff?"

Sarah laughs at her own illogical assumption and says, "You got me there. But really, what did you believe it took to turn water into holy water?"

"How would I know what you Catholics believe? You seem to believe in some very strange things. You have poor Jesus dying on the cross all over the place. You believe he walked on water, don't you? You think he healed sick people, right? Isn't there something about turning water into wine?"

"Water into wine…hmmm… that could be what this is all about; wine. Wine shipped out in gallons. Wine used for the Eucharist at mass."

Once again lost in the confusing traditions of Catholicism I ask, "What do wine and this Eucharist thing mean?"

"Oh, when Catholics take communion the bread represents the body of Christ and red wine is used to represent…"

"Please don't tell me the blood of poor Jesus."

"Oh yeah, that's exactly it."

"So incredibly morbid! Then you eat and drink this stuff? And you people think Islam is a violent religion? I mean really…"

"Abby, this isn't the time to debate religious philosophy but it is time to confirm my suspicions."

"Which is that the cathedral blessed all the wine into Jesus's blood and then shipped it out to churches?"

"I'll forgive that horrible question because I know you don't mean to be disrespectful, which, by the way, that question is. But anyway…"

"I do not mean to make fun of your religion. I am so sorry. I am trying to understand. After all, what about Islam with its Jihads against people who are not Muslims? This is just as difficult to explain to non-Muslims as the communion is to non-Catholics, isn't it?"

"I think so. But anyway, back to my suspicions. I think what this cathedral was shipping out was wine but not because it was blessed, because the whole blessing thing takes place during the mass by the priest…forget that part. I think this wine shipping thing had something to do with the church having wine during Prohibition and shipping it to churches to sell on the black market! What a way to make big money, a constant inflow of wine during a no-alcohol allowed era. And, who knows what other kind of booze they could flow the church network."

I wipe the thick dust off the cover of another ledger book and see no indication of a label. With Sarah's suspicions in mind I begin looking at ledger entries in a different way.

"You are right. Get this. This book is for Irish whiskey! I.W. from Dub… as in Dublin I bet! And this one, I'm guessing the VDK stands for Vodka!"

"And that stuff over there," Sarah says, pointing her flashlight on the wood and metal heap in the corner. "That is probably an old still. The church wasn't just shipping the stuff, I'd say they were making it, too. They must've been making moonshine; some really high potency stuff."

"By the look of these ledger books I'd guess they had to manufacture booze as well as import it to keep up with such a huge demand. As long as they could make moonshine down here, they could always keep up the trade with that and any church wine they could get their hands on."

Since our knowledge of the Prohibition Era is limited, we go see what Frank and Randy knows about the topic. They are still fiddling with the lock on the third room, which, apparently, is different from the locks on the other rooms. They strongly believe Sarah's assumptions about the contents in the second room are correct. Randy is sure that the Prohibition Era was between the years 1920 and 1933. Since all the ledger books we looked at had dates within this time period, we feel we are definitely on the right track. He is also pretty sure, but not positive, that the Catholic Church as an institution was allowed to serve wine during Prohibition. As our group historian, so to speak, we take everything Randy believes to be true as fact.

Frank, of course, takes a logical approach to analyzing the theory. Although he agrees strongly that a Prohibition black market smuggling network ran out of these belowground cathedral chambers, he does not agree that the Catholic Church was capable of handling such a widespread network as the ledger books indicate existed. Convinced that the mafia and the church had to be working together on a project of such magnitude, Sarah and I return to the second room to search the old records for any sign of a mob connection. This is what we are doing when we hear Randy cry out.

"It's open! Finally, this thing is open. Whoever chose this lock for this room was definitely trying to keep people like us out of here," he says.

"Or whatever is inside the room from getting out," Frank cautions.

Side by side, Sarah and I slowly approach the third room. Frank and Randy look at each other rather than at the door knob. Finally Frank says, "I'll do it. If anything jumps out at me I swear I'm going to lose my mind."

I feel my stomach doing somersaults as the door is slowly pushed open. Having no light inside makes it impossible for me to see anything from the angle I am standing at, so I watch Frank's face to measure how alarming the contents of the room are. At first he seems confused; his eyes squinting and his eyebrows arched. Then his eyes dart around erratically as if he is trying to piece together a complete picture of what stands before him. Finally, he flings the door wide open and steps back, as if inviting us to look inside for ourselves.

"It's a weapons arsenal and I mean arsenal. Look at it all. I've never seen so many weapons in all my life!" Frank turns around and says to me. "This makes anything we've ever seen in the past look like kid stuff."

*****

The four of us investigate every inch of the below ground chambers before we decide it is time for us to leave. Sarah is the most eager to go as is evidenced by her constant nagging about the time. Frank is logically trying to figure out how best to depart without leaving a trace of evidence behind. Although Randy has agreed we should be on our way out, he keeps stalling for just a moment longer to look at just one more of this or another of that. I seem to be the only one comfortable with what we have done and what we need to do next.

"Listen, we've done a great job. We've learned a lot about our enemies tonight. First we know that they are ruthless murderers that have the power to cover up the deaths they cause. None of us recall any of the people in room number one being declared missing, right? This means that they were killed in this area without so much as an investigation. That takes a lot of power. Way more than even the mafia has," I say.

"True enough. And, if we don't get out of here we'll be missing too," Sarah adds.

"What about the dead people's families? What were they told when their loved ones were gone? And who told them?" Frank asks. "Think about it. If I had a brother or a father or sister, whatever, that went missing, I'd expect the police to do something until he or she was found dead, wouldn't you? So what were the family members told that made them stop hunting for their dead loved ones?"

"Good point," Randy says. "Obviously they were told a lie by some very high ranking and well regarded officials whom they believed. That is a mighty powerful enemy."

"From the second room we know that this place was used during the Prohibition. That means the tunnel down here must lead to the water, right? Now, how does that tie in to the enemy we're facing now?" I ask.

"Or the tunnel goes to more than one destination," Frank says. "That's a whole other consideration. The question remains, though, does our enemy need the tunnel or not?"

"I can't see them hauling in an arsenal like we just saw in the third room through the cathedral, can you?" Sarah says. "My guess is they brought in the weapons through the tunnel. That's probably how they got the dead bodies down here too."

The discussion about the new information we gathered tonight breathes enthusiasm into all of us. I am extremely relieved this is happening because I know we have to face the one thing I've not wanted to worry about all night. "Now that we're going upstairs we need to figure out how we're going to leave the cathedral. We can't go through the front doors because we know they lock from the inside. This leaves us with emergency exit possibilities and side doors. This means we may have to deal with alarms going off when the doors are opened."

"I've been thinking about this," Frank says. "I believe we have to do what we have to do. This is one of those occasions where there are no good decisions to be made. No, we must pick from the bad decisions and hope it works out okay."

"That's a rather nonchalant attitude." Sarah stoops down to get inside the crypt area of the chapel below the main floor of the great cathedral.

Following Sarah I add, "Yeah, it is a rather laid back attitude considering that we're breaking into a sacred building in Boston; not to mention the fact that I'm Mohamed Haddad's sister."

Frank, who is the last to leave the below ground chambers says, "It is illogical to waste time considering better choices when none are available to us."

Having no argument for this obvious truth I change the subject. "I think someone from this cathedral has to know something about what's happening below these floors. Mohamed told us some man helped him and Carlo inside when they were hiding. Maybe it's a janitor and not a religious man but it's got to be someone with keys and alarm codes."

Sarah dusts herself off as she watches Randy carefully reseal the hidden doorway that leads to the secret below ground chambers. "I agree. What I'd like to know is who are the dead people down there and who killed them," she says.

"I'd love to know why those people were killed. I'm also curious about what all the weapons are for," Randy says.

"It's true we have unanswered questions but we have answered the question we came here to answer: let's not forget our purpose for being here," Frank reminds us. "The weapons we found are definitely military weapons. There are M14 and M16 rifles, semi and full automatic rifles and all sorts of assault weapons only the military is supposed to have. There's even grenades in there."

"Let's not forget the machine guns," Randy adds. "You don't see those on the streets every day. I'm not sure even gangs have weapons like that. Hey, maybe the machine guns they have are older models but they look mighty deadly to me."

"Okay, so we can connect this cathedral chamber of horrors to the mafia in the present day through Carlo Bertoni. We can connect it to the mafia of olden days through the Prohibition era bootlegging network. And we can connect it to the military through the weapons arsenal. That means General Kulik is tied to this place, too. This certainly is progress." Turning to make sure both Sarah and Randy are ready to go up the stairs, I continue my thought, "But the bigger question remains. What, if anything, does this have to do with the Weather Weapons Program, the crazy storm and whoever is trying to kill Arnie?"

With these questions asked, the group begins theorizing what horrible things might be happening in this area and who our enemies may be. The whole time Frank leads us back to the main level of the cathedral, he logically assesses each of these theories. When we reach the area where the Stations of the Cross are located, the subdued lighting casts an eerie glow upon their statues. We all inspect the ceiling, walls, and floor for signs of an alarm system, and we determine there isn't one. My immediate relief is tempered when I remember that the lack of an internal system does not mean that the doors and windows are not alarmed. Although we are fairly confident we are alone, we remain perfectly quiet as we tiptoe to the offices. My vague recollection of an exit at the rear of the building earlier in the night weakens as we come closer to where I imagine this escape door to be. This may be due to an inner feeling that the door I'm picturing is just wishful thinking or it may be because the door is actually not where I think it is. I am hoping for the former.

"I see a red glow," Frank says, as he approaches the corner. "You're sort of right, Abby. There's an emergency exit door at the far end. Not an exit door; an emergency exit door."

"What difference does that make?" Sarah asks.

"Emergency exits are sometimes alarmed…as in loud alarms blaring to let others know there's an emergency inside," Randy explains, in a complaining manner. "Some may even be wired in to the police or fire departments or a security company."

"How will we know whether the door is alarmed or not?" Sarah asks.

"It'll have a sign on it like 'Alarm Will Sound'," Randy says. "So, now's a good time to pray that the door doesn't have a sign like that."

We quickly pass by the empty offices. In my peripheral vision I see the dim lights of computer screens and on/off buttons. The soft hum of machinery is almost calming. When I reach the office where I saw the woman with the briefcase leave earlier, I notice a red light among the typical greens and golds so often seen on computers. *"It figures this woman's stuff would be different from her co-workers,"* I think to myself.

"Don't waist your prayers. It's got that exact sign." Frank keeps his flashlight beam on the sign and stares at it. "Which leaves us with the body of the cathedral."

"Which, for all we know, is alarmed to protect the gold chalices and holy relics," Sarah says.

Randy makes a low growling noise. "But getting in there is useless if there aren't any side doors. Ugh, it figures we'd pull everything else off without a hitch but we can't find a way out of this holy fortress."

"We can't leave through the main part of the cathedral; the front doors are locked from the inside and there aren't any other doors in that part of the building. This back emergency door is also not a good choice. That leaves us with the two side doors or staying below ground overnight?" Frank announces.

"It's after one a.m.," I point out. "What time do you think people get here? Eight?"

"Every minute we stay here we're at risk of being discovered by the enemy," Sarah points out. "Getting caught inside this place by a man of God is one thing. Being caught down there by the devil of an enemy is another. If we stay here until morning then we hide up here."

"Being up here doesn't teach us anything," Randy is saying when we all hear a distinct banging noise. Between the acoustics of the building and our location we can't tell where the noise came from. Like animals in the wild, we instinctively freeze in place waiting for something else to happen. The next noise is more distinct because it is closer. It is the sound of male voices. Jolted into action, I attempt to return to my previous hiding place: the vestment closet. I'm not surprised to find it unlocked as this is how I left it just hours before; however, I am surprised we barely have enough time to cram our bodies inside of it before a fluorescent light shines from down the hall.

"No one, okay?" a gruff sounding older man says. "There ain't no one here I tell ya. That stupid motion sensor thing near Maureen's office; it's hum bug bullshit, it is. Why she insists on having her office alarmed separately is crap too. She's a prima-Donna prissy with way too much attitude she is."

The thought of the red blinking light I saw inside her office moments ago hits me hard. I've made a terrible mistake by ignoring it and now we may all have to pay the price for it. I desperately want to confess what I've done to the others but I don't dare make a noise. Instead I wallow in self-hatred.

"Check the doors," the second male voices says; this one younger and more refined. "I believe you are right, but let us be sure. After all we don't want to find out something precious was stolen because we didn't take every precaution we could, do we?"

"I suppose not."

In my mind I play out the mysterious old man turning the door knobs of the doors in the hallway expecting them to be locked. They all will be, of course, except this one. Unless...

"Push over," I whisper between Frank and Randy.

As I squeeze between them I aim my flashlight on the key board. I quickly find the spare key marked 'vestment closet.' I slip the key inside the lock and the locking mechanism snaps into place. Petrified that the males investigating the silent alarm call may have heard me lock the closet door, I instinctively begin to pray as my mother taught me when I was a little girl. I stop myself and switch my prayers to the dead Jesus in the stained glass window picture thinking that if I am in his church, it is he I should be asking for help.

Chapter 13
Boy Scouts

Sweat drips down the side of my face while the male voices on the other side of the closet door bicker about the alarm that brought them to the cathedral this night. My mounting fear that one of them will attempt to open this closet is finally addressed when the door knob jerks about as far as the lock in it allows. I hear not one sound coming from the others hiding with me, but I can feel the suspense filled anxiety we are creating. When the unmistakable sound of keys jingling seeps through the heavy door, Frank's comforting arms surround me. The voices begin to argue again, someone leans up against the door, more words are exchanged and then I hear the men leaving the area.

"Whoever they are they're none too happy to be here tonight. They don't like each other much either. I didn't catch everything they said but I believe they're checking out the room where the altar stuff is kept...someplace out front like a sanctuary or an apse or...I don't know. They're out front and the exit door on the other side of the building is unlocked and not alarmed. We have to get out of here now...this is our one and only chance." Randy does not allow us to debate our situation, but rather, opens the closet door and leads us through the back office area.

Using the spare key, I lock the closet door from the outside before leaving. With Randy, Sarah, me, and then Frank forming a line we slither by the Stations of the Cross quickly and quietly. Without a moment's hesitation, Randy pushes open the exit door. The four of us have successfully escaped in a matter of minutes. Too afraid to jinx our good fortune, I refuse to celebrate until we are safely out of Boston.

*****

We are all awake when the sun rises at the Otis Village Trailer Park. The sleep we managed to get these past few hours was seriously encumbered by the lingering excitement of our ordeal at the cathedral, as well as our anxiety about our plans for today.

"Listen, its Wednesday and we've got a lot to get done before the craft fair on Saturday and before Frank and I start work on the base. For starters I have to go back to the base with the paperwork and to meet with Arnie. I told him we'd figure out a way to keep him safe from whoever is threatening his life and we need to do that. I think Frank needs to come with me." I gulp down some coffee allowing the caffeine to rush to my brain. "That has to be a priority. Then there's the Boy Scout office. Sarah has to go there and pretend to do an interview with the scout executive to find out more about the old homestead on the property and the cabin in the woods. Is her stepmother's press pass doctored up for her yet?"

"Yeah, it's all set," Randy reports.

"And I've done research on the Boy Scout Council out here. I know where to go and who to talk to and all of that," Sarah adds.

"As for Arnie, I'll call and meet with him. You can come with me if you think you should, but I think Sarah could use your help more. Maybe you can pose like a photographer using Randy's good camera." Frank scans my phone for Arnie's cell phone number. As an afterthought he says, "I hope you can find out more about Jinkins while you are there. He makes me nervous."

"I'll go with Sarah," I agree.

Randy plops down on the couch with an open bag of cookies. With his untidy head of hair and wrinkled t-shirt, he looks as if he just rolled out of bed. "I'll go check on Mohamed and tell him we're going to General Kulik's house tonight. I also want to know more about Agent Brown's wife. It seems to me that she just may know more about her father and his evil doings than we think she does. What if she's not just the daughter of a really bad man but a partner in his crimes as well?"

"All of this would be a whole lot easier to figure out if we knew what the enemy was trying to do. All we know for sure is the enemy is using weather weapons against Boston. That, in itself, doesn't mean much." Aware that the tone of my voice is betraying my growing frustration I decide to reveal some of my private thoughts. "Okay, I'm aggravated because we have so many things to look into, but no clear idea of what we're hoping to find out. We know there's an enemy using weather weapons and that this enemy is trying to kill Arnie. We believe this enemy is connected to the mafia, the military, and whatever remains of what was Eurabia. We also believe the enemy is tied into whatever horrors are being run through the underground chambers of the cathedral. So what does it all mean?"

Sarah nods. "I don't know what any of it means and I don't know what makes us think we should be involved in figuring this out. Yes, if we do we may be able to help Mohamed get a second chance at life. Yes, if he helps us bring down this enemy he may be allowed to secretly go free in some distant place on this Earth. But is this a long shot or wishful thinking? Do we really believe we can bring this unknown enemy to justice?"

"We're just frustrated because we don't have enough pieces of the puzzle to even start forming a picture yet. We need more time. We need to get to know more about Kulik. I'm telling you, that creep is the key to this: and his daughter Alena, Agent Brown's not so patriotic and wonderful wife." Randy changes his focus to the bag of cookies rather than continue with his rant. This indicates to me that he is hiding something and whatever his secret is it has something to do with the General or Alena Brown; maybe both of them. Before I can tactfully try to get to the bottom of his mysterious behavior Frank, begins to deliver one of his calming speeches.

"Randy's right, we need to be patient. We need to think logically and plan strategically. Things will come together for us like they always do. These things take time, we all know that. I think our past experiences with espionage have made us impatient and foolish. Both of these behaviors are dangerous. We must allow the information to come together as events unfold."

Too tired to listen to reason, I interject. "Well I hope things come together soon because I believe Carlo wants Mohamed found and killed because Mohamed has knowledge that can be used against him, such as the existence of the chambers below the cathedral. And what Carlo Bertoni wants, he gets. I also believe there is a connection between Carlo and the US mafia, the Russian mafia and General Kulik. I don't know a lot about the world mafia system but I think it's very possible that a network of mafia power is behind this."

"Okay, so what is its purpose of using these weapons against America? And why Boston?" Frank questions me in a challenging tone, as if he is trying to prove his point that making statements without logic to back them up is foolish and impatient behavior.

"To prove to whatever regime it plans to sell the weather weapons system to that the technology works. I believe that the whole thing is about selling the weather weapons technology to other foreign powers. I'm guessing that the network is doing it in Boston because the weapons system is located at the Otis Base on Cape Cod and Boston is the nearest big city. It's the capital of Massachusetts, too."

"Reasonable conclusions that only time will substantiate. I, however, have a very different reason for believing why Boston is the target." Frank slides a street map of Boston out of a manila folder. He carefully rubs down the creases as he unfolds it. He uses his index finger to trace some bright pink highlighted marks. "The pink circles represent scientific centers that were in the path of the tornadoes of the storm. They include Boston University, the NSF building we were in, Northeastern University, and MIT. Is it just coincidence that the storm would hit that many places with advanced science labs? No, I don't think so."

"Whoa, now that is one freaky storm path." Randy moves closer to the map. "There's no way that just happened. No, the path of the storm was definitely planned. And that fits in with what I've been thinking about. I believe the weather weapon storm could only have been created by the government in a government owned and operated facility. Unless such a place has been hijacked by Carlo and General Kulik, then the weapon storm was fired off; so to speak, by government employees. Since it's doubtful that these employees were acting on the orders of Uncle Sam, whom I assume would never attack his own people, then whoever did this must be an inside enemy."

"Okay, if that's true, then why would Carlos and General Kulik want to release a weather weapon storm from Otis Military Base and attack science centers in Boston?" Frank asks.

"I don't know. I imagine Kulik is …" Randy is in mid sentence when Mohamed bursts into the trailer. For the first time since we've reconnected, I can detect anxiety on my brother's normally calm face.

Leaning over to put on our small TV he says, "Haven't you been listening to the news?"

"No. But we did…" I begin to answer.

"Carlos Bertoni was found dead on Cape Cod during the night! Dead! They're saying he was murdered mafia style!" Mohamed closes his eyes momentarily. He takes three deep breaths before adding, "I doubt the mafia killed him. If they wanted him dead his body would never be found. No, he was killed by the other Eurabian…the ninth Eurabian and, for some reason, they want everyone to know he's dead. You all believe Agent Brown's father-in-law General Kulik is this unknown enemy, is that correct?"

"Yes," Frank says. "But why would he kill his partner in crime?"

"The answer to that has to be inside General Kulik's cottage." Randy insists while jumping to his feet. "And that's where we're all going tonight. Damn it, that's where we all should have been last night, just like I said. If we had gone there maybe Carlo would still be alive. Maybe he could have told us something."

Sarah reaches for the cookie bag while saying, "Or maybe whoever killed Carlo Bertoni would've killed us too."

*****

As planned, I go with Sarah to the Cape Cod Boy Scout Council. Armed with the fake press pass that Randy made from her stepmother's authentic one and dressed in casual business attire, Sarah indeed looks the part of a college journalism student. I, in a similar outfit but carrying Randy's expensive camera, make a passable photographer. My first impression of the lengthy, stone one level structure is that it belongs to a different era; one from the recent past. My second impression of the place comes to me upon entering it. The décor screams 1970's with its wood paneling and the orange, tan, and avocado green color scheme. The office furniture is mismatched and so dated that I have actually never seen some of the desk styles before me. A great number of trophies line the mantle of a huge stone fireplace, which, although beautiful, just doesn't seem to fit in an office setting. The walls are covered with awards and commendations as well as scouting posters. In the corner of the large open room that occupies at least half of the building is an American flag proudly displayed before an oil painting of a bald eagle. A sense of true red, white, and blue patriotism washes over me while Sarah talks to the old lady at the counter.

"She's going to tell the Chief Scout Executive that I'm here. I'm glad I called first because it sounds like the man is really busy with camp related stuff. I told her you were going to take some pictures of him and then roam around and take candid shots of the place." Sarah flips open her reported style notebook. "I'm glad I managed to think up so many questions. This will keep us busy for awhile. You should have plenty of time to snoop around."

"I hope so." I fumble with the canvas camera case. "This camera is sort of complicated for me. I'm setting it on automatic so I don't have to adjust anything."

"Good idea. There's no sense stressing over pictures we'll probably never need." Sarah looks around and says, "This place is a bit of a blow back in time, isn't it? I'm wondering when Smokey the Bear is gonna show up."

We're still chatting about the ambiance of the council when the older woman tells us the Chief Scout Executive is ready to meet with Sarah. His name is Mr. Victor Trumbell and he is in his late forties to early fifties. He is a handsome man although a bit chubbier than I pictured for a hiking scout of the forest. He has light blue eyes that twinkle when he smiles, giving him a childlike playful appearance. What I like most about him is that he has deep dimples that appear every time he smiles. He has the face of someone you know you can trust with your life. As I take pictures of him it becomes obvious that he is also a very photogenic person.

With the freedom to snoop anywhere I want, I leave Mr. Trumbell's private office and poke my nose inside the other offices. One has two desks and is marked as the Finance Department, too boring for any more of my attention. One is occupied by a man quite a bit younger than Mr. Trumbell. He is on the phone and does not seem to be in a good mood. I hasten past his door to the next office. This one has a young woman in it. She is typing away on the keyboard of an old model computer. Situated all around her are astonishingly high piles of papers.

"Hello," I say.

"Oh, hi. You must be from the newspaper. Mr. Trumbell told me you'd be coming in. My name is Holly Cardoza, do you have any questions?" She looks up at me momentarily. "Let me just finish entering this little guy into the data base and you can have my full attention."

"Oh, well I'm the photographer not the reporter but…well, she often tells me to screen the staff for stories in pieces like this," I say, the lie rolling out so convincingly I almost believe it myself.

She makes her last keystroke with a bit of flare and invites me to sit down.

"Ask away," she says, invitingly.

"Okay, how long have you been here and what do you do? Why did you choose to work here? You know, what's your work story?"

"I've been here two years. This is my first job out of college. It's entry level and not at all what I want, but it's a start. I'm in charge of all the computer systems including, unfortunately, tons of data entry. I find I love working with the folks here, they don't get any nicer than these people, let me tell you. And, there's a ton of young men connected to the Boy Scouts with me being the lone single woman. What can I say but that's one fringe benefit I really love."

"Got it, but not thinking my reporter will want to write abut that side story."

We both laugh making the new bond between us strengthen.

"What about the kids, the boy scouts? Do you have any interaction with them?" I ask.

"You can't work at a Boy Scout council and not have interaction with them. They're, for the most part, little dolls. They're the best of the best little boys. They wouldn't be in scouting, if they were terrors. And if they're terrors when they join scouting they're straightened out in no time. You know, I used to think this scouting thing was stupid. I thought it was, like, for nerdy kids and all that. But now that I know about it I understand that what it does is teach boys how to become responsible and respectable men and that starts with being good kids."

I'm unsure how sincere Holly is about the scouts because I can tell her response about them was scripted. Realizing that she's been coached for a possible interview I decide to skip past the niceties and go after something of substance.

"How about the business part of this scouting council? Is the money situation good?"

Holly's surprised reaction to such a direct and unexpected question spin her off script. Not wanting to allow too long of a silent pause she appears to have answered with the first thing that came to her mind: the truth.

"It is, now that the council sold the Trumbell land."

"The Trumbell land?" I hide my growing curiosity by focusing on note taking. "Where is that and why was it sold? Is it related to your boss, Mr. Trumbell?"

"Yes. Mr. Trumbell's family owned a huge chunk of land. It was a family thing; complete with a homestead house and barn and the whole farm thing, you know? Anyways, when Mr. Trumbell's grandfather died he left the entire piece of property to the scouts rather than break it up between his seven children. It was a big deal to the Boy Scout council people as you can imagine. Anyway, they used the property to build a scout camp; it's really nice. They also developed hiking trails, built some log cabins, made places on ponds to keep boats, and they even developed a Christmas tree farm. It was great…until the council needed money and the real estate taxes became a problem and there were some… legal matters that needed settling and…anyways, the land was sold to this guy…um…trailer park guy…um…Jin…something."

"Oh, so they sold the land to this guy? Do they still use it for the scouts?"

"The council kept the part of the land where the camp is located and sold the rest to…um….Jinky? No, kinsman? No…a J, it definitely begins with a J."

As tempted as I am to tell her the man who bought the property is Edward Jinkins, I don't because I know it could blow my cover. Instead I give her another moment to try to recall the name before asking her more about him.

"The Otis Village Park is connected to the land. Jin…Jinkins…that's the guy's name, he owns the trailer park and campsite that abuts the Trumbell property and he's the one that bought it. It sold for somewhere about $1million. I know that for a fact; got the info from our finance director. Anyway, I never could figure out where Jinkins got that kind of money."

"Really, so you wouldn't call him a respectable businessman?"

"I don't think so. The guy gives me the creepy crawlies. A total freak if you know what I mean."

"How did he get to own the Otis Village place if he's such a weirdo?"

Holly leans over her desk and lowers her voice. "I have no idea and I shouldn't be talking to you about him. Mr. Trumbell knows him. They grew up together in this town. I think you need to ask him. All I know is that Mr. Trumbell doesn't like the guy and he hated selling the land to him. Real sore spot for him, you know? In fact, he may not even talk about Jinkins with you. I don't think he will."

After filling Sarah in on what I learned from Holly, Sarah questions the Chief Scout Executive about the land sale. As Holly predicted, Mr. Trumbell avoids the subject of Edward Jinkins. His evasiveness about our strange landlord is so deliberate that I feel I have no choice but to interrupt the questioning.

"It's quite a coincidence that we're renting a trailer at Otis Village, and, according to the map I got from the store there, the land you sold is in that area. Hmmm, is Mr. Jinkins the person who bought the Trumbell property from the Boy Scouts?" I ask, as innocently as a guilty person can.

Mr. Trumbell leans back in his black leather desk chair. He looks between me and Sarah several times before speaking. "Edward Jinkins is the man who bought my family's land. That's a matter of public record as every reporter knows. Your interest in him is, however, more than coincidental, isn't it?"

"Yes and no," I quickly respond. "We're doing the article on this council because Sarah needs the experience. If you don't believe that, check out her stepmother on the internet. She's a reporter, too. Sarah used her stepmom to make connections...well... you know how that is."

Mr. Trumbell looks at Sarah. "Okay, I believe that part because you were so well prepared with your questions for the interview. So tell me, what's with all the interest about Jinkins? Do you really rent from him?"

"Yes we do, but just for the summer. The reason we're so curious about him is because he's been so curious about us." Sarah leans over the desk taking on the posture of a friend about to reveal a secret. "He sneaks around following me and Abby. I think he's even looked in our windows. And that daughter of his...whoa...she's something else, too."

"His twin daughters are both quite odd. The whole family is...and was... odd. Edward and his daughters are all that's left now."

Mr. Trumbell silently stares at us apparently waiting for us to speak. I'm not sure what Sarah is doing, but I'm just waiting for him to continue. After a few very awkward minutes he gets up to close the office door.

"This is totally off the record. And I mean totally." After Sarah agrees he continues. "Rumor has it that Edward Jinkin's father beat his mother to death and made Edward help him bury her. As insane as that sounds, I believe it because Edward has been messed up since he was a kid in middle school and that was when his mother supposedly ran away. Yeah, the story was that she left town because she was afraid of her husband and all that, but, no way, that woman was too afraid to do anything like that. No, I think they buried her deep in the woods. Anyway, when Edward was an adult he straightened out long enough to get married and have the twins, then, wham, his wife falls through the ice on some pond and drowns. Then his father dies in a car crash a few years back."

"It sounds horrible. Talk about tragedy." Sarah's empathy softens her tone.

Fearing she will allow the conversation to get off track I ask, "So, how did I guy like Edward Jinkins get $1 million to buy the Trumwell property from the Boy Scouts? That's a ton of money for the child of a trailer park owner, isn't it?

"Life insurance money: that's how. That's why everyone believes Edward is a murderer. Too many accidents and too much money involved. He could've pushed his wife through thin ice. He could have caused his father's accident. Heck, he could have actually been the one who killed his mother. Who knows?"

"So what is his interest in us?" I see Sarah shudder as I ask this question.

"I couldn't say but I doubt that he just wants to be neighborly."

****

Like Sarah, I leave the Scout Council office building in a bit of a daze. As much as I try to convince myself that Edward Jinkins is not a murderer, but rather a very unlucky life insurance benefactor, I can not.

"I have a bunch of messages from Randy. He wants us to call. He says it's an emergency." Sarah presses her boyfriend's number while still walking toward the SUV. I only half listen as she begins talking, but I give her my full attention when I hear the anxiety ridden tone in her voice.

"Change of plans!"

"What are you talking about?"

"Arnie's missing! Frank and Randy have been looking for him for over two hours and still can't find him. His work said he never came back from lunch. He's gone!"

Chapter 14
A Plan Diversion

Sarah doesn't end her cell phone call with Randy until we drive up to the trailer. Before I have the SUV parked, Frank comes out to greet us. He is so flustered by Arnie's disappearance that I have to remind him to lower his voice before someone nearby hears our incriminating conversation.

"There's no where left to check. We've been absolutely everywhere we can think of. If he's not on the base and he's not around here then where could he be but…well…in harm's way? The man is not a fighter and he could never defend himself. How can someone kidnap a person right from a military base without anyone in authority knowing anything?"

"If whoever took him from the base works at the base then anything is possible," I whisper. "Did Dr. Ritter know anything? You did meet with our new boss, didn't you?"

"I couldn't ask Dr. Ritter questions about Arnie because I didn't want him to know I even knew him. As a matter of fact, I wasn't even sure they were looking for the same person at first. Apparently his real name is Maxwell Arnold Thorpe and he uses his middle name, as in Arnie. If I didn't hear someone he works with refer to him as Arnie I wouldn't have made the connection."

I nudge Frank inside before he can say anything more. Sarah and Randy are having a similar conversation in the small kitchenette. The smell of burnt popcorn tangled with the scent of pine from a scented candle reminds me of just how helpless our boyfriends can be when it comes to handling even the simplest of tasks.

"Tell me again exactly what they said happened." I blow out the candle, open a nearby window, and fan out the unpleasant smell.

"I was told he went to lunch saying he needed to go for a walk. Because I know he saw me when I came in, we can assume he was going outside the building to meet with me the same way he did with you, Abby. So, I expected to see him in the parking lot when I got out, just like you did. Well, it ended up that I had to wait for Dr. Ritter for over forty-five minutes. I'm a bit suspicious about the wait because he was supposed to be expecting me, but the man is a bit eccentric so it could be that he just got sidetracked. Anyway, when Ritter finally came in we went through the new employee stuff and all the forms and all of that. It took about a half an hour. I left expecting to find Arnie waiting for me, but instead I found a few people looking for him. Of course I stuck around and said I'd help them look for him. There was no sign of him anywhere. With all the excitement about him being missing, no one even bothered to ask me who I was; they must've figured I belonged there. So I stayed awhile and there was no sign of Arnie: nothing."

"And they kept looking for how long?" Sarah asks.

"They were still looking when I left. I saw Dr. Ritter hanging around his building's door so I decided to leave before he noticed me."

Randy runs his fingers through his mop of hair saying, "Arnie isn't answering his cell phone. It's off, as in turned off dead."

"Think about this for a second. Someone shoves Arnie in a van, right? Then drives him off base and brings him somewhere to keep him prisoner. Where would that be? Well, if the perpetrator is connected to the military or government, maybe Arnie's abductor brought him to another official type of place. So...where is there an abandoned government facility in this area?" With machine like precision Frank begins naming government owned facilities in the area. I don't ask how he came to know this information off hand because I don't want to sidetrack our conversation; however, I am quite curious.

"That's quite a list," Randy growls. "We're assuming, of course, that the abductor intends to keep him as a prisoner. There's no guarantee whoever has Arnie cares about him being kept alive."

Sarah absentmindedly tidies up the cluttered kitchen counter. She moves the dish washing liquid to its proper spot, makes a neat pile from odd paperwork that has been strewn about, and then rinses out soda cans for the recycle bin. Her behavior tells me she is extremely nervous.

"Hey, are you alright?" I whisper while Randy and Frank are busy noting down additional government owned properties.

"If Randy's right about someone killing Arnie, then maybe we need to go back to the chambers below the cathedral and see if his freshly killed body has been crammed in a body bag and added to the heap down there. I'm not being sarcastic either. We really do need to do that if we can't find him."

The grim picture takes shape in my mind before I can blot it out. Not sure what to say since her point is exactly right, I just nod.

*****

We spend the remaining hours of the afternoon looking for Arnie. Randy and Sarah take the truck and scout out places in the Boston area. Although we don't truly believe Arnie returned to the city of his own volition, we all agree the possibility needs to be investigated. Frank and I use the SUV. We search the national cemetery located near the base, the state prison property which is also in the area, and the Cape Cod Mall site, which, although not owned by the government, is a big place where a body could be easily dumped. We return to the trailer frightfully discouraged. We have just enough time to compare notes when it is time for someone to go get Mohamed so we can all prepare to go to General Kulik's cottage. I quickly volunteer to go for the walk. Frank eagerly joins me. Once deep in the woods I'm a bit shaken at how still and isolated it feels to be this far out into nature. The sound of moving wildlife unsettles me more than I will ever admit. The smell of dampness and stinging pine greenery is neither pleasant nor unpleasant, it is just overwhelmingly present.

"Do you feel that he's dead? I know you don't know whether he is or isn't but your woman's instinct, do you feel that Arnie's dead?" Frank does his two handed knuckle crack then adds, "I just have to know what intuition is saying rather than rely on logical evidence."

It never ceases to surprise me when my logical minded boyfriend turns to me for a purely emotion based opinion. It is as if his logical brain disallows him to experience any kind of intuition at all. In cases like this I have to wonder if he believes I can conjure up some sort of psychic ability to connect to a supernatural power. I also wonder why someone with Frank's deductive reasoning even values instinctive feelings. As I said, he never ceases to amaze me.

"I don't feel that he is gone…dead…yet. In my gut I think he's alive right now because the enemies believe they need him for something. Maybe they do, maybe they don't but it feels like they think they do. As long as Arnie can convince them he is valuable to them alive then he'll survive."

"Arnie's personality isn't prone to acting. I believe that his Asperger's Syndrome makes him unable to process facial expressions properly. If that's true then he can't use facial expressions to act which will be…"

"Which will be perfect. Don't you see? Arnie legitimately doesn't make a lot of expressions therefore he can lie straight at someone without flinching. He's got the best defensive weapon he can have against the enemy…himself!"

This rather odd advantage causes us to laugh just enough for our mood to lighten while we make our way to the Boy Scout cabin. Once there, we find Mohamed inside waiting for us, completely packed with everything he thinks we could possibly need for the mission ahead. After taking a quick look around I realize that Mohamed has made himself at home in this little place; very likely the best home he's had in many months.

"So you say Arnie is missing? This is not surprising. We must do all we can to find this young man." Mohamed closes the cabin door. "I would have helped you search for him today had I known of his disappearance. Instead I spent the day planning for tonight."

"I can see that by the size of your backpack," Frank says.

"You really can't be out riding around during the day, anyway. Now that Abdul reported where you were last seen…well… even though we got you out of Boston you still have to be careful that no one sees you," I add.

"Ah yes, Abdul's betrayal, we are two brothers who can never be reconciled."

"He must have spoken directly to Agent Brown."

"I surmise that Abdul somehow figured out my general location and reported sightings of me to Agent Brown. From there it would have been fairly easy for Homeland Security to watch for me until I was located. Oddly, I am not convinced the agent meant to capture me."

Frank stops walking and asks, "What do you mean? You think Agent Brown deliberately let you go?"

Mohamed nods. "I absolutely believe he did. In fact, I believe he wanted me to know his own people were on to me before they found me. Although I have no concrete evidence to prove I am correct, I am convinced he helped me escape discovery."

"Like how? Did he let you know you were being watched somehow?" I ask.

"For one thing, two of the places I spent nights in were noticeably disrupted yet no one ever came for me in either of them. Also, I was followed one time by a person I knew to be an official. This follower could easily have captured me but instead he got close enough to look me in the eyes before passing by me. Either I was deliberately tipped off about the Homeland Security surveillance or the agents assigned to my case were extraordinarily clumsy. I believe the latter to be the case."

"Why would Agent Brown do that for you?" Frank begins walking, but at a very slow pace. "Even if he believes you have changed and should go free would he jeopardize his job for your benefit?"

"It would seem so, wouldn't it? Unless, of course, he feels it is beneficial to him to have me free for his own purposes. That is the only other possible reason for his actions, is it not? It makes for many interesting theories as to what is happening with the weather weapon storms and how Agent Brown is related to the enemy, if, in fact, he is."

*****

Crammed inside Frank's SUV, the five of us talk about what needs to be accomplished tonight as we ride to General Kulik's cottage. I have a sense of déjà vu because we have done this sort of thing so many times before. The uncomfortable ride accompanied by gut gripping fear: oh, how familiar it all feels. And how recognizable the insistent talk about the plans we laid out so carefully. Plans that we all know, but refuse to say, are likely to completely change due to just one small unforeseen circumstance. I find it bizarre that no one mentions the similarities of tonight to the many nights we have been in this exact same predicament, albeit in a different place. But then again, I don't mention it either. Perhaps it is because it is best not to remember the past when there are so many things in the present to focus on.

The street that runs behind General Kulik's cottage has some homes, several stores for the year round residents, and a hokey touristy business strip with an ice cream shop, a clam shack, and an artist cooperative gallery that features the work of local artisans. Across from the clam shack is an ecological nature trail through a marshland which is the home for endangered bird species native to Cape Cod. This nature preserve has wooden walkways and pathways throughout the area, which, Randy explains, will lead to an empty tract of land behind General Kulik's cottage. This empty land is owned by General Kulik and remains undeveloped.

The plan is for the Frank, Randy and Mohamed to use the nature preserve pathway to get to the General's property. If the cottage is empty they will get inside and find out everything they can about this man and his ties to the now dead Carlo Bertoni. Since the General must drive on this street to get to his home, Sarah and I are assigned to watch out for him. Should we see him coming we will call the men who will then have plenty of time to leave the cottage before the General returns. It's a simple plan, which, as far as I can tell, is fairly foolproof.

With Mohamed, leading, the men quickly set out for the cottage. When they are gone, Sarah and I settle in the front seats for what we expect to be a lengthy stakeout. In the first half hour she eats a pint of fried clams and two clam cakes. I, perpetually weight conscious, sadly refuse the greasy delights.

"A black sedan with U.S. government plates, right? Well, there can't be all that many people driving cars like that around here, can there?" Sarah leans back in the passenger seat and yawns. "If I wasn't so nerved up about everything I'd fall asleep."

I, too, am tired but too stressed for the threat of sleep to be an issue. "I didn't say anything to anyone else but I'm really angry with Abdul for trying to hurt Mohamed. I know turning him in makes sense, and is, technically, the right thing to do, but I can't shake the feeling of his betrayal. It's all about himself, Chelsea and her family, that's all Abdul cares about."

"He is what he is. You can't ask him to feel for Mohamed the way that you do. Abdul is looking forward in his life and his future is all about Chelsea and being a doctor. You're still looking back. You're trying to help Mohamed find a way to survive in a world that despises who he was… or is…or whatever. You're both in very different mindsets right now, that's all there is to it."

"Yeah, well, it's not so easy to think about the future when you love someone who doesn't have any hope for one. I mean, Mohamed has nothing if we can't find a way to find him some sort of life he can call his own. And now, while I help one brother, I can't even turn to the other one for help. Abdul and Chelsea have always been part of helping us battle the enemy and this time…well…I feel that they are the enemy."

And so our conversation continues until we spot a black sedan. It is not heading toward the cottage as we expect it to, but rather, is coming from the general's cottage. At first we think it is just some ritzy person on an evening drive because it just doesn't seem likely that the first car of this type we see would be the one for which we are looking. But as it passes by we instantly realize otherwise.

"Holy cow, it's freaking him!" Sarah shouts, in the middle of a sentence. "The government plates, see them?"

"He must have left his cottage a good ten minutes ago," I quickly start the SUV. "Well, this is an opportunity we can't let slip away. We're gonna see where this sneaky old general is off to."

"You're gonna follow him? You know that's not the plan."

"Well, you know what people say, plans are made to be broken."

"They don't say that. Laws are made to be broken, that's what they say."

I pull out into the street careful to keep a safe distance between him and us. Having never tailed a car before, I begin to get anxious. Within minutes, I feel my heartbeat increase while sweat forms at my hairline.

"Do you know just how lucky we are to have a chance to follow this creep? I'm telling you this is big; really big," I say to Sarah. "Yes-sir-ee, we'd be fools not to follow him."

"Okay, if you say so. It's not exactly like I can stop the car anyway. Well, I'll call Randy to let him know what's going on."

The talking coming through Sarah's cell phone is so loud she holds it several inches away from her ear. I can clearly make out her boyfriend's angry words which are then followed by Frank's equally angry voice. I would attempt to argue the reasons for my actions but I am much too consumed with trying to safely tail the General's speeding car. I almost lose the general when he slides through a yellow light and we get delayed as the light flips to red. The next time we encounter a similar situation, I bolt through the turning red light without a second thought. By the time we reach the major roads I've also mastered the practice of coming to a roll rather than to a complete stop at stop signs. I'm ignoring merge signs and blinking yellow lights pretty much all together. The number of traffic violations I am making adds up quickly.

"How did you get off the phone?" I ask, now that I am more comfortable with what I'm doing.

"They're all mad, Mohamed too. The thing is they can't stay all that mad because they'd have chased after the General, too. Besides, it's not really dangerous if we stay inside the car. We're just going to find out where he's going, right?"

"I guess that depends on where he goes. It's possible..."

"Oh man, he's heading on to 495. That means he's heading north or west or northwest," Sarah interrupts. "He's leaving Cape Cod."

"Interesting, isn't it. He could be going to Boston. He could be going to another military place. Or maybe, he's on personal business."

Because Sarah promised we'll remain in almost constant contact with either Frank or Randy, I have to listen to a blow by blow description of where we are, as well as the possible places we could be heading. Since much of our beginning drive goes through rural towns I don't hear Sarah mentioning many likely destination points for a while. As we enter larger more suburban towns I hear talk of possible places the general could be heading but none of them seem plausible to me. This is the case until we reach the city of Taunton. It is here that many possible government related destinations become apparent. I am so excited when I see the black sedan take the *Bay Street Taunton* exit that I actually yelp.

"Randy is saying that as far as abandoned government facilities go there's one not far from this exit. He's thinking of the old Taunton State Mental Hospital. The place was mostly closed back in the 1970's but had some straggling patients up until recently. He says the last of them were moved to the western part of the state not too long ago," Sarah reports, cell phone pressed to her ear.

"I remember the brouhaha on the news," I tell her. "I also remember the Ghost Busters show going there because the place is supposed to be haunted by abused mental patients. Remember that? They used to call it the Taunton

Lunatic Asylum or something awful like that."

Sarah repeats my comments into her phone and replies, "Randy says that people think it's haunted because it has creepy looking architecture, weird looking laboratory rooms, and underground tunnels. He's also saying that all old hospitals for insane people have horrible stories about them."

While Sarah alternates between explaining to Randy exactly what turns we are taking and asking him questions about this historical hospital campus, I wonder how hard it will be to get on a property which was erected to keep people on the grounds instead of keeping people off of them. I find this topic so interesting that several times I have to stop my mind from thinking about it because I need to focus on my driving through city stop signs, stop lights, and rather thick traffic. The space between us and the black sedan is uncomfortably growing when a police cruiser pulls out of a side street right behind us. Helpless to do anything else, I watch General Kulik drive away.

"Oh man, this is bad luck times two," Sarah yells out for my benefit, as well as Randy's. "We'll have to lose the cop and assume Kulik is heading for the hospital."

It is known to everyone who has ever had a police car following them that it is difficult to obey the speed limit in an area that doesn't have posted speed limits. Yes, I know, this is something we learn when we take the test for our driver's license. One speed limit exists for neighborhoods while a different one exists for congested neighborhoods and another for city streets. However, with everything else on my mind, I can't recall a single speed limit law other than thirty-five miles per hour on side streets, which is exactly how fast I drive through the city streets. Finally the cruiser bangs a left hand turn into a housing development and we are free to have Randy guide us to the old Taunton State Mental Hospital campus. Oddly, the entrance of the hospital is also the dead end of a city side street.

From the safety of the SUV we gaze at an eerie Victorian era insane asylum full of buildings with barred windows. Guarding this daunting place is an enormous two-door wrought iron gate that hangs between two brick columns. I surmise that this gate was made for vehicular access to the property. On each side of it are side gates made for pedestrian use. Each of these smaller gates is attached to tall iron fencing topped with coils of barbed wire, which, I assume, were installed to prevent patients from scaling the fences should they have decided to attempt escape. The almost majestic appearance of the moonlit property appears to be something far more elegant than a penal system building.

"Randy says some of the unused buildings were torn down in the 1970's when the majority of the patients were moved. From what he gathers from the website, the main building is still up, which, from his description, should be the one with that big dome up there on the hill." Sarah looks around the street. Not finding what she is looking for she gets out of the SUV and walks up the sidewalk.

"Hey, where's General Kulik's car? Do you think he unlocked the big gate and drove in?" I call after her.

"I don't think so. Look, this side gate is still unlocked. He went through here. We have to find his car and then park ours away from his."

After a bit of snooping Sarah spots the General's car hidden behind a dumpster in back of a boarded up business building. Although there is more room in this mostly vacant parking lot, I parallel park the SUV between two cars further up the street. Since parallel parking is not something I do well, it takes me several tries before I manage to do an acceptable job. By the time I meet up with Sarah at the front gate she is already on the phone filling Randy in on our whereabouts. She doesn't have to tell me he is ordering us to return to the car; I can hear his screaming words from three feet away.

"Tell him I'm going in. I promised Arnie I'd help him and so I will. If that science geek is being held captive in here by General Kulik then this may be our only chance to save his life." I step through the side gate silently telling myself to be brave.

Chapter 15
Taunton State

Overgrown grass, weeds, and unkempt remnants of once beautiful flower gardens grace the front lawn of the hospital grounds. The long tree lined driveway offers us plenty of cover to hide within, yet the feeling of being watched by onlookers is not something I can shake off. Sarah and I haven't spoken of ghosts since she first followed me inside this place, but the haunting moonlight mixed with the echoing sounds made by the wind flowing through the massive buildings is a constant reminder that unhappy souls of long ago tortured patients may well be around us. With ivy covered crumbling brick walls looming overhead, we hesitantly approach the front door.

Sarah whispers over the sound of a distant hooting owl, "Figures the front is locked. I have a feeling nothing is going to be easy in this horrid place. As much as I absolutely hate to suggest it, we have to split up and check all the other doors, don't we?"

"Yeah, we do. You take the right side of this building, I'll take the left, and I'll meet you out back. If you find an unlocked door just keep going, okay?"

I've learned over time that if you really want Sarah to do something that she doesn't want to do, you can't give her any time to think about it. So, before she can answer, I hurry away. As I search for a way inside this frightening building, I notice that beneath the bars on the windows is a layer of thick screen which causes me to wonder just how caged up the patients were in this place. Here and there I see that attempts were made to improve the appearance of the hospital. Well worn windowsills with a thin coat of newer paint. Missing bricks filled in with cement. Cracked glass taped up with clear packaging tape. To me, the repairs seem almost insulting to a place with such majestic presence. When I turn the corner I am surprised to see that the side entrance door is a new design. This gray steel door has no windows nor does it fit in with the architecture of the building. I'm a little disappointed, but not at all surprised, to find the door to be locked. On my way to the back of the building to wait for Sarah, I try to imagine a reason why she would find an unlocked door when I did not.

Like most people, I find time passes incredibly slowly when I am waiting for someone. This is especially true when I am frightened like I am now. The first five minutes drag by leaving me a bit anxious. After three more minutes pass I feel my stomach knotting up. Four minutes more and I set out to look for Sarah. On the side of the building she went to, I find a similar door as the one I encountered on my search. My hand trembles as I turn the doorknob; it is unlocked. My knowledge of Sarah warns me that she would never go inside this place willingly, but with little other choice, I slowly pull the heavy door open. I jump back when I feel something tap up against my foot. I bend down to feel the ground for the intruding object. It is Sarah's cell phone. Knowing for sure that my friend is in serious trouble, I ward off my paralyzing fear and push forward.

Brick walls, worn tiled floors and leaky ceilings surround me in this dreadful institutional place. The only real sounds within this tormented structure are dripping water and the winds rattling loose window glass. Unfortunately, I am haunted by imaginary screams of pain and desperate calls for help echoing down the unfeeling hallway. My mental state seemingly deteriorates with each step I take. If not for my deep feelings for Sarah, I would, undoubtedly, run out of this place screaming. Keeping my purpose for being here in mind, I make every empty hallway, vacant room, locked door, and open door leading to unknown areas a place to investigate. My eyes and ears tell me nothing of Sarah's whereabouts, I smell nothing nor does the atmosphere change in any way that indicates she can be found above or below the level I am currently on. Oddly, I feel that my internal senses are blocked off from my reasoning, making me nothing more than a machine moving through a maze of dead ends.

When Sarah's cell phone begins vibrating in the pocket of my sweatshirt I realize we're long past our check-up time with Frank and Randy. As much as I'd like to call them, I don't dare speak as the acoustics inside this empty brick mausoleum could surely wake the dead, nevermind a living general and his prisoners. Up ahead I see a balled up tissue on the landing of a stairway. I don't just look at it, I inspect it. I wish I knew if Sarah left the tissue behind. I wish I could connect her to the light blue tissue in some way. I wish I could remember that we have blue tissue hanging around the trailer or in the SUV. But other than the fact the tissue isn't dirty enough to have been where it is very long, I know nothing more about it. I take notice that the stairs in front of me are not the standard size used today; perhaps a bit steeper or maybe a smidgeon narrower, but the size differential is just enough to make my descent in the darkness uncomfortable. I consider using the flashlight but proceed down without it. I move slowly. On the last couple of steps I get a whiff of food. Knowing that General Kulik did not stop for food on the drive in, I prepare myself for a second enemy.

Think, Abby, think. You need a weapon. Okay, what have you seen? Busted up furniture, paper, junk, bathroom stuff you can't carry, office stuff...um... file cabinets....the unhinged doors...the dentist room...the arm for the light... on the floor...it's metal, heavy, but I can carry it. I retrace my steps back to what was once a dentist office. The filthy white metal cabinet doors are open revealing nothing but disintegrating towels inside. The dentist chair is covered with inches of peeled paint that dropped from the ceiling long ago. I have to carefully make my way through debris as I walk to where the metal light arm lies. When I retrieve the metal device, I am pleasantly surprised to find that its one joint is rusted in place making the piece a bent but long, metal sword of sorts. Although the piece that once held the dental light on to the arm is long gone, the sizeable rusted screw that held the light in place can actually be used to stab an enemy.

Weapon in hand, I follow the smell of food down a hallway. As much as I try to convince myself I am prepared for a fight, I know I am in no position to investigate this area. Yet I continue on until I hear voices.

"Yes sir." A deep voice says from the darkness. "I understand completely. She has no car keys on her. This means another intruder, a driver, is also snooping around. I will find this person."

I would give anything to be able to duck inside an empty room, hide behind a large post, or even crouch in a dark corner; however, those immediate remedies to the problem of the approaching man don't exist. Instead I have to move toward the life threatening voice with hopes of stumbling upon such a hiding place. No such break appears. What does appear is the sound of the enemy whistling, which, thankfully, I can use to track how close he is to me. As the whistling gets closer I lower my expectations of an acceptable hiding place. Now I look at some old iron pipes running up the brick wall with an eye of possibility. I realize that if the pipes will hold my weight and if I can climb them high enough, I will be able to hide myself behind one of the arches in the long empty hallway. Without a better alternative, I check the sturdiness of the pipes. Satisfied, I carefully lay down my weapon amongst a pile of rotting wood and wiggle my way up the pipe. I am struggling very hard to climb, making slow progress at best. The whistling is getting louder. Knowing I don't have the skills I need to climb further, I grab hold of a pipe attached to the ceiling and pull myself up. The pipe groans under my weight but it holds me as I perch myself into a sturdy position. The whistling man comes into sight. Despite the awkward angle I am in, I can clearly see that he is not a large man. He walks beneath me without hesitation. When I am sure he is gone I slowly make my way back down, grab my make-shift weapon, and continue on my way.

*****

"Ah yes, you look very familiar my blonde lady friend. In fact, I believe I know who you are. But, once your companion is located I will be sure of your identity. Until then, my dear, you will just have to hang around...if you will pardon my pun," General Kulik is saying while sitting in an old desk chair. "I am sorry you and my other guest, Maxwell...oh that's right, he prefers Arnie, must be manacled to the walls as screaming insane lunatics once were a hundred years ago, but I don't think it is wise to let you go free just yet."

Sarah and Arnie are shackled to the wall in a room I can best describe as a torture chamber. Although this may not have been the original use of the space, it is now an orderly and well furnished area that is perfectly suited for interrogating prisoners. Along with manacles, chairs with leather straps, what appears to be an electric chair, very large porcelain tubs, a wide array of whips, and unidentifiable things that I sense are equally horrifying, this space also has accommodations for the people taking care of the prisoners.

"I have told you, I know much about the weather weapons system, which is true. But I know nothing about you or why you would harm me in this way. Let us go and we can forget this happened." The monotone quality of Arnie's voice seems to irritate the General who, I imagine, thrives on the emotional responses his torture tactics bring upon his victims.

"I tire of your lies Maxwell Arnold Thorpe. I'm well aware of your work at Boston University and the NSF. Say what you will, but I know you have access to the highest level of weather weaponry technology. I also know you would not be at the Otis Military Base if you did not suspect something...or someone..." The General turns away from Arnie. "No, I will not be baited into saying more. You are a threat to me and that is all you need to know."

The General casually looks at Sarah and says, "And where is your friend? With whom did you come here?"

I am horrified to see how frightened Sarah is. She is pale and outwardly shaking. Her lean body is stretched to accommodate the manacles that hold her upright. I expect to hear her voice tremble but instead she screams, "Shut up! Shut up! Shut up!"

The General responds to this outburst by slapping her across the face.

When Arnie yells out in her defense the General punches him in the stomach.

"Do not think I will not kill you. I think nothing of killing those that threaten me. In fact, I collect corpses of traitors like some people collect coins or stamps. And you two, ah yes, you will be part of my collection if you do not cooperate very soon." the General growls.

"You mean you're going to kill us like you killed Carlo Bertoni?" Sarah says. "Was he a threat to you, is that why you did it?"

General Kulik's chest puffs out while both hands clench into fists. "So, you know more than I thought you did. That validates my fear that you are a threat. But I can not destroy either of you yet as you two are not the prize. No, the real prize I seek is Abia Haddad. Don't deny you know her Arnie…I saw you speaking with her yesterday on the surveillance feed at the base. As for you, Blondie, you are her friend. I know that, too. You see, once I have Abia I can use her to get who I really want…the real threat to me."

"Mohamed? You wish to capture Mohamed Haddad? I see. You realize that his sister's safety is perhaps the only thing that can get Mohamed to come to you so you kidnap her. So, tell me, why do you want him?" Arnie's inability to make eye contact with the General sends his gaze my way. Although I'm not sure, I believe he caught a glimpse of me.

"It's because General Kulik is the ninth Eurabian and Carlo Bertoni and Mohamed Haddad are the only people who can identify him," Sarah replies for the General. "Well, at least he believes these are the only two people who can identify him, there are probably others who can. I mean, surely you can't wipe out everyone you've known…."

"I do not have to answer to you! Just remember, I could kill my brother if I had to so taking your life and that of your friends requires little more than a passing thought." The General spits at Sarah.

"You do not make sense. You are connected to the Weather Weapons Program in so many ways. The government committees you sit on and your military career for example. This cannot be the real threat I pose to you." Arnie shakes his head. "There is something more."

"In a sense you are right, little man. Since I can dispose of you without fear of investigation, I will give you something to think about in your final hours. You are expendable not because of what you could prove about my misdoings, but because of what you can prove about the misdoings of others. You see, I may have had a part in the weather weapons storm that hit Boston, but I am not responsible for it. Oh no, the person who is directly to blame for the storm is not a person at all. No, you fool, it is a government; your government." The General waits for this information to sink in before adding. "And I don't want you to expose this unfortunate betrayal of the United States Government against its own people because, my friend, that information is my card to play."

*****

It is the way the General is laughing, in an almost insane manner, which triggers me into action. Armed with the metal dental light arm and the element of surprise I burst inside the room. When the metal arm strikes the General on the shoulder, I hear a thud as his gun drops from his hand. Before my enemy can assess what is happening to him I swing the arm for the second time. This time I land the blow on the side of the military man's head. I watch him stumble and then fall. Dragging my weapon behind me I crouch down beside my bloody victim.

In an amazingly calm voice Arnie says to me, "You must secure him. I doubt that you have killed him even though he is an older man. I fear he will awaken soon."

"Let me get you two off of the wall first. I need help. I'm shaken..."

"That is not possible," Arnie states. "The General does not have the key. The other man does."

"Are you for real? Um...what is around here...I can't get him in a manacle..." I am saying while I watch the General slowly trying to get up.

"Stay calm, Abby." A hysterical Sarah blurts out. "You're going to have to use the General's gun. It may be the only way to completely control him and the other man...the other man will be back."

"What?" I ask, flabbergasted at the suggestion. "You expect me to hold a gun on people?"

"It's by the chair...grab the damn thing!" Sarah shouts.

With gun in hand, I point it at the General. Not sure how well he can see, I aim it at his head and hope he isn't brave enough to challenge my willingness to shoot him.

Arnie studies me for a moment and says to me, "I suspect after all you have been through that somewhere along the way you have learned to use a gun, have you not?"

When I don't answer Sarah says softly, "We've all taken lessons on a shooting range these past few months. What do you think we need to do?"

"You must cripple the General. That is best done by destroying his ability to walk. A bullet in each kneecap will accomplish this objective," Arnie instructs me.

The only way I can perform this duty is to imagine the General's bent knee is nothing more than a target on the range. With both hands holding the gun steady, I take aim and press the trigger. The sound of the gun going off is amplified by the brick walls around us. The General screeches in pain as a bullet lodges itself in his knee. Now that he is awake and helplessly trying to move away from me, it is much harder to shoot his second knee. My shot is either on or close to the mark.

"Now you must gag him," Arnie states. "I believe you can use the handkerchief in my pocket for that purpose. I apologize that it is used but…"

Before he can complete his unnecessary babbling explanation I dig the balled up wad of linen from his front pants pocket. Whether the General is in shock or too weak to resist me, he allows me to gag him.

Before the second enemy returns, Arnie explains that the man insists on being called "the Jailor." Arnie reasons that he is little more than a paid thug in the General's network of criminals. He confirms that this man is small in stature but warns me that he is surprisingly powerful. When I hear the approaching footsteps I duck out of view. The steps slow down as they get closer, but the Jailor doesn't enter. Confused, I cautiously take a peek into the hallway. I never see his arms grasp me around the neck but the squeezing of my windpipe is evidence that I am the Jailor's next prisoner.

"Who are you and what have you done?" the Jailor screams, as he drags me into the light. "Did you kill him? He's bleeding to death! How did you… where's your gun?"

I am half on the floor unable to scramble to my feet because of the hold the Jailor has on me. I twist and flail about until I get what I consider a decent shot at my assailant. I aim the gun in the direction of the Jailor's body and press the trigger. The Jailor makes a guttural noise. Warm sticky blood reaches my arm and then his grip on me loosens. I elbow his gut and then his groin until I am free from his arms. Before I can run away my enemy grabs hold of my hair. I desperately claw at the fingers entangled in my curls but to no avail. I can smell the foul odor of the Jailer's breath; our faces are now very close together. The metal from his gun is pressed firmly above my ear, my every move threatening to be the last I will ever make. From the distance I hear Sarah screaming, "Gun. Abby, use the gun!" I feel the grip of the gun still in my hand as the Jailor kicks me in the ribs. Rather than move away from his leather boots, I grab hold of one of them. I roll over on my side forcing his body off balance. Scrambling to my knees I have only managed to aim the gun in his general direction when the first shot goes off. When I see the Jailor jumping up, I deliver the second shot. This one takes him down.

*****

With both guns packed away, we slowly make our way out of the building. Of the three of us, Sarah is the strongest as she has suffered the least amount of physical and mental harm. Although she is seldom one to take the lead role, Sarah bravely pulls, pushes, and prods us down the long driveway and off of the hospital campus. I can sense Sarah's relief to find the SUV where we left it. She tells us to wait inside the vehicle while she takes care of things. I silently watch her jog down the street with a blanket and a towel from the back of the SUV dangling from her hands. Suddenly the General's black sedan appears. Because there are no homes directly near the entrance to the hospital, she is able to take her time as she literally drives the vehicle into the iron entrance gates. When the hood of the car is bent upwards, the headlights are broken, and from what I can tell at least one of the front fenders is hanging down, she leaves the car taking the towel and blanket with her.

"The blanket and towel will cover evidence of fingerprints and DNA should an examination of the car be made," Arnie says to me matter-of-factly. "That was my idea. Randy and Frank agreed it was a good."

"How long were you two talking to the enemy? How long was I…out of it?"

"You weren't exactly out of it. You were, technically, in shock. When a human being has experienced…"

"Never mind the medical stuff; I get it. So what else did they say?"

"I will let Sarah inform you of that as I am not one to deliver bad news."

Unaware that saying what he did was worse than saying nothing at all, Arnie attempts to make small talk with me as we wait. It is a long couple of minutes.

"Frank? Randy? Mohamed? Are they still waiting for us? Is everything okay?" I ask Sarah the second she returns. "And General Kulik's cottage. What did they find there? Was it worth getting inside?"

"They're all fine and they're still in the preserve area waiting. And yes it was definitely worth them getting in there," Sarah says.

"They found things that connected the General to Carlo Bertoni. Of course, now that the General confessed to us that he killed the mafia boss that is a moot point. They also found evidence that he has a very close business partner. It seems this is a new partner, someone who took the place of a partner he replaced years ago."

"Who?" I ask.

"The partner who was replaced was his brother, Stefan Kulik. Why he was replaced is the question. We are all wondering what this old man can tell us." Sarah drives the SUV toward the highway. "As for the newer partner, it's his daughter, Alena. Yup, Agent Brown's wife Alena is totally an enemy of the state. And, from what Randy told me, the whole marriage to Agent Brown, his career at Homeland Security, and their whole lives have been setups. Things were going fine for them until the Eurabia thing broke open. That's when Agent Brown must have figured out something was wrong with his wife and father-in-law. And now…"

From the back seat I hear Arnie state, "And now, like Carlo and Mohamed, Agent Brown is a threat to General Kulik and He too must be disposed of."

Chapter 16
Abduction

My battle with insomnia last night leaves me sluggish this morning. To add to my misery I still don't know the fate of the two men I left wounded at the abandoned Taunton State Hospital. My logical reasoning is telling me that if General Kulik and his side kick were found, their rescue would be headline news. My compassion begs for them to be in stable condition at a hospital. My patriotic inner voice whispers that they deserve what they got and their fate is not my responsibility. At this point, I think not knowing is worse than having to convince every portion of my mind that I did what I had to do and I must put it behind me. Caught within my own emotional inner struggle, I've blocked out the rather testy discussions happening all around me. Besides the on-going debate about what to do with Arnie, who is currently hiding with Mohamed, there are many other topics in dispute this morning.

For one thing, there are endless discussions about the government's attack on Boston. Like Frank, I believe the attack was orchestrated to destroy the research done at the city's universities and colleges on the Weather Weapons Program. We further believe the target of the attack has to be a particular subject within the research that Uncle Sam finds threatening. Randy, a patriot down to the core, is having a difficult time accepting that his country would harm its own people unless it had no choice. His description of "having no choice" is not easily reconciled with scientific research being done at universities; therefore, Randy does not totally believe General Kulik's claim that our government created the storm that ripped through Boston the other day.

Another controversial subject being tossed around this morning is how we should handle Agent Brown now that we know for sure his father-in-law, General Kulik, is an enemy of state. Of course, we assume that Agent Brown already knows this and also suspects his wife Alena of being involved in her father's evil doings, but how can we be absolutely sure? And should we tell Agent Brown that his wife Alena replaced the General's brother Stefan as an accomplice in his crimes? Do we ask our agent friend to help us find Stefan Kulik? And what about our suspicion that General Kulik intends to kill Agent Brown? Does our agent friend suspect that he is a target? Does this twist in the family fate somehow connect to why Agent Brown has allowed Mohamed to go free?

Feeling a bit overwhelmed, I interrupt an argument between Randy and Frank saying, "I've had enough of this talking in circles stuff. I don't know what the right things to do are and I don't think I'll be able to come up with a decent suggestion until my head has had time to clear. All I do know for sure is that we need to find Stefan Kulik and figure out why the General replaced him as his partner with Alena? Did they have a falling out that broke up their partnership? Is Stefan even alive? Is he still involved in the crimes but in a different way? What can we find out about him?"

"While everyone else was arguing I did some research on the internet. Stefan Kulik is twelve years older than the General, putting him in his early eighties. Like his brother, Stefan was a military guy but he wasn't so much involved in battle stuff. Instead, he was more involved in the military research side of things. I can't find out more than that, because basically, what is written about Stefan is really nothing more than a sideline in articles written about his more famous brother." Sarah reaches for a donut. "He lived north of Boston. I didn't see anything about him being married or having kids, at all. His pictures show him to be a rather… well, not a good looking man."

"He's ugly?" Randy snaps.

"Sort of. Look for yourself."

Randy and Frank peer over Sarah's shoulder.

"That's one big birthmark or whatever all down his face," Randy says.

Frank bends down for a closer look. "That's not a birthmark, it's scars from burns. It looks like the poor devil was in a fire. Maybe a military related wound of some kind. I'd say he's been like that for a long time. It could even be that the scarring is what prevented him from basking in the limelight like his younger brother."

"Can you tell if he's still alive?" I ask.

"Is that article you have there from last year?" Randy asks.

"Early last year. He's just mentioned as being retired military. That's the latest one I can find. He was alive then," Sarah replies.

"So how do we find him?" Randy asks.

"Well, think about this. We believe that by this morning the General will be found, right? Surely someone has reported his car being smashed into the hospital gates by now." I rub my tired eyes and continue. "That'll mean some story about what happened to him has to come out. General Kulik can't tell the truth. The General will surely want to talk to Alena about things so she'll be with him for some amount of time. But, business partners have to keep up the business when their partner are laid up. So, Alena will be busy doing whatever on behalf of her father, right? And, is part of his business Stefan Kulik?"

"Now that's an interesting proposition. While you girls go set up at the craft fair maybe we'll follow Alena around and see what she's up to." Frank looks at Randy. "We better bring a wide variety of tools with us. Who knows where this surveillance will lead us."

*****

Buzzard's Bay Park is situated near the Cape Cod Canal. The park has a well kept gazebo surrounded by flowering shrubs, an American flag pole with a giant flag flapping in the ocean breeze, and surprisingly nice grass considering the amount of people who must walk on it. With the craft fair being this weekend, there is also a great number of canopy tops covering set-ups of every type of art and craft imaginable. As Sarah and I drag cart loads of her items to her assigned booth space, we pass by a candle maker, a wood carver who specializes in birds, and a photographer with an interesting array of seascapes. At a glassblower booth, I stop to marvel at the intricately colored perfume bottles he's designed with hints of gold paint. At the corner of Sarah's row is a candy booth filled with fudge, nuts, and so many chocolate covered delights that my mouth starts watering. We find her spot, which is across from a vender who has so many wares to sell she's rented two adjacent spaces. This double sized temporary shop specializes in hand made clothing, housewares, and other items. One middle aged woman and one elderly woman smile from behind their racks of doll clothes, quilts, and women's clothing. I courteously smile back, not sure if anything more is required of us as we are not yet familiar with craft fair vendor etiquette.

"There's no other jeweler around you which I imagine is important," I point out. "You also have two nice ladies across the way."

"The leather dude to my left seems nice, too. Maybe he's a bit eccentric with the leather skull caps and bikers' gear but, heck, he did welcome me." Sarah begins setting up her pop-up tent canopy. "My neighbor on the right is probably okay, too. Anyone who makes soaps and lotions has to be nice, don't you think?"

I nod as I grab hold of the metal canopy frame and help pull it out into its full square shape. While we secure the canvas top and then the four legs, I watch the hustle and bustle of all the people planning to work at this event. Having never been to an outside craft fair before, I'd never given such a place a passing thought. Now that I'm here, and actually part of the action, I appreciate the circus type excitement of all those involved with making the event come together.

With the heavy tables in place, we begin to look through the plastic boxes. Sarah is making a list of items she needs to bring tomorrow morning. Her mind is so involved with the craft fair booth that I'm beginning to think it means more to her than just a cover story as to why she and Randy are on the Cape this summer.

"They have guards for security all night so I can leave my stuff here. I'm not putting anything out though. I'm afraid the tablecloths will get damp from the morning dew and then if there is any wind…" Sarah says out loud, although not necessarily for my benefit. "The signage will stay in the case. The racks back in the truck… I want here though. I'm going to hang things from them so I want them secured to the canopy frame today. They can both fit in one cart. And the cooler…I need that too."

Not wanting to hurt Sarah's feelings, I pretend to care about the booth and I even offer to get the items she's requesting from the truck. The wagon bumps along the grass as I pull it to the parking lot. I soon find that although the racks Sarah wants are not heavy, they are incredibly clumsy. I quickly decide to gather everything else from the list first leaving the racks for last. Finally, face-to-face with the rickety metal monstrosities, I perch them on the tailgate and push them down so they lean against the truck. Pleased with myself, I am configuring how I will secure them on the wagon when I feel a tap on my shoulder.

"You look like a damsel in distress who could use some help. I'm Burt and I'm a volunteer for the craft show. If you want I can help you get those things to where they're going."

Burt is drop dead gorgeous, a bit older than me, and has the muscles of a dedicated weight lifter. His t-shirt does indeed identify him as a volunteer so I eagerly accept his offer.

"I have a golf cart near the gazebo. Walk with me to go get it."

"Yeah, okay."

"There are so many vendors showing up all at once I've been running non-stop all day."

"That's crazy. Maybe they should have more volunteers. How many guys like you are out here helping? You're the only one I've even seen so far."

"Really. Well, there's more."

"What's at the gazebo, anyway? The sign-up booth is at the entrance so what's the tent for?"

"Um…just set-up people."

In a flash, I picture the sign-up area complete with free refreshments, information on upcoming events, and hand trucks leaning up against a tree. If an area with set-up people existed it would surely be there; not such a distance away. Now that my suspicions are piqued I notice Burt is leading me off to the left of the gazebo, more towards a shed like building that is part of the park.

"The gazebo is straight ahead. Why are you bringing me to the shed?"

Burt stops walking so he can face me. With his hands up and a smile on his face he asks, "What's with all the questions? I just wanted to see if the bigger cart was behind that shed that's all."

"You know what? I think I can manage on my own. Thanks anyway but I'd rather just deal with those…"

"Think again Abia Haddad. Think again." Burt grabs hold of my arm while putting his other arm behind me. Now speaking in a Russian accent he says, "If you don't know what I'm holding to your back allow me to explain. It is a gun, Abia Haddad. Now, you will come with me because there is someone who desires to meet you."

Having been in precarious positions such as this in the past, part of me expects something to happen that will allow me to escape. Maybe Frank or Randy will unexpectedly pop out of nowhere and bop my assailant over the head, allowing me to break free. Or, perhaps, Agent Brown will spot me and come over to question who I am with and what I am doing. If nothing this deliberate occurs then an upset not connected to me would suffice such as a mild earthquake, a group of playing children running us down, or even a loud distracting noise like a backfiring car. But none of these things are happening. Instead, I am getting closer to a part of the parking lot where there are no people mulling about. Desperate to avoid being abducted by my assailant, and sure that my only hope of salvation must come from me, I put into action the first non ridiculous plan that comes to mind.

"I'm going to be sick. Please, I'm going to be sick. I need to go to the bathroom," I plead.

"Keep walking."

"My knees are weak. I can't. I'm going to be sick." Teetering on my heels, I slowly drop to my knees. Alternating coughing and gagging noises, I successfully draw the attention of passing people.

"She'll be okay. She's just got morning…I mean afternoon sickness," my assailant says, proudly. "It's our first."

Before I can object to his bold lie he whispers in my ear.

"I've exchanged my gun for a hypodermic needle. I had wished to avoid drugging you but you have given me no choice. How very unfortunate. You will feel a pinch…ah, yes, you just did. Now my dear, you will be very calm, and by the time we reach the parking lot, you will be ready for a very long nap."

*****

The smell of this place is unpleasantly familiar; a dry but musty odor that can only exist when the living enter an area long forgotten. As determined as I am to open my eyes I am simply too weak to overpower whatever is weighing my eyelids down. I feel that one of my hands is outstretched enough to explore my immediate surroundings so I focus my fuzzy brain on everything in which this seemingly distant limb comes into contact. It seems I am lying down on a low platform of sorts and one of my arms is dangling down from it. Beneath me I feel a rough surface, one that is neither dirt nor stone but a mixture of both. There is nothing within my reach but cool air. Relying on instinct rather than sight, I sense I am in a dark place; a dark and isolated place.

I awaken with a shudder. Realizing I've been asleep since being with Sarah at the fair, I slowly open my eyes finding that this time, my eyelids flip open effortlessly. My instincts were correct; I am in a very dark place. I move slowly and carefully since I have no light to guide me. My hand rubs against a coarse cloth that is holding me above the ground. It feels like a canvas of some type. The cloth is connected to a sturdy yet small wooden frame. I am lying down on a cot in a dark room that is cool, a bit damp, and has a distinctively familiar odor to it. I position my body on my hands and knees so I can crawl around without harm. I quickly realize I am in a small room with some awkward things inside it. I eventually identify an oddly shaped contraption my fingers touch. My heart beats with nervous excitement; I am inside the middle room in the hidden chambers below the Boston Catholic Cathedral! The young man who abducted me from the park brought me to this place, where I am to meet someone with higher authority than he holds. Perhaps General Kulik himself wishes to speak with me. Spurred on by escalating wild deadly thoughts, I find the entrance door. Not expecting the door to be unlocked, I stumble through the doorway onto the ground in the large chamber. I slowly come to realize that my captors did not lock me up because they did not expect me to know my way out of this place.

Smart enough to realize that my drugged brain is clouding my judgment, I force myself to calm down and think. The more I do the more it becomes apparent that I'm in a remarkably good position considering I've been kidnapped. Although Sarah and Arnie were his prisoners, they never told General Kulik that they knew about the cathedral tunnel; therefore, he brought me here thinking the chamber down here was a prison in and of itself. Little does he know that I am quite familiar with this place, and, most importantly, how to get out of it.

Without any light to guide me, I do find it difficult to find the tunnel that leads out of this chamber, but eventually I do. As quietly as I can possibly maneuver in such a difficult space, I make my way up to the chapel crypt area. All that stands between me and the frescoed area is a secret panel door. Not knowing if the space is empty of visitors, I peek inside the chapel as discretely as possible. My view is, of course, limited by the angle I am at, as well as my unwillingness to open the crack I am looking through any wider. My body is trembling in fear as I slither into the vacant chapel, careful to close up the secret passageway to the hidden chamber behind me. On wobbly knees, I reach out for the pews to support me. I slowly work my way to the stairs leading me out of here trying not to panic when I hear approaching voices. Quickly, I get into a kneeling position in one of the pews and play the role of an emotionally distraught praying Catholic. I am surprised to see that my skin and clothing is stained and dirty from whatever happened during my abduction.

The voices belong to a young couple, who, are apparently, are on vacation. Their tourist-based interest in the cathedral is somewhat understandable although their dire need to examine the details of the chapel crypt before me seems a bit overzealous. Since it is easy to see that I am not only of no interest to them, but also somewhat of an intruder in their private picture-taking world, I make an unnoticed exit up the stairs. The cathedral itself, however, is not empty. A place such as this, always streaming with visitors with whom a person can blend in with, would be most helpful if my clothes were not stained with dirt. Nonetheless, I venture out of the side exit door without drawing a great deal of attention. It is very late in the afternoon, and thankfully, still light outside. On the bustling street of Boston without money, cell phone, or an acceptable excuse for my disheveled appearance, I find I am dumbfounded as to what I should do.

I don't know for sure what inspires the business man in the pinstriped suit to assume I am a homeless person in need, but without making eye contact he slips me a dollar bill and mumbles, "God bless you." My automatic response of thanks leads to an older lady rummaging in her large pocketbook for change. Her donation to my cause is three quarters and a dime. Too relieved to be embarrassed, I set out for a pay phone only to find that these convenient modes of communication are basically extinct. There are none on any street… at all. Nor is there one at any of the stores in this area. I finally locate one inside a dumpy bar with patrons that frighten me almost as much as my abductor. I call Frank, who is half insane trying to find out what happened to me. He pleads with me to stay on the phone with him until he gets to Boston, but I can't because I don't have enough coins to keep feeding the phone. I'm filthy, mentally confused, and have no money to buy a drink. As pathetic as I feel I'm grateful to be alive. Outside of the bar, taking cover in an alley way, I wait to be rescued.

*****

Although I am fearful the entire time I wait for Frank that my abductor or General Kulik will come looking for me, this does not happen. Instead the hour or so wait involves little more than a lot of thinking on my part as I watch the sun go down. With the darkness comes city lights, more traffic, and an increase in noise; all of which make me feel safer. When I see Frank's SUV turn onto the street I finally allow my guard to come down. The first twenty minutes we are together we speak of nothing but the abduction. Once I have said everything I can think of about the event, as well as answered every question my boyfriend can think of, we move on to other topics.

"Tell me about what happened to you and Randy today?"

"We were on Alena's tail when Sarah called us. When I told you she was hysterical I'm not sure you understand just how freaked out she was. Anyway, Alena went to the hospital. I assume she went to see her father. This was when the news was breaking about what allegedly occurred at the old Taunton State Mental Hospital."

"Which was what? What exactly is the official story?"

"Well, the guy you referred to as the Jailor, Jay Taylor, supposedly captured and attacked General Kulik for undisclosed reasons."

"What? How stupid is that? What did the news say about the General being shot in the knees? And how did the General, with blown out knees, get the gun and shoot Jay the Jailor in the stomach?"

"Nothing is being said, except that Jay captured the General and tortured him for undisclosed reasons."

"Well, we figured there would be a cover-up so here it is. Is there anything else?"

"The neighbors near the hospital are all over the news saying all sorts of things. That's what's worrying us. Sarah and Randy are scouring every news station to make sure you two weren't seen. Even though it was in the dead of night when all this happened, it's possible someone witnessed something. So far, no neighbor has mentioned you or anyone else being there."

"I wasn't thinking of that. I guess it'll take a lot of luck for the General and Jay to live and for us to have gotten away completely unnoticed."

Frank's silence says more than his words already have.

"Jay the Jailor guy survived, right?"

I hear Frank gulp while he reaches for my hand. Visions of the Jailor…Jay Taylor… falling to the floor inside the abandoned hospital torture chamber overtakes my mind. My stomach acids rise into my throat while my body begins to shake. It takes three attempts before I can ask; "I killed him?"

"The cause of death is gun shot. Officially, of course, General Kulik killed him. Whether it was you or someone else that delivered the fatal shot…we may never know."

Chapter 17
Project Tin Man

I waken to Randy's hushed, but obviously angry, voice coming from the trailer kitchen. Having spent yet another stress filled night trying to sleep rather than actually sleeping, I'm in no mood to deal with arguments this morning. In fact, now that I believe I'm actually a murderer, I don't feel like dealing with anything right now except thinking of a way to lessen the burden of guilt I've carried since finding out Jay the Jailor died. While I lay in bed listening to Randy, Frank, Sarah, Arnie, and Mohamed exchanging words without actually processing what they are saying, the smell of coffee slips through my bedroom door. Occasionally Randy is unable to keep his voice down whereby his loud outburst is followed by reminders that I am still sleeping and had quite an ordeal yesterday. If it weren't for the new aroma of baking cinnamon rolls from a pop and fresh tube, the kind with the white icing that melts over them, I don't think I'd get up for another hour or so.

"Then what? Do you all really believe the enemy will leave us alone just because we want out? It isn't going to happen. General Kulik knows who and where we are. He also knows we're on to him; at least partly. Sure, he's out of commission now with two blown knees, but he's got an army of goons to do his evil work for him," Randy is saying as I slip into the room. "What makes this so hard is we don't know what all the enemies look like."

"That is indeed unfortunate," Arnie states.

The group pauses to wish me a good morning, however, the heated debate continues, within mere seconds.

"I understand why they want us. After all, we're deliberately interfering in their plans, but why you?" Frank asks Arnie. "What have you done to upset them so much they'd kidnap you from the base? I mean, specifically? What is General Kulik so worried about? What do you know that incriminates him? Have you done something in your research that threatens him?"

"It's not what I've done, it's what I know. I have knowledge regarding a government project, a top secret project. I'm not sure I should even be telling you about it." Arnie seems to shrink down in his seat. "It is what I intended to work on this summer. Much of what I am researching now is unofficial. The official research is, I believe, completed. The results are known only by the governmental committee that commissioned the studies at various facilities, including the NSF and other universities and colleges in Boston."

Arnie's confession of undisclosed knowledge unleashes a stream of fury in Randy that dwarfs his previous rants of the morning. Red faced and double fisted, he stomps across the cramped trailer and yells, "Are you freaking kidding me? The girls risk their lives to rescue you, we shelter you, and you hide top secret important information from us? Are you out of your mind? Are you trying to get us all killed? What is wrong with you?"

Mohamed and Frank both pull Randy back before his violent temper explodes into physical violence. Arnie is very pale and visibly shaking. Sarah goes to her boyfriend's side. Her usually calming words seem ineffective.

"No, I won't calm down and hear the stupid nerd out! He's endangering all of us with his top secret stupidity. To think we were willing to treat him like one of us…well…"

"Come on Arnie, let's go out for a walk," I suggest. "It's time you came clean and I think it's best if you get away from Randy while you tell us everything."

"Mohamed, you should come with us. Let Sarah calm the beast down," Frank says. "We'll walk to the cabin."

I am the last to step outside. As I close the door I hear something made of glass smash against it. Rather than get upset I breathe in the calming aroma of pine trees and take my place beside the others.

"It's called 'Project Tin Man' as in the tin man character from the Wizard of Oz. If you remember, the Tin Man was really intelligent but had no heart. That's what the Weather Weapons Program is like; all intelligence and no heart for the devastation it creates. Also, the movie was all about tornadoes… get it, storms?" Arnie stutters.

"What is Project Tin Man? Start from the very beginning, will you?" Frank asks, with a forced calmness.

"The project was started by the government…the U.S. Government…as a result of some research that indicated that the military's Weather Weapons Program may have inadvertently contributed to…or been responsible for… well…some…um…"

"Spit it out…some what?" I ask. "Just tell us."

"Global warming."

Arnie's confession is followed by dead silence which is then followed by more silence. It is Arnie himself that restarts the conversation.

"What is theoretically possible in science often has, um, consequences. The manipulation of weather patterns and the science of weather in general are possible, however, once mankind starts to manipulate nature for its own purposes...sometimes..."

Frank cracks all his knuckles at once before clearing his throat and asking the unimaginable question I am too frightened to ask, "The United States may have caused global warming while making weather weapons? And they know this? So, instead of stopping the program or admitting to the problem or...? Instead of facing the consequences they created, the government created Project Tin Man which is an investigatory research project named loosely after the Wizard of Oz movie? And the purpose of this project is what?"

"Assess the damage," Arnie reports.

"Has the damage been assessed?" Mohamed unsuccessfully tries to make eye contact with Arnie. "You said only the committee who commissioned the project knows the research results; however, do you personally know if our government is responsible for global warming?"

"There is both a scientific opinion and a political opinion regarding the damage. We, the scientists, believe the weather weaponry program is responsible for a great deal of the global warming problem in recent years. We have been able to prove as much in various studies. I know this from piecing together research I gathered from other groups working on the Project Tin Man project. The politicians on the committee who oversee our work do not agree that the damage created by the weapons program was...or is... as devastating as the science is indicating. At least this is what I've been able to gather. You see, I am not supposed to be gathering the information I have brought together. My analysis of the combined results of Project Tin Man research is illegal. The research was deliberately split up and done by different science labs so that no scientists or group of scientists would have a definitive answer to the questions being asked. The question, of whether the United States created global warming while developing its Weather Weapons Program, was not to be answerable by any one person or group of people other than the government itself. Do you understand? "

"Who is on the government committee who oversaw Project Tin Man?" I ask.

"It's a top secret committee. Some of the politicians who deal with HAARP – which stands for..." Arnie says.

"High-Frequency Active Aural Research Program based in Alaska and jointly managed by the military. It's the scientific program at the heart of weather weapons," Frank explains to Mohamed. And me.

"In your search of General Kulik's cottage did you see him involved with this HAARP?" Mohamed asks.

"He's all over it," Frank says. "And also a committee linked to HAARP called UNFCCC or something like that?"

"It's the UNFCCC as in the United Nations Framework Convention on Climate Change. If the Weather Weapons Program is causing global warming the United States is in big trouble on the world stage. This U.N. agreement was signed by the United States in the early 1990s, and in the opinion of the scientists, the country is in direct violation of it," Arnie explains. "You see, this agreement promises that no country that signs it will cause damage to the environment of other countries or areas beyond its jurisdiction. The facts are clear. If the United States created global warning, it has, in a very significant way, caused immense damage to the entire world."

*****

With so much ground to cover in such a short time, our plans for today have us split apart more than I'd like. Sarah will go to the craft fair by herself. Although she will take every precaution to never be alone so she is not vulnerable to abduction, I fear she will be taken just as I was yesterday. Randy, who is still agitated by Arnie's earlier disclosure, will drive into Boston in his truck, where he will do surveillance at Agent Brown's house. Frank and I will be in the SUV nearby. Randy's mission is to get inside the Brown's house to see what he can find that may help us unravel the mysteries of the weather weapons storms and General Kulik. Since Agent Brown lives in the house, we are not expecting Alena to leave clues about nor is it likely that Agent Brown leaves anything of importance hanging around; however, any little thing could be of major help to us at this point. On the chance that Alena is home when Randy arrives, he will alert me and Frank when she leaves. We will then follow her. If she is not home, Frank and I will come up with another plan for the day.

Frank and I are waiting in the parking lot of a big box store strip mall when Randy calls to tell us that Alena is home. He then reports that a nautical blue metallic Toyota Avalon is in the driveway, which he believes belongs to Alena. Because the car is out of the two stall garage, he further believes she intends to go out somewhere today. There is little more to say about the activity at the Brown's home since Randy states that nothing is happening, so he begins to speak about the little we know about Alena. He is discussing how Alena majored in Russian studies at some university I never heard of when he lowers his voice to report that she is leaving the house. This news instantly changes us from bystanders into surveillance detectives.

Alena's car slows to a stop at the stop light in front of the plaza. Frank instantly pulls out onto the main street, slowly cruising in the breakdown lane as if he is lost. Alena looks straight forward as she drives past us, her large designer sunglasses masking her face. I don't take a normal breath until we are comfortably on her tail; far enough behind her not to be noticed but close enough not to be at risk of losing her in the thick traffic. She seems to maneuver her car as if she has a clear destination in mind. She doesn't switch lanes or run through yellow lights, instead she merely keeps pace with the flowing traffic. I can't be sure, but I think she is speaking on a cell phone. My obsession with determining whether or not this is the case occupies my thoughts until she pulls onto the highway.

"I can't say I ever expected her to leave the city." I tell Frank. "With everything going on in her life what in the heck is Alena doing?"

"She has to be doing something for her father. If her car was outside when Randy got to her house then she must have been out this morning. My guess is she went to see her father and he gave her instructions for the day." Frank taps on the steering wheel. "She's driving the speed limit; not one mile per hour more. She doesn't want to be stopped today, that's for sure."

We continue to drive for about twenty more minutes when Alena takes an exit. My heart beats faster as we follow her through some suburban streets. After several turns and a scenic ride through a rural area, we arrive at a beautifully landscaped property with a three story white building.

"This is a nursing home. This has to be where Stefan Kulik is!" I blurt out.

Frank parks a distance from Alena's car, slipping the SUV behind a handicapped van to prevent her from noticing it. We wait for quite a while before realizing that she is not getting out of her car. To find out what is happening, Frank sneaks through the parking lot to investigate. When he returns his bright eyes sparkle with excitement.

"You were right, she was on the phone," he says.

"Well? Who was she talking to?"

"I'm not entirely sure, but I did learn some extremely valuable information."

"Okay, what?"

"Stefan Kulik is inside this place and she is here to make arrangements for him to be released into his brother's care. General Kulik is taking him home!"

"Did she say why?"

"She said to whoever she was talking to that he was one of the people on the list of people who are loose ends and need to be dealt with. Agent Brown is too. Mohamed is another. Of course, we already knew Arnie was on the list. And now, after what happened at the abandoned Taunton hospital, so are we."

*****

Since neither one of us have ever been in a nursing home, we imagined it to be a much different place than the one in which we enter. I expected a front desk person who smiled as we passed by on our way to visit our pretend elderly loved one. I expected a busy hospital atmosphere where our presence would be barely noticed. I expected to see residents here, there, and everywhere making it easy for us to pick out an unfortunate one we could claim was a relative, someone who no longer had the mental facilities to know whether we were telling the truth or not. In my mind this visit was going to be nothing more than the simple task of play acting. I quickly learn that is no to be.

"Excuse me, young couple!" A heavy nurse with a deep loud voice beckons from the front reception desk. "You cannot just barge into this facility without signing in. Now come here and identify yourself and the patient you are here to visit."

"Oh, we're sorry," a polite Frank says. "This is our first time here and we aren't familiar with the rules. In fact, we are here at the request of my mother. It is her aunt we are here to check on."

The heavy nurse slides a sign-in book at Frank and says, "Whatever you say. So, who are you here for?"

Frank's eyes stay focused on the crucifix that hangs below the entrance sign that says *Saint Theresa's Nursing Home.* Before he speaks, I know he will say the first popular female Catholic name he knows. "Mary. We're here to see Mary."

The nurse snickers sarcastically and snaps, "We have a lot of Marys and Marias in the rooms of this place. You'll have to do better than that."

Aware that our cover is cracking fast, I decide to step in with a rescue attempt.

"There really is no need for you to be so rude," I say loudly enough to draw the attention of other staff members. "How dare you complain about how many Marys are living here! I'm sure each and every one of them is important and special in her own way. To treat them…" I set my gaze on the woman I guess to be the head nurse and continue, "Treat them like they're nothing but useless women with useless names…"

The woman in my line of vision hurries over as I hoped she would. After a few soothing words of apology about the heavy nurse's insensitivity she says, "You see we have Mary Gomes, Mary Amaral, Mary Smith, Mary Houston, Mary Leddy…"

Frank interrupts, "Mary Leddy is my mother's aunt. Please give us her room number and we won't trouble you anymore."

As we make our way to the elevator with room number in hand, I feel the burning eyes of the heavy set nurse on my back. Alone in the elevator I say to Frank, "You better hope Mary Leddy is senile or mute because she can blow our cover in two seconds if she's not."

"I didn't sign in our real names. It's not much but at least I did that."

With no further discussion, we find Mary Leddy alone in a single bed room. She looks to be incredibly old which gives me a rush of optimism. On closer examination her hooded eyes look cloudy but not unaware. Unlike the other parts of the nursing home we've been in, her room doesn't smell unpleasant but has a scent of lilacs and lavender. Mary Leddy is far too old to still be attractive; however, I can tell that she most certainly was a rare beauty in her younger years.

"Who are ya and this young man and why ya here?" Mary says in a cracked fragile voice. "I don't know ya."

Stunned by her aggressiveness, I look over at Frank helplessly.

"Whatcha lookin at him for? I'm the one askin the questions, not him," Mary snaps.

"We came to see his great aunt but you aren't the..."

"Is that the story? You're here to see Mary Leddy but I ain't the right one? Praise Lord that's the dumbest thing I ever heard. Whats the true story? Are ya here tryin to get inside info about this place and how they treat us? Work for a newspaper or magazine, is that who ya are? Got a camera in your pocket to snap pictures of us being abused and getting beatins?"

"No, of course not," Frank interjects. "This is just an innocent mix-up, that's all. So, if you'll pardon our interruption we'll leave you to..."

"Leave me to what? Lookin out the winda? I ain't got nothing to do so you aint interruptin nothing. But there ain't no abusing of the old people goin on here either so you're wastin your time tryin to find some. Nope, they're all nice here...most of them anyways."

"Well, we met one coming in here that wasn't so nice," I say. "She's heavy set with dark hair and ..."

"Ha, that there is Fatsy Patsy we's call her. We wouldn't pick on her weight if she wasn't so damn mean but she is. She's always mad cuz she'd rather be eatin than takin care of us. Yeah, Fatsy Patsy has been in trouble so many times I figure she'll be fired soon. Ya know, workers here come and go a lot. She'll be goin next I'd say."

"Well, that's interesting but we really do need to get going," Frank says, once again trying to end the visit.

"Not till ya tell me who ya really lookin for." Mary says. "You don't tell me and I rat you out. Ya tell me the truth and I keep ya secret. Ya see, I don't have much goin on here so you comin in here is exciting to me."

Mary laughs with her mouth wide open exposing a set of clean, well made dentures. I know Mary has won this small battle when I hear Frank sigh.

"We're here because we think a man named Kulik might be here," Frank explains in a low whisper.

"Kulik, ah yes, the patient in the big double room downstairs who doesn't have no roommate. Yep, he's a mysterious man he is. He's related to someone with powa or money or both. He's in the corner room…first floor. He's been here awhile and sort of keeps to himself, he does. Well, he did til the Alzheimer's grabbed him. Ya know when people get real sick with that they stop talkin about today and go back in time… to the past. That's what's happenin to him. Always mumblin on and on about things that don't make no sense. The Cold War, the Kremlin, secret spies and the KGB… good God in Heaven he sounds like a spy novel! He don't mean no harm… no he don't. He seems like he was a good man in his day. His day has just done passed him that's all. Yep, bottom floor in the corner. Everyone knows Kulik because he's the only one that has a big double room and doesn't have to share it. I had to wait years to get me a single room I did. Years of smelly grumpy roommates before I got this here room. Him? Came in to a double room paradise on day one he did. Like I said, he must know someone. Tell me, who is he connected to?"

"He doesn't need connections. Stefan Kulik is famous all by himself. He's a military hero of sorts. That's why we came here. We want to interview this incredible man," I say convincingly. "But, if he suffers from Alzheimer's then that might not be possible."

"Sorry kids, but old Kulik is crackers. Last time I tried to talk to the old fool he was telling me about some tunnel made during Prohibition! You betcha, he was goin on and on about how it splits into two and one end goes to the water and the other end goes somewheres else…I can't remember exactly now. Then he started yapping about weapons. I suppose he was thinking about weapons that moonshiners had? Who knows. Alls I got out of that entire conversation was that the weapons were like money, ya know. Weapons like money…. what does that mean?"

"Maybe it means the weapons are used as payment when someone performs a service for the people who have control of the arsenal below the tunnel," Frank whispers to me.

"Yessa, weapons in a tunnel. Kulik is crackerjacks. Go see for yourself. He's downstairs…the corner room. Ya can't miss him. But I tells ya, since he got the sickness alls he talks about is a tunnel and the Prohibition dry years. Makes no sense if ya asking me."

I lean over and whisper to Frank, "it makes a lot of sense to me. Stefan's sickness has him talking way too openly about the past and secrets that his younger brother doesn't want anyone to know. And that is not only way Stefan was replaced as General Kulik's partner, it's also why the old man has to be silenced…as in murdered."

We wait patiently outside of Stefan's room in hopes of spotting Alena. Unsuccessful, we eventually venture out to the lobby. There between the atrium garden and a Steinway grand piano is Alena and a handsomely-dressed woman in an expensive looking business suit. They are standing close together in a way that implies they do not want their conversation to be overheard.

"This is our chance," Frank whispers as we sneak back down the hall.

We find the elder Kulik sitting in a chair by a large window in his room. His view of cars driving in the parking lot has captivated his attention. His slender body is hunched over and his white hair has thinned to the point that his scalp is clearly visible. Although he looks directly at us when we walk in, I don't believe he actually sees us.

"Mr. Stefan Kulik?" I hear Frank ask. "Do you have a minute to talk to us?"

The old man says nothing.

"We're wondering if you know why you're brother is taking you out of this place?" Frank probes.

Stefan shifts to the right while allowing his toothless mouth to drop open. He mumbles rather than says, "The room is in the tunnel and the key is at the twelve. The tunnel goes to the water. Shhh…there are dead people down there. Deliver me one and I'll give you a gun. A poem…ah yes…Alexi? Do you remember that poem?"

Frank is about to respond when the door flies open.

"Abby Haddad and Frank Stiller, is it not?" Alena says forcefully. "I thought I recognized you on the lobby surveillance camera. How dare you come here and frighten my uncle! How dare you…"

Chapter 18
Alena Brown

"We came here for your help, not a lecture," I say, grateful I'd rehearsed my confrontation with this woman many times this morning. "We can't risk going to your husband directly for many reasons which I cannot explain to you. But there is something critically important for us to discuss with him. We need you to give him this packet. It explains where and when we can meet so no one will ever know. This is critical to us. Please, Mrs. Brown, we trust you to help us. We're sorry if we didn't handle meeting you properly but we are so scared and…"

As planned, Frank steps forward and hands Alena an envelope containing instructions to meet us at the baseball field that is attached to the park where Sarah's craft fair is being held. My boyfriend surprises me by adding to my pre-planned speech, "Mrs. Brown, I don't know how much your husband has shared with you about all that has happened to us these past couple of years, particularly the last few months. But what is happening to us now is even bigger than that. Please, tell him that we said this so he will understand how urgent it is that he finds a way to meet with us secretly."

Alena taps the envelope against an open hand. Her attractive face is neither soft nor hard; it is simply void of emotion. "I'll give this to Zac as soon as he comes home. Is there anything else you can tell me about what is going on?"

"No, just give it to him, he'll understand." Her obvious lack of concern disturbs me. I am nervously biting the inside of my cheek while no words are spoken. With the exception of a tweeting bird near the open window a silence fills the room.

"Then we'll be leaving now. Thank you." Frank, while squeezing my hand, pulls me away.

Alena says nothing to us as we leave her. I notice the staff in the lobby watching us as if to ensure we exit the building. Not sure how closely we are being monitored by possible grounds security systems, we drive up the street and ditch the car at a fast food restaurant. We cautiously sneak back onto the nursing home property with aspirations of getting below Stefan Kulik's window. As simple as this plan sounds, we find it is complicated to implement because of a steady flow of coming and going vehicles.

"Let's hope Alena didn't close that window," I say to Frank as we approach the property.

"Well, even if the window thing doesn't work out, we gave Alena the envelope and the meeting is set. She'll either give it to her husband or she'll give it to her father; either way we've spurred something to happen."

"If she plays it safe and Agent Brown shows up we can tell him all about Jinkins," I suggest.

"And if they don't and the General, Alena, and some thugs show up…well, we'll be prepared."

"Will we be?"

"We're working on it. We're figuring out every possible detail that we can."

With that, we enter the parking lot which we pass through without a hitch. Frank crosses the lawn area first. When he is safely hidden in the shrubbery below Stefan's window, I prepare to follow. I take cover when a car unexpectedly comes from around the front of the building. A white SUV approaches. I assume the driver is either distracted or in a hurry because the vehicle swerves through the rows. When the SUV turns into the row in front of me I make a plan to wait for it to pass by before seeking a different hiding place. Even though the white vehicle doesn't slow as it passes me, I recognize the driver all the same: it is the Russian thug who abducted me from the Buzzards Bay Park.

*****

By the time I successfully join Frank hidden within the thick shrubbery below Stefan's window, he is already aware that my abductor is at the facility. This is because Alena and my abductor, whose name is Jenk, are in Stefan's room. Frank quickly updates me on their intention to transfer Stefan to General Kulik's cottage on the Cape. The plan, however, has been complicated by the General's unfortunate physical ailment caused by having been shot in the knees. Apparently, one of my shots did indeed cause major damage to his kneecap, which required immediate surgery to correct. Although my second shot did not actually hit the kneecap, it still made for a painful leg that is having difficulty bearing the weight of the bad leg. From Alena's description, her father's use of crutches is not going well.

"Shut up, Uncle Stefan," Alena snaps at the mumbling old man. "He goes on and on, Jenk, he won't shut up. I have to keep him near the window, with it cracked open, with his robe on and his stupid corduroy slippers or he totally flips out. Even when I do all of this he drones on and on."

"This is why he must be taken care of, as your father has said. I understand he cannot be moved until it is proven that your father can care for him, but with all of your family's influence, can't this technicality be overlooked?" Jenk's thick Russian accent sends a shiver through me. "Can't you hire a nurse?"

"We did hire a nurse but these things take time to get into place. Meanwhile, this old fool saw pictures of my dad on the news because of the Taunton Hospital incident and has been sputtering on ever since. He's talking about the tunnel…I can't believe it."

Frank looks at me with raised eyebrows.

"All of this mess because of those kids!" Jenk says. "How did that girl, Abia …how could she have escaped from the tunnel?"

"My father is right when he concludes that Mohamed must have rescued her. Only Mohamed, Carlo, and the Bishop know of the tunnel. Carlo is dead and the Bishop has an alibi. That leaves Mohamed. He saved her." Alena lowers her voice. "We're not sure if they escaped through the cathedral or out through one of the tunnel exits."

A silence follows. Overcome by curiosity, I slowly creep up to peek inside the window. It doesn't occur to me that I am much too short to accomplish this until I am looking up at the bottom of the window. Frank stretches up beside me. He quickly pushes me down and whispers, "Alena and Jenk are in each other's arms. I believe she is having an affair with this younger man."

"Oh brother, as if things aren't complicated enough."

"Stefan is asleep; the poor soul. He has no idea they're scheming to get him out of here so they can kill him!"

"It may be for the best any…."

I stop talking mid sentence when Jenk says, "Alexi wants the scientist, what is his name…Maxwell or Arnold…dead soon, but I can't find him."

"My dad is upset about that loose end, too. I'm glad he killed off the Jailor when he did so at least that loose end is tied up. And no one will ever know the Jailor was murdered because it looks like my father was defending himself against that madman."

"I liked the Jailor, Jay. I wish he didn't have to die. I told your father that."

"Jay was okay but he talked too much. He also had a drinking problem. Add those two qualities together and you've got trouble."

Frank squeezes my hand as we silently celebrate the news that General

Kulik, not I, killed Jay the Jailor. Alena's voice seems to be nearer to the window as she says, "If the scientist, Maxwell, Arnold, or whoever, has proof that the United States is responsible for much of the global warming problem that plagues the world today, then he can leak this information out to the media, hence to the world, at any time. This information must only be known and provable by one person; my father. You see, my father needs to be able to blackmail the highest officials in Washington to assure that our escape to Russia with the Weather Weapons Program is assured. How else can we do this unless we have a secret that forces the US powers to do as we say?"

Alena's voice is definitely nearer to us but has stopped moving. "When we are all safe in Russia, we will have control of the only weather weapons program on the planet. Surely you understand what this means? The power, the money, the…"

"Yes, my love, I do understand," Jenk replies. "But what assurances do we have that the United States will dismantle their program just because it has been proven that the country caused global warming while creating it? Will the American people demand that the best weapon they have, a weather weapons program that no other country is even close to rivaling, be destroyed?"

"If the American people believe that the Weather Weapons Program created and continues to create global warming they will demand it be destroyed before their very eyes. Think of the polar bears and wildlife campaigns that will be broadcast all over the airways. Think of the pressure from the rest of the world! The United States will have no choice but to dismantle its weather weapons while we, in Russia, bring our program to life! We stole the technology, we have the scientists, and we have proof through the recent storm in Boston that it works! We have it all!"

We continue to listen to Alena and Jenk until they are interrupted by the nursing home manager. This woman is, not surprisingly, reluctant to release Stefan Kulik from her custody until social services has deemed it safe for him to be placed with his brother, General Kulik. Despite Alena's insistence that the transfer be made and Jenk's explanation that he drove in from Boston just to transport the elderly man, the manager firmly denies their request. When she leaves the room, Jenk leaves Alena to call her father with the bad news.

"It sounds like the General isn't happy about this change in plans," I whisper to Frank. "I think we should wait until both Jenk and Alena are gone before getting out of here. I don't want to risk being seen."

"I'd love to talk to Stefan again. His mind is cloudy, that's true, but inside there he knows something important," Frank says.

"There's no way we can sneak back…"

Alena's voice sounds soft, as if she is speaking to a child. "Okay Uncle

Stefan, I'm sorry if I was angry with you earlier, but things haven't gone the way I expected and Alexi is upset. So, you won't be going to see Alexi today after all."

"Alexi? Ah yes, is he in the tunnel? Oh…a shipment is coming you know. And…the new plans Alexi has made. He is so brilliant. I am going home to Russia soon. He told me when I leave here I'm going to Russia."

"Uncle Stefan, no one is to know about going home to Russia, remember?"

"Secrets? A life time of secrets. Dead bodies…so many in the tunnel. And guns…weapons…the big weapon I worked on so long ago…at the beginning in the military laboratories…"

"Uncle Stefan, please, you must stop talking about such things. Think of other things. Think of the cottage on Cape Cod. Think of how you loved it there."

"Ah yes. Hickery, Dickery Dock. The key is in the clock. Open the door. Below the floor." Stefan's deep laugh is instantly followed by the slamming of his door. Alena has seemingly left in disgust.

*****

On the ride back from the nursing home I get a call from Sarah who sounds, I am relieved to hear, very calm. She speaks in an almost reporting fashion as she updates me on Randy's escapades inside the Brown's residence. Once I inform her that we met with Alena and set the stage for the meeting at the baseball field, our conversation is interrupted by Randy butting in on her end and Frank butting in on mine. Rather than play go-between we give up the phones to our boyfriends and listen to them hash out a multitude of different plan ideas. While this is going on, I feel exhaustion creeping up on me. Frank's voice is slowly becoming more distant until it sounds as if he is talking through a long tube. I find the sway of the SUV and the humming of the tires incredibly relaxing considering what I've just been through, but I suppose sleep deprivation has an odd effect on people, and…

"Abby, wake up. We're back." Frank's gentle touch barely moves my fast asleep body. "Come on. Everyone is inside waiting for us."

"Really? I was asleep the whole way home?"

"I'd hardly call this box of metal and bolts a home but we are back on the Cape at the trailer."

"Okay. Did I miss anything?"

Frank grabs both of our backpacks and slams the SUV door. I follow him inside, still weary from the deep sleep.

"Yeah, you missed Randy and me arguing about the plans for our meeting with Agent Brown or Alena or whoever shows up at the baseball field. So, no, I guess you didn't miss anything that important."

The trailer smells of fried bacon and toast. On the crowded kitchen counter is a plate of lettuce and sliced tomatoes. An open mayonnaise jar with a knife sticking out of it is standing beside the toaster. As I greet Sarah, Randy, Arnie and Mohamed two pieces of toast pop up.

"Take those," Sarah says. "They're for BLTs. We've already each had one so you two should have one before we do seconds. There are chips too."

"Wow, supper is ready and everyone is home safe? It seems too good to be true." I gratefully begin to assemble a sandwich. "I don't know why I have a sense like there's something you all need to tell Frank and me, but I do. So, am I right? Is there some sort of news we need to know?"

"Your senses are correct," Arnie states matter-of-factly.

"And it is what?" Frank asks.

Mohamed looks over at Randy, who I now notice has a clenched jaw, a slightly reddened face, and narrowed eyes. Having seen his angry face many times before I am sure something has gone terribly wrong.

"I think it best that I explain it," Mohamed states. "It seems that my hiding place is not as secret as we would like it to be. My first inkling of this possibility is when I noticed a few things within the cabin being moved about. However, as is usually the case in such situations, I assumed I was mistaken and the items were where I left them even if I did not remember leaving them in those exact spots. To test my theory I set up a few traps. I planted a couple of my hairs on paperwork and I made small pencil marks in the exact place I left my keys to the trailer. And then, upon returning to my cabin I found..."

"The stuff was moved around! The hair wasn't on the papers and the keys weren't lined up with the pencil marks. So someone moved the stuff and none of us moved it!" Randy blurts out. "So, when I got back today, Mohamed and I secretly watched the cabin to see who the intruder is. At first no one came but we were patient. And then we saw him coming."

"Who? Was it Kulik's man? Agent Brown? Someone from..." I stammer.

"Not even close!" Randy breathes in heavily. "Jinkins! Can you freaking believe it! Edward Jinkins is on to the fact that someone is hiding out in the old Boy Scout cabin."

"This is indeed a serious problem, considering it is Mohamed who inhabits the cabin," Arnie unnecessarily points out. "However, we are not yet sure if Edward Jinkins knows Mohamed is the person in question."

"What do we know for sure, about what Jinkins knows?" Frank turns his attention to his sandwich as if he needs to fuel his body before tackling the immense problematic development before us. "Perhaps my question should be, do we even know what Jinkins knows about who is staying in the cabin?"

"We can not be absolutely sure, but we can make some fairly certain assumptions. Since I have also noticed Jinkins nosing around this trailer, I assume he has connected whoever is in the cabin to all of you. I also surmise he knows the inhabitant is male by my clothing. Since I do not keep much in the way of food in the cabin, I believe it is also safe for us to assume he is aware that I am dependent on you for my survival." Mohamed shifts his body and focuses his piercing dark eyes on me. "It goes without saying that it is best for me to find a different hiding place. One that is quite distant from all of you."

"No, that can't happen," I immediately respond. "It won't work."

"It's dangerous for Mohamed to stay in a place now where someone knows he's there," Sarah says. "I think he should stay here with us. It's risky, I know, but he's better off here than in the cabin."

"I think we need to know more about what Edward Jinkins is up to before we make any major decisions," Frank calmly states.

"I think Jinkins is a murdering creep that did away with his wife and father for the money to buy some forest out here and won't think twice about murdering Mohamed for the ten million dollar reward that's tagged to his fugitive head," Randy snarls. "I've been saying all along that jerk is huge trouble and now that we know he is I think we have to deal with him."

"What, precisely, do you mean by deal with him?" Arnie asks.

"Randy, you aren't seriously suggesting we kill the creep are you?" I ask, truly astonished at how angry Randy is becoming.

"Such a strategy is not only wrong, it is illogical. If Edward Jinkins disappears due to his death his daughters will notify the authorities who will then comb every inch of this area looking for him. It will put all of us, including Mohamed, in the precarious position of being in the spotlight of law enforcement." Arnie, whose inability to make eye contact causes him to look at the wall while making this profound observation, calmly folds his hands while waiting for someone to debate his point of view.

"He is correct. My leaving is the only answer to this problem," Mohamed says. "I will do so tonight."

"No, I think we need more time to think things through." I hear desperation radiate from my voice. "And we need some more information. At least let Frank and me do some investigating on Jinkins and his daughters tonight before a final decision is made."

Although the back and forth arguing continues, I'm fairly certain I'll get my way when Arnie starts to update his personal episode computer log. Like most of his daily routines, Arnie performs it only at specific and precise moments.

His log is updated at the first opportunity available after what he considers 'an episode' occurs. In this case, the episode is the discovery that Edward Jinkins knows that someone is staying in the cabin. It is completed in Arnie's mind for now because the next entry will focus on what we learn when spying on the subject tonight. It turns out Arnie is right. I will be out investigating the Jinkins family in less than one hour.

Randy takes the lead position while Frank and I follow about fifteen feet behind. We are all careful to stay hidden in the darkness while we make our way to the old trailer office located in the central circle at the park entrance. As expected, the office is open because the adjourning campsite area welcomes campers until as late as ten o'clock. Thankful there is no one in sight, we become a bit bold as we sneak out from behind the park store Sarah and I visited the day we arrived here. With nothing to conceal himself, Randy sprints across the park entrance to the back of the office. I go next and then Frank. The three of us are squatting below the back windows of the office trying to make out the owners of the muffled voices we hear. I vaguely recognize the daughter I met in the store by her sluggish uninspired tone; however, for all I know her twin may have a similar vocal presence. The male voice, in my opinion, is most definitely Edward Jinkins. It takes quite some time before I realize Jinkins is speaking to someone other than his daughter, who, I believe, is continuously butting into his conversation. The lack of a third voice indicates that the person Jinkins is speaking to is on the other end of a phone. When the talking stops, the door opens and closes. We verify that the daughter has left the office.

"It's almost closing time and none too soon. I'm getting eaten alive by the mosquitoes out here," Randy whispers. "Let's hope Jinkins packs up and leaves as fast as his daughter did."

"She sounded mad to me; the way she slammed the door and all of that," I say softly. "I don't think she totally agrees with her father, which, for such a young girl, surprises me. She can't be much older than fifteen."

Frank huddles us together. "I heard her say something about her sister. They're fighting about her sister I think. Anyway…"

Although it is not quite ten o'clock, the door to the trailer slams shut. The sound of gravel below walking feet is followed by a truck door opening and closing. From around the corner we watch red taillights turn into the entrance of the trailer park. Careful to track the lights to get some idea of where Edward Jinkins resides, it is several minutes before we begin working on the back door lock. Randy's experience with lock picking quickly overcomes the mediocre style lock before him. With not even a moment for celebration Randy pushes the back door open. When it doesn't budge he gives it a harder push which is also unsuccessful. His third try, a body slam, flings the door far enough open for us to slither inside and find that he has shoved a file cabinet out of place. I look down at some scattered papers and wonder how we will put them back on the cabinet in the same places they had been.

"We'll relock the door and push the cabinet back. We'll have to leave through the front door. We won't be able to re-lock it so we'll have to hope Jinkins thinks he forgot to when he left tonight. There's no other way. We can't possibly put the cabinet back in place and leave out the back door, it can't be done!" Frank announces.

"The heck with that," Randy presses redial on the landline phone. "By the time noted on this last call I'd say it's the one we overheard; the one his daughter kept interrupting." Randy waits for Frank and me to get near the phone. We all hold our breath while he pushes the button. The call is answered by a woman with a very familiar voice; it is unmistakably Alena Brown.

Chapter 19
The Clue

Another bad night of sleep is met with relentless sounds of arguing in the cramped kitchen and living room area of the trailer. The main topic of debate is, of course, what we do now that we know Edward Jinkins, and at least one of his twin teenage daughters, are enemies working for Alena Brown. The second source of discourse concerns how we are to play out the meeting we have set up at the baseball park. It seems that agreement can not be reached on how we should proceed should Alena, Agent Brown, or the General himself should show up. And thirdly, there is Frank's and Arnie's obsession with deciphering Stefan Kulik's Hickery Dickery Dock rambling, which, they both insist, is an important clue of some kind. I delay joining the tension bursting crowd as long as possible.

"Is Sarah already headed out to the craft fair?" I ask, greatly upset to find Frank, Randy, Arnie, and Mohamed are all present, but not Sarah. "I was just abducted from the park. How could you let her…?"

"She's actually getting a newspaper. Believe it or not they printed the story she, or was it you, wrote about the Boy Scouts. That Chief Scout Executive, Mr. Trumbell called to tell her. Not only that, the paper is looking for more articles. Go figure it would work out like this when you two weren't really even trying." Randy shrugs.

"Well, besides the newspaper and all the arguing this morning, what else should I be caught up on?" I ask.

Frank pours me a cup of coffee while saying, "Randy's visit to the Brown's residence clearly shows that Agent Brown and his wife do not share a bedroom. This implies that not only is the marriage on the rocks but also that their children are aware of the situation."

"From the kids' rooms I've learned that the son's name is Taylor and he's in kindergarten. I think he's five, almost six. The daughter, Brittany, is ten and she's a dancer. We're talking trophies for tap, ballet, modern dance, and stuff liken that. I even got the name of her dance studio," Randy reports.

"Interesting, but is it helpful?" I ask.

"It sure is. I'm a kid from a divorce and if there's one thing I know for sure it's that kids know a whole lot more about what their parents are fighting about than you can ever imagine. It might be worth tracking Brittany down and seeing what she knows." Frank picks at his fingers and adds, "I think the little boy is too young but Brittany is ripe for us to get the inside scoop."

"Tell Abby the rest," Mohamed says to Randy

Randy goes on to tell me where Alena's health club is, the addresses of some of her relatives, and that the house is remarkably clean of paper receipts. He goes on to describe a few oddities he found in the garage which include an odd collection of license plates from various states, several boxes of clothes marked for donation, and expensive looking skis that appear to have never been used.

"So there's nothing alarming in there. Lots of people collect license plates, donate clothes, and buy sports equipment they never use, right?" I ask.

"That's what I thought at first too. But the boxes of clothes looked like they'd been there a while, and considering what we know is going on, I thought it was weird that Alena would be cleaning out closets right about now. So I looked inside the top box and saw just a bunch of shoes and girls tights, almost junk really. The middle box had toddler clothes, stuff that had to have been from a long time ago rather than just cleared out of the kids' rooms. The bottom box had good clothes that looked like the clothes inside the kids' rooms now. And, tucked between the clothes I found a brand new prescription inhaler for the little boy and a newly filled bottle of some pills for him. I think he has asthma or something like that because I saw some kind of air purifier in his bedroom. Anyway, finding current clothes and medicine so neatly packed away tells me that box wasn't intended for donation at all."

"I agree. That box is packed away for the kids to go somewhere; most likely in a hurry. But who is taking them and where are they going?" Frank asks.

*****

Sarah and Randy head out for the craft fair early enough for them to call Frank from the baseball field adjoining the park. I listen to the plans for the meeting tomorrow night. Details of the actual field, dugouts and nearby buildings are under review. Meanwhile, Arnie and Mohamed continue their debate over how to handle the Jinkins family. The interlocking calm logic of these two men both intrigues and frustrates me simultaneously. Unlike the others present, my mind is spinning with questions about Alena's knowledge regarding Mohamed if, in fact, she knows about him at all.

When Frank ends his call with Randy, we all turn our attention on him. "Randy feels the ball field is remote enough for privacy during the meeting we've set up yet also close enough to a crowd of people for some element of safety. He says the last game should end no later than 8:00 assuming it doesn't go into extra innings. So, with our meeting time set for 8:30, we should have plenty of time for the field to clear out and the lights to go out before our clandestine meeting begins. Randy, Arnie, and Sarah will be stationed nearby to help Abby and me if we get in trouble. If need be, they will attract attention from the people in park next door to prevent our abduction or any other act of violence against us. Even if someone other than Agent Brown shows up, all we have to do is get the crowd over to the field before we get hurt. As a second precaution, Mohamed will be available to follow us, if somehow we are taken from the park despite the safeguards we have in place."

And so, the plans for tomorrow night are set; at least temporarily. With the whole day ahead of us I am eager to hear how we can make the best use of our time as possible. I soon learn, however, that the three men want to focus entirely on the Hickery Dickery Dock thing, which I believe to be a colossal waste of time. Their interest in this topic is so great, in fact, that no one argues with me when I quietly announce I am going out for a walk. I set my sights on the Jinkins family as I enter the vague trail that leads to Mohamed's cabin.

I find the cabin empty. I see no signs that anyone has been inside the place since yesterday, although I wouldn't exactly know what would signify that any of the Jinkins had been there if they had dropped in. I casually look through Mohamed's meager belongings noting that nothing about them indicates who may be their owner. I even rummage through his clothes pockets wondering if a receipt of some kind, or some other random slip of paper, may have given his identity away. Other than a crumbled up tissue his pockets are empty. I find myself killing time inside this small abode while half hoping Jinkins or one of his daughters will show up. I even consider starting a fire to see if the wisps of smoke attract one or more of the spies that haunt us. But, a solid hour passes without as much as a sound from another human being. I let a mixture of relief and discouragement settle within me before deciding what to do next. Then, with a sense of conviction, I march through the woods toward the spot where I believe Edward Jinkins' home is located. Of course, I lose my way before coming out on a side road of the trailer park. Not allowing this minor mishap to discourage me, I determinedly hunt down the Jinkins home.

I'm not sure why I'm surprised to discover that the Jinkins' trailer is a double wide deluxe unit in impeccable condition, but I most certainly am. I quickly cast aside the images I had of a ramshackle dumpy place to focus my attention on how I can determine if anyone is home. The first thing I learn about surveillance in a trailer park with few trees and shrubs is that hiding spots are hard to come by. The second thing I figure out is that the homes are so close together finding a hiding spot is a bit of a challenge. So, with little time to think and less time to get out of view, I do the very first thing I think of upon approaching the Jinkins property: I make a beeline for the fenced in backyard of the trailer. There, squatting between forest green patio furniture which is tastefully displayed on the nicest stone patio I've ever seen, I inspect the rear of the trailer. The back entrance has only a screen door, indicating the home is unlocked. Not sure if this is good or bad news, I mentally map out a path to the closest window. Staying as low to the ground as possible I go from the patio to a barbecue grill to an eating table and then to a sizeable clump of hanging garden hoses. As I knew I would be, I am far too short to see inside the window, so I simply wait to hear something that will alert me as to whether or not it is safe for me to go inside. No such give-away noise occurs for such a long time that I decide to change plans. On tiptoes, I edge my way to the screen door. I find myself looking inside a modern kitchen with stainless steel appliances, marble counter tops, and a tile floor that is so shiny I am actually petrified I will leave sneaker prints on it. I don't know why I go inside without weighing out the risks, but I am passing through the kitchen before I've had time to really think my actions through. There is no one inside the breathtakingly gorgeous living room area either so I walk soundlessly on the plush carpet down the hall. I pass a bathroom and then a bedroom, which, by the adolescent color scheme, I assume belongs to one of the twins. It is in this room I duck inside when I hear the front door open.

"I'm telling you, Dad isn't gonna put up with you much longer," the twin daughter from the store says.

"Shut up Kileen. He's such a jerk I don't care what he thinks anyway."

"Katie, I'm telling you, Dad is really mad at you about this. You gotta just tell him what he wants to know. If you saw the guy then just tell him."

"I don't know who he is, okay? I saw some guy in the woods near the cabin. I told Dad and now Dad knows he's there so let him figure out who he is. Besides, if he isn't gonna tell me who he's getting paid to tell about this guy then why should I tell him what I know?"

"Katie, I'm warning you. Dad knows you saw him and he knows you know more about him than he does. This guy you say, how old was he? And how often does he hang out in the trailer with the two young couples?"

"Listen, I'm not sure I can trust you anymore, but alright, I'll tell you if you tell me who Dad's mixed up with. I want to know what Dad is up to, is that so bad? I know he's spying on the young couples and the cabin guy so just tell me who and why. If you do I'll tell you all about the guy I saw."

There is a silent pause of at least ten seconds when Kileen says, "Okay. You go first."

"The guy I saw is with those couples all the time. He's tall, thin and wicked nerdy. Oh, and he wears glasses; total nerd glasses. And he has short hair, no beard or mustache. Definitely not a sun tan dude. Pasty white if you know what I'm talking about. And he seems distant in a weird sort of way. I can't describe it really; he just seems to himself somehow."

"And his name? Have you caught his name?"

"Nope, but I almost did because he wears a work badge of some kind. I think he has a badge from the military base."

"Hmmm…a nerdy military guy? Wow, wouldn't expect a guy like that hiding out in a cabin would ya?"

"Your turn; tell me who is Dad selling information to."

I hear Kileen let out a long drawn out sigh. "Some general guy and a woman named Alena. Actually, it's not just information he's being paid for. I think, well maybe, he might be negotiating to, um…"

"Dad's a hit man?"

"I don't know for sure but I do know he'd do it for the government and that'll make him a hero. Hey if the nerdy guy is a bad guy then Dad has to do what a big general asks, right?"

Hearing this astonishing bad news hits me so hard I temporarily forget where I am. When I come to my senses I realize I am trapped in the home of a man who is, in all likelihood, negotiating the price for killing me. Not wanting to press my good luck further, after all what would be the odds that I'd be inside the trailer when the twins would be discussing exactly the topic I so desperately needed to know, I hide in the closet to gather my courage.

"I'm not telling you anything else," Katie's voice is saying as it seemingly enters the bedroom I'm hiding in. "The only reason I agreed to talk to you now is because I had to know what Dad was really up to. I'm not like you, Kileen. I don't believe in him like you do. I don't think he's such a good guy deep down inside."

"Why can't you just accept the fact that Mom and Grandpa died…"

"I'm not talking about them anymore. I think Dad murdered them and that's that. Now leave me be. Dad'll be home for lunch any minute and I want to be long gone from here before he gets back. Besides I need to get back to the store."

"That's another thing. You need to be home more."

"Forget it Kileen. I'm staying as far away from Dad as I can. Consider yourself lucky you ran into me today. If it weren't for Dad being all in a fit because the trailer was left unlocked tonight, I wouldn't have been around this morning."

"I was with him last night. I left first so it was up to him to lock the place. But, so what? Nothing was taken. I don't get why he's so upset."

"Exactly my point. I may only be fifteen but I'm not an idiot. Dad is acting like a paranoid freak for a reason and that reason is because he's up to no good."

I hear the bedroom door close. Seconds later the closet door opens and I am face to face with a prettier version of the twin sister Kileen. Our eyes meet, our mouths open, but thankfully, neither of us screams.

"Be quiet. I'll get you out of here in a minute," Katie says, while she grabs a black blouse off a hanger. "Oh, it's nice to finally meet you, Abia Haddad."

As promised, Katie helps me escape. I am back in the trailer explaining what has happened before it finally occurs to me as to just how very lucky I have been today.

*****

After being scolded for taking such extreme risks without discussing them with the others, our afternoon debate is almost solely focused on Katie and Kileen Jinkins. I am as confused as I can be as to why Katie helped me because she said very little to me after our brief closet encounter. The other topic of discussion is the crazy Stefan Kulik babbling. I find myself contributing little to any conversations. The tedium is unexpectedly broken when Mohamed stands.

"I believe I may have solved the Hickery Dickery Dock clue. My interpretation of this odd rhyme is based on my memory of the Kulik cottage."

"Okay. Hickery Dickery Dock. The key is in the clock. Open the door. Below the floor. Can you get past the clock thing?" Frank shrugs.

"Inside the cottage I saw no grandfather clock, no cuckoo clock, no fancy silver or gold plated clock, or any significant timepiece. I do recall an old plain kitchen clock above the sink and an alarm clock in the bedroom…but those are hardly worth noting. In the sitting area there is not clock above the fireplace but there most certainly is something of significance in that room that has to do with a clock, do you remember what it was, Frank?"

"Above the fireplace is a picture of…men in a room….men in suits… like bankers in the 1800s or businessmen or…" Frank mutters.

"Politicians in a senate chamber I believe they were. Most interestingly, however, is the pendulum clock that is on the wall in the picture. I noticed it because one of the men in the picture is pointing up at it; as if to say that time is wasting while the politicians argue the matter at hand. I believe this is the clock referenced in the rhyme."

"And the key in it is?" I ask.

"The key isn't in it, it is in the painting. I believe the key is the time on this clock," Mohamed explains.

Frank nods. "Of course. That makes perfect sense. That old family heirloom picture holds the key. So what time is it on that clock?"

"I don't know. I am so sorry, but I didn't notice." Mohamed sits beside me and adds, "Open the door. Below the floor. This part of the rhyme takes on a different meaning now that we know we're not looking for a physical key. I thought long and hard about a door beneath the floor of the cottage. The cottage has no basement; it is built on a slab foundation and nothing more. There can be no hidden door leading below. However, we already know where the door beneath the floor is because we've been there. Just think about...."

"The cathedral?" I ask.

"Exactly. So whatever the time is on the clock in the picture could be a clue as to where and what is of importance below the cathedral. Something that means a great deal to the Kulik family is in that tunnel. Something that must tie into their weather weapons storm program and the Kulik's traitorous plans. And Stefan Kulik, in his senile state, is repeating aloud a childhood nursery rhyme that was adapted to be a reminder of the whereabouts of the secret hiding place in the tunnel. That is why the General needs to eliminate his brother. Every time he says the Hickery Dickery Dock rhyme, Stefan is inadvertently revealing the location of General Kulik's most valued possession!"

Before I have a chance to think better of it, Frank, Mohamed, and I are in Frank's SUV. Although the night is young, it is dark enough for the scattered streetlights to light up the roads to the Kulik cottage. Mohamed and Frank talk non-stop the entire ride. When we arrive the three of us quietly slip out of the truck, the dinging car door sound somewhat blocked out by the wind coming off the ocean. At the side of the cottage Frank peeks inside a window.

"Oh, man." He gasps. "Someone ransacked this place. It's a total freaking mess."

"What about the picture? Is it still there?" Mohamed asks.

"Yeah, it on the floor. We have to get inside to see it."

The back door is wide open allowing us easy access.

"Can you pick through the piles and get to the picture?" Mohamed asks Frank, who is the first to enter the living room.

"Yep, hold on a second and aim the light on my path, okay?"

Frank tiptoes through the scattered furniture, careful not to touch anything. Using his shirt sleeve as a glove he picks up the heavy oil painting. "The clock says it's twelve."

While Frank picks his way back to us I notice a familiar odor. On the floor, near a pillow that has been sliced open, is a jar candle. "Frank, doesn't that candle over there smell familiar? It's an odd flowery yet minty smell. I just smelled that somewhere?"

"Yes, I smelled it too. It was while we were sitting below Stephen Kulik's window. It's a weird smell."

I wait eagerly for Frank to retrieve the candle, again using his sleeve to avoid leaving fingerprints. His brow wrinkles while he struggles to read something on the label.

"I'll be damned. The label has Stefan's name written on it."

"They do that sort of thing at nursing homes in an effort to keep track of the patient's personal belongings. So the question becomes, why would someone bring Stephen's Kulik's candle here? And does this candle have anything to do with why the cottage has been torn apart?" Mohamed asks.

With the information we went to retrieve in hand, we leave the cottage without further delay. My spirits are high when we get back to the trailer. We are welcomed by Sarah and Randy who immediately ask why Arnie isn't with us. Although the others pass off his absence as part of his quirky behavior, I can't stop worrying about him. Remembering his obsessive concern about retrieving his car from the military base, where it was left when he was abducted, I picture him walking to the base in the darkness.

"I'm going out to look Arnie. Just to see if he went for a walk," I announce, car keys in hand.

With the new information about the Hickery Dickery Dock clue in hand, no one bothers to question me. I retrieve my military badge pass from the glove compartment of the SUV and head out to check the parking lots of the base. Once again, the soldiers at the guard booth ask me more questions than they likely ask any other badge holder before allowing me to enter. The lot near the science building is not completely empty so I do a quick drive-by investigation of the few scattered cars, quite aware that my every move is being watched by soldiers and recorded. When I don't see Arnie's car I simply drive off base allowing it to be obvious to anyone concerned that my reason for being here was to look for someone. With no more hunches to follow, I drive slowly down the winding road. I am surprised to see a military jeep speeding up the long roadway that leads to the Veteran's National Cemetery which abuts the base. I drive a bit further. In my rear view mirror I another jeep leaving the cemetery. Intrigued, I turn the SUV around. With my lights out I steer the barely moving vehicle along the side of the dark road. Ten minutes pass and then twenty. Finally, headlights coming from the cemetery appear. This time a military green truck slowly comes into view. It is towing a car, Arnie's car.

Chapter 20
The National Cemetery

I decide not to search for Arnie without first getting help because Frank is still aggravated with me for my solo escapade at the Jinkins' home earlier today. I'm also petrified to face off with the U S military; a power player I never expected I'd be calling an enemy. So I do my best to set aside my gut gnawing, spine chilling, head bursting fear and return to the trailer. Upon arriving, I see that Randy's truck is gone. I hurry inside to find Sarah anxiously picking through a bag of hard candy while she chats with Mohamed.

"Oh Abby, I'm so glad you're back. Randy and Frank went after Jinkins. He's been driving by the trailer all night. We don't know what's going on." Sarah shoves a butterscotch candy in her mouth.

"I never should have gone snooping around their place." I taste a bit of blood before realizing that my nervousness has me aggressively chewing at the inside of my cheek. "Well, forget about that for now. I found Arnie… sort of."

I explain about the military base, the jeeps, the cemetery, and Arnie's car being towed while Sarah and Mohamed prepare to search for the young scientist. We hurry to the SUV. Sarah glances at me as she gets behind the steering wheel; this is her way of letting me know she wishes she wasn't to play a part in tonight's danger. A hundred feet before the cemetery entrance, Mohamed and I disembark.

I expect the Veterans Administration National Cemetery to be a well organized immaculate place with a tasteful amount of respectful patriotism and it is exactly that. At the entrance stands a sturdy stone wall with regal gold lettering. Following the entrance, there is a flag lined lengthy drive to the burial ground. Mohamed and I trot down the drive to a brick and stone building, which is, of course, locked up tight. We find nothing out of place on the circular patio near the building or around the low brick wall that surrounds the facility. We venture off into the nearest burial section. Unlike traditional cemeteries where headstones reflect the personal taste of either the deceased or their loved ones, the grave markers here are all identical in shape and size. They are also placed in perfectly aligned rows.

"There's nothing here. We can check over there but I doubt we find anything." I look at Mohamed. "We can't find anything because we don't know what we're looking for or where to look. Let's think things through. Arnie would never have gone to the base by himself on foot at night. I don't believe it. Yes, he's been worried about his car, but he wouldn't go get it by himself."

"He was also concerned as to how he would explain his disappearance to his boss and co-workers," Mohamed reminds me.

"I know. He assumed that General Kulik made up some story about his being missing and he was afraid that his boss would believe the General's story rather than the truth he would tell him."

Mohamed, while stroking his beard, seems to be running a number of possible scenarios through his mind. "This makes me believe that someone called Arnie and convinced him it was safe to come to the base; perhaps he also picked him up."

"Arnie is fooled into thinking he can trust someone, like his boss, and then something happens and Arnie's car is here and…"

A set of bouncing headlights come up over a slight hill. We hide behind headstones while watching a dark colored compact car slowly pass by. The car turns into the first left hand row forcing us to shift our positions in order to stay hidden from the driver. Minutes pass before the driver comes out of the car. He is middle aged and wearing civilian clothes. Despite an ocean breeze I clearly hear what he calls out into the darkness,

"Maxwell Arnold…I know they found your car here. Please come out and I'll help you. I found your smashed up phone at the base. You wiped out all the information and then destroyed the unit. Why did you do that? Did you think the military was monitoring your calls? Is that why you ditched your car? Was it because you found a GPS tracking device on it? Tell me what spooked you and I'll help you. I'll drive you to a telephone that's not at, near,or connected to the military base. You can call your family."

Separated from my brother by several cemetery plots, I can't discuss with him the stream of thoughts running through my head. I'm confident that the man here in the cemetery is Arnie's boss, but I'm not confident if he is a friend or foe. I listen to this man's words, trying desperately to determine what his intentions are, only to discover that what he is saying reveals nothing but his desire to find Arnie.

"I'm on your side. Please believe that. That's why I picked you up. I wanted you to get your car and whatever you needed from your office. Listen to me…"

Arnie's boss stops speaking when another pair of headlights enters the cemetery. These belong to a military jeep. My stomach twists as the jeep passes by. Although I am much closer to the action than I want to be, I feel too vulnerable to move. Crouched down as low and as small as I can make myself, I watch Arnie's boss calmly greet two soldiers. Suddenly, I see a flash of light followed by a loud bang which echoes through the dead night. Arnie's boss crumbles to the ground. One soldier places something on the ground before he joins the other one inside the jeep. Without hesitation they drive away.

When I turn to speak to my brother I find he is gone. For a full minute I feel utterly abandoned. Finally I see Mohamed's darkened image near the corpse. On legs that tingle from having been crouched on for too long, I hobble toward my brother.

"Is he dead?"

Mohamed nods. "Of course he is. Trained soldiers never miss such easy targets. I'm afraid Arnie's boss was betrayed by the very people to whom he betrayed Arnie. The reasons for this are unknown and they likely do not matter as the end result can not be changed. After all, dead is dead."

"For this guy to be out here looking for Arnie that means Arnie's still alive and not caught. Also, if this guy was right about what he was saying, then Arnie ditched his car here because he knew it had a GPS on it. And he ditched his cell phone for the same reason. All of this tells me that Arnie is out there somewhere trying to find a way to call us for help."

"In this day and age where would he go to find a pay phone? What other public use phones are there?"

"I don't know. Check out what the soldier put down over there and let me think about it. Arnie wouldn't go back to the trailer for fear of hurting us. No, he'd go someplace he's been before. He doesn't go out much at all so…"

"It is the remains of Arnie's cell phone. I recognize the cover. The soldiers planted this near his boss's corpse as a way to frame Arnie for this man's murder." Mohamed carefully retrieves every piece of the device. "Our government is quite a formidable foe when it has an enemy of power within it."

*****

It seems to be a very long time before Sarah picks Mohamed and me up.

Even though we have no reason to suspect that anyone from the base would be looking for us, we know they are out here somewhere searching for Arnie which means a military jeep could pop up at any time. Since hiding behind trees is neither comforting nor comfortable, I do not give much thought to Arnie's whereabouts while we await Sarah's arrival. Thankfully, she has pushed her brain into overtime since we called her.

"The Bourne Package and Variety Store. I bet that's where he is. He's been there with Randy and Frank a few times. He likes the people who work there because they never make small talk, which he hates. And, they have a phone right near the cash register. I see the clerks answering it sometimes. I bet that's where he is." Sarah heads out to this destination without waiting for either of us to comment. Instead, she asks us for more details about the murder in the cemetery. When we arrive at the store, Sarah looks in the rear view mirror saying, "Mohamed, even though we're parked far from the building you need to stay hidden in the back just in case there are cameras. I'll go inside while Abby walks around out here. Hopefully Arnie will see us and come out."

The night air is a bit foggy, making the atmosphere feel almost movie-like. I walk along the side of the building all the way to the back without seeing or hearing anything that can be connected to Arnie. I turn my attention on a restaurant parking lot next door. I attempt to assess the parked cars with Arnie's mindset. First, I notice the cars are not perfectly aligned. Nor are they sorted by color, shape, or size. These factors, in themselves, would annoy Arnie to the point that he may chose to hide within the vehicles. Next, I consider that there is a pronounced presence of pounding rock and roll band music escaping from the rear of the building. This immediately tells me Arnie would not be hiding where he could hear the beat since he cannot tolerate such sounds. Latly, there is the brightly colored flashing signage at the front of the building. Such lighting is another of Arnie's quirky no-no's, which makes it extremely unlikely he is hiding anywhere within sight of this illumination.

"He's not inside and hasn't been in," Sarah whispers from behind me. "Is it possible he hasn't reached here yet?"

"No, but it's very possible he's too scared to go inside. You know what? If I were him I wouldn't hide behind the store because there's nowhere good to hide. I wouldn't hide in this parking lot because there are too many things in here that freak him out. So…he's got to be on the other side."

"A closed veterinarian? Let's check it out."

And this is where we find the frightened young scientist, hiding between the coops of two separate large dog kennels. The kennels are empty with the exception of one very large St. Bernard which is leaning against the fence with his paw in Arnie's lap.

*****

Randy and Frank are in the trailer impatiently awaiting our return. Like us, they are hyped up by their adventure tonight. A room with six adults all trying to speak at once is not just loudly chaotic; it is, as Arnie points out, an unproductive setting in which to accomplish a nightly reports session. We speak first about our adventure. Then, because Arnie insists he speak last, Frank and Randy take the floor to tell us about Edward Jinkins.

"Jinkins is watching us very closely. After he drove by here tonight for the third time, we got in my truck to see what he was up to." Randy tries to pace back and forth through the overcrowded living area. When he realizes there isn't enough floor space to accomplish this, he shifts from foot to foot as he continues.

"So he goes back to his home and stays there. One of the twins is home with him and the other one is at the office. Time goes by and off he goes to check on us again, this time on foot. He comes back. Then he goes off into the woods, where I assume he goes to the cabin. He's doing almost hourly surveillance of us. That's why I've closed the shades; the creep just keeps coming by."

"There's a bigger problem and that is that as our landlord Jinkins has a key to this trailer," Frank says. "So, he can come in here and snoop around whenever someone isn't here."

"Another complication," Sarah notes.

"Ah yes, a complication in that neither Arnie nor I should be here. Remember, we are both in hiding," Mohamed adds.

"Other than him spying on us constantly, did you learn anything more about Jinkins?" I ask.

"Sure did. We were listening in while he was talking with his daughter Kileen. They were arguing about the twin named Katie. Dad isn't happy with her, that's for sure. Anyway, he tells Kileen that Katie is the least of his problems because he was supposed to do something to both of our vehicles tonight and he can't finish the job because one of the cars isn't around." Randy picks up a small black plastic boxy unit. "This here is a GPS tracking device that I eventually found hidden on my truck. I guess Jinkins planted this one and has been lurking around trying to put one on Frank's SUV."

With GPS as the topic of conversation, it becomes Arnie's turn to talk. He puts his paperwork in a perfectly neat pile on his lap. When the pile goes off the slightest bit he straightens it a second time. Then he looks at each and every person in the room without making eye contact with any of us. It is as if he is memorizing who is sitting where. He clears his throat before beginning.

"My boss at the base, Dr. Chaves, called my cell phone quite unexpectedly. He claimed that he knew what had happened to me and wanted to help. He asked if he could pick me up. I, being untrusting at first, said no. I also insisted on keeping the call short so it could not be traced. Instead I made arrangements for him to meet me on the street near the base. I gave him a time and indicated I would be dropped off from a distance away. I also indicated that I wanted to get inside the base to retrieve my car. He agreed. I immediately left here for the meeting place. He got there early but I got there first. We then went to my office at the base."

"Did he seem okay to you?" Sarah asks.

"As you are all aware I am not accomplished in the field of analyzing personal behavior. To me, Dr. Chaves seems like he always is. When we were inside my office, it became apparent to me that he was just asking me questions rather than exchanging dialogue. Not one for a sense of communication oddities in complex situations such as the one I was in, I tested my boss by seeing how well he answered my questions."

"What did you ask him?" Frank asks.

"I asked who abducted me. He claimed he did not know. I asked how he knew I was abducted. He stated that when I never returned he reported it and he was told I was taken by an unknown person. When I asked what else he knew he claimed he knew nothing and was trying to figure out what was happening from questioning me."

"So he was trying to get information from you without providing you with any information?" Frank asks.

"Yes, it seemed to be this way. So, I played along with him. I asked him for something I knew was only on his computer. While he was retrieving it, I powered up my computer to see if I could access my work files. They were locked up. I then checked the work I'd secretly performed under another name. I gained access and found that some of the research I had created was completed. I copied that research on to this thumb drive. Taking every precaution, I destroyed my cell phone and threw it away. I took my car and drove to the cemetery to see if I would be followed. When I saw the military jeeps come, I ran away. Eventually I was found by the girls." Arnie takes the drive from his shirt pocket and says, "This should contain the personal histories of Alexi and Stefan Kulik. Shall we see what it says?"

Randy moves quickly to get his laptop. We all impatiently wait for the information to appear.

"Alexi and Stephen Kulik were both educated at Ivy League schools. Alexi majored in political science and military history. His younger brother, Stephen, majored in Russian studies. It seems that their choice in majors is what first caught the attention of Uncle Sam. We must remember that when these brothers were in college the threat of spreading communism was dominating the minds of Americans," Arnie pauses, as he scans over the words. "From what the file says it would seem that the government eventually came to believe that these brothers were not a threat, but rather could be an asset to the country. Yes, two Americans of Russian descent battling communism; it could be made into a political tool as far as some politicians were concerned. And so the brothers were employed by Uncle Sam after they graduated."

"How clever," Randy mutters.

Arnie tilts his head. "It says here that Alexi went into the military and became deeply involved in the Russian and Afghanistan War. He then became a key military advisor during the Cold War. He was a highly respected authority on anything to do with Russian military matters. He was rapidly promoted to general and became a superpower within the Pentagon. Although the tension between the United States and Russia lessened when the Cold War ended, General Kulik managed to retain his immense military power."

"Okay, so what about Stephen?" Frank asks.

"Let me see. Okay… it appears that Stephen was never as high in profile as his older brother. But his IQ is notably higher than the General's."

"What did he do for the government?" I ask.

"He worked undercover for the CIA. The files indicate he was in Moscow for quite some time. Then the files drop him. This is odd. It's like he disappears. Oh wait, here he is. It is years later when they pick him back up. It's noted that because of his 'work' he never marries nor has a family. He is then employed in an undercover capacity to infiltrate the Russian Mafia. He does so both in Russia and in the United States. He then disappears again. There is a notation in his file that he is no longer commissionable."

"As in he took sick with early onset Alzheimer's or senility or whatever is wrong with him," I add. "And now he's bumbling around in a nursing home in the suburbs of Boston starting to tell old secrets with Hickery Dickery Dock poems."

"So the Kulik brothers get themselves in tight with the government, but for reasons of greed, decide to become enemies of the United States rather than loyal citizens," Randy says. "General Alexi Kulik joins Eurabia because…"

"Belonging to this group enabled him to gain the power he needed to pull off his own plans to help out his homeland of Russia. It was the Eurabian politicians that helped him climb up the ranks of the military and become a general of immense power," Mohamed explains.

"General Kulik became empowered in the military and then he found out about Operation Tin Man. This research proved that the United States was responsible for many of the global warming problems of the world. So, using his power on the oversight committee in conjunction with his military power, he authorized a weather weapons storm on Boston. This wiped out the research that implicated the US in creating the global warming crisis while also demonstrated the power of the Weather Weapons Program to his Motherland; Russia."

Arnie rubs his hands together. "The General is indeed a genius. Over time he must have amassed the technology of the Weather Weapons Program. He told the Russians he has it but does not give it to them. Then he snuck out copies of Operation Tin Man. When the storm in Boston wiped out other evidence found in this research, it left Kulik with the only full set of data. Now he is ready to implement his plan."

"Which is?" I ask.

"He will sell the Weather Weapons Program to Russia while controlling its secret technology. He can use the Operations Tin Man information to blackmail the United States powers while he and his family escape to Russia. Then, regardless of what he promises, he will leak the Operation Tin Man reports to the media. Once it is known that the Weather Weapons Program is responsible for the global warming crisis, Americans will demand it be dismantled. This will leave only one of the United State's super powerful weather weapons program left operating on the planet: General Kulik's in Mother Russia."

"And the General is currently eliminating anyone who threatens to disrupt his plans," Mohamed notes. "Carlo Bertoni could link him to Eurabia; therefore, he was murdered. The General believes I can also link him to Eurabia; therefore, I too must be killed. Arnie must be eliminated because Kulik somehow discovered that he also has amassed information from various Operation Tin Man research sites that can prove the US weather weapons program caused global warming. The General can't risk Arnie having this knowledge, so he must be murdered. And now the four of you must be eliminated because…"

"Because we got ourselves involved with a very powerful and unexpected enemy." Sarah reaches for a can of cashews. She pops open the lid and sighs. "Okay, let's assume everything that was just said is true. Kulik has to kill his babbling old brother, and most likely Agent Brown, too. Maybe even some people at the Boston Cathedral like the bishop? If that takes care of 'the who' is there anywhere else the General needs to destroy?"

"Why, of course. Otis Military Base." Arnie cocks his head to the side and wrinkles his forehead. "There is not only Operation Tin Man research there. That is why I came to work there this summer; important parts of the weather weapons technology is also there."

This news causes everyone to start speaking at once. After a while, I reach over for Arnie's papers. Eventually I call the others to attention.

"This is a government file on Agent Brown; Agent Zachary Brown. He was an excellent student who majored in Russian studies. His intent was to become a diplomat at some point in his career. To this end he did some time in the military as an officer and then applied for a position in the CIA. Despite being more than qualified for the position he sought, the CIA did not hire him, but instead, he was mysteriously recruited by the Boston Homeland Security office. As you know, he is a man of much power here and has been for many years." I flip to the next page. "He and Alena met at government functions. This means her father, General Kulik, brought her to these events rather than his wife as his date. I'd call this an odd choice for a married man, unless of course, he was deliberately trying to match his daughter up with someone who would also be attending the event, like Zachary Brown. Alena and Zachary Brown marry after a short courtship."

"You think General Kulik deliberately had his daughter marry Agent Brown so he could then transfer him to Boston?" Randy asks Arnie.

"I don't know this Zachary Brown. But I believe having the head of Homeland Security unwilling to take harsh actions against family members who are also Russian traitors is, indeed, necessary for a betrayal of this magnitude to succeed." Arnie states.

"You don't think Agent Brown would turn his wife and father-in-law in as traitors? Of course he would!" I exclaim.

Frank stands. "I'm not so sure. Not if his children's lives are at risk. That's why there is a box of the children's clothes and medicine packed up in the Brown's garage. Someone, be it Alena or Zachary Brown, intends to kidnap the Brown's children. And I believe it will happen very soon."

Chapter 21
The Brown Family

I didn't fall asleep last night until I watched Ed Jinkins attach a GPS device onto Frank's SUV. Why this devious act helped me release my tension that built I'm not totally sure, but I think it has something to do with the overused psychological concept of closure. This morning I am the first one to wake. With sounds of heavy breathing, grunts, and snores coming from all around the trailer, I pause to reflect on how thankful I am that we are all alive. It wasn't so long ago when I was secretly leaving notes and money for Mohamed in an ancient cemetery. Back then I thought I was taking a big risk just being in contact with my fugitive brother. Now, he lies on the floor in one of the tiny bedrooms where he is neither really hidden nor protected. I realize that the risks we are all taking now are astonishingly brazen. But I know this is necessary because we are all too deep inside this web of espionage to break free without first winning the war against two very dangerous enemies; an evil Russian traitor and our own government.

"What are you doing up so early?" Frank whispers as he tiptoes by a sleeping Arnie. "I figured I'd get a head start on making plans for the day before anyone else awakened. I've been thinking about things all night. I'm convinced what we need to do now is focus on stopping General Kulik from escaping to Russia with the Weather Weapons Program. To do that, we need to get our hands on whatever he has that allows him to bring this technology to Russia while also keeping the U.S. Government under his control. We know he's blackmailing the government with the findings of the Operation Tin Man study. We also know he somehow has his hands on all the technology he needs to steal or develop a weather-based weapons system in Russia. We don't know what format this information is in, but we know where it is. It's below the cathedral in the tunnel. The clue to finding it is the number twelve. So…"

"The number twelve can hardly be called a clue. It's just a number that has no specific meaning," I remind my boyfriend.

"It does have meaning in the Catholic religion. Just like the number five is important to Muslims with the Five Pillars of Faith, the number twelve stands for the twelve apostles of Jesus Christ."

"That's right."

"I thought of it last night. My mom always told me those catechism classes would pay off some day."

"I remember you and Sarah complaining about catechism as kids. You had to take the religion classes to make your First Communion or something, right?"

"And Confirmation. The holy sacraments of the church." Frank shrugs off the memory. "I'm guessing the clue is hidden in a picture inside the cathedral. We find the painting with the apostles and we should find the clue, I think."

"Why would General Kulik allow a clue like that to still exist? As long as he and Alena know where the information is hidden, why leave a clue hidden inside the cathedral?"

"I was thinking about that all night. I finally came up with the answer; because they have no choice. I think the clue is there and it's not in their power to remove it."

This intriguing thought hooks my imagination much like a fish is hooked by a fisherman, in that I just can't break free of it. Even when our conversation shifts to the plans for the day I find different ideas about the apostle clue wandering into my thoughts. This continues to happen all morning, even after the others wake.

"Abby, do you agree?" Mohamed asks as he nudges my arm. "You have not been listening to the debate. Randy is suggesting that the GPS Jinkins placed on his truck be attached to a neighbor's car so it will appear as if the truck is moving without revealing its true location. The GPS attached to Frank's car will then be attached to Randy's truck. This will make it appear as if the SUV is at the craft fair park all day rather than off in Boston."

"Um, sure, that sounds right," I reply without actually giving the proposal a thought.

"What about all the plans for tonight's meeting at the baseball field?" Sarah asks. "Were you listening to them?"

"Kind of. I know we'll be prepared for whoever shows up and that basically, we have to play things by ear."

Frank shakes his head saying, "I know you can't stop thinking about the cathedral thing but we have to go check things out with Alena Brown before we can even think about going there, okay?"

"Alena Brown and the kids. Yup, I know. If we suspect she is attempting to kidnap her kids today we contact Agent Brown. Got it."

I half listen to Randy and Arnie review the list of what they need to take to the ball park today. When this is done Sarah speaks about some craft booth jewelry business with which she needs help. It isn't until I hear Mohamed's deep voice that I turn my attention from the cathedral back to the conversation.

"I must be hidden during the day. I also have no means of transportation. However, I plan on spending the day watching the Jinkins family, and if possible, making my way unseen to General Kulik's cottage. I will call for help should anything important develop on either front."

With everyone's plans set we begin the complicated routine of getting ourselves ready for the day. As the six of us share one bathroom, one tiny kitchenette, two private bedrooms to dress in, and a very limited amount of hot water, I wonder how efficiently we move about. I do not feel able to relax until I am alone with Frank in the SUV on the ride up to Boston.

Our first stop in Boston is the Brown house. We are disappointed to find that no one is home. Relying on the information Randy previously gathered, we then drive to Alena's gym. Her car is nowhere to be found. Next we travel to the shopping center she frequents. Her car is not at the grocery store or the pharmacy. We proceed to her daughter Brittany's dance school. The studio is located in a busy upscale strip mall. The front windows are decorated beautifully in the pink and white tones most people associate with ballet dancing. The decorations are arranged to prevent people from looking inside to watch the dancers. Even though Alena's car is not parked in the lot we feel we should verify whether or not Brittany is inside the studio, so I have no choice but to go inside and perform this task.

My dancing days began and ended when I was a very young child. According to my mother I was not only an unwilling participant in the dance troupe, I was also a major distraction to the girls who did want to dance. I only vaguely remember this experience but I do remember one thing about my childhood dance school that I despised: the mean old lady instructor who yelled all the time. And so, with fears of coming face to face with yet another intimidating dance professional, I quietly try to slip inside the studio unseen. The first thing I notice is the girls turning to see who has entered the studio. The second thing I see is a young woman instructor pointing for me to take a seat off to the side. The third thing I see is the area with chairs where mothers of the dancers have silently gathered. Wishing I were invisible, I slither to the appropriate location and slip down into a folding chair.

The dancers are of all different ages, sizes, and coloring yet they look astonishingly similar. Each of them is wearing dark tights with loose a fitting top. Their hair is either in a bun, a ponytail, or cut very short. Only a few stand out as being obviously not Brittany Brown. On closer observation I eliminate several other dancers. But, with only but memorized pictures of Brittany to refer to, I am unsure if she is dancing on the floor before me or not. Wanting to leave before I am asked why I'm here, I quietly make my way back to the exit. I pass by a heap of strewn duffle bags slowly hoping one of them will jump out at me as belonging to Brittany. Of course, no such luck occurs. But I do notice a door on the far side of the room which leads to, what I gather, is an associated business.

When I get to the door of the adjoining business I feel a tinge of hope sparking inside me. I can feel the atmosphere change as I leave the dance studio and enter what I can now see is a gymnastics training center. In front of me are boys standing on and hanging from various pieces of gymnastics equipment. And there, off to my right on the uneven bars, hangs a five-or-so-year-old Taylor Brown. I know it is him because not only do I recognize his little face from a picture Randy provided us, but also because he is wearing a football jersey t-shirt that says Brown on the back. I make my exit with little fanfare.

Frank is relieved to see me return to the SUV with a smile on my face. When I tell him that both of the Brown children are inside taking lessons, we sit back to wait and see who will arrive to pick them up. It doesn't take long before Zachary Brown himself drives into the mall. We duck down in the seat even though he doesn't drive near us. He gets out of his black agency car using the remote key fob to lock the doors. He pauses in front of the dance studio but then enters through the gymnastics center doorway.

"Stay here. I want to see what's inside his car." Frank dashes out before I can ask him what he expects to find. He whips around the black car quickly pausing for a brief moment at one of the rear windows.

"So?" I ask upon his return.

"The box from his garage is in the back seat. His trunk must be jammed with other stuff he needs them to have. He's kidnapping his kids...right now! Alena must have dropped them off and he's getting them before she comes to pick them up. I bet..."

"Look! The three of them are coming out of the dance studio door. The kids are carrying their stuff...they're not changed. The time...it's..."

"It's twenty-five of eleven. I bet their classes end at eleven or eleven-thirty." Frank starts the engine. "No other kids are leaving. Class isn't over for anyone except Taylor and Brittany Brown."

Frank quickly has the SUV a safe distance behind Agent Brown's car. We're not sure if Agent Brown was ridding himself of us or being hypervigilant to not be followed during the abduction, but his driving tactics make it impossible to stay on his tail.

*****

While waiting at the strip mall for Alena Brown to return for her children, Frank and I listen to the local news. As expected, the lead story is about the mysterious murder of Arnie's boss. Because Mohamed removed the planted evidence that would have made Arnie a primary suspect in this crime, the legitimate law enforcement officials have no leads as to who may be the murderer. We learn that the officials are trying to piece together information from the military base security footage, which, of course, both Arnie and I are on. Thankfully, neither of us has been mentioned on the news as of yet. It's being reported that information gathered from the base implies that Arnie's boss was selling top secret information to someone whom, the authorities believe he secretly met in the veteran's cemetery. It's suspected it was this person who murdered Arnie's boss in a deal gone bad scenario. We are discussing how ludicrous this story is when our waiting is finally over.

"Here's her car," Frank announces. "It's eleven thirty on the dot."

"Look. All the other kids are leaving the places now."

"Alena will flip out when she finds out they're gone. Then she'll go somewhere. It's the somewhere she goes next that matters."

"You should keep a safe distance behind her even though she'll probably be way too upset to notice us tailing her."

Frank nods. "She's in. So I give this a matter of a minute or so before the excitement begins."

Alena runs out of the dance studio door. She leans on her car for a solid minute, as if she is trying to pull her emotions together. Once inside her vehicle she gets on her cell phone. She drives as fast as she can in the Boston traffic; slowed by frequent stop lights, pokey drivers, and pockets of congestion. We are having no problem staying on her tail. She pulls into the strip mall where her gym is located. We park about fifteen spaces from her, which is where we sit and wait for a good five minutes before she leaves her car.

"I have to be the one to go in after her because she may be meeting someone in the ladies' locker room," I tell Frank, confident that he has no argument with this obvious fact.

Frank rolls his eyes and replies, "She's not here to work out. We both go inside."

"Don't you think that'll look obvious? It"s bad enough I don't have a membership card to get in, but with both of us getting tangled up at the entrance we'll lose her for sure. I'm thinking it's better for me to sneak in after her."

"Abby, think about this for a minute, okay? You're highly recognizable as Mohamed's sister. Do you really think you can just slip through unnoticed at any entrance that checks for identification?"

Since I can't argue this unpleasant fact I get out of the SUV saying, "No time to argue! Now she's on the move."

The gym building is quite large with coloring of a modern mix of dark blue and steely silver. I assume it is an expensive place to join as there are no signs announcing the price of membership or special discounts being offered. For reasons I'm unsure of, Frank stays a ways behind me while following me to the gym. At one point I stop to allow him to catch up. When he doesn't, I assume he has devised some type of plan and return my attention to Alena's behavior. Rather than go through the inviting front entrance, she enters the health club through a side door by swiping a badge in a card reader. She slips inside and the door slowly starts to close. Despite making a mad dash for it, it is already locked by the time I reach for the knob. I turn to Frank who shrugs his shoulders, again making no effort to join up with me. More frustrated than frightened, I march inside the building.

Standing cross-armed at the front counter is a muscular young man who barely notices me reading the signs that are on the wall above and behind him. As indicated at a countertop display, I pick up a visitor's badge. Barely making eye contact, the attendant mumbles that I need to give him ten dollars for the badge, which I eagerly give him. To authenticate my cover as a visitor I rent a towel for an additional $2.00. He rings up my transactions as if he's done it hundreds of times. His lack of attention to me is indeed helpful as I am not even carrying a gym bag. I wonder about his total disregard until I notice a set of blonde beauties sitting at the nearby juice bar. Their flashy white smiles and hair flipping flirtations convince me that the male attendant standing before me has much more on his mind than people coming in to work up a sweat.

Thinking that Frank will go through an identical route of easy passage, I wait for him in a nearby hallway. When a full five minutes pass by I assume he has made other plans. Luckily it doesn't take long for me to discover where the side door through which Alena entered is located. This section of the gym contains the offices as well as private rooms for massages and other such services. With my ear up against the doors, I listen for voices. I am straining to listen through a closed door when someone pushes the crash bar on the heavy door leading into this hallway. There is nowhere to hide other than inside an unoccupied room. Hoping my ears haven't failed me, I quietly open the door of what I believe to be a vacant massage room. I hear myself sigh with relief when I discover I am, indeed, alone. Through a crack, I watch a big muscle man with a fine collection of tattoos head my way. Although dressed very differently, he is the same man that I saw with Alena at Saint Theresa's Nursing Home. As he passes by, I notice his mouth and eyes are tight, almost as if he is grimacing. He walks to the largest office and forcefully pushes the door open. I hear the door smack up against something inside the room, presumably a piece of furniture. He doesn't close the door which allows me to hear him tell his visitor that he is not pleased she has come by. Then I hear Alena say, in a pleading tone, that she had no other alternative. Although she demands that he closes the door for privacy, it remains open.

"I told you to stop coming here. We agreed not to take chances like this..." the muscular man says.

"I came here because...because Zac took my kids... please...," Is what I make out of Alena's now deliberately hushed voice.

"What can I do about that? You don't need to be here. I never agreed to meet you or your father here. I gave you the door pass for emergencies only! I demand to have it back, immediately."

Alena makes another inaudible hushed response before she is silenced by what sounds like physical struggling. I can only assume the large, strong man is fighting for the door pass, although violence over such a small thing seems a bit extreme in my opinion. Somehow the door slams shut. I am debating whether or not I should dare to get closer to the room to listen to the argument or if I should stay in the safety of my hiding place when I hear the now familiar sound of the door at the entrance of the hallway opening. Having been in such stressful situations more times than I care to remember, I calmly hide from view and await the newcomer.

"Hey, what's going over here?" a very deep but definitely female voice hollers out. "I can hear you fighting in Workout Room C, through the damn walls. I'm trying to warm-up for my incoming class and..."

The muscular male steps into the hallway. With a half smile that I'm guessing would charm many females he says, "I'm having a few words with a...um...love interest if you know what I mean. I'm sorry. We'll take our business elsewhere."

"Whoa Mr. Dubkova, I didn't know it was you, sir. Hey, this is your place and I work for you so you can be yelling all you want, sir."

"No, it is not appropriate and I apologize. Now please return to your warm-up routine. The classes we offer here are very important."

"Okay, sir, whatever you say."

From this brief encounter I learned that Alena and her father are tied to the owner of this gym; Mr. Dubkova. I also learned that their partner has a Russian surname, a lot of muscles, and an enormous amount of charm. And from the way he calmly returns to Alena, this time quietly closing the door so I can't make out a word being spoken, I learn he is smart enough to get control of his temper when need be. I am still undecided about how to proceed when Frank tiptoes past me.

"How did you...." I begin to ask.

"No time for that. I slipped in when that girl came down. That guy...the owner...he was on his cell phone making plans with someone about going to the ball park tonight. Then the call was interrupted and I followed him down here. Is this where Alena went?"

"They're both in there. And he's not happy she's here."

"From what I just heard he and some other people will be meeting us at the park tonight. There was no mention of Agent Brown."

"Okay, so now that we know we're coming face to face with deadly Russian traitors tonight, what do we do now?"

Frank leads me inside a room that smells of herbal lotions and calming candle scents. A massage table stands in the direct center of the space; its light purple blankets smell of lavender.

"They're planning to get to the park two hours early tonight and kidnap you. Then they're going to use you to convince Mohamed to come out of hiding."

I shudder and say, "What'll that do?"

"Wait a second. Stay here while I listen through the door. Maybe they're saying more."

My stomach acids churn while Frank stands unhidden in the hallway. He periodically presses his ear even harder against the door which indicates to me that he can, in fact, hear something. As much as I'm tempted to have him return to the safety of the small and pleasant massage room, I am just as tempted to have him stay where he is to learn all that there is to learn. When sounds of moving furniture leak out from behind closed doors, Frank hurries back to me.

"This is really intense. They're planning to blackmail Mohamed into killing Agent Brown for them by threatening your life! Then, once Mohamed does that they're going to kill him too."

"This is...it's...diabolical. How can they pull off abducting me in such a public place?"

"They go to the ball park early figuring we'll be scoping out the place early too. Before we're totally prepared, they grab you. Then, to distract people from coming to your rescue, they have another surprise in store for us."

"Like what?"

"They know how to launch those mini fire tornadoes. They can't control a lot of them at one time but all they need is a couple to get everyone in the park hysterical."

I immediately picture the spinning fire cones whipping through scattered groups of people, craft booths, and the food area of the craft fair. As much damage as these horrid fire bombs can create, their effect is greatly intensified when people panic rather than work together to combat them. Having seen this exact reaction not long ago I shudder nervously.

"It would absolutely work," I say, resigning myself to the fact that our enemies have an arsenal of weapons far greater than anything we can acquire to battle them.

"Alena is pleading with muscle man to change the plan for tonight. She wants to get her husband there and use holding us and the crowd hostage to get her children back. Like she said in there, 'There is no use pretending Zachary and I are not on opposing sides anymore. His taking my children before I had a chance to send them to safety proves he knows more about me and my father than I wanted to believe.'"

"Will he go along with what Alena wants?"

"Not unless her father agrees. That's what all the arguing is about."

"So tonight we'll have fire laced mini tornadoes to deal with? How can we possibly fight that?"

Frank glances at the office door saying, "I don't know except that there are two people in there that may have to die for us to win tonight's battle."

Chapter 22
Complications Abound

It becomes obvious to me that it is more difficult for Frank and I to leave the gym without garnering suspicion than it was for us to sneak inside the private offices of this place. The first obstacle we face is that even after Alena leaves, muscle man Mr. Dubkova stays inside his office for quite a long time. I don't hear him talking, moving around much, or shuffling papers, yet he is busy doing something in his private quarters which keeps firmly planted in this space. When he finally heads upstairs, Frank and I take the opportunity to search his office for anything that ties him to the Kuliks and their diabolical traitorous scheming. Unfortunately, our efforts go unrewarded. On our way to the door in which Alena entered the building, we run into our second obstacle: a female employee toting a duffle bag. We quickly dash into an empty office to let this petite woman pass by and then wait for her to settle herself inside one of the massage rooms. Once we're convinced it is safe for us to again head out through the side door, we tiptoe down the hall. Frank cracks the door open, but instead of opening it so we can pass through, he gently closes it and pushes me back. Again we hide until another employee makes his way inside and prepares to work. After we finally escape, we decide that with Alena now off of our radar screen we should head for home. While Frank drives, I contact Sarah who gives me a detailed update on her day with Randy and Arnie. I then tell her about Agent Brown kidnapping his children and Alena's meeting with her burly gym-owning boyfriend. When I learn that she has been unable to get in touch with Mohamed all morning I feel my nerves starting to fray. When she reports that Randy has been by the trailer twice and my elder brother was nowhere to be found, my stomach churns. With thoughts of the Jinkins' family and General Kulik's cottage on my mind, I punch in the number of Mohamed's prepaid cell phone. As I expected, there is no answer. I don't need to convince Frank that we need to go to Kulik's cottage to check on him, because, like me, his instincts are telling him that my brother is in trouble.

We park the SUV on the side of a narrow lane near the cottage. Oddly, a slight ocean breeze coupled with the warm sun makes me feel a bit more relaxed. The scrubby bushes and plants along the road provide little cover for us as we make our way toward the cottage. My anxiety increases as it occurs to me just how exposed we are to anyone who should happen to pass by. Although I'm thankful we can move quickly to reduce the risk of being spotted, I secretly wish we could delay facing the horrors that await us inside the cottage.

"The General is here…or at least his car is. Look at the government license plate." Frank studies the small yard and says, "We can go to that big tree with the hammock under it. From there, we go to the shed. Then on to the patio. Got it?"

We set out together, casually jogging to the tree. Using the hammock as cover, I try to peek into a side window but I find it is dark due to a shade having been pulled down. I follow Frank to a spot behind the shed. In this semi-safe place I catch my breath. I look at the back of the cottage to study two small windows. They are also darkened. I then trot to the patio where I crouch behind a wicker couch. From this closer vantage point I can see there are shades blocking the view in every window.

"All the shades are pulled down. Something is very wrong in there. What if Mohamed is…hurt…or…" Unable to say what I truly fear I simply look up at Frank.

"What are we waiting for?" he says, seconds before he bolts to the back door of the cabin.

When I catch up with him I learn the back door is locked. I call Mohamed's name through the door. Even though I hear no verbal response, I'm sure I do hear something falling over inside. Frank wraps his hand in his jacket and then breaks the glass in the door window. We both stand quietly to listen for someone to respond to the noise this action creates. When no one does, he reaches inside the door only to find that it needs a key to be unlocked from the inside. Since this means we cannot open the back door to pass in or out, Frank leaves to check the front door. When he leaves me I strain to see inside the darkened cottage. I feel a warm pain as the window glass that is stuck in the door frame cuts into my leaning body. I hear another thing fall from inside the cottage making me believe that someone inside knows that we are here. On the side of the door I notice a fairly sizeable window. I drag a wicker chair to it, hoping that if I break the glass I can get inside. Suddenly, Frank is behind me, explaining that the front door is locked and also needs a key to open. When he sees what I'm planning to do he immediately picks up the patio table and uses its legs to shatter the glass. Bloodied and full of sweat, I watch Frank remove glass from the window frame as quickly as he can. He then helps me keep steady on the chair as I pull myself up and through the window. I land inside the cottage on a hard floor. Scrambling in the darkness, I tear at the window shades to allow the light to guide me to who I hope and pray is my brother.

I enter the living room totally unprepared for the butcher scene the light reveals to me. There, splayed out on the floor, is Stephen Kulik's dead body. He has bloodied holes in his chest from where he's been shot multiple times. I am staring at the corpse when I hear a piece of metal clanging to the floor. This time I'm close enough to realize the noise is coming from the room at the front of the cottage. I force myself to walk by the corpse despite a rubbery feeling in my legs. The nasty sight mixed with the hot stale air inside this place has me sweating profusely. As I pass through the hall, I reach up to lift the shade on a window. When my eyes adjust to the bright sunlight I make out the shape of my brother. His back is toward me and he is strapped to a chair that is secured to a heavy oak bed but I am sure it is him. I rush to his side as he frantically jerks about. On the floor near him are the objects he managed to knock over to get my attention; including a lamp, a brass candlestick holder, and a thick book.

I carefully remove the gag from his mouth expecting his first words to be those of thanks and love for me. Instead he says, "We've got to get out of here. Jinkins did this; Ed Jinkins! Now he's off planting a jar candle that belonged to Stefan Kulik in our trailer to make it look like one of us did this!"

"What? Why did he kill Stefan Kulik and steal his dumb candle?"

"That isn't just an ordinary candle. Apparently Stefan has very rare and valuable coins hidden inside the candle wax. This explains why he rarely actually burnt the candle, which was a quirk of his that was well known at the nursing home. It seems that some people figured out the candle wax is really a hiding place of sorts although they didn't know what Stephan was hiding in it is worth millions. Of course, now that you and Frank have been seen by many witnesses at the nursing home visiting with Stefan, a plan was put into place to make it look like you hunted him down, found him here, killed him, and stole the candle and its valuable contents."

"So we're being framed for killing the old man for something hidden inside the candle? Okay, that's problem number one. Now, you said Ed Jinkins killed Stefan, right? And he locked you up here?"

"It is clear to me now that Ed Jinkins knew I was staying with you and in the cottage for some time now. He found me while I was in the woods walking to his home to check on him and the girls. He took me by surprise; I was not on my guard as I should have been. Then he drugged me and brought me here. He intends to come back for me very soon. In fact, I am quite surprised he is not yet back here."

"Where does he plan to bring you?"

"To his boss, General Kulik."

"Okay, we better get out of here before he returns. Frank is outside."

It is quite a struggle for me to untie Mohamed's hands but once this is accomplished he unbinds his own ankles. His legs wobble a bit when he stands. "Now that this has happened we have no choice but to...silence Jinkins. I am sorry to have to tell you this."

I don't verbally respond to my brother's remark but my gut silently churns at the though of a dead Ed Jinkins on my conscience.

Mohamed is climbing out of the cottage's back window when I notice that his face and arms are bruised. When he drops down to the ground he stumbles, indicating to me that his legs have also been beaten. With no time to waste asking about his injuries, Frank and I lead Mohamed to the parked SUV. Frank glances over at me when the white vehicle comes into view. For a brief moment hope of a successful escape seems probable, until moments later, coming from an invisible source, bullets blast toward the three of us. Frank and I instinctively retreat. Mohamed limps after us at a much slower pace. I turn back to help my brother, not knowing if Frank is following me or continuing forward. The bullets whiz over me as I crawl over the dirt road. Somewhere along the way the shooting stops. I slowly rise.

"What's happening?" I whisper.

"It could be a trap. Jinkins may be pretending he gave up just so we go to the SUV to check it out. Once we're back there he'll start shooting again," Frank suggests.

Mohamed nods saying, "He may simply be reloading his weapon. We need to continue to run."

We are about to do so when, from behind the SUV, a tall man holding his hands out in front of him appears. His empty hands assure us he is not armed so we wait for him to come closer. I can tell by his build he is not Ed Jinkins. Then, slowly his body shape becomes familiar. I then recognize the mystery man.

"Agent Brown?" I yell out. "What? I mean how? Um..."

I feel Frank's protective arm take hold of my shoulder. Panic ripples through me when it occurs to me that my fugitive brother is with us. As much as I try not to be so obvious, I turn around to see if Mohamed is still in sight.

"Yes, Abby, I know all about Mohamed. I am not nearly as stupid as you seem to think I am. I have my reasons for allowing him to be with you. I've had those reasons for quite some time now. I also have my reasons for letting him go freely with you today if you fully cooperate with me now…and quickly." Agent Brown looks past me at Mohamed and asks, "How badly are you hurt? Do you need medical attention?"

"No. Jinkins did not want to harm me too badly. I suspect he was told to save that privilege for someone else." Mohamed limps toward the agent. "I believe, sir, I owe you a debt of gratitude."

"I suspect I owe all of you some gratitude as well." Agent Brown turns his attention to Frank and me. "So what would you have done if I didn't take my children from the dance studio? What would you have done if Alena came back for them?"

"We would've called you. We knew what her plans were at that point. I guess you did too," I reply.

"I did. And what else do you know?"

"We know many things that we do not have time to explain in detail right now. Frank can highlight them quickly, but we must meet later. We must also get evidence that…" Mohamed says.

"I have the candle Jinkins planted in your trailer. Whatever was once inside the wax has been removed. I assume because this planted candle has Stefan Kulik's name on it and you're here that Stefan is inside the General's cottage?"

"Sort of, he's dead. Jinkins killed him and is trying to pin it on us. Frank and I went to see Stefan at the nursing home he was in, so making it look like we murdered him is a believable plan," I reply.

The agent looks at Frank. "Update me quickly. Then I'll give you the candle. I want you three to hide it somewhere in case we need it. Help me get Jinkins body to the cottage and then get out of here. We'll make plans to meet later. I'll take care of whatever murderous mess is inside Kulik's cottage."

Frank is about to begin talking when Agent Brown turns to Mohamed. "I have to know for sure, did you know I was protecting you from my own agency?"

"Yes, but I didn't understand why." Mohamed looks deep into the agent's eyes as if he is trying to read his thoughts while hearing his words.

"You will learn why later."

Mohamed walks closer to Agent Brown. He retrieves a small dirty plastic box from his pocket; an old pill case. He hands it to Agent Brown and says, "Kulik and Alena planned to abduct me and then threaten to kill Abia if I did not assassinate you. When I learned of this plan earlier today, I stole these from Ed Jinkins' car. There are enough narcotics inside this case to kill me. I would have killed myself before I killed you."

The silence that follows Mohamed's revelation says far more than

Frank's ensuing explanation of all we have learned about General Kulik and his evil plans.

*****

As soon as we are back at the trailer I call the others. Sarah, Randy and Arnie are relieved when we tell them how we joined forces with Agent Brown. I thought Randy would be upset to lose complete control of our mission, so when he tells me that he is glad I instantly know something is not going well at the baseball park. Since I am unable to get any details from him about any ensuing problems, I have Frank speak to him. Soon Frank walks out of the small living room area, leaving Mohamed and me to wonder what secret my boyfriend is hiding from us. With hopes that my imagination is conjuring up far worse disasters than what really is happening, I impatiently wait for an explanation.

Frank puts down his phone and sighs. "It seems that Sarah is having an emotional melt down. She was fine until the little league kids showed up for the first game to be played at the ball field. When she saw these innocent children she started flipping out about what would happen to them and others like them if they were around when the weather weapon storm hits tonight. She's right. There are all sorts of activities planned at the fair tonight which means tons of kids will be there. Fire will surely kill some of the children who are in the path of these flaming twisters."

"I don't want to imagine the damage a storm such as that which hit Boston would do in a park full of families. I am hoping it won't come to that. I am hoping that our enemies will only release such a storm if needed, and that somehow, we can prevent them from doing so." Mohamed pulls back the window curtain to look out into the street. "Perhaps Agent Brown can help prevent this catastrophe. He should be here soon."

"It's too late to totally prevent it." Frank nervously bites at his fingernails. "According to Arnie, who is monitoring air pressure and all sorts of weather science readings, the storm has already been set in motion. The sky above the park is turning that weird gray color. Clouds are forming, too. We should be starting to feel the change in weather here very soon."

"Sarah has to stay at her booth for Alena and the General to believe everything is on track. We can't let her leave now. I can calm her down. I know I can but to do so I have to be with her," I say in a more confident manner than I truly feel.

"Let's hope so. Randy and Arnie completed all the preparations in the ball field that they could before the first game was about to start so Randy has been with her and he says she's inconsolable." Frank spits out a fingernail and adds, "She's going to be even more upset when the enemy starts to show up. She's already imagining they're being watched now. She's totally paranoid."

"Well, it is four o'clock, so maybe some of the enemies are there. They did plan on getting there early," I suggest.

"That is a valid point. Since their plan is to abduct Abby, then they are not sensitive to time. In fact, they may not actually plan to meet with either of you at all. It is more likely they will take Abby as quickly as they can. Perhaps, they intend to start the storm early so that there will already be chaos at the park when Abby arrives making it all the easier to abduct her. Does this not tie in with such an early start to the storm?" Mohamed backs away from the window. He sits beside me. "Abby, I do not think you should go to the park at all tonight. Yes, I understand they are expecting you, but now that we know they plan to abduct you to blackmail me I think it is best if you hide where they cannot find you. It is best to play it safe."

Before I have a chance to argue against this proposition, Frank is agreeing with my brother, making it two strong opinions against one. We are in the midst of a heated debate when Agent Brown walks inside the trailer unannounced. His hair is disheveled, his clothing rumbled and his shoes full of dry dirt. He wipes his feet on the mat as he listens to tidbits of our discussion.

"There's no need to argue as to who will do what this afternoon into tonight. I have everything figured out. First and foremost, I will take care of the park including the brewing weather storm attack. I have a plan to evacuate the area before the storm hits. My plan will also trick Alena and her father into believing that you were there waiting for them just as you told them you would be. I will then have my wife and father-in-law chase after some of my agents that I will have dressed up to look like you. While they follow the decoys, Randy, Arnie, and Sarah will be safe."

"How will you do that?" I ask.

"There will be a sighting of Mohamed Haddad in the park this afternoon. He will be seen with two people who fit both of your descriptions. The entire Homeland Security force and military back-up from the Otis base will be out looking for you three. Of course, none of you will be anywhere near the park. Having you around is a risk I simply cannot allow. In fact, you will not be on Cape Cod at all."

"And where will we be?" Frank asks.

"Doing the one thing that only you can do and doing it when the enemy will not be anywhere around to bother you." Agent Brown stoops down to open up a neatly packed and well stocked tool box. "You'll be underneath the Boston Cathedral looking for the Operation Tin Man evidence and whatever my father-in-law has in regard to the technology of weather weaponry."

*****

The entire drive up to Boston is dominated by communication with Randy. It seems that Arnie is too obsessed with weather readings to speak on the phone and Sarah is too shaken up to speak much at all. What is making our situation difficult is that in order to make the plan believable, Agent Brown can not show up at the park until after the so-called Mohamed sighting is set into motion. We are all the way to Boston and on the city streets when Randy reports that this has happened. He describes an influx of law enforcement, some in uniform and some in plain clothes, sweeping through the park. He reports that they seem to be trying to prevent a panic while simultaneously searching for America's number one fugitive. He then describes how he and Sarah are being watched so closely that he feels it best to end the call which he then abruptly does.

I put my cell phone away and refocus my attention to Mohamed and Frank's conversation. I notice they seem to be very much in agreement on how to handle situations; therefore, I don't even bother offering out my opinion. As much as I don't like the idea, I agree to drop the men, the backpacks, and the tools off behind the cathedral and go off to park the SUV. Their plan is to find a way inside the cathedral before I get back. Relieved that no one seems to have noticed the drop-off, I drive to the front of the cathedral, which I find has white flowers and garland decorating the majestic stone stairs to the entrance door. Two limousines parked in front of the building confirm that there must be a wedding going on inside. After driving around for a short time, I realize the size of this wedding must be quite large because there are no parking spaces anywhere nearby. Panic begins to rumble my stomach when I can't find even an illegal spot four blocks away from the cathedral. As I was taught as a child, I resort to deep breathing to keep myself calm. Unfortunately, the breathing exercise becomes increasingly less effective as more time passes. I am barely able to control my frustration when I head the car back toward the cathedral. Praying to a nameless Catholic patron saint of parking spaces, when I don't even know if one exists, I weave back through the streets through which I've just been. As if the nameless saint has indeed answered my prayers, a space is about to open up before me. A young mother is coaxing her child into the back seat of her van while balancing a toddler on her hip. I have to wait until the family is all strapped in and on the road for the space to be available, but just knowing I have succeeded keeps my patience in check.

I silence my cell phone as I walk to the cathedral, noticing that almost fifteen minutes have passed since I dropped the men off. Relieved to be at my destination, I carefully duck into the darkened alcove behind the cathedral. Neither Frank nor Mohamed are there. I frantically look around for a note, a backpack, a tool, or anything that tells me they will return to this spot for me. I realize that for some unknown reason I have been deserted.

Chapter 23
Plans Gone Wrong

Alone behind the cathedral fighting an escalating panic attack, I force myself to think logically. If just Mohamed was missing from this dark alcove it could be that he was afraid of being recognized by someone who may have spotted him. After all, Agent Brown has set up a fake manhunt for him on Cape Cod making it likely his face is on news broadcasts at this very moment. For that matter, Agent Brown has orchestrated the search to include Frank and me, who, supposedly, are with Mohamed. Therefore, it is also possible Mohamed and Frank are not here because of the staged search on Cape Cod. But, if we have theoretically been seen on Cape Cod, then why would anyone in Boston believe they're seeing Mohamed or Frank here in this city? No, this doesn't make a lot of sense. Okay, then I can assume that their absence is due to the unexpected wedding ceremony. Or, perhaps an opportunity to get inside availed itself and the Frank and Mohamed pounced on it. Yes, that could be as well.

After careful consideration I decide to check the side door of the cathedral. My hopes that the Frank and Mohamed have found their way inside and await me there are not high because if this were the case, one of them would surely come out to find me. The sound of organ music seemingly leaks out of the cathedral during my short walk up the sidewalk. Before I try to open the side door I wait for there to be no cars around. I give the door a hard tug, and of course, it is locked. I remind myself that the wedding ceremony itself may be the cause of our plans going wrong. Temporarily placing myself inside the cathedral I imagine the observant guests who could be wandering about inside, or people standing near the side altar where the exit door is located, or perhaps the bride and groom are about to exchange vows, whereby any noise at all would be extremely noticeable. With nothing else to do, I continue on to the front of the massive stone structure.

The limousine drivers are chatting in front of the white flowery garlanded stone steps. The smell of the flowers floats in the slight breeze adding to the ambiance of this beautiful wedding scene. Again I here the organ pipes roaring. This time the tune is the traditional "Here Comes the Bride" song. As if by magic, the doors to the cathedral open and I see the bride and groom standing in front of the altar. They walk down the long aisle as if they are royalty. The guests clap, cry and laugh; surely no one will notice me regardless of how poorly I am dressed for such an occasion. Once the receiving line forms on the front steps, I politely wiggle my way up through the descending guests. Using one of the side entrance doors, I'm able to get inside where just a few straggling guests are scattered about. I pretend I have important business to attend to while I march past the pews. I reach the side altar door I need to pass through to get to the stairs that lead to the bottom level of the cathedral feeling confident. I am about to step through to the back side of the building when a quiet but growing sense of foreboding convinces me to sit in a pew before continuing on. I slide inside a pew and kneel on a kneeler as if I've done this many times before. With my head bent down, I look around for anything that will help me decide what I should do next. Five minutes pass and almost all of the lagging wedding guests are gone. Less than a minute later and I am completely alone.

Convinced now is the time to make my move, I push myself up on shaky legs. I fight for my bravery to come like an athlete fights for the strength to win a race. The side door creaks open; a sound I don't recall hearing the last time I was in this place. Once I'm amid the familiar world of the Stations of the Cross, I stand still and listen for any sound that can lead me to where I should go. At first I hear nothing but inside silence and distant sounds of outside activity. After taking a deep breath I take twenty-two steps down the hall hoping that if I get closer to the offices in the rear of the building some sort of clue will present itself. Once again I stop. I glance to my right at another Station of the Cross and make eye contact with the tortured face of the man named Jesus. I briefly wonder if this person was indeed the son of God. This one second of silent wonderment is long enough for me to notice a familiar humming sound. Like a wild animal fearing hunters, I stay perfectly still and listen until I know where the sound is coming from. I follow it to the end of the hallway and peek around the corner into the row of offices. The humming is clearer now and recognition of it begins to take shape in my mind. I picture my mother sitting at her antique roll top desk reviewing the case files of some of her more troubled patients. I can hear her humming this same exact tune. It's some old Arabic lullaby she claims she sang to us as children. I don't remember being soothed by it as a baby or young child, but I certainly remember hearing her hum it now and then when she was engrossed in work of some kind. This could only mean that Mohamed is down here somewhere and that he is trapped.

Focused totally on where the humming sound is coming from I am startled by the differing harsh sound of clanging keys. An adrenaline rush sweeps a healthy dose of bravery inside me. From around the corner, I zero in on a gruff looking older man listening through the door of what I remember to be the office of the worker with the briefcase named Maureen.

"Stop the singing. Don't know who you are and what you want but knock off the noise. What's that about anyway? Huh? Is someone else snooping around in here too? You just pipe down until the bishop gets here. You're lucky he wants to see you before I call the bloody cops, that's all I got to say." The older man kicks the office door, fumbles around for a lighter, and then stokes up a smelly cigar.

To keep from becoming overwhelmed, I focus on a short term goal which is to get a key to the office where Mohamed is being held prisoner. I silently congratulate myself for remembering to bring the key to the vestment closet that I stole the last time I was here. Remembering the board with the hanging keys inside this closet, I tell myself a key to Maureen's office must be here somewhere. With my sights set on getting to this location, I retrace my steps back to the main part of the cathedral. I make quick and steady progress across the building pausing only briefly before the intimidating ornate altar which is overcome with wedding flowers and banners. When I reach the closet I find it locked but my key gets me inside with no problems.

"Abby." I hear Frank whisper from behind the hanging vestment. "Get in here and tell me what's going on. Is Mohamed still being held prisoner? "

"Yes, and some old guy is guarding him."

"He's waiting for the bishop. He's the maintenance man in this place. We've got to get Mohamed out of there before the bishop gets here."

"How do you suggest we do that?"

"It looks like we have to fashion weapons out of what we have inside this closet. Then we go rescue him."

"Like this thing? What is this anyway?" I hold up a tall thin metal pole that I find leaning against the wall.

"I believe that is an Advent wreath stand where a candle is placed for every week of Advent. There are four holders for these candles and one in the center for Christmas..."

"Don't need the Catholic lesson. It's pointy so it'll be a decent weapon. Let's see what else we have in here."

"This altar flower vase is heavy. It doesn't have a long reach but it has a big kick."

"It's long enough, that thing is at least three feet," I comment while switching the pole for the vase. "You use the pole to get the guard off his game and then I'll knock him down with this thing."

Together we tiptoe to the end of the hall. Frank peeks around the corner and gives me a thumbs up indicating that the old man is in position to be attacked. Momentarily, Frank lunges forward. Rather than make a wild beast roaring sound, as the heroes in movies always seem to do, he sort of slithers up to the old man unseen and then clocks him over the head.

"What in blazes?" the old man screams out.

I hit him a second time with the vase. This time his knees buckle as he collapses. When I am sure the old man is alive I say, "Please forgive us but we need to do something and we can't have you interfering with us. So, we have to get you out of the way."

"Are ya gonna kill me?"

"Don't be ridiculous. Of course not."

I hear the door open and I look up. Mohamed claps Frank on the back before looking down at the floor where the old man is with me. "We're taking him with us. When the bishop gets here and doesn't find him he'll be too confused to know what to do next. That'll give us time to get done what we need to do."

The old man squints up at Mohamed. "Which is what?"

"We can't tell you that. In fact, we can't even let you know where we're going. Believe me, it is for your own good that you remain ignorant of our activities here. While I was your prisoner I took the liberty of fashioning a gag and a blindfold out of a scarf I found in your co-worker's drawer. Ah, and I also discovered the location of the altar wine."

"What you need that for? Having a cordial drink are ye?" the old man snaps.

"Not me, I never touch the stuff. But you are going on quite a bender tonight. In fact it will be one so intense you'll have difficulty remembering your own name never mind where you've been!"

Turning to Frank and me, Mohamed says, "I have also solved the mystery as to why this office, the one belonging to the woman named Maureen, is the only one locked up at night."

"I couldn't even find the key in the closet for this office," Frank says. "What is going on with her?"

"I don't know what is actually going on with her personally, but I do know she had these locked up in her files. They are maps of the tunnels beneath the cathedral. One leads to the waterfront. As we discussed, it was used to smuggle alcohol in and out of the city during Prohibition. The other tunnel leads to somewhere of much more intrigue: the Cyclorama building. The reasons for this are, I expect, more complicated. But for now, we must deal with this maintenance man."

*****

After struggling with our belligerent and surprisingly powerful captive for some time, we realize that our plan to bring him below ground and force feed him enough alcohol to intoxicate him to memory loss isn't going to work. Unfortunately, it's taken precious time for the three of us to draw this painful conclusion. With the bishop's expected arrival now estimated to be no more than ten minutes away at best, I look down at the gagged and bound elderly man in sheer frustration. Even though the steps to the lower level of the building are just a few feet away, there is simply not enough time for us to get this wiggling man hidden below ground before the bishop arrives for the meeting.

"Desperate times call for desperate measures," I announce. "We have to knock him out, plain and simple."

Frank nods, saying, "Dead weight will be easier to handle than defiant weight."

"I'm afraid you are right. Perhaps a concussion will be easier to recover from than a severe hangover," Mohamed adds.

Our agreement on what needs to be done does not, however, lead to action. On my part I am fearful to hurt this man because he is so old any blow to the head could kill him. I imagine Frank and Mohamed feel the same way although they aren't voicing their thoughts. Fearful another five minutes will pass without action, I hand the altar flower vase to Mohamed and turn away. After a drawn out period of silence I hear the sound of the vase cracking against the old man's skull and then a thud as his body goes limp onto the floor. When I turn around Mohamed hands me the vase; his face is sullen but determined. Frank helps Mohamed hoist the elderly man up and carry him below. I follow behind them, closing doors and erasing evidence of out escape to the tunnel. The silence of the old man bothers me but I don't dare ask if he's still breathing, knowing that if he isn't I may lose control of my emotions. We pass by the chapel frescoes and into the tunnel area quicker than I had hoped. Since there is no sign of the bishop anywhere, I judge our escape to be a success.

"Now that we're here, how do we go about looking for the evidence about Operation Tin Man? The only clue we have from the painting we found at the General's cottage is that the time on the clock said twelve o'clock. So, what down here screams out twelve?" Grateful that my question seems to have changed the solemn atmosphere I add, "Frank, you said something about twelve apostles?"

"Yes, the twelve apostles. I have a list of them in my pocket." Frank flashes light on the doors of the three rooms. "That is just a wild guess. The Operation Tin Man stuff could very well be in the locked rooms."

Mohamed stands before the rooms saying, "Staring from left to right we have a room with dead bodies, a room with evidence that these tunnels were used during the Prohibition, and a room with a small modern day military arsenal. As intriguing as the identity of the dead bodies may be, I do not believe they will lead us to the location of the hidden Operation Tin Man evidence. As for the Prohibition-related stuff, excellent information to use to blackmail the Catholic Church, certainly, but not useful to us at this time. The military weapons…ah…we have learned this arsenal is used to make payments for crimes committed by murderers in need of superior military grade weapons. No, there are no secrets hidden within these walls."

"Then where do you suggest we look?" Frank asks, his head leaning to the right in a questioning pose. "You've spent more time down here than anyone else in the group, so where else is there for us to explore?"

"The tunnels?" I point at a deteriorated but still functional brick archway. "It's pitch black in those tunnels and all we have are three flashlights. Is that enough light to get to where we need to go?"

"The main tunnel branches off into two smaller ones. The one to the left I am a little familiar with. It is the one that leads to the water. I've never been in the other tunnel; however, I'm convinced that is where we will find what we are looking for." Mohamed bends down near the old man. "We cannot take him with us. Although he is acting as if he is still unconscious, I believe he is starting to awaken."

"Then what do we do with him?" I ask. "The bishop could call the police and report him missing and…"

"It has not been long enough for a missing person's report to be filed with law enforcement," Mohamed states. "We have time before that particular complication needs to be addressed."

"When we are sure the bishop has been here and is gone, we can lock him up somewhere within the cathedral. Then, when we are done with our mission, we can release him," Frank says.

"He knows too much," Mohamed says, his voice void of emotion.

Preferring not to hear more details about the maintenance man dilemma, I say, "I'll sneak up and check that the bishop isn't here. By now he should have been here and left, I'd think. Then I'll look for a place to hide the maintenance man. There's a kitchen on the lower level, which I'm guessing will have a pantry of some sort. Maybe there's a good place in there."

When neither Frank nor Mohamed makes an effort to stop me, I scramble back up to the lower level of the huge cathedral. I detour to the kitchen area where I get an eerie feeling that I've entered a time warp and have been transported back to the 1950s. The stove, refrigerators, and counter appliances are white porcelain with heavy silver metal bars and knobs. The surfaces where paint has chipped off these old relics have a dull black finish, revealing the sturdy metal below the pretty paint. On my way to a closet, I run my hand over the lime green linoleum counter top wondering who chose this color and what the reasoning was behind the choice. The closet door opens easily. Inside I smell a mix of spices, flour, and sugar which I assume are sugars. Hanging above my head is a chain, which, when I pull it, lights up an unadorned light bulb. This closet is a pantry; its shelves are fully stocked with canned and dry goods. The pantry floor is worn and dull, but remarkably clean. I mentally assess this tiny room as an excellent place for the old prisoner to be kept while we explore the tunnel.

Next, I tiptoe up to the main level of the building. My stomach churns more with each step I take. I crack open the door where the hallway with the Stations of the Cross are and listen for sounds. I find it amazing how many noises one hears in a silent building. I enter the hallway slowly and I carefully close the door behind me. Then I steal a look into the main cathedral area. I don't see anyone. I drop down low and inch into the side altar area for a more thorough inspection. No, there is nobody in sight. This leaves the office area in the rear of the building. To ensure the second hallway is also clear, I decide to use it to get to the offices. I crack the door open, listen, and peek in before slipping into it. I feel my confidence building with every step I take. I reach the end of the hallway and stop to listen. Again, I hear nothing but building sounds. I prepare for the cursory corner glance when I hear the low but audible buzzing of a cell phone that has been put on silence. I instantly fill up with terror realizing that it must be my phone. I slide the phone from my pocket and finger the button to shut it off completely when I notice a text message from Frank.

"Help."

It instantly occurs to me that the bishop must be with the Frank and Mohamed in the tunnel below the cathedral. Having had our plans thrown into a complete frenzy so many times already tonight, I manage to proceed to the tunnel with a peculiar sense of de-ja-vu. It seems that, as far as tonight goes, I've come to accept that whatever is about to happen must be predestined to be so. The now familiar trail down to the tunnel is quiet. When I reach the bottom I find Frank nervously pacing at the bottom of the stairs. Behind him is Mohamed. He is pointing a military style rifle at the bishop and the cathedral custodian.

"I know this isn't at all as we planned, but it's where we are now. The bishop figured we were down here. He's known about the tunnel all along. He's…" Frank begins to explain.

"My children," the bishop says in a soft spoken calm voice. "There is nothing that has happened that cannot be undone peacefully. There has been no real harm. Jack here," he gently rubs the back of the sitting janitor, "Jack has not been seriously injured. Yes, he is an older gentleman, but he is quite hardy, as many of the old Irish are. We can blame any injury he has on a fall. He can be thoroughly trusted to remain quiet about the events of tonight if I ask him to be. He has been keeping secrets for me for a very long time."

Mohamed opens his moth to speak, but says nothing. Frank is also silent.

"Okay, Bishop…" I start.

"I am Bishop Sullivan."

"What do you know about Eurabia and Carlo Bertoni and how they used this tunnel to hide after the federal agents busted up the group six months ago?"

My no-nonsense direct approach does not disturb the bishop at all. He answers without pause.

"I am aware of them and all that occurred here below the holy cathedral."

"Why did you help them?"

"I had no choice. The history of the Boston diocese has been intertwined with that of the New England mafia for decades. To keep this from becoming a public scandal, in a time when the Mother Church cannot withstand yet another scandal of such magnitude, I have had to continue cooperating with these criminals. It is through Carlo Bertoni that the cathedral was dragged into the Eurabia treachery. It was through Eurabia that we have become embroiled in General Kulik's evildoings."

"Do you know who we are?"

"Of course. He is Mohamed Haddad and you are his sister Abia. This is your boyfriend, Frank Stiller, I believe. You have all made national news today. Of course, you are supposedly on Cape Cod…"

"We're on the news?"

"Ah yes, which is why when Jack, yes… the man you have captive with me is named Jack, which is why when he was missing I didn't expect to find any of you below with him."

"Why did you come down here if you didn't know what to expect?"

"I have nothing to fear. Carlo Bertoni is dead at the hands of General Kulik. Mohamed was reported to be on Cape Cod and General Kulik needs me too much to harm me. There is no one else who I am aware of who comes here."

At this point Mohamed cuts in, asking, "Okay, so what business do you think I have down here?"

The bishop rests his hand on the seated old man. "I do not know but I pray that it will somehow free Jack and myself from the clutches of General Kulik's blackmailing iron grip."

"How do we know we can trust you?" Frank asks.

"How do you know you can not?" The bishop replies demurely.

"Okay, then tell us this. What is in these locked rooms," Frank challenges the Godly man.

"In one room is proof of the Prohibition activities of the cathedral. In another room are weapons used to make payment to murderers and other such criminals, an arsenal worth hundreds of thousands of dollars. And, in the room to the far left are bodies of the deceased."

"Who are they and who killed them?" I ask.

"General Kulik killed them. Some are scientists that gave him the information he needed to steal the Weather Weapons Program for his homeland of Russia. Some are soldiers who learned of his traitorous plans. Some are law enforcement, others are his henchmen who became too knowledgeable. And, if I may add, there are spots and odor containing bags reserved for you and your friends inside this room. Ah yes, my children, it seems you have angered the General immensely. He informed me there are five spaces to be filled." Turning to Mohamed the bishop adds, "But not for you, my friend. No, he expects the government will kill you after you kill his son-in-law, Agent Zachery Brown of Homeland Security." Turning to face the three of us he adds, "Now, have I not proven that I am eager to rid us all of this most evil and dangerous criminal?"

Chapter 24
Catholic Confession

The bishop has the appearance and demeanor of a truly holy man, or at least what I imagine such a person to be. He is neither old nor young; to me he just appears to be wise. He is tall, but not extremely so. He is neither fat nor thin, but in a word, proportioned. His facial features are pleasant with a soft forgiveness built into their creases. His eyes are not striking but melting soft, the exact same type of eyes that made me fall in love with Frank. His voice seems to wind him up all together with its calm, reassuring, and loving tones. He moves with the gracefulness of a dancer; his hand gestures sweeping about him in an almost mesmerizing fashion. He seems to me to be on the brink of unworldly, as in part of him has already passed over to heaven or wherever our souls go when we die.

Feeling sure that the bishop means us no harm, I gesture to Mohamed to lower his weapon. He does so, although reluctantly. When I ask Frank to untie Jack, Mohamed gives me a warning glance but says nothing.

"You seem to know more about us than we know about you and this place. Where does the cathedral's history with the crime element of New England begin?" I ask.

"It began locally, with the mafia in Boston during the Prohibition. The mafia knew the cathedral had a tunnel to what is now the Cyclorama building on Tremont Street. The reasons this tunnel was made dates back to soon after the cathedral was built. It was when the Great Moody and Sankey Tabernacle was erected here in Boston, where the Cyclorama stands today. You see, Moody and Sankey were very popular evangelist preachers in both England and the United States. The powers inside the Vatican in Rome, at some point, became nervous that they would lose faithful followers to this charismatic pair. When the time came that Moody and Sansky built a place of worship here in this city, it was just, um, unacceptable. Since the worship place, the tabernacle, was physically close to the cathedral, Rome ordered an underground tunnel be dug between the two. Rome then ordered the cathedral's bishop to spy on the happenings at this rival house of worship and to learn the secrets of this dynamic preaching team. In time the bishop was told to use this inside information to destroy the Moody and Sankey Tabernacle group all together. This plan met with success as the tabernacle closed six or seven years later."

"That's amazing. So the tunnel to the tabernacle was there and the mafia expanded it to the water to smuggle in booze?" I ask.

"Exactly. The tunnel was branched off to Fort Point Channel to be exact."

Frank nods. "Okay, that sounds possible, but deals go two ways. What did the mafia give the cathedral in exchange for the use of the tunnel?"

"Money and protection? I don't know exactly because such secrets have never been disclosed to me personally. I do believe, however, that the powers in Rome know much of the truth." The bishop spreads his hands out before him and continues. "After Prohibition, I suspect the bishop at this cathedral expected to be able to cut ties with the mafia, but as we know, this didn't happen. The mafia doesn't permit such relationships to be severed, never. And so the mafia and this cathedral have had some sort of understanding throughout the years. Nothing blatantly evil, after all we are a religious institution, but we have agreed to look the other way when it pertains to things that happen here, below the building in these tunnels. And so, Carlo Bertoni, a mafia powerhouse, needs a safe haven for Eurabians to hide until they can escape the city? I could not interfere with this."

"And now that Carlo Bertoni is dead?" I ask.

"Ah yes, he was murdered at the hands of General Kulik." The bishop sighs. "The General is also related to the mafia; the Russian mafia. Our ties are to the Italian mafia. Yet, General Kulik seemed to believe that I should obey his orders and pay allegiance to him and his plans just as I do the Italian family bosses. I, of course, refused. The General was angry and threatened to expose this cathedral and Rome for all of our previous connections, if you will, unless we also helped him. And so, we have allowed him to use the tunnels. So far he has brought down corpses which rot in sealed bags. He has brought in an arsenal of military weapons, one of which Mohamed holds in his hands as we speak. And he hides something in a secret room inside the tunnel to the water, which not even I know how to open, while refusing to inform me of what is hidden. For all I know it could be a weapon of mass destruction!"

I feel Mohamed stepping forward before he says, "Tell me more about this secret room."

"The room was made when the tunnel was built. It has three very peculiar locks that require three different keys to open it. It was crafted this way so that it took three, not just one, people to access the content of the room. I never knew the original purpose of this room. I only know that it was built to hold special things as the door to it not only has triple locks but it is also made of steel. Perhaps I should call the room a vault rather than just a mere room. I suspect it was used for valuables such as money, but this has never been verified for me."

"It must have been a place to store cash waiting to be laundered," Frank suggests.

"Perhaps. For safety's sake a full set of the three keys were hidden within the cathedral in case one of the three key holders should lose his key, or if one of the keys was stolen. Remember the key holders were criminals in a dangerous world, so it was not unreasonable to expect one of them to be robbed, kidnapped, or killed at any time. The whereabouts of the hiding place of the three extra keys were known only by one leader at a time. The place is unknown to me even to this day."

"So this hiding place was built during Prohibition in say, the 1920s?" I ask.

"The Prohibition ran from 1920 through 1933," Frank recites. "The picture at the General's cottage…"

Mohamed interrupts Frank before more information is revealed. "Do you know who selected this hiding place? I assume it was one …"

The bishop turns his attention to Frank. "Interesting you should mention General Kulik's cottage. It was the General's father who built the cottage on Cape Cod. Let me tell you of this dead old man. You see, back in the twenties, before the World Wars, the Russian mafia wasn't much of a presence here in the states. As I told you, General Kulik is connected to the Russian mafia. His father was also connected to them up until the day he died. But before his father had connections to the Russian families, he was briefly connected to the Italian mafia here in Boston. I only know this because the arrogant general told me so. Kulik's father was a modest man of modest means, but from what the General told me, he was a talented woodworker. According to the General this man is partially responsible for the incredible craftsmanship that hides the existence of this tunnel from the cathedral itself."

"I see. This would explain General Kulik's insistence on using the tunnels below the cathedral. He is connected to this place through his father. In his mind, this below ground secret has been part of his life since childhood," Mohamed says.

"Tell me of this picture. Perhaps, if you describe it to me, I can make a connection to the hiding place of the keys here within the cathedral," Bishop Sullivan holds his hands out with his palms turned up. "The time has come for trust."

"First tell us of Kulik's plans," Mohamed insists.

"I can only tell you what he has told me. I know he and his brother were spies for the Soviet Union and now Russia. I know Kulik planned to kill his brother who became afflicted with Alzheimer's. I know Kulik has been secretly selling weather weapon technology to Russia. I also know, through his work in various government agencies, he plans to have the United States' weather weapons program dismantled. He will do this by exposing findings from some studies performed by the government that prove the Weather Weapons Program is connected to global warming. This study was called Operation…um…Tin something…Tin Man…that's it. He then plans to ensure that our government never again develops such a program, allowing Russia to be the only country with this omnipotent power of mass destruction. Lastly, I know he and his committees authorized the weather attack on Boston just days ago and plan one for this week on Otis Air Force Base." The bishop pauses. "Is that enough information to gain your trust?"

Mohamed walks to my side and says, "The picture is of some of America's founding fathers arguing in a government room somewhere. There are typical furnishings, most notably, a distinctive grandfather clock striking the hour of twelve. We can't tell if it is midnight or noontime, only that it is exactly twelve o'clock."

"Maybe it doesn't matter whether it's day or night. It's the twelve that matters," the silent-up-to-now janitor Jack suggests.

"But twelve what? The number twelve holds what significance to the mafia, criminal activity, weather weapons, or the like?" Frank asks, notably not mentioning the twelve apostles. "Or does it tie into Prohibition, as in when the tunnel was built?"

"Oh, my new friends, the number twelve has a great deal of significance within the walls of a Catholic cathedral. Ah yes, there were twelve apostles of our beloved Jesus Christ." Bishop Sullivan stands and brushes dirt off his black pants. "And I believe I know the area where we will find the three keys to the secret room."

Mohamed, Frank, and I instantly look at each other. Our knowing glances assure us that we each believe that the bishop's immediate reference to the twelve apostles, which is our own theory on the significance of the number, proves we can trust this man.

"The apostles ate with Jesus at the Last Supper the night before he was arrested inside the Garden of Gethsemane. There is a handsome oil painting of this scene in the side chapel opposite to the one above us." The bishop takes Jack's hand to help him to his feet.

"And I clean around it all the time and I never even knew how close I was to something so important." Jack dusts himself off while stretching his legs. "So tell me. What do the three of you think is inside the room?" Jack asked.

"The very thing the United States government is trying to destroy with weather weapon storms targeting the universities and colleges here in Boston and on the Otis Military Base; positive proof that the weather weapons program did cause the global warming of the earth. It's referred to as Operation Tin Man in reference to the Wizard of Oz movie. Anyway, if Kulik's plans are completed, he will have the only proof on earth that the U.S is responsible for the damage done to the earth's atmosphere. With that he can blackmail Uncle Sam or sell the evidence to enemy countries or..." I explain.

"That's got to be worth what, millions?" Jack asks.

"Try trillions," Frank says, "Perhaps more."

*****

When I think of paintings of the Last Supper, the one done by Michelangelo with Jesus seated at a table with his apostles around him always comes to mind. The painting before me is not this familiar scene but rather one where the apostles are seated on the ground in a garden of trees while Jesus stands among them. Jesus is speaking to them with both arms raised. His face reveals neither happiness nor sadness. It is as if the artist draws us into the garden with the characters and forces us to wonder what Jesus is saying and how these men are reacting to his words. It is a most intriguing painting in that it inspires more questions than it answers about the Christian faith.

Since the painting is not at the center of the side chapel, but rather on one of the side walls, there is no altar below it. Instead, there are only a row of four velvet seated chairs with dark mahogany wood work. Mohamed and the bishop have agreed that the painting must be taken from the wall, but they are still considering how best to do this. Mohamed wants to get behind the picture as quickly as possible. Bishop Sullivan, who is concerned about the cathedral's valuable assets, is insisting on a more careful approach. After offering a variety of alternatives, none of which please both men, Frank and I are quickly losing patience with their inability to work together.

"Alright that's fine. Go easy though," the bishop instructs as Frank and Mohamed slowly lift the painting. "Now unhook the wire from the nails. They're very large nails so take it easy. Okay, a little higher and..."

Jack grabs hold of the bottom of the heavy painting and says, "Lower her down gently. That's right. Okay."

I can't see the brighter white paint of the wall that was behind the painting because all four men are standing in front of it. They are taking turns running their hands over the smooth surface in hopes that they will be the one to feel a secret hole where the keys are hidden. After about five minutes of disappointing failure, the bishop puts his hands together, and, I believe, begins praying to himself. Beside him, Mohamed stares at the painting as if yet another clue is hidden inside this picture. Jack and Frank are arguing with each other about other places within the vastness of the cathedral that may have represented the twelve apostles to the men who hid the key. As for me, I feel as if I am watching the scene unfold before me rather than being part of it.

"Wait! How old is this painting? Was it hanging in that spot during the 1920s? Could it have been in a different place?" I ask.

I don't know," Bishop Sullivan says. "By the look of the faded walls behind the painting I'd say it's been hanging here a long time but...."

"My father was the custodian here before me and his father before that. I've been coming here all my life and I'll be damned if I don't remember a time when that there painting wasn't above the altar. Yes sir, it was right there, front and center. The moved it to this side because the painting over the altar now was donated by some mucky muck who made a big donation. Pure politics you see. Well well, if my memory is right then the keys are over there somewhere." Jack crosses himself as he steps up to the marble altar. He slowly gets down on his knees and looks beneath the altar table. With an extended hand he feels around for a solid couple of minutes before rising. "There ain't nothing down here. Maybe the hiding place is beneath the picture up here. Come on young men, help me get this darn thing down."

Unlike the painting of the Last Supper, I don't find this piece of art particularly inspiring. It is simply a picture of angels with instruments in dreamy clouds; the sort of thing you see in too many places far too often. When the men, once again, begin to bicker about how best to remove the heavy painting without damaging anything, I turn my attention back to the Last Supper picture. I have never seen the back side of an old painting such as this so I gently pull it forward for a peek. The back of the canvas is dark; time worn I suppose. The wooden frame the canvas is attached to is obviously very old and surprisingly wide. While running my hand over the frame I wonder if Kulik's woodworking father made it himself. With this intriguing thought as motivation, I give the frame a much closer inspection. Eventually my fingers run over a slight indentation in the wood. With visions of a secret compartment I inspect the spot only to find it is nothing but a dent. I refuse to be discourages while I examine the rest of the backside of the frame inch by inch. My efforts are soon rewarded.

"Hey guys, I think…" I call out.

"We're not finding anything yet but we're not giving up," the bishop interrupts.

"Well give up because I've found the three keys…that is I can see where they are. Look, here, in the back side of the frame. Three perfectly placed slits cut into the wood with three keys slipped inside them. I can't pry the keys out but I can sure see them. Yep, all three keys are in this picture."

Frank and Jack are wiggling the keys out of the frame in what I believe, to be a quick but careful manner. The bishop is complaining that the antique frame is being needlessly damaged while Mohamed is reminding us that time is quickly passing by. These two men are very different is so many ways, yet so alike in their headstrong insistence to control the situation. It comes as no surprise to me that they walk side by side to lead us down to the tunnel. Once down below, the bishop takes the lead only because he, not Mohamed, knows the location of the vault-like room the three keys will hopefully open for us. Inside the actual tunnel that leads to this room, I increasingly experience a bit of claustrophobia. This is due to the increasing narrowing of the tunnel and also because we are being surrounded by a damp darkness I can only describe as the black of death. Although I don't admit my fears, I secretly run my hand against the sides of the tunnel to assure myself that the bricks and stone work holding up the earth around me are, in fact, as solid as steel walls. I am so distracted by the misery of claustrophobia that I hardly notice when we get to the steel door. It has three bars running horizontally across it, each one with a heavy lock of industrial size. After several tries, Mohamed matches each of the three keys to the correct locks. With the door ready to open, I expect another argument to ensue between the two untrusting men. Instead the bishop steps back and gestures for Mohamed to open the vault door. I, like the others, have to step to the side to make room for the heavy door to swing open. There is no light inside the vault-like room so all of us use our flashlights to explore its contents. It is Frank's powerful flashlight beam that lands on a briefcase.

"There it is!" I yell a bit too loud for such a small and congested space. "We've finally got it. We've finally done something right."

Mohamed lays the case down and attempts to spring it open. "It's locked."

Jack growls, "Of course it is. Ain't nothing been easy has it? Damn thing almost got me killed by you youngins and now…"

"That isn't true." Frank takes the case from Mohamed to inspect it. "We never intended to kill you. However, I understand your frustration."

Bishop Sullivan squeezes past me and says, "The good Lord wouldn't have brought us this far to fail. I believe in divine intervention, and if we all pray there will be an answer."

"It's a simple combination lock. One number for the left snap and a number for the right snap. If we are sure this is what we are looking for we can break the case later with tools from the box Agent Brown gave us. They are back below the cathedral. There is no logical reason to worry about opening this thing up now unless we are unsure of what is inside. Are we?' Mohamed asks.

"Tonight has been full of surprises, so I vote we break open the thing here. As for divine intervention, well, I'm going with common sense. If the code to find the keys was twelve then maybe the combination numbers are also twelve," I say.

"A divinely inspired suggestion," the bishop says. "Perhaps we need only try the numbers one and two and the case will open."

When I hear the spring locks pop open I feel a shiver creep through me. Call it divine intervention or just the good old fashioned creeps, but I definitely get the sense that the case opening represents a turning point for us tonight. We gather around the new found treasure where we see official looking papers, computer flash drives, pictures, handwritten paperwork, and documents on White House stationery with the presidential seal impressed in them. The contents of the case are much more comprehensive than we imagined.

"This is it," Mohamed says in a low voice. "We found the only complete file of evidence of Operation Tin Man that is not within government control or about to be destroyed at Otis Air Force base."

Frank, who is bent down flipping through the contents of the case, adds, "And here is top secret information regarding the science of the Weather Weapons Program."

While Mohamed and Frank repack up the briefcase, I watch the bishop cross himself. I then hear him whisper words of thanks to the Lord. Hearing this man's profound belief that his God, well, our God or Allah or whomever, is on our side gives me more strength than logical plans do. The power of the unknown is, I now can see, so much more powerful than the known.

The bishop's calm voice breaks my thoughts. "I wish we could stop the planned attack on the military base. The unnecessary loss of life is too much for me to bear. I feel obligated to warn people that a storm may be coming; however, given the situation…." Bishop Sullivan wipes a tear from his eye.

"We think the storm may have already started. We'll know more tomorrow when Frank and I start working on Otis Military Base. It's a long story but we have jobs there. I'm glad we'll be on the base because it puts us in a position to know everything that's going on. But, I must admit, being in the line of fire, mini tornadoes spitting out fire balls included, doesn't appeal to me," I whisper to the bishop.

I chit chat with the bishop all the way back to the main floor of the cathedral. It isn't until it is time for us to part that I ask the question that has been nagging at me since I first met this man.

"Bishop Sullivan, what happens when General Kulik comes here to retrieve the brief case and it's gone? Will he believe you know nothing about it?"

The bishop nods silently as he puts his hand on Jack's back.

"I fear for myself, and of course, Jack. I fear equally for all of you. After you have gone back to Cape Cod I will leave a note that I and Jack have had to leave unexpectedly. Then, we will go into hiding until it is safe to surface. Take my cell phone number in case you need us. Do not come back here under any circumstances. Once General Kulik realizes what has happened, this cathedral is one hundred percent enemy territory."

Chapter 25
Back To The Cape

On our way back to Cape Cod we learn that a small fire storm did, in fact, tear through the park where the craft fair was being held and the adjourning baseball field where the meeting with our enemies was scheduled to take place. Of course, the storm was basically harmless as the area had already been evacuated by Agent Brown and his Homeland Security team. Yes, there were some fires in the surrounding neighborhood that caused damage, but most importantly, there was no loss of life. So, Agent Brown's plan to coordinate a full scale manhunt for Mohamed, Frank and me in the exact area where the meeting was intended to occur worked. By the times being reported on the news, I'd say the spotting of Mohamed the fugitive took place well before we were set to meet with the enemy. This means that whoever went to the baseball field to meet with Frank and me instead met with an evacuation caused by the sighting of Mohamed who was allegedly seen in our company. An ingenious plan, in that it implies that Frank and I were indeed on the Cape at the park just as we were supposed to be, even though in reality, we were not on the Cape at all.

"It seems that the news reporters don't know which story to cover more. There are fires from the weather weapons storm that are still being dealt with. Reporters are talking about the mistaken identity sightings of Mohamed that have a lot of people worked up. And there's the breaking news about Stefan Kulik and Edward Jinkins being murdered at General Kulik's cottage. There's no information disclosed about this tragedy yet except that the General is devastated at the loss of his brother. Well, it's just after one o'clock in the morning so Kulik has all night to figure out something more to say." Frank turns to a different news station. "But whatever he comes up with I'm sure everyone will believe him because people with the status of General Kulik don't come crashing down easily no matter how bad things look for them.

There will be many committee and police investigations to get through before this resilient old soldier pays for his crimes."

"How long do you think satellite service will be out on the Cape? I know with Agent Brown overseeing everything that Sarah, Randy, and Arnie are fine, but I'll feel a whole lot better when I talk to one of them." I toss my cell phone into my backpack.

Frank is half way through a rather lengthy technical answer to my question when my eye lids drop. Sleep creeps over me like fog rolls in from the ocean, slowly but without interruption. I don't awaken until we are back at the trailer and I hear Frank saying,

"This is really bad. Damn, this is so bad. They're not here. They can't still be at the park."

"We have no choice but to go to the park and see what we can learn there. But first we should look inside for a note." Mohamed looks out the windows of the SUV. "Perhaps, given what has happened tonight, I should stay hidden in here."

Mohamed lies down in the back seat and covers himself with a blanket while Frank and I go inside. I'm not sure what I hope to find or not find inside our cramped temporary home, but I am sure that I don't feel good about things right now. When the overhead lights come on my eyes dart around the trailer looking for anything that is out of place. Frank searches targeted areas where we often leave notes for each other including the kitchen counter, the table, and near the TV remote. I, on the other hand, take the approach that the note will be hidden if our friends are in trouble. I rummage through the garbage, feel under the furniture, and inspect the pockets of jackets.

"There are no notes of any kind. Also, from what I can tell, the others haven't returned here since they left for the park. This means that they are either at the park, or, for some reason, off doing something more important than coming back. That is, of course, if no harm has come to them." Frank reaches for Sarah's jewelry making kit and gently snaps the cover closed. "I even remember this being left open in this exact spot earlier today. No, they haven't been back."

"Then we go to the park, but if they were evacuated, then what can we hope to find?"

"I don't know, I'm as confused…"

A knock on the door takes us both by surprise. I can feel Frank's fear mingle with my own as he goes to see who is here so late at night.

"Hi, you're our neighbor, right?" Frank asks.

"I've been up all night waiting for someone to come home. I went to the park before to tell your friends how there were people breaking inside your place earlier this afternoon, maybe a couple of hours after you all left. I called the police and, well, no one came, maybe because of the sighting of the terrorist…um…your brother?" our middle aged, motorcycle riding neighbor tells us. "Sorry, Abia is it? I know it was a false alarm and all that, but anyway, me and my old lady took her car to the park to tell any of you that we could find what was going on and no one was around. Not even the blond, Sarah; the one with the jewelry booth. My wife met her at the craft fair yesterday. When we couldn't find no one we got back in the car and we was riding around looking for some help when something really strange happened. Some military jeep started following our car! It was wild! They followed us everywhere. I didn't get it. They didn't stop us…just followed us. When we came back home they jumped out of the jeep and took a look at us and then left! I don't know what's going on with you people but someone is after you and I don't know if you is good guys or bad guys. I just know I promised my old lady I'd warn you about what happened so considered yourself warned."

"Something is definitely wrong," Frank whispers as he closes the door behind our neighbor. "Randy put the GPS he found on his truck on his car. The military planted those GPS devices and followed our neighbor's car thinking it was one of ours. Now they know we were on to them and messed around with the GPS's."

"Randy, Sarah, and Arnie weren't at the park a short while after someone came snooping around in here. That means they've been missing for a while." I look up at my boyfriend. "If they're not here, and someone was looking for them earlier than we expected, then they may have gotten into trouble before Agent Brown was able to prevent something bad from happening."

*****

We find the park to be dark, wind torn, and striped with paths of burnt ground. We drive to the side of the park where the craft fair was being held where we find the remains of what were the craft vendor's tents. Some vendors are still at their set-ups trying to salvage inventory and supplies. Many set-ups appear to have already been cleaned up by their owners as evidenced by an endless sea of black plastic trash bags all around us. As Frank and I eagerly trot to Sarah's tent, I hear a couple who sell wooden plaques cursing the authorities for not allowing them to pack up their things before they were evacuated. I smell the burnt wood of what was their inventory as we pass by. When we get to Sarah's booth I am shocked to find that most of her inventory is in cases. The tables are knocked over, the canvas tent top is ripped to shreds, and her supply boxes are lying on their sides yet her jewelry inventory has been safely stored in cases.

"She packed up before the evacuation, but why?" I ask Frank.

"Because whatever happened to Randy and Arnie had already happened," Frank replies.

"Okay, if that's true then she left us a note, right?"

"Right, but not anywhere anyone like the enemy would look." Frank nervously bites his fingernails and looks around."

I begin to put the contents of the booth back into place. As the tables, chair, and display cases slowly return to the positions Sarah had them in, I am better able to think as she would have thought during this afternoon's crisis. Because she knew the canvas tent and banners would be completely destroyed by the wind and possible fire, I focus on things that would not burn. The metal legs on the folding tables instantly get my attention.

"What's going on? Are you alright?" Frank asks.

"When we were hunting down the Eurabian enemy we found something extremely important hidden in the hollowed out leg of a wooden table. Now Sarah needs to hide a flammable note in a place that can't catch fire; a place made of metal and…"

"And the table legs are metal and hollow!" Frank gasps.

After various dead end attempts it turns out I am right. There, in the bottom of a table leg, beneath the rubber cap that steadies the legs on flat surfaces, is a curled up piece of paper.

If you find this note then my prayers are answered. I have to write fast. Randy and Arnie were in the ballpark. They were to come to me. No show. I pack up and go find them. They're gone. Called Brown. He comes and puts me with agent. Then evacuation occurs. Storm gets way worse. Fires. I run around looking for R and A. Go to equipment Arnie set up. Find cell phone video of R and A being taken away by Kulik and gym owner. Find agent and ask for Brown. Told he cannot be located! Will meet you at the trailer at two. If not two then three, four etc.

When we return to the car we race to the ball field clinging to hope that another clue has been left behind there. Hidden beneath his hood, Mohamed helps Frank and I search the dugout where Arnie and Randy planted electronic equipment for the meeting with the enemy.

From on top of the dugout Frank, calls down to us, "Randy and Arnie set up an audio and visual recordings device up here. The storm didn't knock it down."

Huddled together, Frank narrates as we watch the unfocused and somewhat garbled data. "Okay, that's them. That's Arnie getting the device…see him? He's putting it in place…he's talking to himself, hear him? Ok…the device goes blank. It's only activated when someone goes by. Okay, the device is back on…it's a dog. Okay…it's gone. Ah…it's Randy."

"Can you fast forward to see if anything is on there that matters to us?" Mohamed asks.

"Yeah, sure." Frank works quickly to gather up the equipment. He then runs through the recordings making periodic comments about what he's seeing. When he finally does show us something, it is not Randy or Arnie that we see.

"And who are you looking for my dear husband?" Alena's voice is saying, although she herself is not visible. "Do not attempt to run or call for your loyal agents to help you. If you do Arnold and Randy will be killed. Yes, we have kidnapped them just as you kidnapped my children. Now, come with me and we will discuss what is to happen next."

"Where are they and where do you intend to take me?" Agent Brown asks.

The video picture then shows the side of Alena's head. "Oh now, you know I do not answer questions."

"I would think your father is too busy explaining how his brother and his pal Ed Jinkins were murdered in his cottage to be taking on me right about now."

"You think wrong."

"You can't take me and the kids to the cottage because it's a murder scene now. As for your prison at the Taunton Mental Hospital site, that too has been discovered. So what other secret hiding places do you have?"

"You will find out soon enough. I will only say that there is more than one jail cell in a prison my dear."

When Agent Brown turns to look into the camera I know he is hoping we will find this recording. "Then I suppose I am in for a visit to Taunton tonight."

"I know exactly where they are. When Arnie was being held prisoner at the Taunton State Hospital ruins in that old building he told me that the guy who watched over him, the Jailor, told him there was another special place on the grounds for really important prisoners. He said Arnie was a nobody and didn't matter enough to be brought there. Arnie said the place was at the basement level of what was the research facility of the mental hospital campus. Arnie looked it up and said the building itself has been removed but figures that the laboratory beneath the ground is still there and accessible somehow."

"Okay, it's a start." Frank says.

"Arnie had pictures of the old buildings…" Mohamed pauses. "He showed me how the research building didn't have bars on the windows like the others ones did. If I remember correctly it was located directly behind the main building."

"We'll find it, I know we will. For now, though, we have to get back to the trailer and get Sarah." Frank shoves the electronic equipment into the SUV. "She better be there waiting for us."

I'm overcome by relief when I spot Randy's truck in the driveway. I hurry inside where I find Sarah wrapped in a blanket on the couch. Her face is pale; her eyes are bloodshot and she is visibly shaking. The two of us sob out loud as we clutch on to each other. Be it exhaustion, nerves or fear, I am in no frame of mind to go on a rescue mission, but, I know I will be on one soon all the same.

*****

Frank and Mohamed strategically pack three backpacks with quite an assortment of items we may need on our rescue mission. Many of the things they are bringing make sense, such as tools, a first aid kit, and ropes. However, some of the objects I notice they are packing puzzle me, like three pairs of gloves and a blanket cut into strips. Of course I've been through far too much with these two to question their judgment, so I turn my attention to the task they assign Sarah and me to do, which is to find out what is going on with the Jinkins girls: Katie and Kileen. Since it is not yet sunrise our task should be no more complicated than a nighttime visit to their trailer. Dressed in dark clothing, Sarah and I set out through the woods using flashlights and memory to guide our way.

"Good! The lights are out. We'll go to the back door. Are you sure you can use the locksmith kit to get through the lock without making a lot of noise?" I whisper to Sarah.

"Randy made me practice for months now, so sure, I think I can. Other than finding out the girls are sleeping, what else are we supposed to find in there?"

"Any information they may have about the investigation or anything their father had on us. We can't have the police finding out Ed was watching us because that could make us suspects in his murder."

"It would be a whole lot easier to do this if they weren't in the trailer. I could do it later today..."

"No, you can't. Even though you're not taking part in the rescue mission you're still going with us."

"Whoa, hold on a second. I didn't know that."

"We didn't want to freak you out until we had to. The thing is we need you in the SUV looking out for us and ready to pick us up once the rescue is made. We also have no satellite access here on the Cape, so you'll have the laptop with you and should be able to pull up the site plans for the Taunton dump and the Taunton State Hospital for reference. We may also..."

"Okay, I get it. I'll be okay. Besides, I want to be there when you get Randy out of there. I just hope they're okay."

"They must be okay. Whatever evil plans Kulik and Alena have for Randy, Arnie and agent Brown it most likely is wrapped up in the weather weapon storm planned for the Otis Military Base. So, the three of them may be a bit beaten up, but I'm sure they're alive."

"I know. We've talked this point over in so many ways that I know you're right but I can't help but be scared. You know how it is."

"Well, let's forget about that for now and get this Jinkins thing done. I admit these aren't exactly ideal circumstances to sneak inside the trailer, but it's what we have to do."

Behind the trailer we find evidence that people had gathered out on the patio this past evening. There is a variety of empty soda and beer cans lying around, left over snacks strewn all over the place, and the typical paper trash one would expect from a social gathering. Through the darkness I detect two shiny translucent orbs which I suspect belong to a raccoon who was feasting on the snacks before we showed up. Surprisingly, we find the back door is not locked. Before entering, I peek inside the kitchen. With no one in sight, we slip through the door. Like the patio, the kitchen is a mess. Used paper plates, uncovered casserole dishes, and more empty cans fill the counter tops. My hopes of finding anything inside this mess dissolve quickly.

"If there's anything to find it's not out here," Sarah whispers from the doorway between the kitchen and the living room. "We have to find Ed's bedroom."

"I know which one is Katie's and I have a hunch which one his is, but the rooms are practically on top of each other down that hall."

"I hear snoring sounds which means one or both of the young ladies probably did some drinking tonight. Let's hope they're not just sleeping but passed out."

"Imagine getting drunk when your Dad is murdered? That's totally sick."

Sarah shrugs. "It is what it is. They must have their reasons."

"Yeah, like he murdered their mother for one. I knew Katie wasn't fond of her father but I figured Kileen would be upset. It doesn't seem that either of the girls is all that broken up, though. Maybe they knoew a whole lot more about their father than they let on."

We tiptoe down the hall where I am relieved to find all the bedroom doors are closed. My hunch about Ed's bedroom turns out to be correct. His room is a master bedroom. It is twice the size of his daughters' rooms and located on the opposite side of the hall. Because it has with windows overlooking the road where other homes are located, we close the drapes before using our flashlights. Ed's room is shockingly neat; almost military style neat. The clothes in his closet are hung up properly, his shoes lined up in a straight row and his dresser drawers have folded underwear and sox balled with their mates. This discovery inspires me because such an organized man would keep oraganized records which are exactly what we're looking for. While I look through one dresser Sarah looks through another. We both find nothing. Next I take the closet and she goes through his nightstand. Again we find nothing. A quick look under the bed leads to more frustration.

"Nothing here, which is good news or bad?" Sarah whispers.

"I don't know. It could be there is nothing to find or it could be he already gave whatever he had to General Kulik. Or it could mean that the police already have it. Or it could mean that he hid his stuff somewhere else." I reply.

"Somewhere his girls wouldn't look, which wouldn't be anywhere inside here."

"Maybe not. There's the shed outside. What do you think?"

Sarah pulls the blinds open. "It's worth looking."

Unlike the trailer, the shed door is locked. Sarah works on the lock for less than ten minutes before she has it opened. I am deeply impressed by her newly acquired skill. The shed is roomy but full. It has a riding lawn mower, yard tools, a small wheel barrel, and an array of miscellaneous things that probably don't belong anywhere else. Although both Sarah and I fit inside, it is difficult for us to move around. This is especially true when we close the door behind us. We each search half of the shed, stretching and straining our bodies to reach places we can't get near by foot. I do manage to find a pile of paperwork which disappointedly is only a collection of operational instructions for various pieces of equipment including the lawn mower and some hedge trimmers. Sarah also finds some paperwork, which proves just as useless as it is nothing more than a stack of dated gardening magazines.

"Another dead end." I move my light from the magazines to Sarah's face. "What's with the smile?"

"Why would he have a stack of gardening magazines if he doesn't garden? From what we saw in his bedroom, Ed was way too organized to keep useless magazines around for no reason." Sarah reaches for a tall white bucket and empties it of car cleaning products. Using it as a stool she reaches up for the stack of magazines. I shove aside a pile of outside orange extension cords and step over some neatly stacked cans of paint so I can steady her.

"No dust on these babies. There's no dust on them," she says enthusiastically.

"Good news, that's great news."

It doesn't take us long to find what Ed Jinkins was hiding in this unusual place. Flipping through the pages of the magazines we find, a great number of hundred dollar bills, pictures of all of us including Mohamed, and flash drives which I assume are copies of everything stored on our computers.

"Look at this," Sarah says, as she pulls a list out from the top magazine. "He actually set price tags on this stuff. He has a list of what he has, what he was charging for it, and what they bought so far. Look here, the GPS device line has been checked off. He got two thousand dollars for doing that to us. And DNA evidence – he sold them DNA evidence on all of us except Mohamed. It seems the price for Mohamed's stuff was set a lot higher than ours. What a creep. Hmmm, wait a second! By looking at this I'm not even sure he gave them anything on your brother."

As tempted as we are to continue looking through the magazines, we shove them inside the cloth shopping bag I stuffed in my pocket before we left the trailer. Although neither of us is too worried about being caught leaving the shed, we take precautions all the same. It turns out it is a good thing we do. The raccoon I thought I saw earlier is back on the patio. Its presence would have taken us by surprise if we didn't know he was out here. Then I notice more animals moving about. There are rats dining on pretzels, cheese balls, and stale potato chips. A scream rises in my throat and is about to escape when Sarah's hand clamps over my mouth.

"Abby, don't scream. I know how you are about rats, but you can't scream!"

Chapter 26
The Dump

If Sarah didn't put her own squeamishness aside and shoo away the rats, I might still be in the shed on the verge of hysterics. Instead, we are in the city of Taunton on our way to the dump, which is located directly behind the abandoned Taunton State Hospital campus. Because of Arnie's recent imprisonment and all that followed, the hospital has been much in the news, making it unacceptable for us to be seen anywhere near the place. So, having no other choice but to sneak in through the back of the property, the first leg of our rescue mission takes us through the city dump.

"According to the city's website the dump is closed on Sunday. This means I'll be able to park in the wooded areas within the lanes that lead to the dump entrance without being seen. Then, when you call I can pick you up wherever you are. Now, the map shows you can pass through the dump and get to the rear of the hospital campus. The campus was deserted so long ago it no longer has the structures, gardens, and pathways that are indicated on this internet map, but I don't think you'll have a problem navigating your way up the hill to the back side of the remaining hospital buildings." Sarah scrolls through the screens of one of the many Taunton State Hospital websites she has found, saying, "The building that once held the laboratory was directly behind the main building, just like Arnie told Mohamed. The way to the prison on the lowest level would most likely be where the original stairs were or where an elevator shaft was located. It is also possible that the below ground level floor had a walk out door of some type, meaning it was built into a hillside, but then that wouldn't make for a very secret hiding place would it?"

"With all the studying you have done have you located a good place for us to hide while we're on the grounds?" Mohamed asks

"There are just four structures remaining on the campus. The main building, as we are aware, is currently being used by our enemy as a prison and is now a crime scene. That one is totally off limits. There is also one abandoned dormitory still standing. This building is quite a distance from the hospital entrance and would allow no vantage point at all in regard to watching for anyone coming or going to or from the property. The third building is where the grounds equipment was or is stored; tractors, gardening tools, and stuff like that I imagine. This building is too far down the hill to be seen from the entrance, also making it a lousy look-out site. That leaves the fourth and final building which is what was once used as a medical facility. Apparently, when a patient became ill, he or she was moved to this building so the illness did not spread to other patients. This building is to the right of the main entrance and offers a perfect view of all the places we need to watch today. However, there may be one problem."

"And what would that be?" Frank asks.

"It's in such a perfect spot that it's possible our enemies are already using it for their own purposes."

If Mohamed and Frank were two ordinary men, the conversation about the hospital grounds and the dump would likely have ended here, but these men are not ordinary, in any sense of the word. Therefore, the conversation continues all the way until we arrive at the city dump itself. My first surprise is to learn that a city can have a section of it that is so rural. The street where the dump is located has farms, trees, pastures, more trees, and a whole lot of landscaping that is not at all urban. My second surprise is that the dump is not clearly marked with big signs. Instead, its presence is more subtly made with pleasant signage referring to the landfill. My third surprise is that the dump entrance is set back so far from the main street you have to drive down a fairly long road just to get to the entrance. When we get to it, however, we are greeted by big steel solid impenetrable dump gates, making it clear we have indeed arrived at our destination.

"Thank goodness we can easily get over the fence because those gates aren't opening, no way, no how. So, let's grab our gear and do this thing," I say to Mohamed and Frank. "Enough with the yip yapping. We've got our tools, a medical kit, food, water and weapons. That means we're set to go on a rescue mission."

It turns out there are many more surprises for me at the dump starting with the fact that the fence is not as easy to get over as I thought. When I do get to the other side, I am then surrounded by sights I've never even thought of before, let alone actually seen. As far as surprises go, I never knew a dump could be so full of trash and yet so orderly. In a way, I was expecting the place to be much more disgusting and smelly than it is. Instead it has a businesslike atmosphere to it where the garbage bags, broken furniture, recycled bottles, and countless discarded electronic devices appear to have their own sections. Of course, the dump is not a pleasant place. For one thing the pigeons and other birds are flying overhead in almost unimaginable quantities. And even though they remain hidden I'm sure rats, mice, raccoons, and who knows what other critters are foraging through the trash for tidbits at this very moment. With the memory of the rats in the Jinkins' back yard still haunting me, I push this thought aside.

"The dump entrance is toward the southeast meaning we will not have to travel on dump property very long before we get to the hospital grounds," Frank announces.

"Do you know what part of the dump exactly we have to walk through?" I ask.

"No."

I glance over at Mohamed and shrug.

Frank continues, "Let me see, we should be following a roadway of some kind that will come to an end. Then we will have to hike across unmarked territory for perhaps a half mile before we reach the hospital property."

"It's the whole unmarked territory on the map Sarah showed us that I don't like. I get that the dump website doesn't label where inside the dump certain items are put, but, ugh, after the rats at the Jinkins'..."

"Abia, stop with the rats. You have been hysterically frightened of rats since you were a child and it is time you get over this irrational fear. This is a dump, and I assure you, there are rats about. Please, you need to..."

"Hey, big brother, not a good time for a lecture. Rats or no rats I found the stuff Jinkins had on us, didn't I?"

"Yes, she did," Frank says to Mohamed, ending the spat.

While we walk in silence I take in our surroundings. There are trees, shrubs, and even some grassy areas in this place. But there is more tar, cement, and dirt than anything else. The smell here is certainly unpleasant, but not so bad that it makes me gag. Actually, some of the things around would be sort of interesting if I were here for a different reason at a different time. Like the collection of broken lawn furniture that's in a sizeable pile to my left. I wonder why that stuff is being held separately. And on my right is a tall heap of metal, rusted metal. Who the heck wants that? And up ahead, I can see a whole bunch of appliances cresting the surface of the land. There has to be a whole pit filled up with them, for goodness sake. Who would think so many of them get junked like this?

"Is that what I think it is? Up ahead?" I ask.

"It's a graveyard for abandoned appliances," Frank says.

"You mean like refrigerators, stoves, air conditioners, and that sort of thing?" I ask.

"That is exactly what I mean." Frank turns around and says to me, "There may be some living animals down there as well."

When we get to the pit of discarded metal I feel my stomach tighten into a knot. I look to the right where a metal building used as a recycling center is located and sigh. I look to the left and follow the trench in front of me until it abruptly ends at a tall fence with a barbed wire top. It is obvious that the only way to get past this collection of iron is to walk through it.

"So, tell me how you plan on us getting across this heap of metal junk," I ask.

Frank and Mohamed are inspecting the appliance dump and plotting out routes when I become certain that the wind is picking up. The sun is shining, the clouds are white puffy masses, and I don't feel any moisture in the air, yet the wind is moving in the crazy fashion it did during the weather weapons storms. I step away from the others and call Sarah. When she agrees that the wind is indeed peculiar, I wonder if the storm targeting the Otis Military Base has been set into motion.

"I wish there was a better way, but from what we saw on the dump website, crossing this appliance pit to get on the hospital grounds is by far the easiest and safest route," Frank is saying to Mohamed. "We start at the kitchen stoves, and then go to the dryers like you said. The refrigerators look stable but…" Frank lowers his voice to a whisper. "Could be rats there, though."

"Let's just do this, alright? I can't stand this much longer. If this is the best way then let's just go." With this bold demand I hoist my heavy backpack on and announce, "I'll lead. That way if I fall or freak out you can come to my rescue. Just tell me where to go and what to do and I'll do it!"

"You weigh the least amount; therefore, you are the best suited to test the strength of the supporting structures below us. I came prepared for this. We will tie a rope around our waists so that should one of us tumble…" Mohamed says while opening his backpack.

"Then we all fall down into the pit?" I ask, half hysterical.

"No, the other two of us can pull the fallen back up to safety," he explains.

Knowing nothing about mountain climbing safety ropes, I tie the white clothesline cord loosely around my waist. I slide on my butt down onto the nearest kitchen stove, a stainless steel drop-in model, and although it wiggles slightly it holds me in place. I step over to the next stove, another stainless steel model, finding this one also provides solid footing. When I place my foot on my third stove choice, a shiny black one lying on its side, I hear a rumbling noise. I careful adjust my weight and try again. This time the noise is even louder and the black stove tilts to the right.

"Try the white one to your left. It's more of a stretch for you, but from what I can see it is in a far sturdier position." I hear Frank say from behind me.

To my right I spot the white stove, which I estimate to be at least three feet away from where I stand. I will not be able to test the stove's safety with one foot first, as to do so would require my legs to straddle a distance I fear they can not reach. Instead, I will have to make a slight but deliberate leap onto the stove with pure guts and hopefully some luck.

"Are you really sure it's safe? I'm gonna have to just go for it," I ask.

"Wait and let me pass you. I will do it first," Mohamed says.

"No. It's more likely to give under your weight. I'm gonna go."

With my arms spread out for balance, I leap onto the white stove. A rush of relief floods through me when the hunk of iron holds firmly in place. I make a thumbs up sign and move on to a clothes dryer, then another dryer, a refrigerator, and a freezer. I keep making good progress through the rusted metal relics until I am pulling myself up onto an industrial sized air conditioning unit and feel something run across the top of my hand. I jump back horrified. The jolt of my movement causes the freezer to shift. I feel it move beneath my feet. The freezer shifts again, this time it starts to lean away from the refrigerator I stepped on to get where I am now. I feel myself sliding as the freezer tilts a bit more. I hear rumbling below me. It registers in my head that I am either going to ride the freezer down about twenty or so feet onto a pile of metal with dangerously sharp edges or I will have to ignore what could be a rat to pull myself onto the air conditioner. Frank's and Mohamed's voices meld together in the background making their words useless to me. The image of the rats on the Jinkins' patio taunts me as I lift my arms. With a brutish scream, I grab on to the air conditioning unit. It is not nearly as sturdy as it was on my first attempt, likely the result of the avalanche I've just caused. I feel and see objects flying overhead. As they hit the metal unit I hear the nauseating squeaks of rats. A piece of metal flies overhead and it occurs to me that Mohamed and Frank are lobbing scraps at the rats in an effort to clear them away. Using whatever possible as footholds, I steady myself and look on top of the unit. The first horror I see is the beady eyes of the largest gray rat I've ever set eyes on. Raw terror rushes up my spine. The second horror my eyes fall upon is what this stubborn rat refuses to leave behind despite being hit by various thrown objects. Lying just a foot or so from my face is a chewed up dead rat. What is left of its head is close enough that I can see its now empty eye sockets. If it weren't for the pressure of the rope around my waist being pulled on by Mohamed, I truly believe I would faint.

"Abia. Stop it. You must do this for the others. For all you know they are covered in rats right now! Get up there now! Push the rat and the corpse off and wait on there until I can get over to you! There is not time for a faint heart. Abia, you must do this for those that you love."

The rat eating another of its kind and I are frozen in time; each of us just waiting for the other to move first. The only movements I notice are the half crazed birds soaring and diving nearby. Although I envision my arm sweeping the horrid creature and its disgusting meal off the air conditioner, my limbs will not move. I mean this in the literal sense; I am paralyzed by terror. This is completely illogical as I've been in far more dangerous situations before this of which I have found the bravery to cope with quite well. But, as hard as it is for me to understand the immobile state I find myself in, I am unable to move all the same. That is until a stern jerk on the rope around my stomach forces me back so far that I either have to pull myself up onto the air conditioning unit with the dreadful rat or fall into the pit. My survival instinct knocks my horrified hypnotic state aside and my arms pull my body up. My stomach slides over the edge of the unit and my chest hovers above the scurrying live rat. I find myself with just the half eaten rat corpse to contend with. I use the side of my arm to swish it over the side of the unit. It isn't until this crisis is over that I realize I'm very close to hyperventilating.

"Stay where you are. I'm coming to get you. I will help you the rest of the way. It's not that much farther." Mohamed skillfully balances on less secure objects than I stepped on. I can tell he's keeping a protective watch over me. "Just stay focused on me, okay?"

"Why? What's wrong? Is something else wrong?" I feel a prickling sense of panic grab hold of my stomach. I fearfully look to my right and left, not quite sure what other horrors to expect. "Is it behind me? What's behind me? Are there more rats? Is it where those birds are?"

"Just focus on my movements. I think this dryer over here will be good. Yes, it will require an extra few feet of travel but it looks the safest, don't you agree?" Mohamed says while forcing a cheerful smile.

"I'm going to look behind me. You saw something I didn't notice and I'm guessing its more rats. Is that it? Do we have to pass through rats to get out of this damn appliance pit?" Rather than wait for an answer I slowly turn my upper body. To my left I see nothing unusual so I turn to my right. For the first time I notice the appliances in this area are moving, but I can't see what is making this happen.

"What is happening over there? I need to know?" I look at my brother and then Frank. "Please just tell me the truth. I can see movement over there so tell me what's causing it. I can't see over that huge metal hunk of junk to see what's on the other side but I can tell by both your faces that you can. Please tell me, is there some dreadful creature over there? Is it dangerous? Does it bite? Is it worse than a rat eating another rat?"

"It is best if you don't know," Frank says.

"Stop it! Just tell me what is over there and do I need to go near it to get to the hospital grounds?" I say in a deliberate manner. "No more of this. I want to know, now!"

Mohamed is within a few feet of me. I feel his hold on the rope tighten about my waste as he says, "First you must come to me onto this heap. The air conditioning unit you are on is no longer secure and you need to move laterally to me. The pile I am on is as steady as a ship on a calm sea, I promise."

"Since when do you speak like that? Steady as a ship on the calm sea? Tell me…" I complain.

"When you get here and are safe in my arms you will look over the side and see the horror as you call it. Is that not fair?" Mohamed asks.

There is something in his almost black pleading eyes that convinces me I am better off not knowing the truth until I am out of danger. I can feel the pile of dead appliances move beneath me every time I shift my weight, so I know my brother's concern for me is legitimate. I also know that my awareness of any appalling sight may be enough to cause a second frozen-in-time panic attack on my part. So, with as much grace and balance as I can muster up I stand on the platform below my feet. When the unit pitches to the right I don't panic. However, when a metal on metal scraping sound groans up from below me my heart beat does quicken a bit. I then mentally measure the leap I must take to reach Mohamed. I prepare for the jump by making sure all my hair is pulled back and adjusting the weight of my backpack. Then, as if I've practiced this jump routine many times before, I leap into Mohamed's grasp without incident. It was a perfect leap; a perfect ten in Olympic scoring terms. Frank is beaming at me. For the first moment since I entered the dump I feel good, I feel confident, I feel energized, I feel like we will conduct a successful rescue without a problem because we are…

"Ahhhhhh! Oh Allah in heaven, Jesus on the cross, and Moses in the desert, this is too much for me. Oh no, this is way too much for me!!!!"

And so it was that I set eyes on one of the most disgusting combinations of sights imaginable. When I consider that I've seen fresh dead bodies, someone's head explode from a gunshot, and stored corpses in plastic containers in various stages of rot, I am a bit surprised that there is anything left that I can find so revolting it surpasses them. But this particular image is almost beyond description. It seems that some people didn't empty their freezers and refrigerators of food before they discarded them in the dump. Since I know units such as this must have their doors removed for safety reasons before being dumped, I can't imagine how such a crime went unnoticed. It appears there are several of these food units involved, perhaps from an apartment manager of some sort. Now there is rotting food spewed about the appliances in this dump with every type of scavenger creature conceivable fighting for their share of the feast. The number of rats is too high to count. To me they look like a moving blanket of brown, grey, and black swarming below just waiting for a fresh body to fall. There are snakes tangled amongst rotting frozen vegetable bags; at least that is what they look like from where I stand. There are insects forming a somewhat shimmering moving sheet as they crawl amid the refuse. I imagine these are maggots trying to grab as much as they can before the bigger animals arrive. There are raccoons, possums, and creatures I cannot identify. And birds. There are crazed birds of all kinds. Black ones, gray ones, white ones, and small birds, large ones, hawks, and I don't even know what else. And some of these creatures are protecting their turf by fighting each other. Until now I couldn't place the noises I heard; I thought they were distant animal noises. Now I see that they weren't distant at all.

"The dumping of these units while they are filled with old food is illegal. This means that this was done when the dump was closed. Also, by the shear number of creatures below us, I would say the food has only been available for a matter of hours not days. I'm afraid this can only mean one thing." Mohamed looks at Frank.

"Someone with access to this dump was here earlier allowing this mess to be made and that someone may still be here or may return at any time," Frank says.

"Ah yes, our assumption that we are alone in the dump today because it is Sunday may, in fact, be erroneous." With that said, Mohamed looks for the next appliance on which to move.

Chapter 27
Rescue Mission

I lean heavily on Mohamed and Frank as we make our way from one dead appliance heap to another. When we at last arrive at the fence that guards the hospital grounds, I stare up at the well-over-six-feet-tall ancient black iron fence. As the poles come to an end they taper into sharp spears, which, I assume, were created as a deterrent for people like us who hope to get over the fence.

"Well, at least it isn't barbed wire," I say. "But those spear shapes at the top of the fence poles still look mighty sharp to me. Of course, now that I see how tall this fence is I don't exactly know how we'll even get up high enough for those spear things to rip into our flesh anyway."

"We've come prepared," Mohamed states matter-of-factly.

"I have a rope ladder, the type people use as a fire escape in apartment buildings. I have heavy gloves and these." Frank holds up a pink rubber ball with a cheerful smile. His efforts to encourage me fall flat. "These will be pushed onto the spears so that we will not be hurt by them as we pull ourselves over the fence."

"We really are well prepared, I must say that. We have our backpacks full of tricks .Our enemies don't know we're here. And, if our enemies show up, we have binoculars to watch them with. We also have weapons should we need them. How can we fail?" My attempt at cheerful banter makes Frank briefly smile. "I'm okay, really, I'm better now that the rat thing is done, well, at least for now. I know we have to come back this way but I'm not going to think about that right now."

Mohamed sets up the ladder and the pink balls without a problem. He gets over the top of the iron fence with no struggle whatsoever. He waits for me on the other side of the fence with assurances that he will help lower me to the ground to avoid my injuring myself. I find climbing the ladder awkward but not difficult. When it comes to getting my body over the ball-topped speared fence poles… well, that is not so easy. Because my arms are not strong enough to hold me up while I slide my legs over the top of the fence, somehow I end up dangling sideways from the top of the fence with no idea how to jettison myself to the other side. Thankfully, Frank comes to my rescue. His powerful arms push my me over the fence while keeping a firm hold on me to prevent a fall. I feel Mohamed's hands waiting to ease me down.

"The wind is weird," I say as we crouch down in the overgrown lawn.

"I feel it too," Frank says.

Mohamed looks up into the sky. "If a storm is starting and it's not a natural storm, then is it the one aimed at Otis? Why now? Have they decided to attack Otis because their plans from last night failed?"

"If so, then there's some logic to their actions. But, under the circumstances right now, it isn't time for us to figure it out. We have to rescue the others first." Frank steps forward and points up the hill. "Let's go."

The hike up the back hill of the hospital campus would be pleasant under other circumstances. Sure, the grass is overgrown, the bushes are straggly, and the once beautiful flower gardens are pretty much destroyed; however we are in a natural haven of peacefulness that any human could appreciate. Of course, this temporary reprise is short lived. There, atop the hill, the remains of a building beckons us to enter the abandoned world of an institution left behind by time.

"There's what's left of the old dormitory. According to Sarah, it's almost directly across from the foundation where we believe the old laboratory prison is." Frank pauses at the crest to scan the horizon. "There's no one in sight. Let's run for our destination point."

As I sprint across the open overgrown lot, I stumble on rocks and other debris hidden beneath the grassy weeds. I am recovering from a face first fall when I hear the distant sound of an automobile engine. I spot Frank waving his arms as a warning sign for me to get down. Just seconds later, I make out a black SUV coming up the entrance driveway. The pain in my two hands and right knee increases in intensity as I crawl as quickly as I can to the closest decent hiding spot, which is merely a clump of straggly overgrown weeds. Flat on my stomach, I try to convince myself that whoever just arrived will not notice me because no one is expecting to find anyone on the property. It seems like a very long time before I finally poke my head up to see what is happening. When I do, I am shocked to see a large man dressed in dark clothing coming toward me. I know I have been caught, but I must somehow convince this enemy I am alone so Mohamed and Frank can continue the rescue mission, which I hope will now include rescuing me. I get up on my knees and lift my arms. Before I can stand and announce that I am unarmed I hear a muffled gun shot and the man in the dark clothes falls to his knees. Within seconds a second and third shot are fired. I don't need to get closer to recognize that the man in front of me is now dead.

I am still staring at the corpse of the newly killed man when I feel Mohamed's arms lifting me up. His deep voice has a soothing tone to it as he repeatedly tells me that everything will be alright. The revolver with the silencer attached to it is sticking out of his jacket pocket: its weight making the garment sway awkwardly.

"You got that gun from the cathedral?" I ask even though I am fairly certain the answer is affirmative.

"I got many weapons the night we were there. It is a good thing I did, too. This man, whoever he may be, is an enemy. Of that I am certain. If I did not do what I did he would have…" Mohamed stands over the dead man's face-down body. He uses his foot to lift up the corpse's right side. "See, his right hand is holding a gun! He would have killed you Abia. I had no choice but to kill him first."

I am stunned that I didn't notice the man was armed. Feeling weak at the knees with the realization that my life was saved by a matter of mere seconds, I grab hold of my brother's arm and whisper, "What can I say but thank you?"

"No, Abia, for all you have done for me you will never need to thank me. After all, are you not risking your life so that I may find a way to earn a pardon for my past evil actions and I may make some type of life for myself someday?"

"Yeah, that's part of it. But…"

Interrupted by a half-crazed Frank barreling our way, we let the emotion packed moment pass. After we gave all calmed down from my near execution, I go up to the foundation where the belowground prison should be located while the men deal with the corpse of the man in black. At first, this area reveals nothing out of the ordinary, but after I examine the ground beneath the overgrown weeds and bushes, I observe the ground drops off on one side. Moving to a different spot, I can now make out how the building foundation was once exposed, allowing for a walk-in door. Although no entrance is visible, I study the ground for footprints and disturbed earth. Again, my first impression is that there is nothing to find. But then, slowly, I detect a vague path leading to the foundation wall. Since the wall is completely covered by heavy vegetation, I paw through vines of all kinds to find a door. My arms are bleeding from scratches when I finally find what I'm looking for: a locked metal door leading to what I believe was once the below ground mental institution laboratory.

*****

"The door is locked. Check the dead man for keys," I tell the Frank and Mohamed as they lug the corpse to the iron door.

"I heard keys jingling around in his coat pocket." As soon as the body is put down Frank locates a key ring. The sheer number of keys on the ring makes me wonder what else this man did with his time. My patience is tested as key after key is tried in the door lock. Finally, a key slides into the slot and turns the tumblers open.

Frank pushes the metal door but finds it fits too snugly into the frame to open easily. Using the weight of his body to force it open, he is the first one inside the dark and exceptionally smelly place.

After a couple of uncontrollable gags I manage to ask, "What in the world is that ghastly stink?"

"It's stale air, human waste, and I'm not sure what else. I have Vicks Vapor Rub to put beneath out nostrils to help us cope with the odor. It is an old police trick I learned watching TV." Frank smears the strong vaporized jelly beneath his nose and hands the small plastic jar to Mohamed, who does the same.

"I'm going in. Give me that stuff," I say.

The not unpleasant smell of vapor rub may sting the skin lining my nostrils, but it is a pleasant sensation compared to having to smell the horrific odor I know is lingering inside these walls. We enter as quietly as we can. We are only about twenty feet inside the dark room when I hear movement. I stop walking and point to where I believe the noise came from. With gun drawn, Mohamed takes the lead. Frank and I stay close behind him while the thought of foul odors is replaced by the fear of the unknown.

"Why aren't you yurning on the lantern?" Agent Zachary Brown asks hoarsely. "Don't you want to get a good look at your prisoners?"

"Yeah, don't you think the three of us have done the pitch-black bat cave thing long enough?" Randy's scratchy voice calls out.

"Arnie?" I yell, unable to control my growing excitement. "It's us. Are you okay?"

All of a sudden, a mismatched chorus of elated voices breaks out. While Mohamed follows Randy's instructions to light up old but surprisingly efficient oil lanterns, I stand on tip toes and look through the small barred window of the thick metal door that stands between us and the prisoners. Inside the room being used as their prison cell are three very old cots with moth-eaten wool blankets. There is a toilet overflowing with filth and a sink which I doubt is hooked up to water. The walls have light green lead paint chipping off of them, revealing a coat of yellow lead paint chipping beneath it. The floor is so dirty I can't make out what it is made of. The odor from inside is so disgusting that the vapor rub is not strong enough to stop me from retching.

With my empty stomach churning, I watch as the prisoners are released. Randy comes out first. His clothes are dirty and torn. He is limping and the right side of his face is bruised. Arnie is the next one out. His dirty clothes are stained with blood, the source of which becomes evident when he steps into the full light of the lantern. His chest and back have sores where blood letting lash marks from a whip are still oozing. The odd scientist appears frail and beaten, yet he cocks his head to the side and politely thanks me for my help. Together, we watch Agent Zachary Brown strut into the light. He is so battered it is a wonder he can walk at all. His swollen face doesn't betray his true feelings but the hate filled blaze in his eyes does.

When the prisoners see the dead body outside the door they explain that he was responsible for much of the torture they endured. As the corpse is quickly dragged inside the makeshift prison, I go to Arnie who has been uncommonly quiet.

"Are you okay? You've been taken prisoner twice now. It looks like you've been beaten, too."

"I am not okay as you phrase it. I believe I am quite traumatized. General Kulik and his army of animalistic thugs will continue to beat me because they believe I know more about the weather weapons technology than I believe I do. After this recent round of questioning, it has occurred to me that, perhaps I am privy to knowledge that I have as of yet fully understood the importance of." Arnie systematically lists off a group of scientific terms of which I don't know the meaning. He then looks at me and says, "Given more time and much needed recovery, I believe I may be able to operate the technology that controls the storms. It is possible. I have thought about this much during both of my imprisonments. That is how I controlled my hysteria. Yes, even people with my mild form of autism feel hysteria although we don't always show it. Anyway, as I've been taught at times of great stress and fear, I focus on minuscule details of a complex nature…"

And so Arnie goes on and on the entire way back to the dump. While Randy explains how he and Arnie were abducted from the park, Arnie is telling me how he tends to speak continuously as a way to release anxiety. Then, while Agent Brown fills us in on everything that happened inside the prison, Arnie speaks of cumulous(which I figure out are clouds) and barometric pressures and other weather related terms of which I don't know the meaning.. I am relieved, for multiple reasons, when we get back to the tall iron fence with the pink balls on the top spears.

"Sarah's calling me," I announce as I take the call. Her news is short and not good. "Oh man, she was in the lane nearest the entrance when the cops came by. She explained her position there by saying she was a reporter doing a story for a newspaper. Thankfully, she has her stepmother's doctored up press pass on her. But he made her move and she's positive he'll be back to make sure she left."

"Did she get the back of the SUV ready?" Randy asks.

"As ready as she can. She figures that Frank will drive and Agent Brown will be in the front. Sarah and Randy and I should fit in the back seat. That leaves Mohamed and Arnie to squeeze in the back. It's going to be really tight, but there's no other way."

"I am quite pliable and will be able to contort my body as need be," Arnie announces. "But I may need help getting over this fence. My limbs have been beaten extensively."

Agent Brown takes hold of the rope ladder and holds his hand out. "Come on Arnie, you can do this, you'll see."

Although we are all tired and beaten creatures, we each manage to get ourselves over to the side of the dump, albeit some of us with more trouble than others. At the edge of the appliance cemetery, we discuss how best to cross while avoiding danger and disgusting sights. Unexpectedly, a man dressed in jeans and a green hooded sweatshirt jumps out in front of us and starts taking pictures of Mohamed. In a voice comparable to a screech he yells out, "I knew it was you! I knew it. I saw you earlier and recognized you," he turns to point at me. "You're Abia Haddad. Mohamed Haddad's sister. I saw you climbing through the appliance pit. I work here and just happened to be here on a side job... allowing some appliances to be dumped and presto! You come in. I was waiting around for a second delivery when I saw you. Damn, and then the rats came for the rotten food and you suckers go through there anyways! And I watched you and knew you were the Haddad terrorist! While you were doing whatever it was you were doing on the hospital grounds, I checked your pictures on the computer and, sure enough, it's you. And guess what? I took your pictures and I'm gonna turn you in and get the million dollar reward and everything. In fact, I'm gonna post this picture on Facebook right now before anything happens to me..."

A muffled bang sounds off from behind us. With his steady hand still extended straight out in front of him, Zachary Brown says, "No, Mr. Dump Man, you will not turn in the man who just saved my life."

The dump man's bearded face grimaces just as he lifts his hand to cover his chest wound. Within seconds, his slightly bowlegged knees buckle. His body bounces when it hits the ground.

"Unfortunately, there will be collateral damage during this battle with my father-in-law, General Kulik, and my very misguided wife, Alena. This man is, I fear, is the first of many. I realize that I am more accustomed to this sort of thing than you, so take my advice. When a situation arises where it comes down to "us" versus "them" do what needs to be done to protect "us,"" Zac Brown says while leading us past the corpse.

"Then you believe I have changed?" Mohamed asks.

"I don't believe in believing. I believe in knowing facts. I know you have, for whatever reasons, become a die hard patriot of this country, determined to right the wrongs you did in the past. I believed this when you helped to expose the Eurabian enemies. I know this now because you risked your life to save mine; a risk you took because you realize that freeing me is the only way to save the United States from serious political ruin and from slipping from the primary to a secondary military world power. If the Russians have the weather weapons program that our country developed while our own program is destroyed, it will be disastrous. But to also make it so that this country cannot rebuild a weather weapons program because it is public knowledge that doing so causes global warming…that is a situation beyond disastrous. No, this cannot be allowed to happen and you believe that you need me to stop General Kulik and Alena from making it happen. And I am afraid you are right; you do need me."

*****

I'd rather not think about our return trip through the appliance dump or the close call we had with the local police when Sarah came to pick us up. To keep myself from losing what is left of my sanity, I will simply push these ugly thoughts aside. Instead, I think about Agent Brown and wonder what this man now intends to do with the group of us now.

"Agent Brown…" I begin.

"As I told Randy and Arnie, call me Zac. I believe once people have saved your life you should be on a first-name basis."

"Okay, Zac, how long have you known Alena and her father are traitors?"

"I wanted to believe my father-in-law was not guilty. Sometimes, even the strongest of us are weakened by emotions, however. But Alena's change in behavior toward me, coupled with her growing closeness to her father, started to make me rethink things," Zac explains.

"Okay, so your attention has been on them lately and…" I am interrupted by Zac's laughter. "What's so funny?"

"You're fishing around to find out what I know about you leaving notes and money for your brother in that old cemetery. Yeah, I know all about that." Zac faces the back seat to look over my head at Mohamed. "The truth is, I didn't know what to do about you. Yes, you're a terrorist fugitive, but you're also an American patriot hero. Now you've saved my life. Damn, you don't make arresting you and making you face the death penalty easy."

"Perhaps we should take the death penalty off the table, at least until General Kulik's plans have been stopped," Mohamed says calmly.

To change the unpleasant topic, I quickly say, "So we know that the U.S. government developed weather weapons and while doing so inadvertently created global warming, right?"

Arnie clears his throat saying, "Yes. Kulik sits on the political committee that discovered this unfortunate fact through its research titled Operation Tin Man."

"So the government decided to destroy the evidence by creating a storm to wipe out the evidence from Operation Tin Man at the it did last week. And now it is sending a storm to Otis Military Base to do the same there."

"That is also accurate," Arnie states. "However, there is one complete set of documentation on Operation Tin Man that is still held by General Kulik."

"Was held by Kulik,, we have it now." Frank says."

"You found it yesterday? In all the excitement I didn't ask. I assumed if you did, you'd have said something, " Zac says loudly. "I've looked everywhere for the Operation Tin Man files. I've searched my house, his house, offices…"

"We have it all right. And we got to know the bishop of the cathedral really well, too." Frank provides a detailed explanation of the events of our mission yesterday.

Since I lived the experience at the cathedral and don't particularly wish to re-live it a second time, I allow myself to drift off to sleep. I am snapped awake by earsplitting thunder. When my mind clears, I hear Arnie saying, "From everything I've been able to learn about the Weather Weapons Program, once a storm is set into motion, it cannot be stopped. This means that we are literally driving into what is likely to be the worst storm this country has ever seen to battle with the evil enemies that created it. Our lives will be threatened not only by our enemies but by the storm as well. If my mental calculations are at all accurate, this hurricane-like storm will rival those that have made history. Of course, with fire spewing tornadoes as part of its ferocity, as you can well surmise, we are in for quite a great deal of peril."

"How we can destroy our enemies and save the people on the military base and surrounding area without revealing the role the United States has played in making this storm and the one that hit Boston? To betray our country's secrets, regardless of how wrong they are, are an act of treason that we could be taken into custody for, right?" Sarah asks.

"So we have to play heroes without any government help other than you," Randy says to Zac. "Can we even do this?"

"Actually you have no government help at all. You see, General Kulik has compromised me with Homeland Security. As far as I know, I am now considered an enemy of the state…just like Mohamed." Zac breathes out a long sigh.

"Getting back to what happens if we expose the government's part in creating these weapon storms. What exactly would they do to us if we leaked out the truth to the media?" Sarah asks again.

When Zac remains silent, it is Mohamed who answers. "I have no doubt they will kill all of us before such a thing is allowed to happen. And, I believe Zac's silence indicates he agrees with me."

Chapter 28
Jack

The closer we get to Cape Cod, the stronger and more frequent the wind gusts seem to be. We also observe an erratic presence of thunder and lightning as we drive east. Rather than appearing in clusters, these storm disturbances come and go with no discernable pattern. Arnie is commenting non-stop about the weather phenomenon we are experiencing, but of course, I understand little of what he is saying except that the storm we are driving into has to be a weather weapon storm rather than one created by nature. As tired as we are all feeling right now, not one of us is sleeping. Be it the trauma of what we have all just been through, the craziness of the storm, or anxiety about what we have yet to do, all seven of us are wide awake. After listening to Frank and Randy question Zac about a number of things I decide to get some answers for myself.

"Speaking of our jobs on the military base, why did you agree to get Frank and I jobs at Otis?" I ask Zac.

"I did it for two reasons. Number one, I wanted the bullet that killed Dr. Azar returned to me. It is the only evidence that exists of the governmental cover-up of what happened in Boston two and a half years ago, and, quite simply, I want control of it. I only gave it to you to sneak it out of the Homeland Security Office, I never intended for you to keep it as long as you did. The second reason is that I need Mohamed's help with this battle. I knew you were in contact with him and I knew that if you asked him to he would help you, or should I say us, bring the General to justice."

From behind me I hear Mohamed's deep voice, "Why do you need me?"

"General Kulik planned to kill me because I know far too much about him, Alena, and their treason. To do this, he intended to kidnap Abby and use her as bait to get you to come out of hiding. Once he had you, he would set you up as my murderer, an ingenious plan because of its believability and simplicity.

Eventually he would kill you, too. With you dead he could then build evidence that supported the theory that you were the ninth Eurabian and not himself. He could also blame you for many of his treasonous actions. So, knowing all this, I knew you would fight against him to protect your sister and yourself."

"That is all true but it does not answer my question. Why do you need me to fight General Kulik?"

"Well Mohamed, it's come down to this. For us to accomplish what needs to be accomplished, which is to kill Kulik, save the people on and around the military base from the storm, and destroy whoever is controlling the storm, we need to keep every set of official eyes off of what we're doing. Otherwise, as well meaning as law enforcement may be, they will complicate matters and inadvertently enable Kulik and Alena to accomplish their traitorous goals. To keep local law enforcement busy, we need them chasing after someone they want more than anyone else. And that someone, Mohamed, is you. We tested using you in such a diversionary plan in order to disrupt the meeting set at the baseball field. Although our plan failed overall, because Kulik arrived at the field much earlier than we anticipated, the diversion part of the plan worked by keeping the state and local authorities so busy they had no idea of what was happening around them. The strategy of using you to distract the authorities is a good one, but it is not foolproof."

"So, while we are doing whatever we can to stop General Kulik and protect innocent people from a killer storm, Mohamed is going to do what exactly?" Sarah asks.

"He is going to be himself, only a more public version of himself. In other words, I think Mohamed has to make a few appearances." As if he recognizes the horrified look forming on my face, Zac adds, "Oh don't worry, he will never get caught. He is to be seen and heard but never caught. Oh no, I don't intend to ask Mohamed to turn himself in. On the contrary, I am asking him not to turn himself in, but instead to play hide and seek with the authorities just long enough for the rest of us to save this country from disaster!"

"I very much would like to learn more about these public appearances you would like me to make. I am fascinated by the concept, but confused with how to accomplish a sighting without endangering myself. Are you suggesting that I be recorded or make live sightings?" Mohamed asks.

"Carefully planned and executed live sightings that I will personally work on. I realize this requires you to trust me, which you may not…." Zac stops to think. After a long pause he adds, "In the next day or so, you and I need to come to an understanding. We need to trust each other with our own lives, as well as the lives of those we both care very much about. You have no reason to trust me as I am a federal authority who is sworn to hunt you down and bring you to justice. I have no reason to trust you as you are known as and admit to being a terrorist who attempted to bring unspeakable horrible death to this country. Yet, due to very strange circumstances, we have both demonstrated that we will protect each other from harm. I have known of your location these past six months but have never turned you in. In fact, I have deliberately covered up your hiding places from my own staff. And you have just saved my life, plain and simple. Therefore, be it reasonable or not, an element of trust does exist between us already. I believe the best way for us to move forward at this point is to speak openly and honestly to each other. So, on that note, I will ask you a question."

The quietness inside the SUV is neither awkward nor welcome, it simply exists until Zac continues. "What do you want to happen for the rest of your life? What do you hope will be your future? How do you expect your life to play out given all that has happened?"

"My future is tainted by the mistakes of my past. This is a fact I cannot alter despite my deep heartfelt wish to erase the unforgivable things I have done. When I was involved in the terrorist attacks in New York, New Jersey, and Boston I had convinced myself that the United States was evil and deserved to be punished. I cannot blame those that taught me to believe these untruths, for I agreed to believe them to be true. Yet I am, and was then, an American who should have known better than to believe this country is rooted in anything but truth, justice, and equality. My life was turned upside down after the 9/11 attacks. I was an all American young man about to marry the girl of his dreams, when suddenly, a terrorist attack turned me into someone vile and evil…all because I am also a Muslim. I was angry when my relationship was ended by my beloved's family. I was angry by the way my friends now looked at me because of my faith. I was angry at the way people I didn't know despised me because I would not say all Muslims are evil. I was angry at the way my family advised me to give the country time to heal from the Islamic terrorist attack before judging all Americans as unworthy. I sought solace in others who shared my anger, and as we know all too well, these new friends of mine were terrorists. So I, like them, chose jihad as a way to vent my anger. That decision has ruined my life. You ask about my future as if I have one, but how does one describe something that doesn't exist? I don't have a future. No, I only have a past that I can never run away from and the present in which I keep trying to run. Is there a future for me, Mohamed Haddad? No, there is none. My life will play out one day at a time, and then, some day, I will be caught, found guilty and brought to justice. I assume I will receive the death penalty, which I rightly deserve. I wish I could face the consequences for my actions now, but I am not brave enough to bring such sorrow to those I love, so I continue to run away from the ever gaining monster of my past."

"What do you mean you're not brave enough to face the consequences because of sorrow for others?" Frank asks.

I feel Mohamed's warm hand on my shoulder. He kisses the top of my head and says in a voice just a tone above a whisper, "I keep running because of you, Abia. Because you do such things as hide disguised packages inside cemeteries with the hope that I will find them. Because you give me money I know you cannot afford to give away. Because you believe that I am pure of heart, despite evidence to the contrary. My conviction and subsequent death will be too painful for you. Do you not see that my persecution will murder your spirit?"

Holding back sobs I manage to say, "So…when you made sure I … the world knew you weren't attacking the United States six months ago…when you helped to expose the real enemy the…Eurabians…"

"I exposed the real enemy to clear myself for you, Abia, because I know you can not live your life in peace believing I am still the evil terrorist I once was. Unfortunately, I now find I am believed to be one of the enemies I helped to expose, ah… but such is life."

"Okay, let's just put all the touching, loving family stuff aside. We get it. Mohamed doesn't think he has a future because of his past. That pretty much answers your questions, Zac. So, we're almost back to the trailer and it's time for Mohamed to ask a question." The mental and physical abuse Randy has suffered has weakened his usual crusty exterior. Although his comment is meant to sound impatient, I can tell the interaction between Mohamed and me is stirring up heartfelt emotions he would prefer not to display.

"I have but one question. Is it possible for you to allow me to see my family, privately, before I am taken into custody? I do not deserve the privilege, I am aware, but I would like to beg their forgiveness before I am a prisoner."

Agent Zac Brown spews out a great many words but doesn't actually answer Mohamed's question. I'm not surprised, really, as even if he had an answer he wouldn't want to disclose it in front of the rest of us.

As we get closer to home, we have to stop and clear the road of tree branches and other storm scattered debris quite often. In fact, in the center of the entrance drive of the trailer park a branch from a white birch tree is dangling down so low Frank has to swerve around it to get by. The wind gusts are now blowing between forty and fifty miles per hour, it is sleeting, and there is still periodic thunder and lightning. There are not, however, tornadoes of any sort including those with fire spewing abilities. We are passing the park office trailer when Katie Jinkins comes sprinting out. She is frantically waving at us. Not wanting her to see everyone crammed into the SUV, I hastily jump out and tell Frank I will meet them at the trailer.

"Is everything okay?" I ask.

"As okay as it can be. The cops still don't know who killed my father but I think it was the creepy General Kulik. Sure he's limping around on a walker because of the shots he took to his legs, knee, or whatever, but he's behind the death of his brother and my father, I just know it." Katie holds down her hair while until a gust of wind subsides. "What would you think if you were me?"

Sensing an opportunity to garner information from this young and somewhat naïve girl, I ask if we can speak inside the trailer. When I see Kileen in the office my guard goes up a bit as I don't trust her as much as I trust her sister.

"I guess, to answer your question, I don't know what to think about your father's death. What was his relationship with this General, anyway? Why was he involved with such a man?"

Kileen snickers. "Oh come on, you know my dad was working for him and part of that work was spying on you."

"But why?" Katie asks. "Why was my dad asked to spy on you and your friends? Is that what got him killed?"

"I don't know, but I do know that General Kulik is a dangerous person and the two of you need to stay clear of him. If you ask too many questions or are too accusatory about him being behind your father's murder, then he may turn on you, too." I warn.

"As far as Kulik believes we hated our dad, which is actually partly true. But, he was still our father and we want the truth to be known." Katie looks at Kileen before adding, "Listen, we both know my father wasn't a good person and that he did some really bad things. We're not stupid. We also know that he probably deserved to die. Kileen and I didn't always agree about him, and to be honest, he sort of put a wedge between us. But we still want to know who killed him and why."

"Is this for your conscious or for some other reason?"

Kileen shrugs her shoulders at Katie.

"No. It's because of this." Katie opens a desk drawer and removes an envelope. "We found this in one of his jacket pockets. We didn't know what else to do with it but to tell you. Maybe we should bring it to the police but....they might not know what's going on like you do. If Dad was spying on you for General Kulik then you have to know what this means, right? It's instructions for tonight." She unfolds the paper. "He was supposed to go to Boston, meet up with people, and then deal with someone named Jack Sullivan?"

I gently take the note from Katie. "This is extremely important and I know exactly what it means. The two of you may have just saved two lives. What your father can't do someone else surely will try to do."

Kileen steps forward. "If General Kulik knows we know about this…"

"Don't tell anyone about this note! No one…ever!" I hear the hysteria in my voice. "Listen, I know the two of you have mixed emotions about your father's death. That's natural. But, for now, keep partying and pretending you're glad he's gone and also that you know nothing about what he was doing. Do you hear me? This is a matter of life and death!"

*****

Back with the others at the trailer we all agree that Jinkins' note implies that he was to meet Kulik at the cathedral. We all surmise that Kulik is going to the cathedral to retrieve his Operation Tin Man evidence and the top secret information he has on the weather weapons program. As for the reference in the note to Jack Sullivan, that is really a reference to two people: Bishop Sullivan and the cathedral's janitor, Jack. Both these men were to be killed tonight because they too know about General Kulik's traitorous plans. Knowing the General's plans for tonight means that all the plans we discussed on the ride home from Boston need to be changed. So a discussion about returning to the cathedral tonight starts up. The conversation is supercharged with energy, anxiety, and fear.

"We need to cease the multiple conversations and focus on the most important matter at hand," Arnie instructs, as if we are unaware that we are interrupting each other. "The question to be addressed first is who is going to the cathedral tonight."

"He's right," Sarah says.

Randy, Frank, and I nod in unison.

Mohamed, who is watching the storm from the kitchen window, turns to face us. "It is foolish for all of us to go. I believe the plan for tonight needs to be made by Zac."

Sarah, Randy, Frank, and I exchange surprised glances before turning out attention to Zac. The agent tents his fingers, clears his throat, and says, "I will go tonight. That is a given. Since all of you are familiar with the cathedral and tunnel, that would put you on even footing except in the areas of physical strength and the willingness to kill if need be. For this reason, I select Mohamed and Randy, both of whom have taken a man's life. I want a team of four which means I can select one other. The logical choice would be Frank, for he is strong, but I would be a fool to underestimate the value of women's instinct. I have always believed females can sense things that males cannot; many law enforcement officials believe this as well. We believe it is related to the maternal instinct. So my selection for the fourth team member is Abby. Her instincts have been tested and proven accurate since I first met her years ago and I have absolute faith in them today. In fact, I am willing to stake my life on them."

*****

I am haunted during the drive to the cathedral in Boston by thoughts of Frank's anger at not being included in tonight's mission. Sure, I expected him to be upset that he was left behind with Sarah and Arnie to work on the project dealing with Mohamed's planned "sightings,"but I didn't expect him to be inconsolably distressed. I even pleaded Frank's case for coming with us to Zac and Mohamed, but they adamantly refused to consider changing the original plan. My stomach is in knots all the way to our destination. It isn't until the dark stone cathedral is looming over us that I am able to push my Frank from my mind.

"What's with the red and blue flashing lights?" I ask, while bringing one of the back seat windows down. "I don't hear construction or smell smoke. It looks like the fuss is right at the cathedral, doesn't it?"

"Damn it." Zac slows the SUV down to a crawl. "Is there any place I can pull off the street?"

"Up a ways on the left," Randy points out. "There's a parking lot that looks full but maybe you can squeeze in there."

"There is something happening at the cathedral. Perhaps the authorities are aware the bishop is missing?" Mohamed pulls his hat down even further on his head. "Neither I nor Zac can be seen here. Randy and Abia must investigate."

"Let us out here and we'll call you to pick us up somewhere else. Get out of here before someone notices you." Randy immediately jumps out of the passenger seat of the SUV and I follow directly behind him. We cross the street as casually as we can considering we are in the middle of snarled traffic. When the cathedral is in sight it is obvious that the police are, in fact, investigating something inside.

"People will recognize me if I ask what's going on, so you'll have to do it. I'll be near that group of people. They look chatty so I may overhear something." I briefly watch Randy watch me as I walk away.

The group I chose to target has eight people, six of whom are women. The oldest two are so upset they appear to be crying. The younger ones seem enthralled in learning more about what is happening inside the building. As for the two men, well, they look like they just want to go home. I position myself about two feet behind them and begin deciphering who is saying what to whom. I soon realize that a corpse was found inside the cathedral a couple of hours ago. It takes a bit longer for me to learn that the corpse was that of a man, apparently an older man that was known to the two older women in this group. Next I listen for information about cause of death, such as heart attack, murder or suicide, anything that tells me what type of tragedy we're dealing with. It takes a full seven minutes before I realize that the group I am with does not know the cause of death. While I seek out a more knowledgeable source of information I feel my cell phone vibrate. It is Randy calling. Instinctively I look around the area for him but he is no where in sight.

"Hi, what's going on? Some guy died but I don't know who or how yet."

Randy speaks in a lowered voice just above a whisper. "The dead guy is Jack…the janitor of the cathedral."

"If he was in hiding with the bishop then how did he die inside of there?"

"From what I'm hearing he was murdered. We need to find the bishop to learn more."

"Okay, I can call him. I've got the number he gave me."

My hand shakes incessantly as I retrieve the bishop's cell phone number. I press the number to make the connection. I am preparing myself to hear a voice mail message when I hear Bishop Sullivan's frightened voice say hello.

"Where are you? What is going on? Oh, this is Abby Haddad and I'm just outside the cathedral but…"

"Oh Abby, what they did to Jack is unforgivable. I will never be able to wash the horrible images from my eyes."

"Forget that, where are you?"

"I am at the Cyclorama. I escaped through the tunnel. They caught us, Jam and me, and forced us to go back to the cathedral and explain where the Operation Tin Man evidence was moved. We both pretended we did not know anything, but General Kulik did not believe us. He started torturing Jack first and he made me watch. I could not stand it so I said the evidence was still in the tunnel and I would show him where. We went below: Jack, General Kulik, one of his henchmen, and me. Then Jack did a most courageous thing. He screamed out for me to run and he used the full force of his body to try and knock them over. I saw the big hulk trip before I ran down the tunnel. Minutes later I heard a gun shot. I fear my dear Jack was killed."

"I'm sorry to say that he was. The police are everywhere around the cathedral. That's where I am now."

"Oh, I see. My poor innocent Jack. He gave his life to protect mine."

"So you went through the tunnel to the Cyclorama and you're there right now?"

"Yes. I have no transportation as Kulik brought me back to the city in his vehicle. He tracked us down by Jack's cell phone. Oh to think such a thing can give away a hiding place."

"Does Kulik know you're at the Cyclorama?"

"Not that I can determine. Oh, it is so sad. And now his body is found inside the cathedral?"

"I don't know where inside because they're not letting anyone inside, but I'm sure it isn't in the tunnel."

"Perhaps he believes I will come out of hiding when I learn my friend was murdered in the sacred house of worship I am sworn to protect." The bishop sighs. "This is terrible."

"That's probably exactly what he thinks. So, logic says Kulik and his henchmen are still around here somewhere."

"Oh yes, that must be true. But Abby, you and I have made a terrible mistake. If the General was tracking Jack's cell phone to find us when we were hiding, then he is also tracking my phone now. This means he now knows I'm here at the Cyclorama. He may also know I am speaking to you and where you are. Oh my God in Heaven help us, we have just made a frighteningly deadly mistake!"

Chapter 29
Betrayal

It takes me three full passes through the crowd at the cathedral before I spot Randy's wild, bushy hair. After unsuccessfully trying to flag him down, I maneuver through the crowd until I can reach over and grab his jacket. The instant his face turns toward mine, I notice it is the ruddy red it gets when he is agitated. I expect him to say something upsetting, but instead he dons what I know to be a fake smile while slipping his arm over my shoulder. I find his pretense that we are a couple out for a nightly stroll who happened upon the cathedral fire to be, rather unsettling. While mumbling a bit of nonsense about getting back to our apartment, he leads me past the onlookers. It isn't until we are far from the crowd that he speaks,

"I saw one of Kulik's thugs hanging near the side entrance of the cathedral. At least I think he's a thug. We can't chance going inside that way with that man hanging around. When I went to the side entrance I saw another big dude. He's hanging out across the street with his eye on the side door. I found the exact same thing at the rear entrance."

"We could never risk going in the cathedral with the cops inside anyway. Mohamed and Zac could never take that chance. I think Kulik and his crew are hanging around here hoping the discovery of Jack's corpse will make Bishop Sullivan come back here. But I know that he won't because I just spoke to him. He's hiding at the Cyclorama. He took the tunnel there earlier. The bishop thinks Kulik found Jack and him by tracking the cell phone, and now that he and I have connected…"

Randy musses his already messy hair in frustration. "Then Kulik knows about us being here, too. Damn it. We have to get to the bishop before they do. Our mission is turning into a huge mess, a complicated mess."

"Not necessarily. We know Kulik and Alena are around here waiting for the bishop, right? So where do you think they're hiding?"

Randy slips his arm off of my shoulder and asks, "Where?"

"They didn't follow the bishop through the Cyclorama tunnel and they're not with him. And I doubt they went through the tunnel that leads to the ocean. That means they're either out here in this crowd or they're still down below the cathedral. I don't see them anywhere out here, do you? And, why would they post look-out guards at the cathedral doors, like you just described to me, if they were outside? They wouldn't. They're still inside the tunnel for some reason and their look-outs are making sure no one interferes with what they're doing. No, they may not be able to find Kulik's hidden Operation Tin Man files, but they're down below the cathedral doing something."

"Okay, so if you're right, we need to find out what they're doing. But how do we get to them with cops and their look-out henchmen everywhere?"

"The same way Bishop Sullivan got away from them. I don't know where the secret tunnel exit door is inside the Cyclorama building, but the bishop found out tonight. He can bring us there and we can surprise Kulik, Alena, and whoever else is below ground with them by backtracking through the tunnel. We simply take the tunnel back to the area underneath the cathedral. They'll never suspect us of doing that."

Randy receives my plan with an enthusiastic grunt. We scramble back to Zac and Mohamed who we find parked in front of a closed tobacco store located several blocks from the cathedral. They both like my idea about going through the tunnel to lay siege on our unsuspecting enemies, so we quickly head out for the Cyclorama. Although we do not reach a consensus on whether or not to include Bishop Sullivan in our surprise attack, we do agree that we need to learn more from this man before ironing out the final details of our plan. When we arrive at the Cyclorama, I am surprised by the size of this architectural wonder, which until now I didn't know existed. I am even more surprised to find Bishop Sullivan eagerly awaiting us outside, as I would expect him to want to remain hidden from his enemies.

"The entrance to the tunnel is not recognizable from the Cyclorama side. I doubt anyone at this establishment even knows of its existence. You see," the bishop says, running his fingers over the torn knees of his pants, "you see, the tunnel ends into a crawl space and you must crawl for about twenty or so feet until you reach a wooden trap door above your head. You then must push this door open. This is difficult and noisy as the hinges are rusted. Then you push your body up through the hole and climb into a very narrow space. When you put the trap door back down it blends in amazingly well with the cement and stone floor of the narrow closet you are in. This closet is in the basement of the Cyclorama building. It is unique in that it has no door. It is more of a pantry than a closet, per se. There are shelves on one side where odd theater-related things are stored. From this pantry closet you can sneak upstairs into the Cyclorama, you can eavesdrop on conversations through the old heating system, as I did before I ventured up the stairs, and you can even get outside through a bulkhead door. Yes, the creator of the tunnel did a remarkable job."

"So, we can all slip into the tunnel and easily find our way to the cathedral?" Randy asks.

"Not easily, no. I did not have a flashlight so it was very difficult for me. As you are more prepared it may be easier for you, but it will not be easy, no. You see, for some reason there are small tunnels branching off the main tunnel along the way. These branches are all dead ends. I do not know their purpose, only that there are forks in the tunnel that must be maneuvered," Bishop Sullivan explains. "Perhaps their original use was simply to confuse those in the tunnel who were not supposed to be there?"

"That's possible. Did you notice a pattern about these branches?" Zac asks.

"No, but I did memorize them and how I got here. I did so in case I had to backtrack to the cathedral for some reason." The bishop's sorrowful eyes momentarily close. "I had hoped to rescue Jack. I fear that opportunity was not given to me."

"You could lead us back through the tunnel, right?" Randy asks.

"I could. In fact, I believe we could make good time now that I know which turns to take." Looking at Mohamed, Bishop Sullivan adds, "Do you think, perhaps, General Kulik is still in the tunnel?"

"I think that is likely. What of Alena?" Mohamed asks, stepping closer to the holy man.

"I believe she is with her father. I overheard Kulik say his daughter would be the one transporting the evidence to Russia. He was upset that she was stalling for time. He blamed her behavior on the fact that she does not have her children and was stalling for more time to find them. The General was insisting that their plans do not change. I assume she will obey her father even if she does not want to. I am sure I heard this correctly. You see, Jack and I were in the back of their van when we were traveling back to Boston and I listened to everything they said."

"I'm surprised they spoke in front of you and Jack. It makes me suspicious as to the truth of what you heard them say." Zac steps closer to the bishop. He focuses on the bishop's face, particularly his eyes, while waiting for a response.

"No need to be suspicious, agent, they did not know I could understand them. You see, they were speaking Russian. Yes, I too speak Russian. I once worked closely with the Russian Catholic churches. Such a coincidence for an Irishman you must be thinking; but not really. My father was one hundred percent Irish, this is true; but my mother, oh no, she was not Irish at all. In Russia her name was Вера, but she was called Vera. My father met her during World War II. He was a soldier in the Ireland army and she was a nurse with the Russian forces. Such different people from such different worlds, yet they fell in love and…well…the rest is history."

"Your mom taught you to speak Russian?" I ask, even though I'm fairly certain the answer will be yes.

"Oh no, actually, she did not. You see, it was her heritage that interested me with the Roman Catholics in Russia. Yes, I worked with this minuscule population among the Russian people from behind the Iron Curtain for some time in my early career. I taught myself the Russian language. My mother was a true blue American and spoke nothing but English once she became a citizen of this country. God bless her soul."

Zac ends our chit chat by barking out orders in the manner of a drill sergeant. Randy and I are to park the SUV in an unnoticeable place that is not too far from the Cyclorama. Mohamed, Zac, and the bishop will wait for us in the Cyclorama basement. Randy's short temper erupts when we find there are no available spaces anywhere nearby. Soon, our definition of keeping the SUV in close proximity expands as our frustration grows. Finally, a car up ahead pulls out from some sort of driveway. My hopes run high as I silently pray that none of the cars ahead of us take whatever spot may be up ahead. The driveway is very short and leads into an unmarked parking area. There are no lined parking spaces or signs, just some cars crammed into this small vacant lot that belongs to some unidentified person. I am about to debate with Randy whether we should park here or not when he squeezes the SUV between a white compact car and a black truck. Because the vehicles are parked so close together, my car door only opens part way and I have to slither out of the vehicle. I don't dare complain though because Randy's scowling red face looks prime to explode at the very next person or thing that irritates him.

When we reach the Cyclorama, Randy's bad temperament has calmed somewhat but he is still very much on edge. Inside, we find that the building has a main room which is circular with screens covering its circumference. It seems like an interesting place to visit under other circumstances. Only after milling around a few halls and opening several doors do we find the way down to the basement level. I briefly wonder why it isn't marked. My wondering stops when I see that the stairs are very narrow, worn, and certainly dangerous. The cost of liability insurance on this place would be unaffordable if the public were allowed to come down here. We find Zac waiting for us.

"Mohamed and the bishop have already gone into the tunnel. Abby, you go first. Randy and I will be last."

As the bishop warned, I find the tunnel is exceptionally well hidden. The pantry-like closet is so filled with items that it is not at all surprising that no one has ever noticed the trap door. With Zac's help, I drop down into the crawl space without any problem. However, my very first thought in this dark dank place is that I am claustrophobic and didn't know it until now. I feel increasingly overwhelmed by a need to escape from this too-tight spot. The walls on either side of me are too close, they touch my body with every move I make. I feel an urge to scream. I am also unreasonably itchy. My skin has the sensation that something is crawling on it, something with furry legs. I can see nothing in the darkness, I can smell my own breath, and I can hear my lungs breathing. I feel like I am, in a way, squished inside a capsule in which I cannot escape. I feel panic rising…

"Go on," Randy urges, while prodding me from behind. "It's only like forty feet or so."

I calculate that forty feet is less than eight lengths of me which isn't very long. So, if I crawl four feet a minute then…

"Abby, you're not moving."

"Okay," I whisper. "I'll go now."

The force it takes me to move my hands and knees across the gritty stone beneath me is minimal compared to what I have to do to get myself to continue to move into complete darkness. This is not darkness like you see in a room where a distant light casts a shadow just bright enough to break up the ebony in front of you. No, the darkness I am in is a completely pitch black with not one speck of light anywhere. As I move forward, I look for the proverbial light at the end of this tunnel. When I at last see a distant light I momentarily feel elated, but then some other feeling overcomes me…a feeling of being unsure…a feeling of confusion. I recall what Zac said back at the trailer about my women's intuition and decide I need to correctly assess my feelings. And then, just as the light in front of me beckons me forward it hits me, something is wrong and my gut is warning me of that.

"Doesn't it strike you as highly coincidental that Bishop Sullivan just happens to have a Russian mother? Isn't it just a bit convenient that he learned Russian because of her? Isn't it strange how his Irish father met her during World War II and they fell in love? I mean, what are the odds that a soldier in the Irish army would meet a Russian Army nurse anyway? Randy, you're a history buff. Tell me, did the Irish army serve on the Russian front?" I stop crawling to wait for Randy's response. I am taken aback when he grabs hold of my back side.

"What did you say? I wasn't actually listening to the bishop's dribble drabble about his parents and I think I missed something. Did you say his father was in the Irish army?"

"That's what he said. His dad was a soldier in the Irish army when he met...."

"Ireland was famously neutral during World War II! Some men from Ireland may have signed up in the British military, but I know there wasn't an Irish army! I'm sure about that. The bishop is lying!"

"Are you absolutely sure of that?" Zac asks. "We have no internet access down here so we can't check the facts but we need to be sure. How sure are...."

"Agent Brown...I mean Zac...I am one hundred thousand million percent positive about this. I may be a political science major but my minor is in history and the World Wars are of special interest to me. I'm totally sure about this. Bishop Sullivan is either lying to us or very confused about his father's history."

"Okay, so if he's lying what does that mean?" I say, thinking out loud. "He helped us get the Operation Tin Man evidence. This means he willingly betrayed Kulik. So this means that he and the Vatican want Kulik stopped, right?"

"They would want the General stopped, I would absolutely believe that. I further believe that they would rather help you to stop him than attempt to do so themselves. The Vatican is surely trying to untangle themselves from involvement in this international mess. Imagine the backlash to the Church if it became known that they aided and abetted criminals such as Eurabia and General Kulik," Zac says. "So, the bishop agrees to help us all the way to bringing us to the showdown with Kulik, Alena, and whatever thugs may be waiting for us in the tunnel below the cathedral. It makes sense for him to do that, so why is he lying?"

"He made up the entire Russian eavesdropping story because he wanted us to believe he was listening in on their conversation, when in fact, he was really part of it?" I ask.

"I think so," Zac says. "If Bishop Sullivan wasn't a hostage in the van, then he was part of their group. That means Jack was the only hostage, right? That makes the bishop complicit in Jack's murder. The bishop is sworn to protect the Catholic Church and I think he sacrificed Jack to protect it."

"And even us," Randy snaps. "That guy isn't any holy friend of ours. We need to figure out what his plan is and how we fit into it and fast."

"Okay, let's take this step by step. The Vatican sends Bishop Sullivan here to Boston because they know about the cathedral's past connection with crime; the mafia connections, prohibition, Eurabia and now General Kulik. The Vatican can't risk any of these criminal connections leaking out because the Catholic Church can't bear another scandal. The bishop's orders are to prevent a scandal at all costs. They choose Bishop Sullivan for several reasons, one being he's fluent in Russian. He may also have been chosen because he is a good fighter, willing to kill and things of that nature." Zac pauses. "So, Bishop Sullivan comes to Boston and pretends to work with General Kulik. He knows about the tunnel and the Operation Tin Man evidence and how bad it'll be for the world if Kulik's plan comes to fruition. When he informs the Vatican of Kulik's plans, he's instructed to try to stop them. Then he runs into Abby, Mohamed, and Frank at the cathedral. He decides to help them stop Kulik instead of doing it himself. He starts by helping them locate Kulik's Operation Tin Man evidence, which in all likelihood, he couldn't find on his own. In essence, he double crosses Kulik. Then, when Kulik learns his hidden treasure is missing, the bishop allows Jack to pay the price for the betrayal. He probably blamed Jack for taking the evidence or leading someone to it. Who knows what story the bishop told about Jack, but he said something that made Kulik believe Jack was the traitor and not him. And here we are with Bishop Sullivan ready to lead us to finish up the ugly job he was sent here to do, that is stop any chance of a scandal escaping from this cathedral. He plans on having us kill Kulik, Alena, and whoever, thereby eliminating the last people who know of the guilt ridden past connections this place has with the criminal world."

"But if his aim is to protect the Catholic Church as a whole, then he'll have to destroy everyone that knows about the cathedral's involvement in this mess; that includes us." I say.

"True." Randy says. "He'll also want to destroy the evidence in the tunnel that connects the cathedral to crime such as the pile of corpses, the Prohibition records, and all the other things that are down there. This means, with us in the tunnel with the General, Alena, the thugs, and everything else he wants destroyed, he's setting up the absolute perfect situation to get all of his death targets in one place so we can be destroyed all at once." Randy swears under his breath. "We've been played for fools by the bishop. He isn't setting us up to kill our enemies, he's setting us up to be killed with them."

While Zac and Randy quickly develop a plan to overtake the bishop, I restart my trek into the darkness. The tunnel has a steep slope as it nears the light cast by Mohamed's lantern, giving me the impression that I am walking up into a light-filled paradise. At the end of the tunnel my eyes take a few moments to adjust to the light. When they do, I make out a body slumped over against a brick wall. It is the bishop, bound and gagged.

"He is not who he pretends to be." Mohamed's deep voice comes out of a dark shadow seconds before he does. "His story of Kulik bringing Jack and him to the cathedral to retrieve the Operation Tin Man evidence and Jack being killed is a lie. His fleeing through the tunnel to the Cyclorama is true, but…"

"We know, but how did you figure it out?"

"I first suspected his story was a lie when he said his father was in the Ireland army in World War II as…."

"I know, Randy explained how they were neutral. Go on."

"I kept asking him questions and he kept giving me answers I didn't like. Then, I asked him why Kulik would bring Jack's body up into the cathedral and have it discovered, knowing this would bring the police in the cathedral right above them while they looked for the Operation Tin Man evidence in the tunnel."

"And he retold the story about this being their way to flush him out and get him to come back to the tunnel, right?"

"Yes, which is also illogical, as why would the bishop return for a dead man? Any good Catholic knows that once the body dies, the spirit is released up to heaven. The bishop would have no reason to be at the side of Jack's corpse."

While we talk Randy, exits the tunnel with Zac close behind. With the four of looking down on the beaten, restrained, and angry Bishop Sullivan, Randy explains his theory about Bishop Sullivan to Mohamed. While he does so I watch the bishop's reaction to the truth being told: his eyes widen, close, look away, and narrow expressively as the details of what the bishop has been doing and planning are revealed.

Mohamed looks down at the bishop and says, "Ah, but there is more. The bishop made a deal with Kulik that Kulik couldn't resist. He tells him that the Vatican will get General Kulik, Alena, her children, and the Operation Tin Man evidence out of the country with no questions asked on the Vatican plane. The plane that carries the Vatican officials, such as the Pope, is not subject to inspections, a diplomatic courtesy few people know about. With this special treatment, Kulik and all he wants with him can easily be smuggled out of this country. In exchange for the use of the Vatican plane, the General agrees he will release the Catholic Church from any further obligation."

Randy scoffs. He looks at the bishop and says, "I can't believe you believed him."

"But he didn't. Oh no, the bishop and the Vatican had no intention of believing such a criminal would keep his part of the bargain. You see, the plane with Alena, Kulik, the children, and the evidence would never have reached Rome. No, it would have an unfortunate accident and all would be lost." Mohamed sighs. "Yes, the bishop admitted this when I threatened his life. With the permission of his bosses at the Vatican, the plane carrying the Kuliks was going to experience a fatal accident. I don't know the details but…"

Suddenly Zac screams out. His hands ball into tight fists. He closes his eyes and breathes in deeply. After a full thirty seconds he slowly walks over to the bishop. Hovering above him like a vulture over his prey has says, "You intended to kill my children making them nothing more than collateral damage in your sick plans to protect a manmade institution. The Catholic Church...."

Mohamed takes hold of Zac's trembling body. "No, do not blame the Catholic Church for the actions of a few. This would be as wrong as blaming Islam for those who insist terrorism, like the 9/11 attacks, are religious based jihad done for the sake of Mohamed. It is not the Pope or the good Catholics in this world who planned the demise of your children. No. Bishop Sullivan admitted his contacts at the Vatican are a few 'old school' officials who do what they believe to be best without the permission of the true leaders. No church is infallible when it comes to having zealots within it...no church, no religion and no worthy cause."

Chapter 30
Parting Ways

Zac, Randy, and Mohamed show little mercy to Bishop Sullivan while getting him to reveal what he knows about General Kulik, Alena, and whoever else is waiting for us below the cathedral. After a considerable amount of persuasive physical encouragement the bishop admits he was, indeed, planning to kill all of us. He further admits that the Vatican plane was intended to crash, although he denies knowing the precise details of this pre-arranged tragedy. Zac, who is leading the interrogation, has to regain his composure each time the plane crash topic comes up because the thought of his children dying on the doomed flight sends him into a fit of rage.

"How in the world did you intend to kill us, Kulik, and Alena?" Randy asks. "You didn't know we'd be here today? You didn't come here planning to kill Kulik. You came here to sacrifice Jack for the stealing of Kulik's Operation Tin Man evidence but you didn't expect to kill him today, did you?"

"I didn't know what to expect," the bishop mumbles through swollen lips. "It was not part of the original plan to help you people to steal Kulik's secret evidence, but it was an opportunity I could not allow to slip away. With the evidence out of Kulik's hands, I was assured that the worse of the potential disasters could be avoided. Kulik and Alena's fate depended on their reaction to this loss. They, of course, believed that Jack was to blame for the evidence being gone. And so, they killed him."

"They wouldn't have killed him until he told them where he put their evidence. So, what did Jack tell them?" Zac jerks the bishop up from the floor. "Did Jack tell them about Mohamed and…"

The bishop's weak neck snaps from side to side. With pain radiating from his voice he says, "I told them that Jack confessed to me about Mohamed, Abby, and Frank before Jack could tell them the truth about my involvement."

Zac lets go of the bishop's shirt and the man falls to the ground. "And so

267

you're a coward as well as a murderer. So tell us, coward, how did Kulik and Alena take the news that the Haddads stole their precious Operation Tin Man evidence?"

Bishop Sullivan lifts his beaten head. Fearing he may die, I try to prevent more physical assaults by reasoning with him. I crouch beside him, take his hands in mine, and say, "Bishop Sullivan, what you did and what you planned to do are horrible. There's no way you can undo that, but you can lessen the sin by helping us make things right. That starts with telling us the truth."

After a delayed pause the downtrodden man says, "After they killed Jack, Kulik turned on me. He didn't believe I was as innocent as I pretended. He threatened to expose the cathedral's historic involvement in crime if I didn't tell him all that I knew. Again, I resisted. Then he threatened to frame me for Jack's murder. That is why the corpse was brought up into a part of the cathedral where it would be discovered by the police. I have no doubt the detectives will believe me to be the main suspect."

"I see. So they believe you are as guilty as Jack. When and how did you escape through the tunnel to the Cyclorama?" Mohamed asks.

"Unlike Kulik, I am extremely familiar with the area below the cathedral and both tunnels. I have spent a great deal of time exploring all that is hidden below the surface. I have also researched the mechanics of this underground network including such things as air ventilation, security doors, and hidden chambers. All of the historic documents that pertain to this deep dark world are intact and I alone know where they are hidden. You see, they are believed to be missing but I stumbled upon them one day; it was God's will that I have them."

"Don't you to dare bring God into this," Zac demands. "Now answer the question! How did you escape?"

"There is a sliding door, a security door, in the area just before the tunnel branches into the two separate tunnels. Near this door is a hidden chamber. Inside this chamber is the crank that operates the pulleys that slide the door almost into place. When it is one foot from the wall, someone on either side of this door can pull it closed and lock it. The door was designed to provide security in either direction, to keep people from getting in from the tunnels or from escaping out through the tunnels. When they were pre-occupied, I hastened away. By the time Kulik's man followed me, I was hidden in this chamber I speak of. Although they tried to find me, they failed. Eventually, once I knew they'd given up, I escaped to the Cyclorama. Knowing my way through the confusing network of dead ends enabled me to get to my destination rather quickly."

"How do you even know Kulik and Alena are still down below the cathedral?" I ask.

"I don't know but I believe this to be the case because hidden inside the secret chamber, I was able to hear their plans. They believe Jack's murder will lure some of you to the cathedral. They think that because he helped you find their evidence that you will want to learn what has happened to him. To prepare for your inevitable arrival, they have men outside waiting for you at the entrances to the cathedral."

"Then we're lucky we left the front of the cathedral when we did," Randy says. "So, they think if they catch one or more of us they can somehow negotiate to get their Operation Tin Man evidence back?"

"Yes, and kill you all as well."

"Well, they're wrong," Zac says. "So how did you plan to kill all of us if they have the arsenal of weapons and you have...what do you have?"

Bishop Sullivan, once again, stays silent.

"I believe I may know the bishop's plan. It is coming together now. When he called Abby and learned she was here in Boston, he concocted a plan to get us together with Alena and Kulik so we could all be destroyed at one time. To come up with a viable plan so quickly has to mean it was something he had thought about in the past for one reason or another. So what could be available to him, below the ground, which is lethal? And how could such a weapon be used without endangering his own life? The answer, I believe, has to do with the air ventilation system down here. Yes, this sub-ground world is ventilated; I learned this when I hid here with Carlo Bertoni. At that time I also learned that there are industrial size kerosene heaters below the cathedral. These units were purchased for use down here but could never be used because the space is much too confined and the carbon monoxide they generate would be lethal to any living creature near them. So, the useless kerosene heaters purchased for this below ground world have been collecting dust in the dark for years now. Surely the bishop is aware of the heaters and their history if he is as familiar with the below ground network as he has proven to be. And so, if you were him and wanted people to perish down here, you could place a heater near an air system vent and let the toxic carbon monoxide slowly poison your captives. They wouldn't even be aware they were being poisoned because this gas is colorless, odorless, and tasteless."

The bishop looks at me with tearful eyes and says, "It is all true. There are such heaters, one of which is in the tunnel not far from the chamber with the controls for the sliding security door I described to you earlier. This one is on a wheeled cart. It was brought there by Jack some time ago. He asked if he could take it out through the tunnel near the waterfront during the night. He claims to have had a buyer for it."

"So if we wheel it back up to the hidden chamber, seal the door, and fire the heater up then we could kill Alena and General Kulik without them even knowing they were being gassed?" I ask.

"Yes. If I help you to do this may I then expect some level of mercy?" The bishop looks up at Zac, his swollen eyes opened a bit wider than I expected they could open.

"There is only one way for you to get mercy and I will explain that to you when I get back. For now, I want you to stay here with Abby while we take care of my Alena and her father. Just to be safe, I'm going to tie you up really tight." Zac points his gun at the bishop's head. "You so much as think of escaping and you're a dead man. Remember this; I can make sure you are exonerated of Jack's murder when things settle down and I will, but only when you agree to my terms."

*****

I am relieved that I do not have to go gas General Kulik, Alena, and anyone else that may be with them. Although I believe these people deserve to die for their evil actions, I definitely do not want to be the one to deliver their death sentences. I soon learn, however, that being here with Bishop Sullivan is not nearly as easy as I thought it would be. It is difficult for me to even look at this man because he is not only physically broken but heart broken as well. It seems that remorse, sorrow, and regret make even handsome people appear unsightly. Thankfully, the bishop and I are able to converse well considering the enormous tension surrounding our circumstances. He preaches to me of faith while I question his ability to have faith in a God that has led him so far astray.

After he speaks to me about the devil, I question how Christians are supposed to know when their Satan is or is not around. With a small smile, the bishop tells me that people of all faiths do know when evil is lurking around them, but, like him, they do not always turn away from it fast enough. Then, as if he knows they have died, the bishop prays for General Kulik's and Alena's souls. He begs for their God to have mercy on them for the evil they have done. Then he prays for Mohamed, Zac, and Randy, who, he believes, also need to be forgiven for their part in gassing Alena and Kulik. I must say this man's beliefs are as baffling as they are intriguing. I notice the lantern light bumping down the tunnel minutes before the men return. Their faces look solemn.

"Is it done?" the bishop asks.

"Yes. I checked the area after the fact. I was very careful. Alena and her father are dead. They were alone." Zac begins to untie the bishop. "While we head back to the Cyclorama I will explain what is to happen next. It starts with me pulling in some favors from the local police. Even though General Kulik has destroyed my reputation with Homeland Security officials, he has not ruined my reputation with the dedicated men and women I've been working with for many years. I will explain about Jack and how you are being set up for his murder. I will tell them to exonerate you and explain how you were a victim of the same people who killed Jack. I will have to bring some of them in on the General Kulik and Alena story, to some point, anyway. Then, I will ask them to allow you to fly to Rome on the Vatican plane as soon as it can be arranged. I will state the reason for this is that it is unsafe for you and your assistant to stay here in the United States at this time."

"My assistant?" the bishop rubs his wrists. "I have no assistant but Jack. But, Jack is no longer alive."

"Now it is time for me to speak to you two," Zac says to Mohamed and me. "Mohamed, you made a mistake years ago; a very big mistake. You were swept up in Islamic radicalism because of your emotional response to how you were treated in a post 9/11 world. No, because of how many Muslims in America were treated during this time. It was wrong of you. It was unjustified. It was illegal, immoral, and traitorous. But it was neither impossible to understand or unforgivable. You were young, confused, and in love with a woman who was suddenly, and without cause, forbidden to marry you. And so, you made the dreadful mistake to become a terrorist. Thanks to your family and friends, your group's evil plans did not succeed, and there was no mass loss of life due to the terrorist attacks you were involved in."

Mohamed stares into Zacs eyes. He remains perfectly still and silent.

"I, too, have erred in my life due to emotions. It is not easy to accept that the woman you loved and married only wanted you so she and her father could betray the United States. It is not easy to look at the children you love knowing they did not come about because of mutual love and respect, but rather were produced as a prop to hold up a fake marriage. Yes, I too have been fooled by my emotions. I was slow to recognize the evils of Alena and her father because it hurt too much to see them for who they were. I'm having a difficult time forgiving myself for this. I feel as if I can only get over my own failings by making things right and bringing Alena and her father to justice. Their deaths just now are the first step in my doing this. But, to totally forgive myself, I need to do more than this. I need to prove to myself that I'm worthy of forgiveness. I tell myself we are all worthy of forgiveness, that we all make mistakes, yet we so easily condemn. Did Alena and her father deserve another chance? Did we not condemn them to death without any thoughts of

Diane Kozak

forgiveness? Was this a proper decision or an erroneous judgment?"

"Some people can be forgiven, even if they cannot change." Mohamed says. "Given another chance, Alena and her father would have continued to live evil lives because they did not see that they were evil. The blind do not look for the light. The deaf do not listen for the sounds. And, the unknowing do not look to know. Alena and the General did not know they needed to look to change; hence, they would not have done so."

"I agree, which is why I did what I did. I just hope we're right. As for you, Mohamed, you did see that you needed to change. And you did change. You've proved it time and time again to me, to Abby, and most importantly, to yourself. So, I believe, if I am to continue on with my life, then you too should have a life. We shall do some penance together, and then, well, we shall see where life takes us. You will be smuggled out of the United States disguised as Bishop Sullivan's assistant. The Vatican plane is not checked for security due to diplomacy; therefore, once you are onboard your escape will be imminent. I will send with you all the things needed to protect you, me, and the rest of the group from our own government should ever any of us be in danger by a rogue official. I have the bullet that killed Dr. Azar. You have the Operation Tin Man evidence including the Weather Weapons Program technology information. You also have the information Jinkins was collecting on your group on behalf of General Kulik. And you have the candle that belonged to Stefan Kulik which proves that you were being set up for his murder, when, of course, you are innocent. All of these things must be gathered before you leave."

I am so stunned I am speechless. Randy is uncharacteristically quiet as well. It is only Mohamed that manages to respond to Zac's incredible announcement.

"What will I do at the Vatican?"

"Wait for me to clear things up here. Then, you and I will become temporary partners and work undercover together." Zac smiles. "You will not be the first of America's enemies that ends up working on secret missions to protect the country. Imagine the influence Mohamed Haddad will have in the terrorist networks this country is trying to infiltrate."

We all talk non-stop about Zac's and Mohamed's future as we make our way back to the Cyclorama. Even Bishop Sullivan sounds enthusiastic as he, more than the rest of us, loves the concept of forgiveness. I am personally so excited for Mohamed that it doesn't occur to me for quite some time that there are consequences of this new life of his that I don't particularly like.

"Um, if Mohamed is off on secret missions, then how will I be in contact with him?" I ask, hesitantly.

272

"You won't be." Zac states, firmly. "Contact with him could easily get him killed. Even your cemetery notes led me to him. There is no way you can be in touch with Mohamed without endangering his life."

"Will the United States government know about him?" Randy asks.

"I know, and in time, others will." Zac reaches up for the trap door that connects to the Cyclorama. "You'd be surprised to know what really happens behind closed doors in Washington, D.C. Let's just say the White House, the United States Capital, and the Pentagon hold indescribable secrets in unimaginable quantities."

*****

Our escape from the Cyclorama building goes well for a combination of reasons. For starters, the place is closed for the evening and is completely empty. Secondly, Randy brought the tools he needed to by by-pass the old-fashioned alarm system that still protects the building. Randy, who has taken it upon himself to become quite adept at disabling security systems, tells us when it is safe to exit through a side door. This is when reason number three for an easy getaway falls into place: there is no one out on the street as we leave the building. Yes, it is night time so pedestrian traffic is expected to be light, but to run into not one person at this crucial moment is surely a stroke of luck. And then, as we walk to the SUV,we have just minimal human eye contact despite our outwardly haggard appearances. In fact, the people that got the closest to us were so inebriated I doubt they will even remember the encounter, never mind who we or what we look like.

"Okay, Bishop Sullivan, how fast can you get the Vatican plane here?" Zac asks.

"Eight to ten hours. I will call His Holiness and explain our guest," the bishop straightens out his bloodied clothing. "And if he refuses to participate in your plan?"

"You're kidding, right? The powers you're working with will do anything to cover-up the Boston cathedral's history with New England criminals, right? Well this is your chance! I will bring all the evidence below the cathedral with me when I come to get Mohamed; everything you are so afraid for the world to see. We exchange Mohamed for the evidence that has been blackmailing you for so long. And, other than the kids, no one is left that knows about the tunnel." Zac explains.

"General Kulik's henchmen do. The ones posted outside the cathedral watching the doors right now," the bishop says, with more strength than I imagined he had left in him. "What of them?"

"I'll take care of them when I go back to deal with Alena's and Kulik's corpses." Zac turns to me. "Where is the evidence, files, the candle…all the stuff you are hiding? How long will it take you to retrieve it?"

"It's hidden in the woods near the trailer," I admit. "It's near the remnants of an old farmhouse."

"Okay, get it when you get back and then never let it out of your sight." Zac looks up into the dark sky. "Hey, the storm is gone. No more wind, have you noticed?"

"It is quite calm, actually," Mohamed says.

"That's freaky. Something must be going on." Randy unsuccessfully tries to contact Sara, Frank, and Arnie. "Get in the car. Maybe there's something on the news."

Randy is correct. The news does tell us what is happening with the weather and it is not at all what we expected. It seems the storm that was spreading out from Cape Cod has mysteriously retracted and is now nearly circle-shaped around the Otis Military Base. The wind speeds are approaching eighty-five miles per hour. The ocean waves are wild and expected to increase in size as the full moon approaches during the next twenty-four hours. There is rain mixed with hail slashing almost vertically through the air. The lightening is sporadic, but when it appears it takes over the entire sky. The thunder is so loud it shakes the earth. Although it has not yet been called a state of emergency, most areas of Cape Cod are being evacuated.

"Drop Mohamed and me off at the chancery in Brighton. I can hide him there until it is time to go to the airport. We cannot go to Cape Cod with you if the evacuation will make it difficult for us to leave the area. The news is describing traffic jams on all exit routes." Bishop Sullivan leans into the front seats where he states to Zac, "You can trust me now; the future of my church is in your hands."

"I can't go to the Cape under these circumstances, either. I have to deal with the mess at the cathedral. I'll go to the chancery as well. Is there a car I can use?" Zac asks the bishop.

While the two of them converse, it occurs to me that I am about to have to say goodbye to Mohamed for what could very well be the last time. I feel my warm tears streak down my face in one continuous stream. Occasionally a sob sneaks out from within me. My heart feels like it is being wrung out like a sponge. My chest is so tight I'm afraid I will hyperventilate. Lodged in the back seat between the bishop and Mohamed, I know they must be aware that I'm having an emotional breakdown, but I do not look to either of them for comfort. Instead, I look down at my hands which lay in my lap and watch my tears bounce off my fingers.

We arrive at the chancery, which is actually a campus of structures used by the Catholic Church Diocese. Even though it is dark, I can see the property is extremely well maintained. The bishop and Zac bid me goodbye and allow Mohamed and me a moment of privacy. Here we are, underneath what I believe to be beautiful mature maple trees. I stand face to face with Mohamed, crying uncontrollably. I cannot form words but can only make incoherent sob based sounds. Mohamed raises my hands to his bearded face and kisses them. He then places them over his heart and smiles. His eyes well up with tears, which when they accumulate, overflow.

"You have believed in me when I did not believe in myself. You have protected me when I would not protect myself. You have loved me when I have not loved myself. And now you must set me free as I do not know how to free myself. I cannot leave you, Abia, unless you tell me to go. I owe you too much to walk away from you, be it here and now or anytime in my future. I am not free to start a new life because I do not know how to take ownership of my current life; my life belongs to you. Do you understand?"

I feel a sense of calm sweep over me as I finally find my words. "If only I had the power to set you free, for if I did, you could stay here with me. But I don't. The only thing that can set you free from the past is distance. We both know this is true. And so, because I love you so very much, I grant you my best wishes for a safe journey into a new life where I hope and pray you take care of yourself as well as I have taken care of you."

Chapter 31
Hiding Secrets

The wind blows so fiercely I fear the SUV will flip on to its side. The sky is still lit up from a network of lightning bolts when the rumble of thunder shakes the road beneath us. On the other side of the highway there is a traffic jam of every type of automobile imaginable, all trying to leave Cape Cod at the same time. On the road on to the Cape there are just a few vehicles, including ours, driving into the massive storm. With the sleet pounding on the windows, puddles slurping up beneath the car, and a sky that is much too dark for day break, I pray every inch of our way to the trailer park. When we get to our temporary home we find Frank, Sarah, and Arnie anxiously awaiting our arrival.

"So, you don't know what Zac plans to do with Alena's and Kulik's dead bodies?" Sarah asks while popping open a bag of potato chips. "And when is he going to meet us here on the Cape? And Mohamed going to the Vatican, how is that going to work?"

While I attempt to answer her questions, I notice Arnie straightening out his already perfectly straight stacks of papers. When he is satisfied he interrupts me, saying, "I have an announcement. I have been theorizing most of yesterday and well into the night, and I now conclude that this storm has to be operating through the Ground Wave Emergency Network through a traffic controller and input/output terminal located at the Otis Military Base."

"Uh, didn't we sort of know something like that?" Sarah asks.

"Yes and no. The part about the controls being at Otis; yes, we knew this. However, I did not know exactly what to look for in regard to a control and command center as I did not quite understand how this particular storm was being generated. Now that I do, what we are looking for on the base is a building with many computers, access to private satellites, high security, and disguised as something other than what the building ..."

"Stop. What are you talking about?" Frank asks.

"It is a long story; however, it began in the 1980s when the Ground Wave Emergency network or GWEN tower system was built. You see, the government built these towers all across the United States for many reasons but stated they were only for emergency communication reasons. Back then, during the Cold War with the Soviet Union, people believed a nuclear bomb could wipe out communications across the country instantly. The GWEN system was supposed to be operational even if such an attack occurred."

"Sounds logical," I say.

"That reason for the GWEN system was logical, however, many people didn't believe that was the only reason the system was created. Americans love their conspiracy theories, and so it came to be believed by many people that the towers were erected so the government could implement mind control over all its citizens." Arnie, looking pleased with himself, waits for a response to this comment.

"What?" I ask. "What do these towers do?"

"Well, specifically, they are capable of ionizing the atmosphere with radio waves, some at very low frequencies. You see, each of these low frequency radio towers, referred to as GWEN towers, are about three hundred feet high with copper wire beneath the ground that can radiate…"

"Forget the specifics and tell us what these GWEN towers have to do with the storm," I demand. "And please, dumb down the explanation for us non-scientific folks."

"As you wish. Basically, and I mean very basically, they can modify the weather. They can enhance storms, create storms, prolong droughts, and produce environmental problems in enemy lands…is this not basic enough for you?"

Randy raises his eyebrows and snaps, "Yes, we're not idiots. So, the storm here, right now, is being made through a GWEN tower. So what?"

"Well, this is the interesting thing. The answer was right there before me the entire time, yet I did not see it until just a couple of hours ago. You see, the GWEN technology is actually rather, how should I say, um…dated. As I noted earlier, it was partially designed for communications even during the worst of circumstances. These included primarily military communications. The communication system was designed so once information is sent out from the control to the tower, let's say to create a storm, it cannot be stopped. Think of it this way: pretend a military order is sent out during a national crisis and then the communication system in the country is damaged. The order must continue to be sent regardless of the damage to the system, should it not? Yes, the order should continue until new communication networks can be established. Therefore, the system was designed so that once orders or communications are sent in certain ways that they cannot be stopped, no matter what. Because of this built in safeguard feature, I believe that this storm on Cape Cod could not be stopped once it was 'commanded' to commence. This is true; however, it is not a fatal failure to our mission."

"Whoa, so what you're saying is we can't stop the storm, but somehow, that isn't really a problem?" Frank shakes his head. "What are you talking about?"

"Until now, I planned for you and Abby to sneak me onto the military base once you found the command center. Then, I was unsure as to how I was going to attempt to stop the storm because the system was designed so that it could not be stopped. I was perplexed as to what I was to do; however, I had developed various possible strategies to fool the system into believing it had achieved its goal. My strategies were just conjecture with no real basis to believe I would be successful. Now I know, after hours and hours of thought, that the answer is not to focus on the impossible or conjecture, which in our case means trying to stop the storm, but to focus on what is possible."

"Which is what?" Randy rolls his eyes and shakes his head. His frustration with the scientist's thought process is obvious to all of us but the source of his frustration.

"Do you not see? I should not attempt to stop the storm. I need only to change its course! I simply need to change the coordinates of the storm and send it out to sea!"

*****

Frank and I bundle up before we venture to the abandoned farm house to retrieve the hidden package of valuable evidence we hid there not so long ago. Although everyone knew of the hiding place, it was us who actually brought the cooler containing the Operation Tin Man evidence, Stefan Kulik's candle, and Ed Jinkins' notes to the hiding place, so it is best for us to go get it. Of course, with the storm ripping apart the trees all around us, our progress is slow. We find the midsize beach cooler intact exactly where we left it; hidden beneath the weedy overgrowth which covers what once were the basement stairs of the farmhouse. With the precious items safely in hand, we decide to detour to the cabin to remove any remnants Mohamed may have left behind. While Frank gathers up the few pieces of trash and a handful of items my brother left behind, I wonder about Katie and Kileen Jinkins. As far as I'm concerned, I can't feel good about letting these young girls deal with the tragic and undignified death of their father until I know they will be safe from inadvertently getting tangled into his criminal dealings. When I explain my feelings to Frank I am surprised, and greatly relieved, to learn he feels the same. Together we leave the cabin behind for what we hope will be the last time and fight the storm to the Jinkins' home. When we at last arrive at the street where the Jinkins' rather luxurious trailer is located, my instincts immediately tell me that something isn't quite right.

"The wind from the storm tore off the Jinkins' front storm door." I say.

"It's dark inside, too."

"That's because all the window shades are closed, too"

We carefully approach the street for a better look.

"Look at that jeep parked at the far end of the street. Do you see it?" Frank holds his arm out in front of me to prevent me from walking out too far in the road. "That's a military jeep. The color looks like it is, anyway. Why would the military be here?

"I bet it has something to do with Ed Jinkins and the girls."

We simultaneously draw back into the woods. "Stay here while I get closer to the jeep. While I'm gone, watch the trailer for activity. Don't go in there without me. And don't forget, we have the evidence with us and we can't risk losing it for anyone, not even the Jinkins girls. So, do not take any chances, okay?"

With Frank's stern warning in mind, I retreat deeper inside the woods where I sit on the cooler of valuable secret evidence. The burden of guarding what I have below me is heavy. Although I still have an excellent view of the trailer, there is nothing for me to see except how the unnatural hurricane that howls all around me ravages everything in its path. In the short time I wait for Frank, I watch several bizarre objects pass by including a baby stroller, a broken patio umbrella, and a bright orange life preserver. I also watch the sleeting rain come and go haphazardly, as if the storm has a brain and can make itself create precipitation when and if it wants. After a while a lightning streak appears. I brace myself for the booming clap of thunder. This storm's thunder and lightning cannot really be described as steady or sporadic. It is not steady in the sense that it is not constantly present. And, it is not sporadic because when it is present it is steady. In non-scientific terms I refer to this storm's thunder and lightning blasts as sporadically steady. I am feeling vulnerable as the storm engulfs me when Frank returns.

"The good news is that the jeep is empty. The bad news is that it definitely is from the military base. And the other bad news is I think whoever brought it here is in with the Jinkins girls. At least it seems like they aren't in any of the other trailers nearby." Frank tells me.

"Then we either go in the trailer and confront them or wait for them to leave. The risk of waiting is the harm they can do Katie and Kileen," I point out. "That is if they'd actually hurt the girls. You know, I warned the girls to keep quiet about their suspicions about their father's connections…"

"I don't think this is about Ed Jinkins' and Stefan Kulik's murder. The latest news about that is that Ed Jinkins murdered Stefan Kulik, which we know is true. The news then said that whoever killed Ed did so after he left the Kulik cottage, which is also true. As far as the story of his murderer goes, the news is now saying that it was an accomplice of his, someone who worked with him on the Stefan Kulik assassination. We know that's not true, but when you think about it, it does neatly close up the case for now, which is exactly what General Kulik wanted. With the cover-up already well in place, I don't see what it matters about what Katie and Kileen Jinkins think, do you?"

"You make sense, so why are there soldiers at the Jinkins' home?"

"I'll go see."

"No," I declare as I jump up. "I'll go. I'd rather snoop around than be stuck here guarding the treasure chest that could save the world; literally save it that is. Think it through. The reality is that the best thing to do is have you safely get that cooler back to the trailer. As for me, even if I get caught at the trailer, I can simply say I was there checking on Kileen and Katie, right? You know, one girlfriend to another sort of thing. It's no big deal. But the evidence is a big deal and you've got to get it away from these soldiers. Besides, I doubt any soldiers plan on killing me or either of the Jinkins girls out in the open like this, do you? "

"They did park down the street."

"They didn't hide the vehicle. They probably just wanted to make a surprise entrance so the girls didn't hide and refuse to open the door for them. Really, just go. I can do this."

Frank runs through a list of cautious advice before he sets out with the cooler. I brace myself for more lightning and go to the street. I carefully make my way to the back yard of the Jinkins' home, a place with which I am quite familiar. A huge web of lightning bolts illuminates the entire neighborhood just as I creep up to the back door of the trailer. I am happy to see that unlike the front windows, which have the shades pulled down, the windows in the rear of the trailer do not. This allows me to climb the back steps and peek inside the kitchen window. I am astonished to see that the cabinets and drawers are all open with much of their contents scattered on the counters and floors. Taking a more daring look inside, I see two soldiers in combat clothing in the hallway between the kitchen and living room. I can't see Kileen or Katie but I can hear them both speaking. It doesn't take long for me to figure out that the soldiers are questioning the girls about something their father had that belongs to the military. Whatever this something is, the girls are claiming they know nothing about it. As much as I listen I can't quite figure out what the soldiers want, except that it has something to do with an eastern roadway. I keep waiting for the soldiers to give up their search so I can talk to the girls, but they are persistent to locate whatever they came here to get. Not knowing what else to do, I sneak to the front of the trailer and knock on the front door.

"Hi, Katie. It's me. I'm just checking on you girls to see how you're making out with the storm. I see you've lost your door out here. Well, my friends can help you with that when the storm is over. You know we're just..."

"Now isn't a good time," Katie says while darting her eyes back and forth to let me know they aren't alone.

"There's never a good time for a storm like this," I say even louder. "If you don't mind I'd like to come in and dump some stones from my shoe before I head back, you know one little pebble can hurt like the devil."

I wink as I push past Katie. "Kileen, you look so flustered. Is this because of your Dad's passing? Oh honey, I'm so very sorry about that. I heard the news, and, well, all I can say is I feel terrible for both of you. But, you know you have friends in all of us just on the other street and we'll do whatever we can..." Standing at the entrance to the kitchen I exclaim, "What the heck happened in there?"

From the hall a young well built soldier says, "We happened, Ms. Haddad. Now join your friends in the living room."

"Who are you and what are you doing here?" I ask, hoping my pretend innocently confused look is convincing.

The second soldier, another male but this one wearing black rimmed glasses, points to the living room.

Seated on the couch between Kileen and Katie the courage I had when I pushed myself inside this place starts to slip away. As is always the case, the actual confrontation with the enemy is so much more difficult than you expect it to be. But, since neither of them has their weapons drawn on us, nor do they appear to be much more than extremely aggravated, I sense we are fairly safe from danger.

"Okay, Ms. Katie and Ms. Kileen Jinkins, if you do not know where your deceased father kept the key and pass cards he was issued for the eastern passway to the military base, then you do not know. Quite frankly, I do not believe your story that these items were never found, butI cannot force you to give them to us. I will repeat, however, that General Kulik himself is demanding their return and I can assure you he will not be pleased that they haven't been located. Do you both understand?" the soldier with the glasses asks.

Kileen and Katie nod.

"Wow, to think the General was working with Ed Jinkins and then he turned around and killed the General's brother," I say, truly flabbergasted that the soldiers admit they were sent here by the General himself.

"No, Ms. Haddad, General Kulik did not issue Ed Jinkins these items! He learned that they were issued to him after his brother's murder! You are a fool for saying such a thing. I suggest you watch yourself very closely, Ms. Haddad. By the way, our other purpose for coming to the Otis Trailer Park was to inform you and Frank Stiller that you are to report to your jobs at the base as soon as possible!"

"What do you mean?" I ask, once again truly astounded.

"The environmental program you are both assigned to is in complete disarray because of this storm. The winds, sleet, atmospheric pressure, and other storm related phenomenon is having a drastic impact on the behavior of the turtles you and Frank have been hired to locate and account for. Both of you must be sent directly into the field to locate the turtles and log where they are picked up. Apparently, if this is not done, the storm will destroy so many turtles that all of the research gathered over the past several years will be useless. That is all I know."

"I see. Well, I guess I need to get home to Frank."

The soldier without the glasses scowls at the Jinkins girls and me. He says, "I've been to the Middle East twice and I know when people are lying to me. Yep, I can sense it. Both you sisters are full of crap. As for you, Mohamed Haddad's sister, I can't believe you're allowed on a military base because you're full of crap, too."

I don't allow either sister to speak until the soldiers are gone and I have them follow me to the shed. They are not confused by my odd behavior for long.

"Don't talk inside the trailer...they probably bugged the place while you weren't looking, hoping that you will talk about where your dad kept those military base keys and pass cards or whatever after they left," I tell them.

"I'm so glad you're here. I don't think they'd have left if you hadn't come. And we definitely would've started talking the second they left," Kileen says.

"So do you know where your father kept the base stuff?" I ask. "If you do, it's extremely important that I have it."

Katie nods at Kileen saying, "Tell her. Come on, we've got to get ourselves out of this mess before we end up as dead as dad!"

I can see that both young women are very much shaken up by the soldiers' visit. With just a bit more coaxing I get them to confide in me.

"I know more about this than Katie because she didn't want anything to do with it all. I kept trying to get my dad to stay out of it, you know? I never really understood it all but I did know all about him and General Kulik and the favors he did for the General. Well, not favors, as you know he was paid well for what he did. Then, one time at the office, I heard him talking on the phone about your group. Of course I was interested, so I tried to listen in. He caught me and went outside to talk. I actually went into the bathroom and perched myself on the toilet to hear what he was saying. I didn't get much, except that something would be dropped off later in the afternoon." Kileen braces herself as a thunder clap temporarily deafens us. "I wasn't there when it was delivered, but Katie was."

"Dad had gone out to the cabin, he knew someone was staying out there and he used to check the place out all the time. Then some military aide came driving up and insisted on handing this envelope to Dad personally. The man sat and waited almost forty minutes for Dad to get back. When I asked Dad what was so important and what he had to do with the military, he threatened to beat me silly for being so damned nosy. That was his way, you know. He was pretty rough. So I dropped it until later that night." Katie looks over and Kileen as if to inform her it is her turn to finish the story.

"That night Dad got a phone call about getting the envelope and all that," Kileen starts. "He went outside to take the call and this time he talked about knocking people off and bringing their bodies to the base! This wasn't going to happen until a storm came...which I'm guessing is this storm. And, he didn't say it in this conversation, but Katie and I knew the people he was told to knock off were you...you, Abby, and your friends. I couldn't believe he'd actually do it. I thought he was just going along with it but wasn't actually going to do it..."

"Forget about that for now. So what happened to the envelope with the military base pass key and pass card or whatever else was in there?" I ask.

The two sisters look at each other.

"Okay, if this is about trust let me tell you something in exchange for that envelope, deal?"

"Like what?"

"How about if I tell you the truth about your father's death?"

Kileen nods while Katie agrees.

"General Kulik paid your father to kill his brother Stefan because Stefan had Alzheimer's disease and was saying too many incriminating things about the past. Your dad was, sort of, caught in the act and was killed by a government agent. The story is covered up a bit because of General Kulik's political power, but the truth will come out soon enough."

"How do you know all this?" Kileen asks.

"I was there and saw it happen. I'm sorry."

Katie and Kileen ask me nothing except if their father suffered. I explain that he was shot and died instantly. Then, while thunder booms overhead, the sisters push open the shed door.

"Come with us to the office. The envelope you're looking for is inside the beat-up old panel truck that our father used to haul firewood around the campgrounds. I saw him put in there along with some other things that…well you'll see. The keys to the truck are under the seat. Take the truck with you, you may need it." Kileen says, as she runs toward the family truck.

We ride to the office together. The old panel truck is rusted and dented. Its dirty license plate informs me that the vehicle is road worthy and registered, quite surprising considering the condition it is in. It is Katie who pulls open its back doors. I expect to see dry fire wood stacked inside, but instead I see rolled up blankets, lanterns, a tool box, and what I can only describe as an industrial sized utility cart of some type.

"I told Kileen when Dad loaded that stainless steel cart in here that he meant to go through with killing you. Why else would he need it other than to move dead bodies around? I also told her that if he tried to hurt any of you I'd call the police. She agreed. We never would've let it get that far…if he really did try to go through with it," Katie says.

Kileen comes from around the open door with a thick white envelope. "This is what you're looking for. It has maps in there, a key, and a magnetic pass card. I think it was for Dad to use to get the corpses on the base," Kileen holds the envelope inches from my open hand. A gust of winds slams the panel truck door closed. "Tell me one more thing. How did Dad know there would be a storm like this one?"

I stare at both sisters for a solid thirty seconds before deciding what to say.

"I'm not sure he believed such a storm would come. That might be why he took money to murder my friends and me. It may be that he didn't believe General Kulik had the ability to accurately predict a storm like this would hit Cape Cod. I think, possibly, your father didn't actually expect he'd have to kill us and bring our dead bodies to the military base during a storm because he never believed there would actually be a storm."

I hope the opportunity I have given them, to think better of their father than he deserves to be thought of, in some way repays Katie and Kileen for their trust in me.

Chapter 32
Turtle Scouting

You would think after having such an exhausting and terrible night in the cathedral tunnel that I'd be dreading my first day working at Otis Military Base, but I'm not. Of course this has nothing to do with the *Eastern Box Turtle Habitat Selection and Hibernation Thermal Ecology Research Project* I'll be working on. It is because I feel that with General Kulik defeated, we can finally deal with the unexpected enemy, our own government. I have very mixed feelings about learning that the United States inadvertently created a great deal of the earth's global warming problem while developing its weather weapons program. On one hand, I admittedly feel safer knowing we have the most advanced weaponized weather program on the planet; a program the Russian government will pay anything to acquire. On the other hand, I know the price my country paid to develop this caliber of weapon is unquestionably too high. However, what bothers me the most is that some leaders of this country are sacrificing human lives to cover up what they did and that they're getting away with it. Sure, it is evil and misguided power mongers like General Kulik who sit on the committee that approved the weather weapon storms on the Boston colleges and universities and now the Otis Military Base. Sure, it isn't a majority of the politicians in Washington D.C. who approved an attack on its own people. But still, these murderous storms were authorized by powerful officials that have sworn to protect this country and its people and this betrayal is hard for me to accept. No, it's far more than that; it's an unacceptable treachery that needs to be brought to justice.

"Come on Abby, Arnie wants to educate us a bit before we go to the base. We better hurry though; it sounds like we have a lot of turtles to pretend to save." Frank drops down on the couch. "Okay, man of science, we're here."

"First, I think it is imperative that I inform you that I have not given your duties on the base my complete thought, as much of my thinking is dedicated to how I can change the course of the storm. My plan to divert the storm out to sea using the transmitters may not be as direct a route as my calculations…"

I wave my hand in front of Arnie's face saying, "Please, there isn't any time for your explanations. Besides, I don't understand what you're talking about, except that once you're on the base you'll be able to talk to some towers or something that is creating the storm through transmitters that may or may not be located on the base."

"I am quite sure the transmitters on the base are, in fact…" Arnie continues.

"Okay, sorry, they're there. Let's get to the turtle stuff," I say, a bit sterner.

"You told me something about the storm harming radio transmissions?" Frank reminds the scientist.

"Ah yes, the storm will harm the radio transmitters which are affixed to the turtles being tracked, as well as harm the turtles themselves. The storm will also cause the turtles to change their normal, or should I say natural, routines which will skew the study results. You see, they are being studied not only to measure their population and how they select microhabitat, but also to monitor their movements such as…"

"And this means what to us?" Frank interrupts.

"It means so much, can't you see? Ah, of course you do not. Well, since the environmental scientists on the base are not aware that this storm is a weaponized storm controlled, in part, by radio transmissions, they will not be aware of why the entire turtle radio transmitting system will not be operating properly. In fact, I will venture to guess that much of the actual rescuing of the turtles will be done by going to their known nests rather than using radios to locate them. The turtles that are disturbed by the storm and have set out blazing new paths to look for safety will, in all likelihood, perish." Arnie, with his head down, sighs.

"Okay, so our boss and co-workers won't understand why their radio equipment is messed up. What does that mean to us and finding the control and command center?" I ask.

"Well, that's just it now, isn't it? The irony of the situation is this, although the equipment they give you will not help you locate the turtles, it will help you locate the control center."

Arnie then provides us with the details about the radio receivers we will be carrying and how to use them. As complicated as I fear this instrument will be, it turns out I feel confident that I can use it properly with just a little practice. With this unforeseen lucky break, Frank and I head out for the base trying not to be overly optimistic.

At the entrance gate I am, once again, treated as a highly suspect visitor. That is until the lead environmentalist on the Eastern Box Turtle Project,

Barry Silversmith, informs the guards that he has been impatiently awaiting our arrival and needs us to report to duty immediately. The soldier at the gate informs us that yet another emergency meeting has been called by Barry because the rescue program is not going well. Knowing what we do about the radio transmitters and receivers not working properly due to the storm, I'm not at all surprised to hear this. We arrive at the building we are assigned to, without delay. It is a typical gray building with nothing distinguishing it from any of the others nearby. Once inside, we find the work area buzzing with excitement. I can truly feel the workers' sense of hopeless panic radiating from their wet and tired bodies. Frank leads me to a space against a wall where the two of us join the in progress meeting.

I watch Barry, who is of medium height but very slim, pace back and forth as he explains new directives for the failing turtle rescue program. I'm instantly fascinated by him. His camouflage clothing is a bit baggy and his jungle type hat has strings hanging down from it which he has tied under his chin. He is soaking wet front head to toe; his wet shoes squeak loudly with his every step. He often pauses while he speaks; sometimes to gather his thoughts, other times for no reason that I can see. But the oddest thing about this environmental man that I just can't seem to get used to is that is head, neck, nose, and eyes look like a turtle. It's uncanny. His face has a smooth roundness to it. His nose is a size too small and his eyes have a beady quality to them that is normally only seen in reptiles. His ears, assuming he has them, are hidden beneath his hat, making them as absent to the eye as a turtle's are. And, most noticeable of all, he is wearing a turtleneck shirt under his uniform. I assume there is a practical reason for him wearing such a shirt, but given his profession, someone needs to tell him that it's not a good wardrobe choice. Putting his odd appearance aside, I find Barry is extremely knowledgeable about turtles and has an obvious enthusiasm for his job.

When I am eventually able to get past Barry's ridiculous appearance, I manage to focus in on what he is saying. He is going into details about the failure of the plans. He describes how each turtle in the program has a radio transmitter on it, where the turtles are likely to be located, and how radio receivers are normally used to find them. He then gives details on the proper capture, transport, and logging of the creatures. With the current plan laid out, he then states that for unexplained reasons the transmitters are not operating as expected. The audience's reaction to this is an outburst of comments and questions, many of which deal with the worker's own frustration with using the ineffective radio transmitters. I listen to the sincerity in the voices around me and realize for the first time that my nonchalant attitude toward the turtle program I've been hired to work on is not only disrespectful, it is unwise.

From this moment on I listen attentively.

When the discussion is over, Barry ends the meeting by handing out assignments. I am assigned to go out into the field with a walkie talkie and a radio receiver and hunt for turtles. My objective is in a specific area of the base where an identified group of turtles is known to have spent time. No one explains to me why turtles left this area, where they went, or what the likelihood is that I will find them there today. No, I am only instructed to look for turtles, verify by their tag markings, which group they belong to, and call in the information to the central control location. Barry doesn't need to tell me that I am assigned this particular duty, because although it needs to be done, it is unlikely to yield a significant turtle find. No, I understand perfectly that I am being sent out on this rather unlikely venture because I am an inexperienced new employee who lacks training with the turtles. To my boss and my co-workers I am, at best, a set of eyes, a mouth, and enough of a brain to follow simple directions.

Frank's fate in the turtle rescue effort is actually less exciting than mine. He is being used by Barry for his strength. Frank is assigned to work at the central control area where the rescued turtles are being housed during the storm. He will basically be carrying, pushing, and pulling crates and tanks of turtles all around the big building as they are prepared and secured for the storm.

"I have to go. Look, I have a badge number, radio receiver, round wire shaped metal antenna, map, GPS, and walkie talkie. I'm ready to turtle hunt. I had a quick lesson on the equipment," I lower my voice to a whisper. "It turns out Arnie was exactly right about how the radio receiver works."

"I'm so mad that I'm stuck in here," Frank complains, as he looks at my equipment. "What's with that canvas bag?"

"The bag is for any turtles I feel I need to pick up. I've got gloves too. They don't actually want me picking up any of the little buggers but I can if it's an emergency. I'm not an official *Turtle Handler*, just a *Turtle Scout* you see."

"Damn it, I wish I was the one going out there. It could even be dangerous in the storm. What if the fire tornadoes start up?"

"I think it may be good that you're in here. You may be able to slip away and deal with the security system issues. Sure, we can get Arnie in here through the Eastern Roadway, wherever that is, but we have to make sure no one becomes suspicious while watching the panel truck drive onto the base that way."

Frank shakes his head, as if he is trying to shake out his anger and irritation. "Kulik must've set it up so that Ed Jinkins could move around the base freely in his truck. The problem is, of course, Jinkins is dead now and everyone on this base knows it."

"That's exactly right. And they're going to find out General Kulik is dead pretty soon, too."

"Well, maybe being in here isn't so bad. I probably will be alone long enough to sneak away. Arnie gave me a pretty decent explanation of the base's security system station and I can at least check out what's going on in there during the storm."

"And there's some land lines inside this place, too. You can call Zac and find out what's going on with Mohamed and him."

Frank reluctantly smiles. "You're an eternal optimist, Abby. I suppose you do make some good points. Let me take a look at your map and check out where you're supposed to go scouting."

Frank runs his fingers over the map several times. After a while, he stands up straight and cracks each of his knuckles, one at a time.

"This X is where we are, at the lab. This area is where you're supposed to go. It'll take you at least twenty minutes to get out there from here. Once inside the woods you follow these dotted lines which represent trails. It's along these trails where you scout, right?"

"Yeah, they told me all that. So what are you looking at?"

"See here way off back there? It's the old military staff residential area which is now abandoned. According to your map it is considered 'off limits.' That doesn't make sense to me. Why should it be off limits? It should be just old housing, right? What's so off limits about old housing? Try getting close to it and see what your radio receiver does. If it starts going crazy then maybe that's where the weather weapons control command center is located. Think about it, this is the sort of place Arnie described to us, right?"

"I'm on it," I say, enthusiastically. "Don't worry about me, I'll be careful."

With radio receiver, antenna, and turtle gear in hand, I hike up the narrow tarred road to my assigned scouting area. The sleeting rain has stopped, but the wind seems to be stronger than it was this morning. The sky is dark, and thankfully there hasn't been any thunder or lightning for at least a half hour. As I walk on the tar, my sneaker-clad feet slip on the sleet, but I do not fall. The cold damp smell of the storm makes me feel uncomfortable. When I reach my assigned scouting area I find that I'm totally unprepared for dealing with the paths in the woods which I find are difficult to locate and even more difficult to follow. Unlike hiking trails, marked with painted dots on trees and rocks along the way, the trails I am following are marked only by the paths themselves. With the greenery growing wild all about me, following a trail is an incredible challenge for a non-naturalist like myself. The wild wind further complicates my mission as wind-strewn tree branches and leaves cover up much of the little evidence there is marking the proper route to follow.

For the first forty-five minutes my radio receiver picks up the erroneous constant beeping Barry described at the meeting. He explained that this steady beeping pattern should not be present; therefore, it should be ignored. Therefore, I focus my hearing on anything that sounds different than this steady pattern of beeps. Finally, at a particularly swampy area near a pool of water, my receiver begins to beep faster. The closer my antenna gets to the water, the more the radio receiver signals to me. Although the beeps are not the correct pattern for indicating I have found turtles, the strangeness of the beep pattern assures me I've found something. Careful not to disturb my prey, I tiptoe into the tall weeds where I can lean over just enough to see the edge of the water. And there they are, several Eastern Box Turtles all in the same general area. I watch the creatures for a few moments and then use my walkie talkie to call in the coordinates of my find. When I am told I can leave the area, I continue on toward the area Frank asked me to explore. The closer I get to this destination, the faster the radio receiver beeps. My heart begins to take on the quick pulse of the radio receiver as my excitement mounts. Standing before the "Off Limits" sign near the abandoned residential area of the base, I make believe I am authorized to be in this restricted area to scout for the endangered turtles. With thoughts of soldiers monitoring my every move, I wave my radio receiver about and follow imaginary leads.

The abandoned apartment complexes Frank told me I would encounter are all identical. They are painted a very pale yellow, have black shuttered windows and porticos over their burgundy doors. Considering that no one is living in these buildings I find them to be in fairly good shape. The strategically placed playgrounds within the network of apartment buildings give off an entirely different vibe. There is nothing creepier than an abandoned playground with broken down equipment, missing pieces, and overgrowth of weeds. The chains for the swings are rusted with only two of the four sets actually being attached to a seat. The ladder to the slide has missing rungs, the slide itself is warped. There are monkey bars with wild shrubs sprouting out beneath them. And, saddest of all, in one of the playgrounds is one lone rocking pony on a bent, rusted spring. The once gray pony's paint is peeling; its saddle is smeared with mud. The whipping wind slaps me as I walk through the deserted cracked tar parking lot. I get to a clump of wind worn trees where I continue on with my turtle hunting routine of waving the antenna around while spying hopefully for small critters. When I crest a small hill, my radio receiver begins to go ballistic. There in front of me stands an old but clean building that is surrounding by a chain link fence. As I approach this long narrow one level structure I notice that it too has an abandoned playground. Although there is no sign labeling this place, I can tell by its doors, windows, and walkways that it once was a school. I walk around the perimeter of the fence which I notice has a padlocked double gate. Oddly, regardless of what angle I am at, I am unable to see inside any of the windows. It is as if each window is blacked out with paper or a shade of some kind. I am positive this building is the weather weapons control and command station, absolutely positive. I'm about to walk around it for a second time when I catch something moving from the corner of my eye. More curious than frightened, I walk over to investigate at the edge of the tree line. Much to my amazement I spot three turtles walking along a fallen tree.

"Good grief. You guys must be terribly lost. Well, I guess this is a turtle emergency my friends."

My gloved hands pick up the rather docile turtles that I assume are either sick or terrified. I gently place them in the canvas sack.

"You know what? You little guys just reminded me that I need to stick to my role. Someone may be watching me, so I need to get you back to the turtle safe house. But before I do, let me note down these coordinates. Ah, then again, maybe not. I don't want any turtle hunters coming up here later looking for more of your friends. Hmmm…I'll have to say I found you somewhere else…somewhere far away from here."

*****

The turtle lab is a series of rooms, some are set up like offices, others like laboratories, and still others like pet shops. There is a feeling of excitement radiating from the staff, who I believe, feel empowered by being included in the rescue effort. The way in which a college intern gently takes the three turtles I've brought in pulls at my heart. She cradles them in a comforting manner which I truly believe sets them at ease.

I leave my little friends to go talk to Frank. What I expected to be fairly easy turns into a nightmare when I discover he is not anywhere in or around the laboratory building.

"Hey, aren't you assigned to be scouting?" My boss Barry walks past me with a cardboard pet transporter in each hand. "By the way, what happened? It looks like you picked up some specimens by yourself."

Thankful that I've developed excellent lying skills these past couple of years I say, "They were up a ways from the area I called in earlier. They were on the move so I figured if I didn't grab them they'd be long gone before someone more qualified than me could get there to capture them."

"I understand, Haddad." Barry looks closely at me. "So, do you need another assignment? There is an area on the eastern part of the base that…"

"Yeah, sure, the eastern side of the base sounds fine," I say, too eagerly.

Barry shrugs, "As I was saying, on the eastern section of the base there is a wetland area that is greatly populated by turtles. We've accounted for and rescued most of them; however, there are thirteen turtles from this area that are still unaccounted for. I need someone to go out there and search for these missing turtles."

"Give me a map and I'll go. I should pick them up if I find them, right?"

"Not if they have formed a small nest. But if they are just one, two, or three together, yes, you must handle them yourself."

While Barry works on my map I slip outside with hopes of spotting Frank. I am disappointed when he is nowhere to be found. When I return for the map, I find Barry is very angry about something. Fear grips me as I assume it is I who has made him angry. He thrusts the map at me and orders me to get going before turning his rage on what is really upsetting him.

While kicking at the side of a metal desk he says to a young man on a landline phone, "Tell them that if a fire tornado does hit this base then the forest will surely catch on fire and the turtles here will perish! What do they not understand? We must evacuate these turtles before a fire starts." Barry grabs the phone and screams, "Yes, sir, I understand all about security measures but I also understand all about the millions of dollars in research spent on the *Eastern Box Turtle Habitat Selection and Hibernation Thermal Ecology Research Project* and what'll happen to it, and my career, if these turtles burn to death! I ordered the trucks for an emergency evacuation and I'll get them on this base whether you like it or not!"

Barry slams down the phone and then, quite unexpectedly, screams like he has been stabbed in the heart. Everyone stops what they are doing to watch him, but no one makes a move. His face gets increasingly redder as the seconds pass. His eyes become watery, but thankfully, he isn't crying. He throws a few miscellaneous items at a wall, balls up his fists and screams for a second time. I am too stunned to do anything but observe the man I now believe may be a madman. Barry whirls around, looking from one face to another. He seems to be making eye contact with someone behind me, someone who has just walked into the building. The voice coming out of his mouth is no longer his, it now sounds like the voice of a creature in a second rate horror flick.

"You, new guy, you've proven to be quite intelligent today. The list of trucks I ordered for the emergency evacuation is on my desk. You get them here before this storm starts throwing fire balls around, got it? Don't ask me how because if I knew how I wouldn't be ordering you to figure it out! Any questions?"

I immediately recognize my boyfriend's voice. "May I have her help me?"

he asks, pointing at me.

Barry raises his eyebrows. "She has proven herself surprisingly useful as well, but…"

"She has political connections..."

"Then take her. Do not disappoint me. My entire career…no… my life is my career…so…my entire life depends on you getting trucks on this base that can save these damn turtles!"

Chapter 33
Coming Together

Having known Frank since we were children, I can read his facial expressions almost flawlessly. The tightness around his mouth, the slight narrowing of his brighter than normal dark eyes and the quickness of his step indicate that he has much he wants to tell me. My whispered attempts to get at least a bit of news from him before we are at what he considers to be a securely private area are met with a scornful hush. So, I allow him to lead me into the handicapped bathroom within the turtle project control center where we can be alone. Of course, should we be seen together inside the bathroom we will have a lot to explain; however, Frank's eagerness to speak with me makes this potential problem unimportant to him.

"I can't believe how lucky we are that Barry asked you to oversee getting the turtle evacuation trucks onto the base. To think that all we have to do is sneak the panel truck with Arnie and Zac in the line of rescue trucks and our problems are over." Noticing Frank shaking his head I say, "What's wrong? Isn't this a good idea?"

"No, I don't think so. But let me start from the beginning. First of all, I spoke with Randy who spoke with Zac earlier. Mohamed is with Bishop Sullivan and they're both safe. The Vatican plane is almost at the airport and all the clearances needed for Mohamed to escape on it have been made and confirmed. He's getting away, Abby, for real." Frank puts a hand on each of my shoulders and smiles. "We did it, Abby, we got him a new chance at life."

"I can't believe it. I won't believe it until he's gone. When he's out of Boston and he's over the Atlantic then, and only then, I'll start to believe he's finally safe."

"Actually, Mohamed is the one slowing down his escape. He doesn't want to leave until he's sure we are successful in rerouting the storm. He refuses to leave Boston unless the mission is done. As far as he's concerned, he's still part of our team until the team has succeeded."

"He's a fool…"

"He's Mohamed Haddad and he does what he thinks is right, that's just who he is and what he does. Anyway, before Mohamed and the bishop left Zac, they helped him drag General Kulik's and Alena's bodies down the tunnel that leads to the water. Randy is driving up to meet them with Jinkins' old panel truck. The plan is to take their corpses here to the base and make it look like they died while controlling the storm from the central command center."

For a brief moment, my head spins while it assesses this information. "Okay, so Alena and the General will take the rap for this storm? They'll be found dead here, at the old school, like they were controlling the storm and somehow got killed doing so?"

"That's exactly right! It's a clean way to explain their demise. I've got to say Zac is good at cover-ups."

"Oh yeah? What story has he created for Jack's dead body found inside the cathedral?"

Frank smiles. "Believe it or not, he implicated Kulik's hit men, the men that were watching all the doors at the cathedral to make sure no one disturbed General Kulik. Truth be told one of them probably did kill Jack, right?"

"But they know the truth about the Boston cathedral's history with crime and Zac promised the bishop all of that would remain a secret forever as long as he helped Mohamed escape." I remind Frank.

"Well, according to Zac, they don't know anything about the cathedral's history. Zac offered to get them out of the murder mess if they told him what they knew. Apparently, Kulik didn't tell his thugs much of anything. The General believed it was best to keep them ignorant, which, in the end, worked out good for everyone."

"Alright, let's get back to my other question. What's wrong with using the eastern roadway to get the panel truck on the base?"

Frank shakes his head. "Nothing, but I don't want to send in the turtle rescue trucks that way because then there would be an official inspection of the trucks. And…"

I hold up my hand saying, "And we can't have that when we have two dead corpses in a truck, especially a General and his daughter. Not to mention Zac and Arnie being the drivers; both of whom have been banned from the base by General Kulik himself. I get it. So what's the plan?"

Frank puts his ear to the door and then opens it just enough to peek outside. After declaring to me that there is no one nearby he begins to explain.

"I've spent a good chunk of time in the security department of the base today. Besides inspecting the equipment Arnie told me about, I also observed how the military officers watch the monitors of all the activity that occurs on the base. Due to the storm, the base is short staffed. That is a very big advantage for us but it hardly solves our problems. I came across problem number one quite unexpectedly. It seems that there is a security tape from the evening that Arnie's boss was killed in the cemetery. On this tape it shows you driving around the parking lot on the base. Do you remember being here that night?"

"Yes, I was looking for Arnie."

"General Kulik has left an order that if Arnie or you get on the base that he is to be notified immediately. The officer in charge has been trying to contact Kulik since we arrived, not knowing, of course, that the General is dead. In the meantime, he is watching you closely and he knows you were up at the school. Thankfully, he bought into the turtle catching thing you did up there, I saw that too. You did a good job fooling them when you picked up those specimens. But, the problem is that you are still very much on his radar screen. In fact, he is probably wondering where you are right now."

"So what do you want me to do?"

"Well, while you and Randy were with Zac at the cathedral, I was with Sarah, Arnie and Mohamed. We worked on creating the diversion film where we used Mohamed as a ploy to get the local police sidetracked away from what we needed to do. We worked a lot with the cameras and film attempting it to look like Mohamed was being seen all over Cape Cod even when he wasn't actually there. I learned a lot yesterday and when I combine that with stuff I already knew, I was able to make some adjustments to the security monitor that covers the school area. All you and I have to do is keep all the soldiers busy watching us while Zac and Arnie drive in that one area."

"What do you mean? And what about the panel truck, won't that show up on the security tape and give them away?"

"No, because I doctored it up so that after they arrive at the school, actually the weather weapons control and command center, old security footage of the school will be played in place of current surveillance. So, what the soldier monitoring the school will see will be nothing unusual, while, in fact, the panel truck and Arnie and Zac are actually there."

"So you're replacing live footage with old footage taken when nothing was happening at the school? That's great. You learned that yesterday?"

"Arnie's penchant for explaining things in great detail can be quite helpful after all."

"All right, so what's the plan?"

Come to find out, much of Frank's plan involves doing whatever I think is best at the time. In other words, he doesn't so much have a plan as he has an idea that he expects the two of us to develop into a plan as we go along. Given the brevity in which he has time to prepare for the arrival of Zac and Arnie, I certainly do understand his position. Because I desire a more solid framework to work within, I catch Frank's arm just as we are about to leave the bathroom and offer out the best idea I can come up in a matter of seconds.

"I've got it. Sarah and Randy use her press pass and come to the military base. They get other protesters to come too. They create a ruckus about the turtles being left to burn! They can contact environmental groups, the EPA, I don't know…the animal rights organizations and…well anyone who will care about the fate of the Eastern Box Turtles. With enough pressure do you the ink the people in charge of this base will let the trucks in to save the turtles? Think of the public relations fiasco the military will have to deal with if all those innocent little turtles fry in a storm tornado fire."

Frank's eyes light up as a grin spreads across his face. "You're brilliant. Let me try to get in touch with Sarah using the Jinkins' office land line and get her on board. After that, we wait a few hours for Arnie and Zac to arrive."

*****

I am not, ordinarily, an aggravating person. I'm not one to make a scene in public about bad service. I would never send my meal back to a restaurant kitchen unless it was inedible. I don't sit too close to strangers, talk too much, or forget to turn my cell phone off in public places. It is because I am, basically, a non-irritant that I'm finding it so difficult to help Frank divert the military officer's attention from the security monitors which will be showing the panel truck entering through the eastern gate and traveling through the outskirts of the base up and into the area where the school is located. Thankfully, the truck can only be viewed on one or two monitors at a time and these monitors are usually set near each other. But even with this set-up, causing explosive distractions one after another is not easy.

Our disruptive diversion plan starts off as well as can be expected. Zac and Arnie's arrival occurs some time after the quickly arranged turtle-saving protest at the main entrance gate to the military base. Between the storm, the protest,and the short staff situation, the staff assigned to the security monitors is a bit distracted before the panel truck first appears on security footage. Luckily, the officer at the monitor showing the panel truck at the eastern gate is, like various other staff, watching the protest on the sea of monitors across the room. The protest footage shows a bunch of people being whipped about by the storm. In the center of them, I spot Randy holding his arm straight up and shouting. Sarah is behind him. Her hair is tucked inside a baseball cap and she, too, is screaming. With a camera in her hand, she is pretending to be covering this breaking news story for a local newspaper. I am quite surprised to see twenty or so protesters gathered at the gate for such an impromptu gathering. My attention is quickly drawn from the screen when the soldier assigned to the monitor that now shows the panel van turns around. Although I am blocking his view, he will bypass me in just a few seconds. I look over at Frank who is consumed with stopping a different soldier from seeing the van on a second monitor. I think of feigning illness, but realize that won't be a long enough distraction. I consider screaming but know that too will be a fruitless attempt to hold the soldier's attention. I feel myself backing up as the soldier approaches, and then, as if by the miracle of a Catholic saint, my hand touches the wire of the security monitor I am trying so desperately to hide. Trying to remember the little I learned in gymnastics as a child, I allow myself to drop backwards just enough to unplug the monitor. Of course, I can't prevent myself from falling all the way to the floor taking more wires and the monitor with me. Within seconds every set of eyes in the room focus on me. Even though what I've just done is an accident, I do what any desperate woman would do in a situation like this; I pretend to cry hysterically. It is several minutes before the officer in charge demands the members of his staff return to their positions.

"I'm so sorry," I say, as I stumble across the room. "I don't know what happened."

The officer in charge is walking me over to Frank, who is acting as a totally unconcerned co-worker. Frank is blocking the monitor with the panel van while he explains to the soldier assigned to it how he intends to get the turtle rescue trucks on the base. I sense that regardless of Barry's assignment, we will quickly be removed from the security department. The officer in charge is just about to bark orders at Frank when I notice the truck disappear from the monitor ion which it was just displayed. I look frantically for the monitor which should now show the truck. I can't seem to find it pictured anywhere. It isn't until Frank offers for the two of us to leave that I realize the panel truck must have reached the school and the monitor of the school is set to old footage.

"Okay, now what?" I whisper.

"I'm going to check with the big man in charge and see if he's changed his mind about the trucks yet. The rescue trucks are on stand by just twenty minutes away. He better give in soon because we've worn out our welcome, and Barry or no Barry, we're going to get kicked off this base. That's not even considering that some people are still monitoring every move you make on behalf of General Kulik. Wile I'm gone, why don't you go see Randy and

Sarah at the protest? That'll keep whoever is watching you busy for awhile."

I find my two friends amongst a crowd that has swelled to an amazing fifty or so people. All the protesters are soaked from the constant sleeting, but their spirits remain high. The wind blows so hard it takes our words with it as soon as they leave our mouths. While we struggle to catch each other up on what is happening, the thunder and lightning bursts start up again. The sky is a dark shade of gray with purplish undertones, an angry color scheme that frightens me. Periodically, I hear branches from nearby trees breaking off or the sound of something heavy hitting the earth.

"Hey, do you have another hat and rain coat or jacket with you?" I yell to Sarah.

"Sure, in the back seat. Help yourself."

"I'm going to use them to hide myself so I can meet up with Arnie and Zac. The security soldiers watching me won't expect to see me wearing anything but what they know I have on now."

"Better yet, I have a poncho with a hood back there, too. It's man sized so it'll totally cover you up. Take that."

"Okay."

"Remember, tell Frank that we want on the base after the gates open. Then we'll all go see Zac and Arnie who, by then, should have this damn storm re-routed out to sea."

*****

I wait with Frank until the trucks are given permission to come on base to rescue the turtles. They will arrive in less than half an hour. Since Barry will oversee the turtle evacuation personally, Frank will be able to meet me at the abandoned school not too long after I get there. While he explains to me how he intends to sneak Randy and Sarah with him to the command center, I watch a gust of wind rip a fledging tree out of the ground.

I begin my journey to the school by going to the turtle rescue command center. Inside the building I don on the large black poncho, securing the hood around my face. I then head out for the school with my turtle scouting gear on full display. Since I know I will eventually be off monitor, when the real time surveillance is replaced by Frank's old footage, I stop the scouting charade as I approach my destination. I find the bolted double gates open chain cutters and other tools lying on the ground beside them. I try to look inside the building before entering, but as I noticed before, all the windows are blacked out. The first door I try to open is locked. So are the second and third doors. I bang on a window only to get no answer. Confused and getting increasingly frightened, I go to the opposite side of the building. I pound on every window until, finally an arm holding a gun cracks open a door. The would-be assailant is Zac.

"Abby, get inside. This is a disaster of enormous consequences!" he yells out into the storm.

I run against the wind, making slow and unsteady progress. "What's wrong?"

Zac pulls me inside and slams the door shut. While he bolts it I look around at what I can only describe as a science fiction movie computer room. The space being occupied is the size of two classrooms. It has computers against all four walls and what looks to be a central command center on a platform in the middle of the floor. The computer monitors are flashing intermittently, some of them dinging while others just hum loudly. The lighting is bright enough to see well but not glaring. I feel warmth radiating from the machines inside what I believe should be a cool room. Arnie, who is perched at the command center unit, is talking to himself. He sounds like he's having a real conversation between one side of his brain and the other. If he were capable of making facial expressions I'd guess he'd look frantic.

"What's wrong?" I repeat.

"Arnie was doing great until someone else started over-writing his commands. Someone, somewhere, is taking control of this storm away from here. And, that someone is attempting to release fire tornadoes all around the perimeter of the base," Zac explains. "I don't know how long Arnie can keep the someone at bay. As it is now, I have to jump on a computer from time to time and follow Arnie's instructions to block out whoever is doing this."

"Did you say fires all around the perimeter? If that happens then whoever is inside here, fighting the storm, will be surrounded by fire," I whisper.

"That's exactly right. If they succeed with the fire tornadoes we either evacuate or burn to death."

Arnie momentarily looks at me. "If I leave this command and control center, the storm programmed into the weather weapons system will kill thousands of people. It will make the storm that hit Boston look inconsequential. Then, when the fire tornadoes are launched, whoever survives the storm will surely burn. Such fires are not only targeting this base, of course, but also the Sagamore and Bourne bridges. If access to these bridges is denied, then everyone still on Cape Cod will be caught in the fire. I do not know how long I can prevent these tragedies from occurring, but I advise you, Zac and the others to do what you can to get off the Cape now. Take a boat, a helicopter or whatever you need to take, but get out before it's too late."

"I'm not leaving you. If I leave, you'll lose your computer fight with whoever else is trying to control this storm. I'm not a computer genius like you but I'm getting dammed good at blocking the intruder." Zac turns to me. "But Frank, Randy, Sarah and you must go."

I walk over to the platform Arnie is on and watch the scientist's fingers fly over the keyboard. "What happens if whoever is trying to take control of the storm away from you gets someone to help them? Will their second person offset Zac?"

With no expression Arnie replies, "Yes."

"Then if this person gets two, three or four more helpers and you don't?"

"I will lose control."

"Then I'm not leaving. No, if you'll risk your life by staying here, Arnie, I'll stay with you. And, I can guarantee you that Frank, Sarah, and Randy will stay here with you, too."

Without looking up Arnie says, "This is not understandable in your case. I will stay because I am a scientist and being here, fighting this battle, this is my dream…this is what I've trained my entire life to do. But you…it is illogical for you to sacrifice so much to do nothing but follow my orders!"

"Arnie, I don't know when you'll ever get it but it has nothing to do with logic. It has to do with loyalty," I explain.

"Ah, now I see. Somehow this has to do with your loyalty to Mohamed?"

"No, Arnie, this has to do with my loyalty to you. I can't fight this battle; only you can do that. But I can prevent you from having to fight it alone. I owe you that."

Arnie ticks his head to the side saying, "Ah yes, emotional actions and re-actions, how bizarre."

*****

As planned, Frank, Sarah, and Randy meet up with us at the weather weapon command and control center. They arrive during the evacuation of all but emergency personnel on the base. Although it was a bit tricky for them to get to us without being spotted by security, they used the turmoil of the evacuation, the protest, and the turtle saving effort to sneak into the woods and hike their way to us. It takes both Zac and I to open the door of this converted old school building to let them inside because the wind is now blowing at constant speeds around 100 miles per hour. Frank and Randy appear to be doing fine considering they have just come in from a wild hurricane laced with sleet and hail. Sarah, conversely, doesn't look well at all. Of course this is to be expected since she is soaking wet, her hair is a tangled heap, and her skin has red blemishes where hail balls have smacked her. But it's the way her blue eyes drift off into some far away place I can't see that grabs my attention. My concern for Sarah multiplies after she and the others learn that Arnie needs our help to battle unknown and unseen enemies who are trying to out power him at the controls of the weaponized weather storm that is fatally churning all around us.

"So, we are in the middle of the storm and there are other scientists, somewhere, trying to get control of it? And they are attempting to do what with the storm, exactly?" Sarah asks, her voice sounding surprisingly calm.

"I believe, they intend to use the fire tornadoes we witnessed during the Boston storm to set fires all around the perimeter of the base," Arnie says, matter-of-factly.

"If their target is to destroy this command center, then why not just send a fire tornado here?" Randy says as he pulls Sarah close to him, his concern for her showing on his expressive face. "I would think that would be the best way to destroy the Operation Tin Man evidence, wouldn't it?"

"That would be the best way to destroy the weather weapons command and control center. The Operations Tin Man evidence, which was created here on this base, this could be located anywhere. I assure you, it is not in this building." Arnie's obvious factual statement slices through my misguided assumptions like a knife. "Did you all believe that finding this command center was the same thing as finding the evidence? Oh, how difficult it is to work with nonsensical beings. Ah, no, the evidence and the command center are not one and the same thing."

Zac lifts his head up from the computer console he's been watching since I arrived. "Okay, Arnie, where is the Operation Tin Man evidence on this base? If we know that won't we know where the first fire tornadoes will form?"

"I see, you wish to discuss more assumptions? First of all, now that the enemy knows we are here, he may send the first fire tornado here just to get us out of the way. Secondly, I don't know where the Operation Tin Man research was performed on this base. I surmise the evidence resides where the research was done, wherever that may be. I believe we will learn where this evidence is only after a fire tornado has been sent to destroy it." Arnie is silent even though we wait for him to say more. After a long pause his head snaps up and to the side. "To station number five: immediately! You will see someone has control of this terminal. You must get to it and then type in exactly what I say. I need to stay here at this main control terminal…"

Frank is at the computer terminal in question within seconds. Randy watches over his shoulder as he and Arnie fight a computer battle with an unseen adversary. I assume, of course, they will win this skirmish as Arnie has won every other one he has fought since I got here. That is until I notice Arnie is speaking increasingly faster while the threat at hand does not diminish. The struggle goes on for almost eight minutes when Arnie calls Randy over to his control terminal and quickly shows him what needs to be done there. The scientist then takes over the terminal Frank is commanding. His thin fingers move over the keys with the confidence of a concert pianist. He cocks his head from side to side as he seemingly considers various options. Ten or so more minutes pass but there is still no victory at hand. Finally, a full twenty-five minutes into the battle, Arnie leans back and raises both hands above his head.

"I am sorry to report we have lost our first battle. There is a fire tornado forming in the northern section of the base. This is a thickly wooded section located not too far from here. If I am not mistaken there are some buildings in this area. Perhaps this is where the Operation Tin Man research was done. In any case, despite the sleet, I expect the fire to move swiftly and be difficult to fight because of the winds. Ah, and so it is, we now have a time limit to win this war. I estimate the fire will reach us in a matter of a couple of hours.

Chapter 34
Battles

We lose a second fire tornado battle to our unseen enemy approximately fifty minutes after the first. This one was lost at Zac's computer station. According to Arnie, the opponent used a different computer code to manipulate the system; this one required him to make major adjustments on his side to prevent the intruder from getting past the system's security firewall. Arnie was indeed close to completing these necessary adjustments; however, the enemy snuck through long enough to launch the second fire tornado. As frightening as this second fire ball is to me, what concerns me more is Arnie's insistence that this tornado has a different component to it. He can't identify what makes this new spinning weapon different from the one that was launched less than one hour ago other than to say it is large, has a fiery bottom, and a frigid top. In my mind this is impossible, but I've come to understand that in the world of weather weapons even the impossible exists.

Now that all of us are assigned to monitor a handful of computer stations our conversation has become nothing more than Arnie shouting out orders and the rest of us babbling out panicking comments as we try to comply with his demands. So far I have waged four computer battles successfully and a fifth one to what Arnie calls a stalemate, whatever that means. I also have two computer terminals that have next to no activity on them, which allows me a bit more free time than the others in the group.

"The winds sound stronger to me. If this building wasn't made strong enough to secure this weather weapons command center, I swear it would fly away," Randy snaps while hawking from one computer screen to another.

"The storm is increasing in ferocity as it was programmed. I have been too busy battling the enemy intruder to attempt to lessen the storm." Arnie taps away on his keyboard like he is playing a high intensity game. "In fact, I have been so involved with battling our intruder I've been unable to even begin diverting the storm."

"What? There's a freaking fire on its way! Damn it! Those suckers are going to beat us because of this damn computer battle," Randy bellows.

"Don't panic! We need to think this through," Zac says, calmly. "Let's give reports. I'll begin by saying my terminals have required the constant use of the blocking techniques Arnie has taught us. I have even had to block two terminals at once."

Frank shakes his head indicating that he is in the middle of a keyboard battle so I speak next. "The activity in my section has actually slowed down a bit."

"That is because of the areas your terminals control and the difficulty involved with penetrating them. I believe our opponents are focusing on more vulnerable areas at the moment."

"Like mine," Frank shouts out.

"And mine too," Randy adds.

"I still have the two terminals that I have to constantly block. My other ones aren't that active and when they are I just tell Arnie and he deals with them."

With Zac leading the discussion, it becomes painfully obvious that unless something in our strategy changes, we will continue to win computer battles but lose the war as the storm achieves exactly what the enemy intended it to: the complete annihilation of Cape Cod and any evidence of Operation Tin Man that is hidden here. My heart begins to physically ache as the reality of our situation dissolves every bit of hope I have left. If it weren't for the odd whizzing sounds I hear coming from outside, I honestly believe I would become hysterical. Instead, I look at the others to see if they hear the new noises as well. Their puzzled faces convince me that they do.

"Come on, Sarah. We'll open the door and see what's happening out there. Let Arnie deal with your terminal activity," I say as I wave her over.

Sarah hurries to me. "You're biting the inside of your cheeks again, Abby. Are you nervous about the mess we're in or opening the door?"

"Both."

Together we get the door open wide enough for us to examine the almost unrecognizable sights outside.

"Oh no!" I hear Sarah yell out from behind me. "This is too much for me. Too damn much."

My first impression of the unspeakable things spread out before us is that what I'm seeing is an optical illusion. I am temporarily convinced that what my brain is interpreting as particular objects is being distorted by some factor of the storm. I stare at the red liquid which is sprayed all around and decide it must be a chemical stored on the base. As for the horrid smelling burnt human body parts…no…they are dummies…yes, arms, legs, and torsos of training dummies. And that thing that just sliced by me…a Frisbee... a toy caught in a tornado…that is all…and the ice on the ground with the red all over it….that is simply chemicals…

"Burnt body parts…shirt…sleeves with something…arm?" Sarah is seemingly hypnotized by the disgusting debris caught in the wind storm. Like me, she is in some stage of shock. Unlike me, she is verbalizing her thoughts. "Bloody body things…I think human…can the wind rip off body parts? It can't be, but…there is so much blood and…something is wrong…and burnt things…how can this be?"

It's not just wind…it is the flying saucer sheets…they are red…can't she see them? Burning…oh no…a fire ball with….oh….

"A head…Ahhhhhh….its a head…."

I'm not sure exactly how long it takes for Frank and Randy to come to us, I just know that when they do I hear Sarah throwing up. Somehow I'm pulled inside and my own stomach churns. As I fight not to be sick, I realize that I am shaking so much I can see my arms moving. Someone - not Frank - is wrapping a coat around me. Randy is wrapping himself around Sarah; I think he is crying with her. From the distance I hear a quick-talking Arnie.

"Stay calm and explain to me in detail what you are seeing. I believe they have unleashed a weapon which I didn't anticipate…I did not know it was fully developed. As I said earlier, the last large tornado was different and I think I now know how. Take a closer look and describe exactly what you see. Are the human limbs ripped off or cut off. Are the edges clean or torn? Can you tell…?"

"Are you freaking kidding me?" Randy yells out. "There's a human head, no… correction, a *burnt* human head rolling around in the wind out there and you want me to inspect it for *jagged* edges?"

"You must go outside and look," Arnie insists, as if he is asking him to do something no more difficult than crossing the room. "If the head is nearby it will be the safest appendage to inspect. If this is what I think it is, then you shouldn't take any unnecessary chances out in the storm. No, you must be careful of…"

"The flying Frisbees? The red icy Frisbees?" I mutter just loud enough to be heard.

"Yes! I mean no. I mean yes to the objects, except they are not the toy named Frisbee," Arnie replies.

Randy throws his hands up while turning toward Arnie. "What are you talking about now? Are you out of your freaking mind? Spare us the scientist speak and tell us what is going on out there!"

"In my research at the university I came upon a weapon that was not fully developed, which, I fear, may be in use during this storm. It would explain the consistent sleet we have seen, as well as the increasing hail stone activity. It too is spew out from the killing tornadoes. The super tornado, as I call it, can not only spew out fire balls but it can also churn out thin sheets of ice that are, in fact, razor sharp. If such a super tornado has been unleashed, then what you are describing outside is possible, correction, quite likely. The ice sheets will slice up anything in their path, including human life. Then the fire will burn it. Or vice versa depending on what gets to the target first."

"Razor ice sheets that cut into people? That's just beyond comprehension," Zac says.

"That's disgusting and cruel... I can't even imagine...but I guess if they have fire in tornadoes, then why not razor sharp ice," I ask.

"If this razor ice is out there then..." Zac pauses. "Then we may not be able to escape here unless we defeat the enemy. You see, if you recall, the tornadoes are attracted to heat and movement so they will follow us."

"Can the razor ice cut through a glass windshield or rubber tires? What about the steel of the panel truck?" Zac asks.

"I don't know but it doesn't matter. At this time all the roads off the base are on fire so escaping by truck is no longer possible. To get away we would need to go out through the woods...there is just one possible way but I do not believe we will make it." Arnie says.

Again, the fact that we are defeated weighs heavily in the room. Arnie again requests someone to go outside to examine the edges of a severed human body part. It is Zac and Frank take on this task. When they return to report that the cuts appear to have been caused by razor ice they both look sickly gray. For several minutes we are all silent.

"Can you use the satellite or the radio waves the weather weapon system is connected to in a way to get that TV working? I want to see what's happening on the news." Randy rubs his head. "We can at least see what the end looks like."

"I have already hooked up the TV." Arnie turns on a twenty-four hour news station.

The wild storm and fire on Cape Cod is the lead story. The news report is showing a map of fires on the Cape, all of which were started by storm tornadoes. There are now five fire symbols on the military base, yet they look insignificant compared to the many other symbols all over the map. We learn that both the Sagamore and Bourne Bridges are closed because they have been damaged by super tornadoes carrying both fire balls and razor ice. The damage to property is almost beyond comprehension, but all of it means nothing compared to the fatalities that are quickly mounting up.

"What strategy is left to try?" I ask. "We've thought it all through already so is there anything even left to think about? We stopped General Kulik and Alena; their dead bodies lie over there beneath that tarp just waiting to take the blame for this storm. We found the weather weapon command and control center hidden in here, an abandoned old school. We got Arnie in here, possibly the only scientist that could get control of the storm. And now there's this unknown enemy that battles with us through the internet because it can't let the storm stop until the Operation Tin Man evidence is destroyed?"

"And while it keeps the storm roaring, innocent people on the Cape are dying. What if we try to communicate with the people on the other side of the computers?" Frank suggests.

"We don't know who they are so how can we know how to begin negotiating with them?" Zac looks at Arnie. "What's happened in the last couple of minutes, since we stopped battling the enemy?"

"There is another fire on the base. This one is to the south of the main gate." Arnie uncharacteristically looks at us. "I am sorry I failed you. I cannot stop the enemy as it is, without question, representatives of our government. Their power is immense."

I don't know when I started to cry, I only know that I am crying when Frank takes me in his arms. I close my eyes and listen to the relentless wind banging on the building wishing that somehow something good would happen. I hear Sarah sobbing and Randy's comforting words. Zac's and Arnie's voices sound distant, as do the reporters' voices on TV. Frank's whispering words of love are tearing my insides apart. A breathy sob pushes out of my chest. I just stay in my boyfriend's arms and wait until someone offers out an evacuation plan, that is if we dare try to escape the fire and razor ice tornadoes that surround us.

"Ah, the distant member of our group is attempting to save us. He said he would not fly out of Boston until he knew we were safe and he, obviously, realizes we are not. Breaking news, Mohamed Haddad has managed to send a press release over the internet!" Arnie says, loudly. "Come, let us listen closely."

Zac looks stunned as he puts the volume higher. After the reporter explains that the following message was uploaded onto the internet a short time ago a grainy picture of Mohamed appears. Behind him is a solid white sheet that ensures no one can recognize where he was when he made the message. He speaks slowly and deliberately, his rage must be obvious to all.

"I am Mohamed Haddad and I am sending this message to you today because I am one of the few people on Earth that can gain the attention of the entire world merely by speaking. The beginning of my message is intended

for a select group of people who, unbeknownst to the masses, have betrayed the American people. They have done so in the past, do so now, and will continue to do so unless they are stopped. I know of them because of who and what I am. They, however, do not know that I have in my possessions that which they seek to destroy. If they do not immediately cease their current activities, I will upload my second message which explains in detail all about this unexpected enemy of the country, how I know of them and what crimes they have committed. When I am assured the people with whom they battle are safe, I will then and only then destroy the second message."

We have watched Mohamed's message three times when we realize that the storm outside is slowing down. A while later we hear the sound of an incoming helicopter. From the central command computer Arnie reports that the enemy is actively decreasing storm activity while rerouting it off to sea. I hear the wind dying down and the sleet pounding less. Everything around us is getting calmer and quieter. Arnie informs us that some of the strange sensations we feel have to do with air pressure changes and other storm science factors, but regardless of the cause, I feel absolutely bizarre. My ears are ringing rather than pounding. The adrenalin my body has been running on for so long is seeping away. From a distance I hear a familiar whirring sound. I look up and there in the sky is a helicopter. It lands in the big vacant parking lot and two soldiers jump out. They come to the command center and bang on the door. With his gun drawn, Zac insists they disarm before letting them inside.

"Agent Zachary Brown? Yes, I was told you were here with a few other national heroes. We have come to rescue you before the fire reaches this facility," one of the soldiers explains.

"I'm not going anywhere until…" Zachary stops speaking when the second soldier reveals his identity.

"Allow me to introduce myself. I am General Radison, the Secretary of Defense. I was sent here to get you at the request of the President of the United States of America, who is waiting to meet with all of you in Washington, D.C. He believes you have uncovered some rogue politicians within the government of whom he wants to learn more. One of these is General Kulik?"

Zac points toward the tarp, "The General and his daughter are dead. They are behind this entire mess, but there are also others."

I leave Frank to stand before the Secretary. "How do we know we can trust you? We've already learned the hard way that our government can't be trusted."

"Your government keeps secrets in order to protect its people, but it does not murder its own. From what I understand, the government has kept some of your secrets for quite some time now? I don't see why you should fear them now." Secretary Radison steps toward the door. "Now, the second helicopter will be landing in less than a minute. We must get footage of your rescue on TV before Mohamed Haddad does something we will all regret."

"How do we know you weren't sent here by our enemies? How do we know the President himself wasn't in on this whole thing? How do we know who in this government we can trust?" I ask as it becomes clear to me that we don't know who within the government we are battling with.

Secretary Radison smiles at me and says, "Abia Haddad, you cannot be sure right now, but in time, you will understand. Let me just say this. Sometimes it is advantageous to not know what is real and what is not because it is this unknown which allows you to have faith."

Afterward

After many meetings in Washington, D.C., I've come to believe that the committee which authorized the weather weapons storms on Boston and Cape Cod did so without the knowledge and permission of the government and its leaders. I also believe that the entire truth behind the Weatherized Weapons Program and its impact on global warming is so tangled in politics, corporate greed, international relations, and egos that the truth of it all may never be known. I will never look at my country the same after this experience; who could now that I know what I do? But even though I'm no longer the naïve red, white, and blue die hard patriot I once was, I still believe I live in the best country this planet has ever had and I am grateful that I do.

As for Frank, Randy, Sarah, and me we are all back at school in Boston. None of us have told our family the entire truth of what happened a few months back, but we all have admitted to enough to get our families to stop asking questions. This is harder for me to do than the others because I have to keep Mohamed's new life a secret from those that I love, which I am finding very difficult to do. Oh, and we have a new neighbor who comes over all the time; you guessed it…Arnie! Actually, we have two new neighbors; Arnie and the St. Bernard from the veterinarian kennel he made friends with the night his boss was murdered. We never knew Arnie kept going to check on the big beast until he came home with him. The dog's name is Bernie, short for Bernard. Arnie thinks it is a logical name. I guess some things will never change.

Zac Brown went to Rome to meet up with Mohamed shortly after he left Washington, D.C. He did not contact us the entire time he was away. As you can well imagine, this lack of communication had my mind spinning with bad thoughts. If I knew who I could call to get information on Zac, I think I'd have caved and made the call, but there was no one for me to contact so all I could do was wait. And wait I did. Finally, on Christmas Eve of all days, Zac came by the apartment! He told me that Mohamed is doing fine. He wouldn't say where my brother is, who he's with, or what exactly he's doing. All he did say was that Mohamed is the best partner he's ever worked with. Zac also said that they often talk about missing the four of us and how we made such a great team. Then he asked all of us to rethink what we wanted to do with our lives. Of course we all laughed at the joke about us becoming undercover spies like Mohamed…well, we all laughed except for Zac. I don't think Zac was kidding.

Also from Diane

Full Circle 911

Abby Haddad is a Muslim teenager living in a post 9/11 America where discrimination and a radicalized elder brother complicate her high school centered life. When she stumbles upon an active terrorist plan on American soil that is based on the events of 9/11, she and her friends follow the clues left behind by the Islamic Extremists to face down the enemy in the city of Boston. The group's heroic actions are complicated, however, when they learn that Abby's brother is one of the enemies. The storyline is further energized by one of Abby's peers whose mental illness causes her to be a direct threat on the heroes and, in turn, on the future of America.

Exposing Eurabia

Through an act of fate, college student Abby Haddad finds herself at the scene of an Islamic terrorist attack that takes place at Harvard University. Because her brother Mohamed is a wanted terrorist fugitive of the United States she knows she must find a way to leave the scene without police notice. While plotting her escape she is horrified when she sees Mohamed walking among the smoky rubble. She soon learns the enemy is really a secret society named Eurabia; a group of European and Arab countries who have joined together to destroy America. As she and her friends untangle the enemy's far reaching network of insiders within the U.S. government, business networks and other positions of power they realize the time they have to expose the enemy is quickly passing. Unsure of whether Mohamed has truly changed from an enemy of state to a remorseful patriot the heroes have no choice but to depend on him to prevent Eurabia from murdering the most powerful leaders of the country.

About the Author

A product of the Great American Dream, Diane Kozak's life began in a typical American family in a typical American town, learning the values of being a good and hard-working person. A determined dreamer with an optimistic nature and receiving a healthy share of good luck, she managed to enjoy many successes in her personal and professional life. At the peek of such success (CEO of a major credit union) she gave it all up to pursue her dream as a writer. Diane Kozak lives in Massachusetts with her husband. To know more about Di, visit her at: http://www.dianekozak.com

CPSIA information can be obtained at www.ICGtesting.com
Printed in the USA
BVOW11s1638030614

355225BV00004BA/7/P